In St. James's Park, the Raven heard the mounting cheers, the shouts, the cries of joy as the queen and her entourage entered the Mall. He smiled gleefully, one finger caressing the shutter release-trigger of his Nikon camera-radio.

As the queen approached Marlborough Road, the cheering grew in intensity. The Raven watched through the camera's viewfinder as she drew near the intersection. The shouting increased, the throngs waved. Inch by inch, she came on. Three hundred yards . . . two hundred . . .

He depressed the shutter release.

The explosion was terrible.

The queen was dead. Long live the Raven!

WILLIAM K. WELLS

CHAOS

TOR

A TOM DOHERTY ASSOCIATES BOOK

Special thanks and acknowledgment to
Jack Garside for his contribution to this work.

CHAOS

First printing: March 1987

A TOR Book

Published by Tom Doherty Associates, Inc.
49 West 24 Street
New York, N.Y. 10010

ISBN: 0-812-51045-3
CAN. ED.: 0-812-51046-1

Printed in the United States of America

0 9 8 7 6 5 4 3 2 1

FOR JANE,
. . . who stood by during my
period of darkness

And for Florence Zazzarino,
who kept the faith

And for Knox and Kitty,
who provided encouragement

The author wishes to thank the brothers Bruce and Keith van Sant for their expertise on railroads, and some good friends all— Gordon and Veronica Thomas for their pointers on London today, Jacques Français and Ed Politz for their knowledge of the Mer de Glace, and Captain John Ward for his lore of the sea.

William K. Wells

I have a rendezvous with Death
At some disputed barricade . . .
And I to my pledged word am true,
I shall not fail that rendezvous.
                    —Alan Seeger

PROLOGUE

New York City, Early May

White clouds drifted high over Manhattan, barely visible from the canyons of rutted asphalt where buses, taxis, and trucks spewed out their daily quota of filth. Rush hour. The streets were packed, commercial and private vehicles fighting for space.

Shoppers headed for subways to jostle with office workers in cars sprayed with the pitiful art of misguided youth. On 34th Street, a gray sedan pulled up in a loading zone fifty yards down the street from the Israeli Travel Center, four stories of crowded offices devoted more to organizing campaigns for Israeli relief than to extolling its virtues as a vacation spot. The sedan's driver was a handsome man in his early thirties, lean, bearded, intense. His dark brown eyes studied the scene through heavy-rimmed glasses.

A block away, a blue and white police cruiser moved slowly up the street. The bearded man started the car, drove around the block, and stopped in the loading zone again. The police car was gone.

The polluted street was hot. The car was not air-conditioned. He kept the window open, seemed to be intent on the Travel Center. He lit a cigarette, drew on it deeply, set it in the ashtray, and reached for a Nikon camera hanging from his neck on a colorful strap. The interior of the camera did not contain prism, lens, or electronic shutter. It housed a complex electrical circuit, a radio oscillator designed to send a signal more than a thousand yards and detonate high-explosive fuses. He sighted

1

on the building. Satisfied, he let the camera dangle, and smoked, waiting.

At this moment, he knew it had all been worthwhile—the months of privation and filth and the never-ending ache of muscle in the training camps of Lebanon, of Libya, and, finally, in the wasteland of Russia. Every time he used the Nikon, he dedicated his kill to someone, to something in his past that made him what he had become. This one was for "dear old Dad," who had never had the time to talk or understand the pain of growing up, to help him curb the need to kill. The wings of flies had palled; the severed jugular of a neighbor's pet had eventually become dull work; the decapitation of homeless drunks had not been enough.

More. It had to be more and ever more. He had come a long way, from a grenade thrown into a restaurant to the hundreds who would die today.

His musing was interrupted by action at the target. Three men wearing light blue coveralls and yellow hard hats left the building. Good. It was going down. Two more blue-clad figures emerged, and finally a sixth. They were all out.

He looked at his watch. Four-forty-nine. The building would close at five. Other buildings would soon start to empty. Perhaps four-fifty-nine would be the ideal time.

He looked up and down the street again. No police in sight. Two buses were crawling slowly from the east, delayed by two gasoline tankers. Three buses were bumper to bumper coming from the west. If he was lucky, they would converge in front of his target in about two minutes. To hell with the office workers. He would go for the buses and tankers.

Somehow, at this point, time seemed to slow for him. Mexico, the Middle East, Thailand—it was always the same. When a job was going down—in those few seconds when it was all coming together—time played on his side and slowed for his enjoyment.

One minute. One block and the heavy vehicles would be in front of the Israeli Travel Center.

Thirty seconds. Twenty. He carefully raised the Nikon to his eye and sighted on the center of the building. It didn't matter if he was accurate. The signal would blanket the area.

Ten seconds. Five. He could see the overloaded buses starting to congest the street in front of his target. The tankers were almost in place. Another twenty feet . . . ten . . . five . . .

He depressed the sensitive shutter switch.

In unison, every window on all four floors of the building blew outward, the shock wave crushing buses and tankers together. Orange flame poured out of the ruined building to engulf the street. Huge chunks of granite tumbled on flesh already cooking in the inferno. Columns of smoke were pushed skyward by the heat.

Ribbons of flame streaked toward leaking valves atop the tankers, igniting the gas collected there. Both tankers exploded, covering the buses and the buildings on both sides of the street with yellow and orange flame.

A few wretched souls ran screaming from the inferno, their clothes aflame. They were already dead, but had not acknowledged the fact. All others—those in the buildings, on the street, and in the vehicles—were consumed in the massive pyre.

The bearded man had miscalculated, something he did very seldom. The act had far exceeded his wildest dreams. Sometimes you got lucky and it happened that way.

He could not drive away from the scene as he had planned. A river of flaming gasoline sped toward him. He stepped casually from the car, the pseudo-Nikon still around his neck, closed the door, and walked away from the scene as gasoline lapped at the tires of his hired vehicle.

Book One

THE DESERT

When night
Darkens the streets, then wander forth
   the sons
Of Belial, flown with insolence and
   wine.

       —JOHN MILTON, *PARADISE LOST*

CHAPTER 1

Palos Verdes, California, Tuesday

When the call came, Philip Alden was in the middle of the eighty-ninth page of his thirty-fifth screenplay and it was not going well. The dialogue was stilted, the characters dead, the plot unrealistic. If it ever reached the box office, it would probably receive a special Oscar for Biggest Bomb of the Year.

So the ringing of the phone came as a relief, a welcome intrusion into his self-doubt. As he walked across the patio, he hoped it might be Harry Zimmerman on the other end to tell him his thirty-fourth script, *The Darkened Heart,* had been accepted and would go into production immediately. Shit, Harry. Let it be you.

It was not Harry Zimmerman. It was Kate. "Hi," she said.

"Hi. Where are you?"

They never addressed each other by names. That had stopped long ago, a year before the divorce. It was a tacit agreement of détente, of recognition without involvement.

"Chicago," she said.

By God, it was good to hear her voice. "What are you doing in Chicago?"

"I'm on my way out there," she said. "I told you."

His mind groped and found it. "Oh. The Warren Stackman picture. I didn't know they were in production."

"Don't you read the trades?"

"Hell no! *Variety*'s become a legal brief. Everybody's suing everybody else. The *Reporter*'s not much better."

Then he asked something he'd not intended, a gesture from a desire he'd thought long dead. "When does your flight get in? Maybe I could pick you up."

"I'm not flying. You know I don't fly," she said, her tone showing impatience.

"Still?" He laughed. "Come on, they've racked up millions of miles of safety."

"Nobody should go around in a big box up in the sky," she said, then paused for a few seconds. "I'm on the Southwest Limited. Arriving Thursday. I don't know what time," she went on. "Call me here at the Drake before six tonight if you're going to meet me. Otherwise I'll book a limo."

"The Drake? What are you doing at a hotel? Who's with you?" he asked, suddenly suspicious.

"Nobody's with me! For God's sake, Phil. Are you going to play the jealous bit?"

"I'm not jealous," he said, sorry he'd asked the question, let the thought slip out.

"And you have no right to be. We're divorced, remember?"

"I remember." He remembered all the good times, too. He still loved her in his own way. They had been good for each other—just couldn't make it work on a permanent basis.

"Anyway, I had to get out of the rain," she said.

"What's the matter with Union Station?" He knew what it was. She had to have privacy and luxury all the time. She felt she'd earned it, and she had.

"Six hours in that dank and dreary dungeon? Are you crazy?"

"For a few hours' layover you have to book a hotel room. Jesus, money means nothing to you." He loved to get in his little dig. "I'll meet you," he said, impulsively.

"You will?" Her voice had changed, taken on a little girl's tone. "Lovely. I hate to get off in a small town and find it empty."

"This is no longer a small town," he said. "We have Lew Wasserman, the Arabs, and countless McDonald's. Very cosmopolitan. Some want to call it New York West."

"I hate the bloody place."

"So do I. Very often."

"You *will* meet me."

"I said I would."

"You're a love," she said, hanging up, getting the last word, as usual.

When he cradled the phone, he had tears in his eyes. He fought them back, standing at the bar on the ocean side of the patio, mixing himself a Johnnie Red with water. *No soda,* the doctor had said. *Soda gets the alcohol into your bloodstream faster.* It was his third that morning.

The IBM Selectric was still humming. He flicked it off and stared at page eighty-nine, then shifted his gaze up, over the stretch of sand and the blue Pacific. In his peripheral vision, a pelican swooped low and dove into the water. He grunted to himself, then sipped his drink and pulled his attention back to page eighty-nine. The characters remained interred, buried in their immobility. The brief intrusion had not charged them to clamor for life and rise up from the white shroud of the page. They remained lifeless, as he himself felt lifeless.

He had finished his drink and sat staring mournfully at the empty glass. Maybe one more would get the juices flowing, burst the boundaries of his impotence, take the harsh edge off reality and call the soothing muse to his aid in the war against page eighty-nine.

He had discovered many years ago, when writing in the late afternoon or evening, that a drink, perhaps two, would relax him just enough to get the first line down. His mind would clear of the day's tensions, the story conferences, the wear and tear on his ego, the ever present worry.

But he could not write when he was drunk, and he was well on the way. It was not yet afternoon or evening and he was on his fourth scotch. He had written only two lines—two lines without blood, without passion, without life.

Then Kate had intruded, reaching out two thousand miles from Chicago to interrupt his train of thought.

The hell with it. This was not a day for working. He covered the IBM and sipped his drink, brooding over the blue Pacific.

He looked down at his naked stomach, at the bulge of

fat drooping over his belt. He sucked himself in automatically and at the same time wondered about his liver. He decided it was probably fatty, too.

Still, for a man in his fifties, Alden was in excellent physical shape. He stood six feet, was lean and muscular. The tire about his middle was not pronounced. His yearly physicals revealed only minor signs of aging, and his heart, blood pressure, and lungs checked out well. He played tennis and could still sail his forty-foot sloop without a crew. He was handsome, gray-haired with just a touch of black, blue-eyed, deeply tanned.

If he was thankful for this, it was with a gratitude tempered by suspicion. He had seen too many people die and he knew the perfidious havoc nature could wreak. Who knew what was going on inside his body at this moment? He did not, nor did his doctors.

He abhorred illness and despised death. But more than anything, he hated his own disenchantment and, in this sense, looked forward to his own denouement.

The disenchantment was not new. It had been implanted years before and had grown slowly, like an insidious cancer. He felt he had been screwed—not himself alone, but his whole generation. Led down the primrose path, lied to, victims of a vast evil duplicity. They were now being held responsible for the failure of their dreams.

He sighed, finished his drink, and wheeled the typewriter under an awning. Inside, it was cool and calming. He loved this house. He loved its spacious, airy rooms, its red tiled floors, its feeling of age and tradition. It was old Spanish Palos Verdes—six bedrooms, spacious grounds, a large pool. It was BD, before the developers. He had bought it at under two hundred thousand. He could sell it now for more than two million.

Truly disgusting, he thought.

He showered, fixed another drink, and called Harry Zimmerman.

"Harry," he said, "how about lunch? Time we got together."

"Sounds good. When?"

"Today."

*   *   *

It had been 1947 when Kate Kavanaugh had first played in Chicago. She had not carried a spear, but it might have improved the role.

She had not been Kate Kavanaugh then, simply Mary Leary from the Marble Hill section of the Bronx. Statuesque, beautiful, violet-eyed, red-haired Mary Leary. The hair was still red, a brilliant copper-red, and lovely. She was still statuesque, at five feet eight, and her face, still beautiful. Yet there had been so many other changes.

Three husbands, for one. Oh, Christ, she thought. Let's not think about that again!

Looking out the window at Lake Michigan, she thought she would like to see the old theater, if it was still standing. But it was raining, and she hated rain. It made her soul feel damp. It depressed her spirit, warped her creativity. She did not perform as well when it was raining.

Turning, she walked into the living room. She smiled. If Philip knew she'd booked a whole suite for six hours, he'd have turned blue.

Kate Kavanaugh's whole life had to be first class. First class on trains and boats, limousines instead of cabs, suites instead of rooms. Sprung from a dour and dreary background, she had made life lie at her feet. Caviar and champagne had replaced corned beef and cabbage.

She had spent three years in the theater as Mary Leary. It sounded dull and distant, not a name to brighten the marquee, to draw crowds. Mary Leary did not contain the element of stardom.

She liked Katharine. Her heroines were Cornell and Hepburn, both Katharines. And, of course, Kate in *The Taming of the Shrew*.

Kate, then, she had thought. But Kate what? She settled on Cavanaugh as a sop to her Irish family, but changed the *C* to a *K*. Kate Kavanaugh.

"Kate Kavanaugh?" Alden had scoffed. "Why not Kate Carstairs? Or Kate Cameron?" He had always despised grandiosity in others, if not in himself. He seemed to cultivate a strange double standard where he was forever right and others wrong. Until he arrived in Hollywood. Then he began seeing things differently. He was not about to tell Judy Garland to change her name back to Frances Gumm.

"I didn't like the name," Kate had said.

"What's in a name?" Alden had replied. "A rose by any other name . . ." He had paraphrased the old expression and then kissed her.

They had been young then, very young. They were doing one of his plays in a small theater in Greenwich Village, she starring, he directing.

She stood now, looking out the window at the slanting, gray rain, eyes moist in remembrance of that most beautiful time. They had made mistakes and had such fun in the process. She tried to remember the names of the other actors, the twenty-year-old producer who was forever waving pages of manuscript in the air, forgetting that Alden was directing as he barked orders and put on a display of pure, unadulterated ham.

After the play's run in the Village, after the excitement, the fun, the delirious success and Broadway offers for both of them, after the shared kisses and the young, idealistic lovemaking, she had half expected him to propose. But, for some reason she never fathomed, he had not. Their marriage had come much later.

After Barbara Lloyd.

Her watch showed one o'clock. Five more hours to departure time. She must know someone here. But who? Of course! Zack Fuller. She went to her purse for her address book. She'd invite him for lunch or a drink. Maybe he could see her to the train. Or maybe she would invite him to the suite and they could renew an old affair. He had been a better than average lover. Star material.

Her purse, made of the finest leather, was large, floppy, with many pockets, zippers, and compartments. It contained a makeup kit, pencils, pens, scraps of paper, two compacts, a hair brush, a wallet, three checkbooks with few stubs completed, emergency Tampax, four packs of cigarettes, and three crumpled hundred-dollar bills. But it held nothing that resembled an address book.

Goddamn! Shit!

She felt like crying. And she did.

A mass of contradictions, Kate Kavanaugh. Offstage,

she could be a klutz. Onstage, she was the epitome of talent and control, commanding all about her—the cast, the audience, the vehicle—with superb poise and perfect artistry. She remembered every cue, every pause, every nuance, every line of the script, including those of the other characters. But phone numbers disappeared from her mind like thieves in the night, and her checkbook always balanced precariously on the edge of disaster.

Why had she divorced Alden after fighting so hard to get him? He had been, and still was, by far the best of the lot.

She mixed a martini and lit another ciagrette. Because he was always so serious, she decided. So guilt-ridden. Christ, you'd think he'd been born on a cross, and he wasn't even Catholic. She was. Not that it mattered—she had not been to mass since the age of fifteen. But she would probably die crying for a priest.

Another contradiction.

She puffed on her cigarette and thought about the Coast, the picture, the shooting schedule. Philip. Would she and Phil get to bed? Was it possible they might make it again—in marriage? She looked into her drink, twirling the stem of the glass. He likes young broads. Always had. She sighed.

Ten stories below Kate Kavanaugh's suite in the Drake Hotel, a tall, thin, bearded young man convulsed violently in a queen-sized bed. He was having the dream again, the recurrent dream that always came after he had killed.

He was running across a field and his father was chasing him, a rifle in his hands. His heart was beating wildly; he was terrified. Tears had formed in his eyes. He wished, he yearned, to have wings, to take to the sky, to fly and thus escape. He wished he were a bird.

And suddenly he was. Taking off into the sky and glancing downward, he saw his father as a small diminishing figure looking up at him.

But then with horror, he saw his father grow wings and spring into the air, the rifle clutched in his talons.

He flew with fury, but his father gained on him. Glancing back, he beheld his father just a few yards away, the rifle held firmly and pointed at him.

"You stinking coward! You *monster!* I'll kill you!" the gray-haired apparition yelled up at him.

He screamed as he watched his father begin to squeeze the trigger.

He woke screaming.

The last time he'd had the dream had been three days ago, on his way from New York to Chicago. He'd lurched awake screaming then, too. For a moment, he hadn't known where he was, until, looking through the windshield of the rented car, he'd seen a sign: REST AREA.

Then he'd remembered. He'd been on the Pennsylvania Turnpike headed west. He had stopped to get out and vomit, then had lain down and fallen asleep.

Waking in the car, he had decided not to drive for a few minutes, had fired up a stick of the best Far East marijuana. After a few tokes, he'd felt better, remembering.

The job had gone well. Cool. Without a hitch. He had pressed the button and the Travel Center had blossomed into a red-orange flower. On the way west, he'd bought a paper at a truck stop. His work had been on page one. Waiting for the fuel trucks had been a masterful stroke. Seventy-nine employees killed; another twenty-eight people died on the street. Fifty on the buses had died, and a hundred and fifty-two were in critical condition. The burn units in Manhattan and other boroughs were filled to overflowing. It had been much better than he had hoped for.

He always approached killing as he approached sex—suavely, coolly, inwardly excited. But after the act, the disgust, revulsion, guilt, the rising bile, would always overcome him. The compulsion was always there, had to be satisfied, but afterward, something within him rebelled. Perhaps the vestiges of decency somewhere hidden in his past—in the alcoholic wasteland of his dear old Dad. This one weakness, this throwback, always followed the act.

As he had on the turnpike, he awakened in the hotel room screaming, sweat pouring from his face. He lurched into the bathroom to spew up the meal he'd had only two hours earlier and the lovely Grand Marnier he'd sipped with such enjoyment.

It was always like this. The only penalty. He stepped under a cold shower, toweled off, dressed hurriedly, and picked up the phone. While he waited for the front desk to answer, he flicked a lighter, lit a joint carefully, and inhaled deeply, pulling the sweet smoke deep into his lungs, holding it for a time, then exhaling slowly.

"This is Mr. Abelson," he said when the connection was complete. "Room 1529." His voice was deep, resonant, totally controlled. "I'll be checking out. Will you prepare my bill?" He listened. "No, I don't need a porter. Thank you."

He checked a few drawers and the closet once again. Finding everything in order, he closed his two Vuitton bags, locked them, and slung his camera case over his shoulder.

He was an American-bred international terrorist, the most feared in the world.

He was the Raven—and he was loose.

CHAPTER 2

Los Angeles, Tuesday

Harry Zimmerman was not tall. He was spare and lean, well muscled, and played a horrible game of tennis. His face was that of an ascetic—sharp, ridged, topped with a cap of neat white hair. His hazel eyes were dreamy and poetic.

He was seventy years of age but looked not a day over fifty. Behind the dreamy eyes lay the cunning of a fox, the shrewd, calculating mind of one of the best literary agents in Hollywood. Producers called him the Killer.

As he raised a succulent bluepoint oyster to his lips, Zimmerman said, "I remember the days we couldn't get these here."

Alden grunted, "Dave Chasen had them."

"Not all the time."

"That made them taste better."

"You think those days were good?"

Alden's eyes took in the fake foliage, the fake leather, their fellow customers. He looked at the Gucci loafers, the Lauren shirts, the designer sunglasses, the actors, actresses, producers, and directors—most high on coke. He couldn't shut out the flow of overly eager conversation.

"Things change," he said

"You sound weary," Zimmerman said.

"I am." He paused. " 'Forsooth, I know not why I am so sad. It wearies me. I know it wearies you,' " Alden quoted, smiling. "Forget it, Harry. It's my self-pity day."

Finishing his oysters, Zimmerman lit a cigarette. He

chain-smoked, even through meals. "I'm very big on self-pity. Let's hear it."

Alden winced inwardly. Harry had been big on *The Darkened Heart*, too, but for over four months he had said not a word about it. This could only mean he was having trouble selling it and was trying to save Alden's feelings.

Alden had come to lunch looking for good news and, instead, was getting silence, the deadly bad. He decided not to pursue it, looked out the window. "I've lost my passion, Harry."

Zimmerman laughed. "That twenty-four-year-old in La Jolla. You don't call that passion?"

"That's sex, Harry."

"You know what I mean."

"No, I don't, but this is my self-pity day, remember?"

The Crab Louis arrived and Alden eyed it with distaste. "Even food," he said sadly. "I've lost my passion for food. This looks like shit."

"Eat it."

"I can't eat shit."

"You've eaten worse. Remember when you were poor."

"I was never poor, Harry."

"That's your trouble. Now, eat your shit like a good little boy." Zimmerman attacked his own with passion.

Alden played hockey with a mushroom cap, pushing it around on his plate. "The script I'm working on," he said. "It's lifeless. The terrorists don't terrorize, and the victims—who cares about them?"

"Leave it for a while. Go down to La Jolla."

"Sex does not evoke the muse, Harry, or cause great scripts to be written."

"But it evokes hard-ons," Zimmerman said, "and causes great strife throughout the world." He stopped eating and lit a Harry Sherman. "Look, you're not the only one. Look at me. I get tired. I lose my passion sometimes. Who doesn't?"

They talked for a few minutes without eating. The dessert came as Alden finally dug into the Crab Louis with gusto. "This isn't bad," he said.

"It's shit," Zimmerman said.

Over dessert, Alden said, "Kate's coming out."

"Yeah, I read. For the Stackman picture. You going to see her?"

"Why not?"

"Because you always start out friends and end up enemies. If I were you, I'd go to La Jolla."

"Look, if you're angling for that little bimbo's address, I'll give it to you. Christ! She doesn't mean that much to me."

"At my age? Don't be a schmuck," Zimmerman said, a lascivious grin on his darkly tanned face. "I can't handle lap dissolves anymore."

"The term dates you, Harry. But you can make believe you're fifteen."

Zimmerman paid the bill and they wandered out to the parking lot. Under the blinding, smog-filled kleig of the California sun, they wandered to their cars, Zimmerman's Mercedes 380 SEC and Alden's 280 E.

They shook hands and looked at each other, incognito behind their sunglasses, aliens in a strange desert.

"What about *The Darkened Heart*?" Alden asked.

Zimmerman looked over Alden's shoulder at something on the cluttered horizon of Sunset Boulevard. "Not much action, Phil."

Alden shrugged resignedly. "All right, so I had to be a jerk and ask. How many turndowns?"

"Stackman said no."

"How many?"

"Ten."

"Don't tell me. I know," Alden said. "It lacks passion."

"No, Phil," Zimmerman said. "It's too personal."

Too personal. The term rankled. As he drove along Sunset, he played with it in his mind, found that the words evoked squalls of anger and bitterness, frustration mingled with depression.

What the hell did they expect? A Pollyanna story about the boy next door, smitten by the girl next door, bringing her flowers, taking her to the local ice-cream parlor and then setting off for war while she remains true? Shit! Today the young bastard would screw her first and bring her coke afterward. Then they'd go to a disco, where he'd get knifed by a fellow pusher. The entire script would be full of grunts and monosyllables without one clear, finished, intelligible line of dialogue. That, they liked.

He could not write that kind of story. He wanted to write his own story, record his own experience on film, reveal *his* viewpoint, *his* evaluations and conclusions of the world as he saw it. It was time for his own testament.

But *they*, the omnipotent *they*, had said it was too personal. They wanted a damned good story. He was tired of good damned stories.

Christ!

He was on Hollywood Boulevard. Why he had driven this route he could not fathom, but there he was, and there they were. He stared out from the air-conditioned interior of the Mercedes in utter dismay.

It was like a silent film. No sound reached him, and the characters on the screen outside moved in a kaleidoscopic show of bizarre gestures and grotesque configurations.

Long-haired, bronzed, bearded men sidled along the sidewalk wearing tank shirts, shorts, and Adidas. Girls in shorts, high heels, with braless bustlines, paraded by. Painted vans lined the curbs. A game of three-card monte was in progress in front of an X-rated movie theater. Pimps lolled against walls; gays walked hand in hand; prostitutes plied their trade. Freaks. Freaks leaving their droppings on the Avenue of the Stars.

Alden saw a parking space near what had once been Grauman's Chinese Theater and backed into it. He needed to look at those stars again. Outside, the smog hit him like a fistful of solid acid. The odors of pizza, hot dogs, and greasy tacos made his stomach burn. The mingled blare of three different rock hits shook his eardrums. But he needed to see the stars.

At Grauman's, he stared down like a ten-year-old at the prints of Marilyn's hands, Judy's feet, Astaire's shoes. He walked on, eastward, head bent, eyes fixed on the pavement, staring at the faded romance of days gone by, at the Camelot of memory. Norma Shearer, Ronald Colman, Cary Grant, Clark Gable, Katharine Hepburn—the stars passed beneath his feet. Humphrey Bogart, Greer Garson, Robert Taylor, John Barrymore, Ethel, Lionel.

God Almighty! God Almighty, what talent beneath my feet! He laughed, almost cried.

A voice disturbed his reverie: "Watcha lookin' for, man? Sensemilla? I got good Colombian. Dollah a stick, man."

Alden raised his head and looked into the black man's eyes. His "No" was almost inaudible. He walked on.

Behind him, the black rasped, "Mothuh-fuckuh!"

Before he could forget about the pusher, two well-manicured sandaled feet blocked his way. Looking up, he saw a slim young man wearing shorts and an ascot. Earrings dangled from either side of his head.

"I'd love to suck yours, old father," the gay said.

"Not today, son," Alden said with a sigh. "Or ever." He eased toward the curb, walking around the man, feeling very subdued, almost bereft, giving up his quest for the stars. The freaks had taken over. He needed a drink.

Across the street, the lobby of the Hollywood Roosevelt beckoned. It won't be the same, he thought. It was not. The bar had been moved. The new orange and white wallpaper was garish, almost obscene in its blatant insult to color and taste. The large, comfortable banquettes had given way to small Formica cocktail tables.

He knew life was passing him by, but where was it going? The place smelled of stale beer and cigarette smoke. The clientele was mostly lower middle class with a smattering of seedy-looking characters mixed in. A simile came to mind. *Key Largo* on Hollywood Boulevard.

When he had located the bar, he crossed to it and ordered a scotch and water from a barman in a soiled white shirt and unpressed trousers. More orange and white wallpaper.

Sipping lightly, he let his eyes wander about the shadowy interior, reconstructing the place as it had been in 1952, a year after he had married Barbara. Kate was in town doing a bit part on a B-picture, and he had felt it wiser they meet secretly, off the beaten path.

"Is she the jealous type?" Kate had asked.

"I guess you could say that," he replied. "Tell me about your part."

"I always wanted to carry a spear," she said. "It's

called *Amazon Jungle* and I'm one of the Amazons. Dressed in a leopard skin, yet. I have five lines and the spear speaks for itself.''

He had smiled. "No kidding.''

"Me no kid. Me Katymumba. Best lay in jungle. Want try me, sahib?''

They had laughed, talked, and drank. Too young to know, yet two professionals, still dreaming, still aspiring, still grasping for the heights.

"I may be testing for Hal Wallis," she said.

"Oh? Who got you to the big man?'' He'd had his share of starlets—damned hard to keep them from your door—but he hated to think of someone like Kate having to play that game.

"An assistant director. At least he said he can get me to Wallis.''

"Be careful of those," he had warned.

Kate switched the subject to his future. "I suppose you've committed yourself."

"Maybe. I'm not sure yet."

"Your father wants that, doesn't he? Wants you to be a writer like him?''

"I suppose." His mind projected a newsreel of the old man, the gaunt yet handsome face, the proud, erect carriage. A list of credits rolled by. He counted the successes and failures and knew his father had died a failure, though most of his life had been full and complete. "Yes, he'd like that," he'd said.

He had booked a room upstairs, but did not know how to broach the subject. It would be his first extramarital affair, but he kept telling himself it was not really an affair because Kate had been first—before Barbara. Yet he was flustered, nervous. And he felt guilty.

"I've taken a room upstairs," he finally said.

The smile on her beautiful face widened. "Let me change into my leopard skin. Me best lay in jungle.''

Upstairs, they had come together and reclaimed the remnants of New York, making of them something they had never been before. It was as though all else had been rehearsal, and this their best, their masterful performance. She did it with her eyes wide open, brimming with tears and staring at him as though he were a god. And she had, in her excitement, cried out to him again and again, "Oh, God! Oh, God! Oh, God!"

It had frightened him, for he was not a god and he felt guilty for the passion.

I was passionate in those days, goddammit! I had passion!

His eyes were fixed on the orange and white wallpaper, but he was staring through it and beyond into the past.

Sensing something wrong, the barman slid a dirty rag along the plastic bartop, stopped at Alden's place. "Again?" he asked.

Philip asked himself where he had to go—what to do. "Again."

Memories of Kate and the old days had brought on a low point of melancholy. He was forced to look at himself, not just failure with Kate and the work going badly. He thought of Barbara and their son, Nicky. Now, there was his *real* failure. His son. Barbara had had custody and had fed the boy her doctrine of socialism. The lad had been smart enough to get out, but had been affected by his mother's ravings—hadn't tried to see his father or call him for five years. Until last week.

And that had been a disaster.

He had wanted to find a bond with his son, to salvage some kind of relationship with family, but he'd blown it again. He had always been preoccupied, a real prick of a father; the boy had been different, withdrawn, a kid without feeling, without remorse for his transgressions.

It had been about noon when the phone had rung. He'd placed the receiver to his ear and heard: "Hi, Pater."

Pater? What the hell? His anger rose; his jaw tightened.

He recovered, tried to sound cheerful and warm. "Well, this is a surprise." But an edge had crept into his voice. He knew it and couldn't control it. Damn! It was going to happen again.

"How's it going, man?"

"All right." Alden hated the expression "man." It rankled and he didn't know why. "Where are you?" he'd asked, his tone colder than he'd wanted.

"New York."

They hadn't known what to say to each other, so a long

pause added to the tension. Finally Alden asked, "Are you coming out this way?"

"I might, I might."

"When?"

"I'm not sure, Pater." Nicky giggled.

Christ! That goddamned giggle! It was a signature of the new generation, Alden had decided, or the herald of the pot smoker. He was not sure which. "Well, let me know," he had said. His voice was still tight, with little warmth to it. He was trying. His gut churned, threatened to throw up the good scotch he'd drunk. A half-hidden sneer, a note of disdain had crept into his son's voice. It always unhinged him. "Well, let me know," he repeated. "You can stay here if you want."

"I might, I might. I might just do that."

Christ! Why all the repetition? Can't the kid say something once and let it go at that?

"Why the call?"

"Just to say hello, Pops. Just to say hello."

"You don't need any money?" Dammit! Learn to keep your mouth shut.

His son's voice had been cool in reply, taking on a hardness only hinted at before. "I told you years ago, Pater. I don't need your help, your pocketbook love. I can make it on my own and I'm doing it."

That had torn it. "Doing what?" Alden asked, out of control. "Doing what? Playing the guitar? Pushing pot? Some seed money to finance your latest pipe dream, maybe?"

"Fuck you!"

"What?" He had been stunned.

"Fuck you! You deaf as well as senile?" The voice had a hard edge then, an edge to cut steel. "I said fuck you!"

A loud slamming in his ear had stunned him. He had sat in his Palos Verdes sanctuary holding an empty silence, tears forming in his eyes.

Tears formed in them now. God, how he hated this goddamned, fucking wallpaper. He threw his glass at the orange wall, put a fifty on the bar, and walked out, not looking back.

Out again into the desert, into the smog-filtered sunlight, the disease that was Hollywood Boulevard.

The car was an oven. Even with the air-conditioning on maximum, it didn't cool until he turned off Hollywood Boulevard onto Highway 101 and joined the streams of metal projectiles hurtling along paths of cracked cement toward doom or assignation.

At the maze of ramps at the junction of Highway 11, he missed the turn and circled twice, wiping the tears from his face with one hand while fighting to see through the mist of his own wrath.

You stupid bastard! He pounded the wheel. You asshole! You miserable fuckup! He calls you because you're his father and he hasn't forgotten. How long will it be before the next call—if ever?

Self-reproach, guilt, and remorse rose up in him like a tidal wave battering a rocky shore long since eroded of strong foundations. He had felt it crumbling and in his own stupid way had given it a push.

Fool!

Ten minutes later, at the Pacific Coast Highway, he turned off, less churned up, more resigned, ready to stop the personal castigation and examine the other side.

Goddammit, the kid had a crust! After five years, to act as if nothing had happened. New York. He could have been calling from anywhere.

"Just to say hello, Pops." Shit! And: "I'm not sure, Pater." What's all this shit with "Pops" and "Pater"? And that giggle. That silly giggle.

Jesus, Almighty, Christ!

Daddy, is the moon up there?

It had all been simpler then.

Daddy, is the moon up there?

It had been simple when Nicky had been little—too young for the Commie prattling of his mother and the preoccupation of his father. Alden pulled into his driveway, threw the keys on a table inside the door, and headed for the bar. He poured a stiff scotch and downed it straight, lit a cigarette, and pulled on it until it glowed red a half inch. Everything I shouldn't do, I do so well. Right?

But the rest? A fuckup. Maybe the kid was right. The old man is nothing but a fuckup.

Daddy, is the moon up there?

Too late.

The Train, Tuesday, 6:00 P.M. Central Standard Time

Kate was a moving hillock of bags, nineteen in all, as she made her way across the station, followed by an aging black redcap who shook his head mournfully at the mélange of leather and cardboard heaped on the baggage truck before him.

Three expensive suitcases sat upon an old, battered theatrical trunk pasted with travel stickers from Paris, London, Vienna, and a hundred-odd other places in Europe and Asia. One beaten-up gladstone bulged with God knew what. Four Gucci totes supported three cardboard hatboxes crammed with odds and ends. One strange zippered contraption with a dozen compartments, looking like something stolen from a gypsy caravan, rested on six garment bags tumescent with gowns, blazers, and furs.

Her secretary had begun packing. But Kate, in her inimitable style and seething anxiety, had taken over. What resulted could only be described as a catastrophe. The bags were not packed. They were stuffed. She had never learned the art and had given up years ago. But her neurosis demanded she have a hand in it, for if packing was left to others, she was sure something would be missed.

"We'll be late," she hissed, stumbling on too-high heels across the station. "I *know* we'll be late."

"Plenty time, missus," the redcap muttered. "Got a full fifteen minutes till train time."

"I know we'll be late," Kate said, leading the way.

The redcap sighed. "To the right, missus. Else we sure 'nough gonna miss the train."

"It's not Mrs. It's miss."

"Yes, missus," he said then. "I'll see you on the platform. Gotta take this to the freight elevator."

At the top of the stairs, she nearly pitched headlong,

then took off her shoes and descended barefoot. At the bottom, she headed in the wrong direction, until the red-cap, coming from the freight elevator, intercepted her.

At the Pullman door, as the porter raised his eyes heavenward at the sight of the mountain of baggage, she gave the redcap a fifty-dollar bill and kissed his forehead.

The Pullman porter's mouth dropped open. The redcap stared at her, dumbfounded. "Missus, you know what you done give me?"

"That's for getting me to the church on time," she said as she disappeared into the car.

Farther down toward the front of the train, an unshaven, uncouth-looking young man boarded a coach behind a line of other passengers. He had no redcap in tow, nor did he carry any bags.

His personal possessions were contained in a neat, tightly drawn pack, strapped to his sturdy back and shoulders. Along with extra jeans, a few worn shirts, a shaving kit, and a good supply of condoms, the backpack contained fifty pounds of C4 plastic explosive.

The bearded young man who had checked out of the Drake as Mr. Abelson was now more than thirty thousand feet in the air flying westward through puffs of clouds that looked to him like cotton candy.

He was traveling first class. The seat beside him was empty. He stared out the window almost dreamily as candy puffs of white moved by more than five thousand feet below.

"May I get you anything, Mr. Bayer?" the blond attendant asked.

"Oh," he said, turning, startled. "Uh, maybe a Grand Marnier. Do you have it?"

The girl smiled. "I think we can rustle that up for you, Mr. Bayer."

"On the rocks," he added.

He watched her walk down the aisle toward the galley. He liked the slight, sexy hitch to her buttocks. He let his mind dwell for a few moments on a fantasy of bedding the girl, then turned his gaze once again to the open skies.

His expression was poetic, but he was not thinking of

poetry. His thoughts were of C4 plastique, fuses, percussion caps, personnel, timing, hostages, and body counts. He thought about the armored car and the plane they would demand. Only time would tell if the government would comply.

If not, the Nikon was always a solution.

He looked at the pseudocamera on the empty seat beside him. Prosaic, unusual, unassuming, but deadly. As a sop to his bitter sense of humor, he lifted it, unsnapped the case, removed the lens cover, and pointed the camera out the window. He took a "picture" of the clouds below. But the shutter release was on "lock." He smiled.

His thoughts turned to Maxon as he looked at his watch. The man he'd hand-picked to run the show should be boarding the train soon. The others would board at various stops later on.

Nothing would go wrong. Nothing could. But if things should, he had the Nikon, and he would have to waste them—blow them all to kingdom come if need be.

Kingdom come.

Thy kingdom come.

Bullshit!

CHAPTER 3

Moscow, USSR, Early May

It was still cold in the city. Greatcoats and fur hats were the dress of the day. Snow still occupied corners and niches where buildings met sidewalks. Winds were crisp and chilling, scattering papers and the remnants of last year's leaves along the streets.

On the fourth floor of a dirty gray stone monolith overlooking Dzerzhinsky Square, Vladislav Grushenko sat chain-smoking in the office of Colonel Dmitri Petrov, deputy chief of the Thirteenth Directorate of the Komitet Gosudarstvennoy Bezopasnosti, the KGB.

The colonel smoked also, but his choice was a Havana cigar. He delighted in blowing smoke in large, swiftly moving and expanding rings. His huge office smelled like the smoking room of a men's club, lacking both ventilation and adequate light.

"Vladik," the gravel-voiced colonel said. "The Raven is an American. Never forget that."

"He's an American citizen, yes," Grushenko said.

Petrov smiled broadly, winking, his rheumy eyes twinkling, his bald pate ringed with creased skin that moved like a bellows as he gestured. "You're so accurate, Vladik. Always so accurate. But remember that American citizens always refer to themselves as Americans. Perhaps at the expense of their comrades in Central and South America, and the Canadians." He blew smoke rings across the desk, into Grushenko's face. Grushenko blew a stream of cigarette smoke directly back. "Where do you get those foul

28

cigars, Dima?'' he asked, coughing, spitting up phlegm
into a handkerchief. The tightness in his chest grabbed at
him, but he ignored it.

Petrov indicated a carton on a table beside his mammoth
wood desk. The printing was in Spanish. ''Our Cuban
comrades provide,'' he said.

The men laughed. They blew smoke at each other again
and seemed to be having great fun. They were friends, had
served together at Stalingrad and in the taking of Berlin.

The smaller of the two, Grushenko, sat huddled in his
chair, still wearing his greatcoat. The office, a great barn
of a room paneled in dark veneers, was not well heated.
Grushenko was a thin, wiry man whose flesh was molded
to the bones of his face like yellow parchment, drawn tight
and delicate. But his large blue eyes were bright and
sharp. Very little escaped them. His skull was almost
devoid of hair. Only a few wisps of gray remained over
his ears. He was in his early sixties.

Lighting another cigarette from the first, he leaned forward. ''What about the Raven?''

Petrov shrugged his huge bulk. ''He seems to be off on
another of his adventures.''

''Taking things into his own hands.'' Grushenko's tone
suggested that the Raven had acted this way before.

''More or less.''

''What is it this time?''

''I'm not sure.'' Petrov blew a large smoke ring toward
the window. It hovered, quivered, then disappeared into
nothingness. ''He's in America again,'' he said. ''New
York.''

''Are you sure?''

''Our sources have seen him there, as of a week ago.
An explosion destroyed the Israeli Travel Center last week.
They think it was his work. It bore his signature well
enough,'' Petrov said, brushing ashes from a stained military-
cut suit of heavy cloth. ''What's he doing right now?'' he
went on. ''I don't know. But I hear he's getting another
team together. Seems to be the biggest one yet.''

''Without our knowledge again?'' Grushenko asked, beginning to see where the conversation was leading.

''Or our blessing. He's a very independent thinker.''

"Most Americans are," Grushenko said. "What do you want me to do, Dima?"

"The Raven is valuable to us," Petrov said. "We'd rather not lose his services, his usefulness. But he should include us in his plans. And ask. If he continues to pick his own targets, sooner or later he will pick the wrong one—step on our feet. Find him, Vladik. Talk to him."

"And if he refuses to listen?" After the endless years, Grushenko never denied the fear any intelligent man would feel. He was simply checking his understanding. He'd seen too many agents lose their heads over a misunderstood order.

Petrov shrugged again. "Comrade General, the decision is in your hands. Do as you see fit."

Although Grushenko held no official rank in the KGB, he had acted as their best roving troubleshooter for a long time. In deference to his age and many years of trouble-free service to Mother Russia, he was respectfully, though not officially, referred to as the General.

Mulling over what Petrov had said, Grushenko reached two possible conclusions: Either the Raven would cooperate or he was signing his own death warrant. If he was ever caught, or killed and identified, his history would lead straight back to Moscow and the KGB, his mentors and teachers in the lively art of terrorism.

As he rose to leave, Grushenko hacked and coughed until he was red in the face—the heavy smoker's cough. The pain came again. He took a drink from a carafe before he said, "I understand, Dima. Exactly."

"One other thing, Vladik. I'm told the Raven has not drawn funds in keeping with his known activities." The flurry of smoke rings emphasized the possibilities.

"He could be a double?"

"No, but he could be in it for the joy of killing and we are not bloodthirsty enough for him," Petrov said. "I'm sure that's it. He may not be a double, but he could have a second control."

"And if that is so?"

"Then we cannot afford to let him live." The message was clear enough and ended the interview. Petrov stood behind his desk, leaned over it to clasp Grushenko's hand.

"You can pick up your passport and identification package this evening, Vladik. Your flight leaves tomorrow."

Grushenko grunted a good-bye.

"And how is Grisha?" Petrov asked, coming around the desk and putting an arm around his old friend as he led him across a vast expanse of office to the door. "A fine lad, yes?"

At the mention of his son's name, Grushenko felt a sudden tug, a pang of pain fused with confusion and hostility. A sour bitterness welled up in his chest. "Grisha is fine," he said. "Someday he'll make a fine man."

Petrov laughed. "This younger generation, Vladik, with their decadent rock and their use of drugs and vodka. We must give them time, my friend. They do not grow as we grew. It takes longer. But you'll see—Grisha will develop into a fine man."

"I hope you're right, Dima," Grushenko said. He kissed his friend on both cheeks in parting.

Outside, a cold wind ripped through his overcoat, but Grushenko padded along the streets erect and proud, his slight figure drawn up to its full five feet six, his bearing befitting the dignity of a general.

Inside, his heart was taut and full of depressed agitation. Thoughts of his son had intruded upon his day. He could do nothing to change the direction of events. He had control over his assignments, but not over his son.

To the left of his depressed heart, a slight bulge signaled a holster and a weapon. Through the years, he'd spurned the KGB's official issue—the Makarov. Operating in the West, the Russian weapon would be a dead giveaway. When Grushenko filled his hand, it was with a .38-caliber Smith & Wesson six-shot revolver an American officer had given him in Berlin in 1945. It hadn't been standard issue for the American either.

As he plodded toward home through the crowded street, he thought of the years of service he'd given the state. He was one of the few able to compare East and West. He traveled in Europe and America constantly, stayed in Western accommodation, ate their food, saw their productive and carefree way of life.

And as he grew older, he wondered—wondered who

was right. Traitorous thoughts implanted themselves in the recesses of his tired brain against weak resistance. He had been doing this too long, had been given too much freedom of action and thought, was growing old and weak. Weak in mind, body, and worst of all, in conviction. At the thought, the cough racked his frail body again.

The rumbling bass chords of the landing gear roused the bearded young man from sleep. He blinked his eyes a few times, getting his bearings, wondering where he was, what he was doing here. Often sleep erased memory for frightful seconds, and his hand would go automatically inside his left-breast lapel to grasp his weapon. He had no weapon this time, of course, because he was aboard a plane, but where in the world the plane was, he knew not. It might be Tripoli or Moscow, perhaps Havana or even Damascus. Then he remembered, and lay back in his seat.

"We're coming into Las Vegas," the flight attendant said with a smile. "Would you please fasten your seat belt, Mr. Bayer?"

"Sure," the young man said, then smiled his number one smile, the one full of very white, strong, teeth. "Tell me, are you laying over in Vegas?"

The stewardess's smile never missed a beat. "Yes, I am."

"Maybe we could have dinner?" he suggested, his own smile never diminishing.

"Maybe." She still smiled. It was a contest of white teeth and handsome faces, one trying to outdo the other.

"I'll be at Caesars," the young man said. "What about you?"

She named a hotel, and the bearded man went on, "Do you like to gamble?"

"I've never done much of it, Mr. Bayer."

"I'll show you," he said, and then winked. "I'll show you how to win. All the time."

The wink signaled an offer to teach more than gambling. "That might be fun, Mr. Bayer," she said.

"The name's Arnie," he said. "And yours?"

"Claire. Claire Bostwick."

The plane landed at McCarron. Passengers were subject

to Vegas's usual welcome: a long ride on a passenger conveyor belt, bombarded all the way by a plethora of commercial messages blasting from speakers along the way—chamber of commerce hoopla recorded by famous performers. Then the unique cacophony of slot machines from the minute of arrival in the terminal—departers emptying cruelly depleted pockets on the way out or arrivals who couldn't wait to get started.

At Caesars Palace, the bearded man registered as Arnold Bayer. He had planned to exchange his driver's license and credit cards for ones in the name of John R. Mallory from the treasure trove of credentials residing in his attaché case. But since making the date with the stewardess, he had changed his mind. She might call him at the hotel. As Mallory, gambling, perhaps dinner, and what lay beyond would be off. In any case, the next alias could wait. He was in no danger yet.

He wondered where the train was now, and whether Maxon and the others were making their schedules.

He looked at the Nikon that lay on the bed and reached over to pat it gently. Would he have to use it, snap a "picture"?

He yearned to—very much.

Not far away, in one of the better suites of the Desert Inn, another Nikon, the genuine article, much used, lay on a small chairside table next to a portable tape recorder.

It belonged to a young woman of unusual beauty, whose ice-blue eyes were now fixed attentively on the man opposite her, Mike Goodwin, a man who epitomized the best in casino pit bosses.

"Tell me something about yourself," she asked. Since this was not a formal interview in front of a camera, she used an opening question that would tell her if the subject was going to open up easily.

"What's to tell? I started dealing illegal shops in Jersey way back," he said. "Worked the islands: Cuba, the Bahamas, Aruba. Set up casinos for the government of Egypt under Nasser. Now I own a piece of this place."

"Quite a history," she said. She had thought this was going to be dull, a filler between more juicy assignments, something to earn the bread to get back to Europe or the Middle East, where the real action was. But it looked more promising all the time. "What exactly does a pit boss do?" she asked.

Goodwin was dressed in an immaculate tuxedo, a picture in black and white. He was partially bald, but the loss of hair hadn't taken away from his good looks. He must have been seventy, but he looked much less. "It's my job to make sure the casino makes money. I can't control how many players will sit down, but I have to maximize how much they will drop. That's on the average. Some will win."

"Is your operation totally honest, Mr. Goodwin?" She always tried to come up with a shocker. This one might do it.

Goodwin had seen it all. He smiled. "All of Las Vegas is honest, Miss Stern. The state of Nevada makes its money from gambling. The setup is totally unique. The state has rigid controls—hundreds of inspectors floating from one casino to the other twenty-four hours a day."

"Why did you say 'Las Vegas' and not 'Nevada'?" she asked.

Allegro Stern was a skilled interviewer, a free-lance photojournalist who had traveled the globe and produced many sensational stories in the late seventies and early eighties. She took several photos of Goodwin while he answered. The man was articulate, but used no gestures. Still, he had a presence, a hidden strength she hoped she could bring out with her lens.

"Some operators in backwater highway stops will have one table and a wheel. They might not be as honest as we are." He slipped a gold case from an inner pocket, flipped it open, and offered her a cigarette, lit one for himself. "We don't have to cheat. The odds always favor the house. We just have to wait for the number of bets to grind it out for us."

"Some people win big."

"And it's good for business," he was quick to answer. "Word gets around after a big win. Players flock in to try us. They believe the flow might be against us."

"And is it—ever?"

He blew smoke to the ceiling, away from her. "Sure. The laws of probability. That's what I meant by 'grinding it out.' If you play long enough, and you're an average player, we will take your money."

"Who do you fear? The big shooters?"

"No. We fear the player who is expert. One who sits at a blackjack table and grinds it out of us."

"How?"

"If you know the exact odds for every hand you are dealt, compared to the one card the dealer shows, you know whether to draw or stand, how to play soft hands or hard. You can reduce the odds to about a half percent in our favor."

"So you still have the odds with you."

"That's when we separate the hard player from the sucker. If the player knows how to handle his money, to bet up when the cards are with him and to lay back when they're not, we have a hard player and I watch him closely."

"Or her."

"Or her, often enough." He smiled at her jab. "I'm not a complete chauvinist, Miss Stern. I'll take money from anyone." He was handsome, impressive. As she studied him, she began to see the steel beneath, the kind of strength she'd felt when interviewing a Mafia capo. This man was far removed from the Mafia, but their kind of ruthless strength was part of him, just under the surface.

"Is that it?" she asked. "They have to know how to play their hands and bet well?"

"No. They have to play a lot of hands. They need the law of averages to work for them. If they stick long enough and have brought enough cash, the cards eventually go their way. They lay back, losing small amounts. When the cards go their way, they pounce—bet up to the house limit, dragging enough back until they're eventually paying with house money," he said, pausing every few seconds to take a drag from the gold-tipped cigarette. "That's when they really get hard. They double up on their original minimum bet, then double again as the money begins to pile up."

"What can you do?"

"Change the dealer. Change the cards. Offer them free drinks. It doesn't work often enough. If the player has discipline, stays sober, and sticks until the cards go his way, he ends up a winner. We're glad to lose once in a while, but when we see a hard player come in, we grit our teeth and play it out."

The interview went on through the same detail for craps, roulette, and chemin de fer. Allegro hadn't intended to take the time she did. The man was fascinating, took her through the inner world of gambling, gave her an insight she'd never imagined.

He was attractive, the kind of man she'd always found herself involved with. Age had never meant much to her. It was the man, his maturity, that counted.

While she worked, while she thought about Mike Goodwin in bed and the complications of the winning hand, a corner of her mind dwelt on the 747 that would take her back to the hot spots of the world. She had recently covered the latest counterrevolution in Iran and had slipped in and out of the country without incident, almost invisible. Her forte was getting in where others feared to tread— and getting out.

Allegro's writing was strong, if impartial. She despised terrorists and their grip on the politics of our time. Her mastery of the still camera filled her photographs with a vivid imagery reminiscent of Capa and Bourke-White.

At the end of the interview, Goodwin stood, offered her a drink. As much as she was attracted to him, she refused. Once in a while she had to use some restraint, and she had a strange feeling something was about to come up to fully occupy her time. It happened that way sometimes.

Downstairs, the hundreds of slot machines that filled the lobby and the area around the bar raised the level of noise close to the threshold of pain. To be understood, you had to lean close and shout. At the bar, she ordered a martini, straight up, and smoked a cigarette. She looked at the menu, but decided not to eat because she was dieting again. Perhaps later, in her room, she would order up a dozen clams.

She watched the action. Little old ladies pulled at their personal clutches of one-armed bandits in a steady cadence, taking coins from paper containers with gnarled hands soiled by money. Each guarded her harem of reluctant slots with a vengeance one might attribute to a lioness with her cubs.

Down the bar, where it curved to the left, she noticed a tall, thin, gray-haired man of about fifty. Definitely her type. But he was obviously married. Wife or lover, the woman beside him was stunning.

Allegro Stern paid her tab, waved a sad farewell to the barman, and went upstairs to bed.

CHAPTER 4

The Train, Tuesday, 10:30 P.M. Central Daylight Time

Some miles west of Fort Madison, Iowa, Kate Kavanaugh lifted her glass and toasted the young man seated opposite her in the dome car of the Southwest Limited.

"Here's to computer programmers," she said, and sipped cautiously, eyeing him over the rim of her glass, liking very much what she saw. He was young, but he had a mature masculinity that was pungent. An aura of sexuality rose from him like an invisible cloud to permeate the atmosphere.

The young man laughed. "I've only been one for a few months."

"What?" Kate had forgotten what she had said.

"Computer programmer. I don't know yet whether I'll like it."

When he spoke, his full beard jogged up and down and his pale blue eyes glinted. His nose was hooked and strong, though a bit lopsided, as was his chin, which veered slightly to the left. But these imperfections did not upset Kate, who took them as signs of character. Beneath them, she suspected, was a raging yet gentle energy, a magnetism that would attract but never repel. He was star material, a leading man, and she wanted to play opposite him. She looked forward to an exciting yet relaxing evening.

"I've seen you so many times," the young man said. His tone was not obsequious, as so many were, but straightforward, the statement delivered calmly, but with some warmth.

"You have? Where?" Her voice held a little girl's tone.

"On Broadway a few times. And in the movies."

38

"Films, young man. Films, not movies. Or pictures, that's even better."

"Pictures, then."

She knew better than to ask him which ones. In the last, she had been ghastly. "What's your name, bright young man?" she asked.

"Carpenter," he said.

"Jesus was a carpenter," she said. She was becoming slightly drunk. Perhaps it was the promise of the evening.

"Lyle Carpenter," he said.

"What a nice name," Kate said.

Later, as she lay next to him in the sumptuous double bedroom, listening to his soft snore and her own breathing, she felt relaxed but thoughtful, unable to sleep.

It had been as she had expected, even better. He had shown himself to be a strong yet gentle lover, a man possessed of a seemingly insatiable appetite, rampant, rough, almost crazed at times, but still soft, considerate, tender—a volcano restrained.

Yet still not as good as Philip Alden.

As she lay there, staring upward in the dark, listening to the thump and clatter of the wheels, letting her body roll with the motion of the train, she thought back on her life and the many men in it. Too many, she knew, and yet not enough.

She knew, or the psychiatrists had told her, that nymphomaniacs don't exist, that she was merely a highly sexed woman. She knew that Philip had never approved of this, and could never accept it. It had been the basic fault, the underlying cause of the fissure between them. The fissure had widened into a chasm.

Fed by his possessiveness, his jealousy had become a consuming flame, their marriage the charred remains of hope. It had never worked out with Philip, it never would. Yet somewhere, deep within, she wished it had.

40   *William K. Wells*

Washington, D.C., Wednesday,
1:00 A.M. Eastern Daylight Time

In his lonely Georgetown condominium, Walter Trask, a man in his sixties, tossed between sweat-dampened sheets, haunted by deeds past and plans for the future.

Trask had been an original Office of Strategic Services field man, had worked for Donovan when the founder of the OSS was the American counterpart of the notorious German "Willy" Canaris. Trask had been a charter recruit when the Central Intelligence Agency had grown out of the OSS, a big, raw-boned Rock of Gibraltar recruit who could always be relied on to give every ounce of his energy to the Company.

Trask had been at McLean ever since, was an old-timer, trusted beyond question, privileged to the inner workings of the CIA, a confidant of Prentice Tredwell, the Agency's director.

He was also a moonlighter with Swiss bank accounts that would make most Wall Street hatchet men envious. The money came from many sources. Trask was a broker of terrorists. His customers, always nameless, were political, commercial, and ecumenical. A sufficient number of U.S. dollars deposited to his credit could work miracles.

The Raven was one of his. When the most notorious of terrorists was not busy with a Soviet project, he worked for Trask. Both the Raven and Trask had no politics or religion. Their god was money. Their pleasure was the sight of fresh blood. Gender, color of skin, political belief—it made no difference to them. Customer or target, it made no difference.

The 34th Street job had netted Trask a hundred thousand. He had paid the Raven the same amount with no expense money. The train job was worth a half million, which he split down the middle. The Raven would pay the recruits, but most worked for expenses. Labor in their business was cheap—no minimum wage, no unions.

Both men paid a penalty. They each had to live with the horror they created. Trask didn't know how the Raven dealt with his guilt, but at his age, the accumulated guilt, like Jacob Marley's chain of cashboxes, was getting heavier every day.

Sleep was elusive. He pulled himself from his bed and opened a cold beer. He sat and looked out at windblown streets and thought about money. Ironically, he would never spend the money. He had no kin. The millions would pile up in Bern. The accounts would become dormant after his death. He didn't know how to spend money, had never learned to enjoy life.

He only knew how to destroy.

The Train, Wednesday, 1:57 A.M. Central Daylight Time

The Southwest Limited came to a jerking halt. Maxon's eyes snapped open to peer through the coach window at the drizzling rain.

Looking at his watch, he realized they had arrived at Kansas City. He could see little through the window. The people leaving and boarding the train were simply dark stick figures, lurching like stiff robots, hands clutching suitcases and packages, feet reaching for support on the car steps.

He did not see her and for a moment he felt a clutch of panic. But it was difficult to make out faces through the dirty pane and he knew she was, of all their group, probably the most dependable. If she had missed the train, she would have a good reason.

He looked around the coach, his eyes flicking from front to rear, waiting to see her face.

To his left, a Chicano family—husband, wife, daughter of about ten and three younger children—awakened by the stop, decided they were hungry and were busily opening packages of yellow cheese, oily tortillas, and a bottle of red wine. The woman was pregnant, obviously close to her time. While she began to shred a browning head of lettuce, the man unfolded a dozen green jalapeños, then proceeded to hand one to each member of the family.

Maxon's stomach churned.

Two seats in front of the Chicanos, a wrinkled white-haired old man, who looked like a Lilliputian minister, turned to the woman beside him and began to bombard her with a whole discourse on his experiences drilling oil wells. His high-pitched voice carried to Maxon and beyond.

Somewhere in the back, a harmonica began to play and the mournful strains of a slow country and western lament drifted lazily through the car.

The blunt end of a cheap suitcase almost hit Maxon in the face. He looked up to see a man dressed like a gambler, complete with string tie, looking for a seat. He looked out of place. As Maxon turned his head to watch the man struggle down the aisle, he saw Miriam Boros enter the coach from the rear.

She was wearing a backpack, much like his own. As she passed his seat, their eyes met briefly, without recognition.

Maxon's gaze followed her down the aisle as she made her way toward the forward coach, her legs long and firm beneath the tight-fitting jeans, her long chestnut hair unbridled. He could not see the ravaged face, the result of a poorly treated case of chicken pox as a child. Her pack was neat and well tied. Satisfied now and free of worry, Maxon pictured its contents: as much C4 plastic explosive as she could carry and a small but powerful shortwave radio transceiver. She was an expert in electronics, had built the radio from a kit.

He sat back, relieved. *Le jour de gloire est arrivé.* The day of glory. The day of freedom for his friends, his comrades.

Comrades. Maxon didn't entirely care for the word. It was too Russian and he had never identified with the Russians and their brand of revolution.

His was a newer, grander, a truly American revolution. One dedicated to the proposition that injustice must disappear. No more robber-baron conglomerates. No longer a great gulf between rich and poor. One class to share the joys that life can give. All to share the richness of the land and its people.

The New American Revolution. Maxon could picture it.

He wondered where the Raven was at that moment. Probably in bed in Vegas. He smiled. If he knew the

Raven, he was probably not alone. The Raven. What a piece of work.

The train began to move again. Laying his head back, Maxon dozed for some minutes, but was awakened by a terrible explosion, an explosion in his dreams.

Even awake, he could still see the flames, hear the cries of pain as the Southwest Limited blew, its cars shattered, mangled bodies flying into the night.

A narrow rivulet of perspiration trickled down one side of his face. He didn't want this. Would they *have* to blow it?

If it became necessary, he wondered how he would react. He had never killed anyone. His thoughts went back to the night before. Would she die? The woman he had been with? The actress?

No. Not her.

Please. Not her.

His fingers fumbled in his pockets, and when he lit the stick of marijuana, his hands were trembling.

Palos Verdes, Wednesday, Noon, Pacific Daylight Time

Alden sat by the pool. He hadn't bothered to wheel the typewriter out. His mood was utterly opposed to work. He smoked sullenly, eyed the window of the upstairs room in which his daughter slept.

He spent an hour or two musing over his marriages, his life. He seemed to be doing too much of that lately, and not enough writing. Alicia's unannounced arrival had been a surprise and not a very welcome one. He wasn't in the mood for a sermon.

He had become very drunk the previous afternoon. Arriving home from Hollywood with the light still in the western sky, he had come upon the rental car in the driveway.

Inside, she had greeted him with a laconic "Hi, Daddy" and then kissed him, doing little to mask her disapproval of his condition. Alicia seldom drank, her extravagance being a glass of wine now and then. But neither did she pop pills nor smoke pot, so she was in a position to play the saint.

Alden smiled. He loved his daughter very much and wished he could see more of her. She traveled often and their meetings were few, their togetherness approaching apartness. Yet she wrote periodically and never failed to call or drop in when she was in the States and within hailing distance. And she paid her own way through life and the broad world she lived in.

Alicia. A name to conjure with, full of warmth, beauty, and lyricism. Kate's idea. Kate's daughter. But then Kate always had shown taste, just as Barbara had always spouted Lenin. Nicky had been the product of that union, one he'd been forced into by false pregnancy. He didn't want to think of the boy. Since the call last week, he'd been low—too bloody low.

He heard noises from the kitchen and looked at his watch. Noon. Alicia had risen from her beauty sleep. He envied her generation. They all slept late, went to school for half their lives, and journeyed through life seemingly oblivious to the temples and institutions that were crashing down all around them.

Some minutes later, Alicia appeared on the terrace carrying a mug of coffee and munching on a hard roll. She slumped down in a deck chair, long legs extended.

Alden eyed the legs admiringly. Well proportioned, shapely. Kate's legs, as was her long reddish hair. Unlike Kate's, Alicia's breasts were on the small side. She had Kate's features, Kate's eyes, but somehow they didn't blend to produce Kate's startling beauty.

He waited, but she didn't speak. Her eyes were on the pool, and for all her attention and recognition, he might as well have been invisible.

He sighed and finally broke the silence. "Sleep well?"

"Uh-huh."

"Got any plans for the day?"

She shrugged.

"Maybe we could run up and have lunch at Ma Maison."

She shrugged again and bit into the buttered roll, crumbs tumbling down on her bosom and thighs.

"How long are you going to stay?"

Her shoulders moved again. "I dunno." Her eyes remained on the pool.

Alden laughed. "You're a scintillating conversationalist. A veritable raconteur."

She made a lemon face. "Oh, Daddy," she said painfully. "I just got up."

At noon, Alden thought, and sighed inwardly. This, then, was the modern world. A vast network of intelligent communicators exchanging data and information at the speed of light, making better things for better living through rhetoric. But not until afternoon.

"It's not a generation gap," he said aloud. "It's a communication gap."

She threw him a weak smile.

She's finally coming awake, he thought.

"The offer of lunch still goes," he said.

"I'll think about it."

"I'll only have one, maybe two drinks."

She looked at him intently for the first time. "It's not the drinking, Daddy," she said, her eyes wide, sad. "It's that I love you."

He coughed uncomfortably. "I love you, too, daughter." Then he cleared his throat and said, "'What are you doing these days?"

"I'm between."

"Have you quit your touring?" The last he'd heard, she had been conducting fat American tourists to places that totally bored them. If it didn't look, taste, and smell like home, they looked for something that did. He wasn't proud of his countrymen away from home.

"It got very boring," she said. "All those hearty half-educated Americans. And the Germans. They're the worst—demanding."

"Are you going back to Spain?"

She looked at the pool again. "I've got a job, in the south of France."

"Doing what?"

"Hostessing, at a hotel in Chamonix."

Alicia never had trouble finding a job. People liked her, trusted her. She gave them value for their dollar. She was attractive, personable, keen of mind, even, and Alden had to smile, articulate when she wanted to be.

Unlike Nicky. Nicky had never worked very hard, had dropped out of college, had followed the communes and the guitar circuit, seemed content to do nothing and amount to nothing.

Daddy, is the moon up there?

The voice was back in Alden's head. The small, baby voice. He could almost see the large brown eyes of his son.

Daddy, is the moon up there?

He had never answered—not really.

Now he gripped his cigarette tightly, almost crushing it. "Have you heard from Nicky at all?" he asked.

Alicia's eyes went to the pool again. "More than that. I ran into him last year. In Paris."

"How is he?" Alden felt his pulse quicken. He could hear the bitter voice: "Fuck you!" His stomach lurched.

"Out to lunch, as usual," Alicia said. "I didn't understand a word he said. I never could. He took me to Maxim's for dinner."

"Christ! In denims?"

"Oh, no. He was dressed to the nines. One of those sharply cut, pinstripe Italian suits, Gucci loafers. He looked real neat, Daddy. He still has the beard, but it's trimmed and barbered now. His hair isn't down to his waist."

Alden too had been staring into the pool. Now he glanced at his daughter questioningly. "Where the hell is he getting the money? Has he got a job?"

Her shoulders levered up and down again. "Don't ask me. I didn't ask him." She rose from the deck chair and and stretched. "I'll get ready for lunch. And it doesn't have to be Ma Maison. You don't have to impress me, Daddy."

He laughed. "We'll see."

They walked to the house. Once inside, Alden waited for the sound of her shower, then darted to the bar and poured himself a double scotch. Much as he loved his daughter, he was uncomfortable with her and didn't look forward to a drinkless lunch under her watchful eye. He guessed it went back a good many years to his fights with her mother and his then acute alcoholic swings. He had not been a good father. But he had tried.

Alden was tired of the world he saw around him—the experiences like the one he'd had in Hollywood the day before, the rapes and muggings detailed on television, terrorism and its control of good men who had fought and worked for what they had won. Like a mental patient, the whole world had become confused, unstable, violent, and paranoid. Whether he liked it or not, he was part of it, was being dragged into it.

It was something he hadn't bargained for, but who was he to bargain? What was the ante he could put up? What could he accomplish?

He was the average man in a civilization bent on destroying itself, either with nuclear bombs or simple sloth. The course of destruction didn't seem to matter—only the fact.

It was as though darkness had fallen over the world, and all were living a nightmare of chaos.

CHAPTER 5

The Southwest Limited is made up at the 12th Street yard in Chicago on the day prior to departure, its complement of sleeping cars and coaches determined by the number of passengers booked between Chicago and Los Angeles. It makes the run daily and is an "all reserved" train.

On a typical day in May, the Southwest Limited is a serpentine consisting of two mail cars, a transition coach for the crew, a baggage car, three passenger coaches, all double-deckers, and a lounge café. The luxurious café car is a clubby affair, with booths and Formica tables for eating, drinking, or card playing, encapsulated by a transparent Plexiglas roof displaying the passing countryside by day and the awesome starlit western skies by night. Following this central eating and drinking car are a more formal dining car and two sleepers. The sleepers are double-decked, containing five deluxe bedrooms, fourteen economy bedrooms, a handicap bedroom spanning the width of the car and equipped with extra-wide doors, and, last, a family bedroom that sleeps two adults and two children.

All of this is pulled by two GM diesel-electric locomotives, one held on reserve for mountain work, the entire train weighing in at three million pounds.

The Limited leaves Chicago at 6 P.M. and covers the 2, 243 miles in forty-one hours at an average speed of fifty-four miles an hour. In the age of the jet, this sounds slow, but the accommodations are luxurious for those who wish to assimilate, at their leisure, the beauties of their country:

48

the flat plains of Kansas, the majestic rise to the Rockies, the blatant, almost unreal colors of the western deserts. It's also a haven for those who fear to fly.

On the flats, the Limited reaches eighty miles an hour. The slow climb up the Rockies and San Gabriel Mountains cuts down the average speed.

The train is crewed by an engineer and a brakeman, both in the locomotive. The complement includes another brakeman, or flagman, at the rear, one conductor, and four train attendants, who work with him checking tickets. This basic operating crew changes three times: at Topeka, Albuquerque, and Flagstaff. In addition, a steward is in charge of the dining and lounge cars, aided by one waiter, a barman for the lounge, and one floater, a waiter working both cars.

The Southwest Limited has a capacity of up to four hundred passengers. It is one of the last vestiges of a fading age.

The Train, Wednesday, 9:45 A.M. *Mountain Daylight Time*

As the Limited pulled slowly out of La Junta, Colorado, Kate Kavanaugh sat in her deluxe bedroom drinking black coffee and puffing lazily on a cigarette.

It was too early to be awake. She was not accustomed to rising before twelve or one o'clock. The motion of the train, the clatter of the wheels, the stops en route, had given her a restless night. She looked at her watch again, then at the timetable. She wondered how the train had picked up so much time. A full hour. It never occurred to her she had left the central time zone and was now on mountain time.

As she looked out at the passing countryside, she reviewed the events of the night before. The young man had been a good lover, yet she felt a darkness inside her as she thought about him, an embarrassment tinged with shame and a touch of sin. She had been somewhat drunk, she knew, but that did not account for all of it. Her libido had been rapacious, an almost uncontrollable force through most of her life and she hated it. It had caused more than enough trouble through the years and she had come to despise her behavior, at times wishing that she had been born with the morals and instincts of a nun.

I am a Catholic, she thought, and smiled.

She found herself thinking about Philip Alden. How did he look now? She had not seen him for nearly three years. Was he all gray by now? Or just that silver tinge at the temples? That lovely silver tinge.

Her eyes moistened and she blew her nose into a very expensive Irish lace handkerchief.

She had ordered breakfast in her compartment because she did not want to meet the young Carpenter fellow in the dining car. She always found it embarrassing to confront a stranger the morning after.

Nor, for the same reason, did she plan to go to the dome car later in the day.

But she knew she would.

In the dining car, the man who had introduced himself to Kate Kavanaugh as Lyle Carpenter, but whose real name was Gerald Maxon, sat over coffee and rolls opposite the dark-haired young girl with the ruined face who had boarded at Kansas City under the name of Gloria Mass, but whose real name was Miriam Boros.

When they spoke, their voices were lowered, carrying no farther than the table, their droning monotones betraying little inflection.

"Lois and Dunk got on at Emporia last night," Boros said. "They're in coaches one and two."

Maxon sipped his coffee. "They brought the weapons?" he asked. "How many?"

"Enough. Eighteen or twenty. Mostly light machine guns—Uzis, like that," she said.

"Good."

Miriam buttered a part of a roll and lifted it to her mouth along with a forkful of scrambled egg. "Judd, P.J., and Valasques boarded this morning about six at Hutchinson."

"I'm glad to have P.J.," Maxon said.

"I told you he'd make it." She lifted her cup and stared

at him over the rim. "What about the others? Where do they get on?"

"The Booth brothers boarded at Dodge City this morning. I saw them." Maxon chomped a roll. "When we get to—"

The man who looked and dressed like a Mississippi gambler passed their table and Maxon continued to chew without speaking. When the man had found a table, he continued. "Most of the group will board at Albuquerque. Two more at Gallup. Chick and Ali Khan in Flagstaff. Joyce and Merit are already in Kingman. If everybody shows, we'll have at least two for every car."

"And the Raven in Las Vegas," Miriam Boros said.

"Yes."

"It's real beautiful. Real well planned."

Maxon had been looking out the window. "Let's hope so," he murmured.

They were silent for some minutes, eating, drinking, dragging on cigarettes. Then Maxon said, "We'll set the charges after we pull out of Flagstaff."

"That's only three hours before Kingman," Boros said. For the first time, her pockmarked face showed expression.

"Best at night," Maxon said. "No problem. Everybody knows what they're doing."

The waiter came and Maxon ordered more coffee. He waited a moment, then said, "It doesn't take long to set the charges. We'll start at ten-thirty tonight. They'll be ready by midnight. According to the timetable, we arrive at Kingman at twelve-fifty-eight." He looked at his watch. "We're running about five minutes behind, that's all."

"When do I contact the Raven?" she asked.

"When I say so. And not before we take the train. All right?" He knew he'd have to be firm with this one. She had a tendency to be pushy, to take over.

"You're in charge," she said, knowing the Raven would check in with her before then.

"You say that as though you don't like it." He was beginning to wonder if he was paranoid about Boros. He'd had run-ins with her in the past. She wanted to shoot first and think later. That was one reason the Raven had picked him to lead.

"I stated a fact."

"In fact, you're right," Maxon said. He lit another cigarette, inhaled deeply, looked across at her. "Let's hope we don't have to do it," he said.

"Do what?"

"Blow up the train."

"We will." Her voice was flat, hard. "Or *he* will."

"Why? How do you know?" He had been on the fringe of bombings before, but never in the middle of one. He wasn't a pacifist, but he sure as hell wasn't a mass murderer—not yet.

"You expect any kind of reasoning or rationality from the people we're dealing with? What are you? Some kind of jerk?" Her voice was rising to a tight, shrill squeakiness at odds with her physical appearance. "They're assholes! Cunts! Cocksuckers!"

Maxon hissed, "Will you be *quiet*, you idiot! Quiet!"

Boros looked down at the table and spoke softly. "The Raven will have to do it, Maxon. You watch."

"And you? Where will you be?"

"Off the train, I hope. If not, somewhere way up in the sky." She looked at him, eyes slits, face creased. "You chicken, boy? We're a suicide team. Remember?"

Maxon blew smoke across the table. "So you die. The rest of us die." He moved his head around the dining car, indicating the passengers. "They die." He paused. "What for?"

"For the betterment of mankind," Boros said, grinning. "For justice. Equality. For the revolution. For ARM."

"You don't seem to value your life much," he said. He believed in the struggle as much as she, but he was a thinker, while she was a blind follower. Violence was not always the answer. No way he was going to die unless it was meaningful.

"I wouldn't have joined up if I did," she said. "Anyway, what's the difference? If I don't go up with the train, I go up with something else. Probably the nuclear war that fink in the White House is cooking up."

Maxon sighed. "I guess you're right." Yet Maxon was aware he did not like her attitude. He himself was in his thirties and had come to value his life more than he had in

the past. Boros was young, only twenty-four, a raw recruit, overly zealous and dedicated, excitable at times to
the point of viciousness. In a crisis, she might well prove
to be intransigent if not unstable. He eyed her surreptitiously, weighing probabilities, wondering about the next
few hours on the train.

After a few seconds of silence, she said, "Why Kingman of all places?"

"It's the Raven's choice."

"I know, but why?"

Maxon shrugged. "He didn't tell me. It's near Las
Vegas. The Raven likes to gamble."

She sipped her coffee. "He's gambling a lot on this
one."

Yes, Maxon thought, our lives, the lives of all aboard
the train. But not his own. He never gambles his own—a
thought that was becoming increasingly bitter.

"We'll get what we want," Boros said. "They'll give
in. If they don't, then we die. So what?"

So what, Maxon wondered.

"Have you written the manifesto?" Boros asked. She
nodded at a blue notebook at his side.

"It's almost done." This was untrue. He had not started
it yet.

After Boros had left the table, Maxon continued to stare
out the window. Then he picked up his blue notebook and
headed for the dome car, intending to write the manifesto
at a booth. He hoped to run into Kate Kavanaugh.

She was not there.

In a garishly decorated coffee shop on the Las Vegas
strip, Allegro Stern sat before her breakfast nudging a fork
at poached eggs, bacon, and toast without appetite.

She felt lost and rather sad, and as she contemplated her
life, her mind drifting back to the past, assimilating the
present and confronting the future, a loneliness crept into
her soul she could not quell.

She was thirty-two, attractive, lovely of line and feature, successful in her work, talented and artistic. Yet
there was little surcease from the loneliness within, and
wars raged in her soul. She felt little confidence and con-

sidered herself a failure, her talent only an amateur's flair,
her beauty marred by desperation and defeat.

Her life was empty—she knew why. She wanted a
husband. She wanted a child. She had neither.

It was her fault, of course. She constantly picked the
wrong men. The pipe-smoking gray-haired professor of
English at Harvard had been one—that merry, articulate
man who had revealed to her the intricacies of Shakespeare, the depths of Dostoevsky, the flourishes of Dickens.

And he had opened up other wonders to her. They had
bedded in a small, stylish motel not far outside Cambridge
for almost a year. A delirious year. Until his wife returned
from Europe.

She remembered the tall, bearded man at Berkeley who
had taught her photography and darkroom technique. She
knew he was married, but by then she had accepted her
apparent role in life. At times, she had hoped he might
leave his wife, but those hopes had never materialized.

She had been with others, many others. All thin, all tall,
all gray.

The senior editor at Time-Life had come closest. They
had been together for two years, and since most of her
work at that time was centered in the States, they had seen
each other almost every day. He owned a dune cottage in
Amagansett, and during the winters, when his wife rebelled against the cold and loneliness of the Hamptons,
they had spent every weekend they could manage walking
the windswept beaches.

She remembered the fireplace in the afternoons and at
night, the meals they had cooked together, the few restaurants open all year in which they had eaten—Gurney's Inn,
the Shagwong Tavern, Herb McCarthy's, if they felt up to
the drive.

And the lovemaking. He had made her feel like a total
woman for the first time, and he always said she made him
feel young again, as though he were starting over.

Then the ultimatum had come. The wife had known, of
course, from the very first, but had borne it, as finishing-
school wives do, stoically and with bitter tolerance.

Allegro had to admit he had tried. He had weighed it,
considering it from all points, had seriously made the first

moves through a lawyer. But perhaps he had been cheap after all, an Ebenezer Scrooge when it came to money versus romance.

He'd had too much to give up. He had not explained it as such, but she could sense his dilemma. The children, the house in Mt. Kisco, his reputation, his job—and his wife's money.

Allegro's thoughts were interrupted by an overly brusque and officious waitress. She ordered another pot of tea and confronted the future.

It wasn't the men she'd chosen, she decided. It was her taste. Why must they all be thin, tall, gray, educated, debonair? Why couldn't she settle for one her own age on the way up? What her mother called salt of the earth types?

The fact was, she did not care for such types. They all seemed to be fat or leaning toward it, and they were all "into" things. Into rock, into computers, into pot. Allegro hated rock, scorned computers, and despised pot and a host of other things of her generation. She very often concluded she had been born in the wrong age. She often wished she had lived somewhere in the past. The future promised nothing new. Only more rock, more computers, more glass buildings without windows, and much more pot. She often wondered who would govern the country in the future, if it could be governed at all.

To hell with salt of the earth. Give me pepper. Something tall, thin, gray-haired, and sophisticated.

But they all seemed to be taken. In her mind, she suddenly saw a flashing image of her father. Tall, thin, gray. They had been close—perhaps too close. He had retained custody after the divorce, and she had lived with him from age ten to eighteen. He had been handsome and brilliant, with a sharp sense of humor and more than his share of adventure and élan. She had been happy with him, and after his death, the void had come. It had remained.

Tears came to her eyes. She lit a cigarette quickly, inhaling the smoke deeply, blowing it out in a cloud as though it would clear the moisture from her eyes.

So I've got a father complex, she thought. So what?

What she needed, she decided, was a new scene, something to bring excitement, adventure, perhaps even danger. This was her way out of loneliness, out of reflection and the cancer of rumination. It had been so for years, ever since the death of her father.

She would finish the article on the Las Vegas casino boss that night, fly to New York in the morning, and pick up one or two money assignments. Then she would be on her own again, free to choose.

She would head for Europe or the Mideast. Perhaps South America. El Salvador. Try to get an interview with Duarte and then a few from the guerrillas.

Yes, I need excitement, she thought. Something stimulating.

The lunch with Alicia had gone well. Alden had had only one drink, a weak scotch and water, and his daughter's eyes had sparkled as she told him about Europe and described the many jobs she had held and the many men she had met—although she still called them boys.

He had laughed at her youthful exuberance and she had laughed at his jokes and twists of phrasing. Afterward, they had driven back to Palos Verdes and walked along the beach, picking up stones and shells, marveling like children at the exquisiteness of nature.

She left that evening. Too early, Alden thought, and too soon.

"Off to France?" he had asked in the driveway.

She was back in her sullen mood. She shrugged. "Yeah. Back to work." Then she smiled, and her eyes had met his. "But I love you."

They kissed and she drove away.

What is it? Philip Alden wondered now as he sat by the pool under an unusually clear early evening sky. What is this gap? What is it? Is it my fault?

He remembered his own father, how he had hung on his every word, drunk or sober. How he had listened, almost in awe, to the old man's comments on the stage play versus the screenplay, on scene, on dialogue, on suspense. He had been voted three Academy Awards for Best Original Screenplay and had been nominated for five. In his cups or out, he'd been the idol of every writer in

Hollywood. An intelligent man without formal education, he had not even graduated from high school, but he had read and could quote from Shakespeare, Shaw, Coleridge, and Tolstoy. He had started as a comedian in vaudeville and had gone on to become one of the highest paid writers in the motion-picture industry.

I wish I could write like him, Alden thought. But I never will. I have one award. And it looks like that's all I'll get. He pulled his mind away from his father and once again focused his thoughts on his children.

And still could not understand the gap, the chasm, the alienation, between the young and old of today. He knew he was not alone. He had spoken with many other parents and it was the same story, reel after reel, fadeout after fadeout. The disease seemed to be epidemic. The family structure was crumbling the world over. The unit was splitting like the atom. Togetherness had become apartness. It had become a question of *me*—what do *I* get out of it?

Yet, he still felt guilty, still could not understand. Had it been the two divorces? The children had been young. But so had he been when his father and mother parted. Had it been Barbara? What garbage had she preached to Nicky? What had she filled his mind with?

Or was it himself? His own fault? His drinking, his need for privacy, his unwillingness at times to open up, to talk about himself, to share his experiences. It all went on paper and not to his children. Was this the curse of writing?

Shit no! He was dramatizing. He was seeing things that were not there, inventing an obtuse philosophy that fit nothing, complicating an otherwise simple situation, and in the end excusing nothing.

Kids were kids. And they were different today. That was all. That was it. And Nicky had been worse than most; no one could have controlled him.

Yet, something gnawed at him, tearing up his insides. He considered a drink, but pushed the thought aside. This made him feel better. He could control it now—had done so for some years.

Other years, earlier years, he did not want to think about.

CHAPTER 6

An hour out of Kennedy Airport, Grushenko, head lolling lazily on his fully reclined seat, was dreaming of his son.

It was a pleasant dream, full of gaiety, exuberance, and joy. His own son was a child again, eight or nine, and the two of them were cavorting in the green fields behind Grushenko's dacha fifty miles from Moscow. The boy squealed and screamed with delight, and they chased each other across the open space toward the woods bordering the northern boundary. Grushenko laughed, too, and somewhere music intruded, a balalaika playing an old gypsy folk song.

But as often happens in dreams, the mood changed. The rhythm of the music slowed and the colors of the field turned dark and somber. The forest became a black shroud, and on the edge of it the boy picked up a long stick and turned to his father. Grushenko grew white with fear. For the stick had become a gun. The boy had grown ten feet taller than Grushenko, and his face was a grinning skull. Grushenko tried to cry out, but his voice was mute. He tried again, and found himself rising into the sky, a black sky full of white clouds tinged with red that looked like blood, dripping and wet. Then he found his voice and cried out a rasping "Uhhhgh!"

People in the cabin turned at the sound, and Grushenko found himself sitting upright, staring at inquisitive eyes and disapproving faces. He felt as though he were naked.

"A nightmare," he said, smiling, as he relaxed back into his seat.

Gazing out the window, watching the bright sunlight bounce and glitter over a rolling sea of white clouds, he reflected upon the dream for some time. It saddened him. The symbolism was stark and simple. It weighed upon his spirits, suffusing him with an inner reality full of dark thoughts and desperation. It connected in straight, uncomplicated lines to the outer reality, and it was this simple clarity that accounted for his sadness, his loneliness, his despair.

The events of the night before had been harsh, unexpected, and brutal. He had returned home from his meeting with Dmitri Petrov to find his son tearing at the strings of his electric guitar in a drunken frenzy. The dissonant, ear-splitting chords reverberated throughout the apartment in an apparent effort to shake the walls and shatter the windows. They made no sense, these chords, piled one upon another like so many stones from different rock quarries, unrelated, knocking against one another to an incongruous beat. To Grushenko's finely tuned ear, accustomed to Beethoven, Tchaikovsky, and Khachaturian, they were the sounds of decadence—the noise of primitive jungles.

They had argued. They had shouted. They had finally fought.

"It's the new wave," his son had argued. "The coming thing. It will replace all the schmaltz."

"It's decadence!" Grushenko had shouted between fits of coughing. "American decadence! English decadence! *Western* decadence!"

"Better than Soviet decadence," the son replied, filling a glass with vodka. "I spit on it! And I spit on you and your precious police state!" And he had, the phlegm landing on Grushenko's left leg, soiling his trousers.

It was then that Grushenko had struck him.

Looking across the room at his son, at this unkempt youth with long hair, at this drunken boy-man who had only a moment before declared himself a dissident, Grushenko had felt the rage well up within him like rising

lava. He had crossed the room and slapped his son across
the face.

"Do you know what you are saying?" he whispered
hoarsely. "Do you know what they could do to you for
saying that?"

"*They* are *you*," his son said. In further answer, he
swung a weak, drunken fist with just enough force behind
it to topple the old man backward to the floor.

His face a pale yellow-tinged mask against the backdrop
of the intricately figured Persian rug, Grushenko had looked
up at his son in horror, and surprise. His voice was a croak
when he said the single word: "Beast!"

Then he found, in one brief and chilling moment of
self-realization, that his right hand was grasping the butt of
the Smith & Wesson the American officer had given him
in Berlin.

He lay there for a long moment, on the thick rug,
staring at the ceiling, listening to the clink of glass and
bottle as his son refilled his tumbler, before he drifted into
a mumbo jumbo of unintelligible drunken talk. Finally,
Grushenko rose, brushed himself off with a hint of
Chaplinesque dignity, left the room without a word.

He had left the apartment early in the morning, leaving
his son snoring on the floor. He caught the early Aeroflot
flight to Paris.

In a toilet stall, in Paris, he had changed from rough-cut
Muscovite clothes to Western, and transferred his new
passport and papers to his pockets. He boarded the Pan
Am flight to New York as Ernst Eisenstadt, geologist
and metallurgical engineer. His German was fluent, his
accent could be from anywhere, for he had lived in many
countries. That was the source of his accent, the man of
many countries.

One fact he was beginning to regret as time played
tricks with his tired body: He had killed many men.

Now, as he stared upward at the acoustic ceiling of the
747, he remembered the ceiling of the previous night as he
gazed at it from the floor. He suddenly realized the true
import of the dream and the reality: He was not afraid of
what his son might do to him, but of what he might do to
his son.

In the dream, he had risen into the sky rather than kill. A father should never murder his son. Nor should a son kill his father. Of these two truths he was convinced.

At worst, they should stay apart. Forget each other. Each had his own life to lead; each his future to decide. Each shall sow sin, each shall find happiness, and each, if luck prevails, shall find love.

The pitch of the engines changed to a whine. He heard the rumble of the flaps as the big plane began its descent into the layer of billowing cloud.

For a while, all was dark and murky. Moisture streaked the window panes, and the huge mass of flying metal bounced and shook in the turbulence.

At last, they burst through the cloud cover again, and Grushenko looked out and down at the flat fields of Long Island, the blue sheet of the Atlantic to his left, and in the distance, the glistening concrete towers of New York.

They landed at Kennedy early Wednesday afternoon. Grushenko immediately took a cab to his hotel, a small, rather dingy, third-rate establishment in the Murray Hill district.

Two packages and a letter addressed to "E. Eisenstadt" awaited his arrival. As he registered at the front desk, he eyed the mail skeptically. This was dangerous. They should have phoned and named a drop. The new generation of agents was sloppy. They refused to follow simple rules, and their ability to think ahead was stunted. They were too concerned with computers. He often wondered what the future held, what would happen when men like himself were gone. Havoc. They would wreak havoc and bring it all down—everything that had been so carefully built.

Leave it all to the sons, then. Leave it to the misguided sons. In his dingy room, he unwrapped the packages. The first contained ten thousand American dollars in various denominations, all used, all genuine and untraceable. Good. At least they had not erred in that.

The second was a small parcel containing a number of different identities—passports, credit cards, driver's licenses, and the like. He placed them carefully in a hidden compartment of his attaché case.

The envelope had been posted at the Ansonia station and

contained a blank sheet of paper folded three times. For
Grushenko, it was a clear message. The Raven had
disappeared—whereabouts unknown.

He crumpled the paper, tossed it into a wastebasket, and
sat on the edge of the bed dejectedly, wondering whether
his long journey had been in vain.

Eventually, he got up and turned on the television. Not
for the games, the soap operas, the dramas, or the come-
dies, but for the commercials. He was fascinated by the
thousands of wonderful and exotic products the sponsors
ran past the eyes and ears of the American people, titillating
their appetites, stimulating their sexual drive, prodding
their greed.

Watching a jeans commercial, he thought that nowhere
in the world were the girls thinner, more angular, more
desirable and sexual than here in the United States of
America. Nowhere were the buttocks so firm and tight yet
so rounded, the waists so slim, the legs so long, the
breasts so pointed.

He felt the stirring of a long dead urge and smiled. It's a
sin to grow old, he decided.

And then he thought, Decadence. A simple case of
decadence.

The trip had tired him and soon his eyes were heavy. He
stretched out on the sway-backed bed and pillowed his
head against the unintrusive, monosyllabic sounds of an
afternoon soap.

He fell into a deep, untroubled sleep.

Late Wednesday afternoon, the bearded young man who
had registered at the hotel under the name of Arnold Bayer
stood at the craps table in the huge gaming room.

His mood was sullen, scornful. Beneath it ran a silent
river of fury.

He had been betting against the dice, and against all
odds, the dice were passing. He had already lost thirty-five
hundred and his luck was not changing. He allowed himself to drop another five hundred and then quit.

He sat at the bar, ordered a Grand Marnier, thought
about his depression, the reasons for it. The girl—the
flight attendant the night before—had given him trouble.

Why do they always give me trouble? Shit!

She had complained he was hurting her.

Why do they always complain about being hurt? Shit!

She had complained he was too rough, he bit too hard, his heavy pounding was making her sore.

"Shut up, for Christ's sake!" he had shouted. "Shut up!"

But she had continued to complain, had begun to weep, and had clawed at him, trying to escape. He had felt his fury rise, his temper coil itself into an explosive spring, the temper he had never been able to quell.

He had struck her. "Shut up and lie still!"

She had looked up at him in shock and surprise, her mouth bleeding, her body a limp mass of pliant servitude. He had gone on to achieve an orgasm and then rolled away from her in disgust.

In the luxury suite with its huge round bed, mirrored ceiling, and in-suite hot tub, the sight of the two of them was exotic. The blood on her mouth and the cowed attitude she'd been forced into had added to his high, had helped accelerate the De Sade approach he most enjoyed.

Later, as she dressed, she felt at her jaw and said, "I think you loosened a tooth."

He had struck her again, blindly, viciously, without thought. Then he had held her chin in an iron grip, looked at her eye to eye, as cold as a desert snake. "If you go to the cops, I'll kill you. I'll kill you, okay?"

He took his hand away, savagely pushed her toward the door. "First, they wouldn't believe you. Second, you'd lose your job." He spit out the last as she turned the door handle. "Third, I'd kill you."

He held her arm cruelly and spoke just above a whisper, menacingly. "You know it, don't you. You can see it now, can't you. I'd enjoy it." He never took his eyes from hers.

She had left with an expression of incalculable fear in her eyes. She had backed out of the door, closed it quietly, then she ran, holding one hand to her bruised mouth.

She had been right to be afraid, he thought. Oh, so goddamned right. Every time he beat on a woman it was as close as he could come to killing and not kill. Every time it was for his sloth of a mother wallowing in her own stupid fantasies and trying to force them on him. Every time he was striking out blindly at the women who had not understood, who had seen him kill and done nothing to help.

God would help. The god he did not worship would give him final absolution in the purity of hell's fire. But by then it would be too late. What was the count now? No one would ever know. The last one—the Israeli Travel thing—had been beautiful, about two or three hundred. The next—the Limited—could be five hundred or it could be nothing. That one would be on the head of the righteous Lucas J. Foreman, president of these United States of bloody America. This one would not be for Petrov and Grushenko, the doddering old men of Moscow who started him in the big leagues but who could not control him— could not stop the blood lust to kill or bring governments to their knees. This one would be for Trask, who provided the lovely money.

He had to have it! He had to see them die!

He rushed for the washroom and flung himself beneath ice-cold water.

Oh, God! Would no one stop him!

And it passed as it always did, leaving him weak and relaxed, but not remorseful—never remorseful. Afterward, wearing an expensive silk robe and being careful not to drop flakes of marijuana, he sat slouched in a chair in the living room of the suite, smiling slightly to himself, sure that the girl would never go to the police.

Hatred rose again in him. The utter fury turned away from himself to the people, the world, and the universe that made him and bade him live as he was. It was his temper at the point of simmer, just below boiling. When he couldn't kill, could only bruise or maim, it made him edgy and suspicious, nervous and unhinged.

The feeling of aloneness, the unhinging, brought on deep depression. The depression made him want to scream and shout, roust about and destroy things, wreck anything in his path, wreak havoc. Its only cure was action— destructive action. *Blood!*

He was fated not to have such action that night. Soon, but not that night.

He had gone to bed, had slept fitfully. His dreams had been full of floating faces—faces of people he'd killed. They'd floated out of a mist, indistinct: white, yellow, brown, and black. They filled his field of vision from horizon to horizon. They filled a village, a town, a city. The numbers escaped him.

Why didn't they stop me—the busy father, the neurotic sloth of a mother, the never-ending parade of professionals in Savile Row suits or white lab coats? Why did they not stop me?

Now, more than twelve hours later, seated at the bar amid the tinkle of ice and glass, the chatter of the crowd, the almost overpowering clatter of one-armed bandits, the depression had returned. He tried to fight it off. He hated this feeling! He wanted to be like others, be happy, high, on a cloud. He had always wanted to live on a cloud.

He looked up the bar at an attractive girl and then into her cleavage.

Why do they always tell me I hurt them?

Shit, man!

Shit!

He turned away from the cleavage and stared into the Grand Marnier. He reviewed his basic philosophy: Find 'em, fuck 'em, and forget 'em. The flight attendant had not been enough. Maybe later he would find another one to help assuage the blind fury.

He looked at his watch, drained his glass, and left the bar.

In the suite, he opened a small suitcase, exposing the console of a powerful radio transceiver. He turned it on, extended an antenna, and waited.

At one minute to six, he lifted the microphone. At precisely six o'clock, he pushed the "transmit" button.

"Raven to Blue. Test one," he said.

He pushed "receive" and waited.

After a moment, he heard the hiss of a carrier wave, then a voice, a young voice. "Blue to Raven. Five square. Ten-four."

The rules were simple. Keep the messages as brief as

possible. Less chance of detection and direction finder, DF, coordination.

The Raven switched off the transceiver, closed it, returned it to the closet.

He left his room and made his way to the bar again, to drink and watch the girls go by.

Perhaps he would find one.

When Gerald Maxon joined the radical left in 1967, he brought with him a deep-seated idealism and a strong dedication to help change the existing order. He wanted to fight the avaricious, high-handed establishment of politicians, international cartels, and labor unions that were misleading the American people. The rich were slowly and subtly depriving the poor of their rights, driving the cost of living up and the opportunity to work down. They were waging senseless wars for copper, zinc, and oil, all in the name of dominoes and national security.

He had been part of the peace rallies, the radical sit-ins. He had marched on Washington, had attended the 1968 Democratic Convention. On campus, he had protested the Vietnam War. Maxon had a flair for writing. His way with words had led him to become a sought-after propagandist for a number of splinter groups.

But, as the seventies came and went, he had seen peaceful protest become aggressive assault, sit-ins become war-ins, dedication change to grim destruction, idealism take on the face of fanaticism. He had witnessed the emergence of violence.

He had not, in 1970, been in the Greenwich Village townhouse when the three Weathermen had blown themselves to their questionable salvation while making bombs. He had not been directly involved with any of the FALN bombings at Fraunces Tavern, the Socony Building, or La Guardia Airport. But his work for the various groups had made him an accessory and he bore the onus with a mixture of revulsion and resignation, accepting the violence and murder of the innocent as the inevitable price for a new world.

It was only when the Raven had come from Europe, a few years before, where he had orchestrated a number of acts of terrorism for the IRA, the Red Brigades, Baader-Meinhof, and the Japanese Red Army, that Maxon had let himself slide from the side of peace to the side of destruction.

Using his consummate talent for organization and planning, the Raven had culled the very best from the splinter groups. He had taken members of the Weathermen Underground, the Black Panthers, the Black Liberation Army, FALN, and other groups and had formed them into one single unit, one group bent on one goal—destructive terrorism. It was large. It was national. It was organized around a cadre of hard-core veterans of violence who had no compunction about casual murder, and to whom assassination was an ordinary, prosaic part of life.

The Raven had founded ARM—the American Revolutionary Mobilization.

When the Raven met Maxon, he had seen in him more than a mere propagandist. He had instantly recognized Maxon's intellectual capacity, his vivid imagination, his ability to organize, plan, and carry through.

The two had talked, hours into the night, night after night. Slowly, Maxon had come over, had been convinced, led down the primrose path of the Raven's inimitable charm and cajolery.

Since then, Maxon had witnessed the blowing up of a General Motors building in Detroit, the destruction of a television station in Phoenix, the bombing of a restaurant in New York's Central Park, and last, the recent fire on 34th Street.

He had seen bodies explode into bloody pulp, limbs fly through the air, heads disconnected from torsos, and children bleed to death in unconscious silence. He had been surrounded by the sheared-copper smell of blood, the stench of loosened sphincters, the inevitable and final odor of death.

Now, as he gazed out the window of the dome car of the Southwest Limited, as his eyes took in the fading colors of the western landscape, he could not escape the memory of the blood and smells. He felt the revulsion rise in him like vomit. While, up to now, he had not led a team, had never pulled the trigger himself, he had been up close and he'd seen the fury of the devil's disciples at work.

Now he asked himself, What was the point? What was its worth when weighed against the horror of death? What did death have to do with idealism?

The Chicano family was trying to pass the hours in a nearby booth. He looked at the children. The small boy was springing up and down in his seat, stuffing a large piece of bread into his mouth. A little girl was working with crayons in a coloring book. The parents were playing dominoes, the woman looking like a bloated melon, ready for the delivery room.

He suddenly visualized them all dead, bleeding on the desert ground, buzzards fighting over their innards. A cold tingling ran up his spine and he felt sweat at his armpits. For a moment, his vision was clouded and he wondered if he was going to black out.

He looked at his open notebook, read what he'd written, made changes, began to reread it: "Citizens of America! This is the voice of the American Revolutionary Mobilization! We call upon you to ARM! ARM against the tyranny of your imperialist government! ARM against the traders in death who sent you off to senseless wars, who picked your pockets while they promised you the moon! ARM against . . ."

"Well, how is my bright young man today?"

He looked up into the shining face of Kate Kavanaugh. She radiates beauty like the sun, he thought. He closed the notebook quietly as he rose from his seat.

"Miss Kavanaugh . . ."

She laughed and sat down. "Miss Kavanaugh? Isn't that a bit formal after last night?"

Maxon laughed with her. "Will you have a drink?" he asked.

"Thanks. A martini sounds about right."

He beckoned to the steward.

Kate was looking at his notebook. "Are you a writer in addition to your other talents?" she asked, smiling lasciviously.

"Not really."

"What were you writing so furiously?"

"Nothing, really." He tried to hide his alarm. "Were you watching?"

"Not really. I just happened to notice. Then you were studying the Mexican family. Is that what you're writing about?"

"They call them Chicanos nowadays." His voice carried a slight edge.

"Chicanos, then," Kate said. "But why not Mexicans? They *are* Mexicans, aren't they?"

"I suppose."

"Chicanos—Mexicans; blacks—Negroes. I used to like 'colored.' Even my maid said she'd rather be called colored than black." She frowned. "I don't understand the need for this new jargon. I'd hate to be called an actorperson."

Maxon smiled lightly, but his eyes were serious, almost grim.

"Why are you looking at me that way?" she asked.

"What way?"

"As if you're studying me, dissecting me?"

"I'm sorry."

"What were you thinking?"

"Nothing, really." He fidgeted in his seat, unwilling for this to go any deeper. He *had* been studying her, dissecting her in a sense. He had been picturing her dead, lying on the desert floor, torn apart, her blood running into the hardpan.

Once again he felt the tingle. The fear. The dread. This was one of his victims. It was unnerving being so close to one he may have to send to a violent end.

"Are you going to L.A.?" she asked.

"No. Kingman."

"Kingman?" She was puzzled.

"Kingman, Arizona," he said. "We get there about one in the morning."

"Oh." She hesitated, then smiled. "That's hours from now. We've got plenty of time."

"Yes," he said. But he knew he would not see her in bed that night. Perhaps never again. The tingling shudder went through him again. His mouth went dry and his gut felt hollow.

Christ, no! he thought. Christ, no!

CHAPTER 7

The Train, Thursday, 12:25 A.M. Mountain Standard Time

Thirty-three minutes before the Southwest Limited was due to arrive in Kingman, the charges had been set and placed. Sausagelike strips of C4 plastic explosive, four to each car, had been wedged between and under the seats, taped in nooks and crannies in the rest rooms, and layered along baggage racks.

The main charges, placed near the center of each car, weighed less than a pound, but had the explosive force of five hundred pounds of TNT and contained a servomechanism tuned to a specific high-frequency radio signal. Upon receipt of this resonant pulse, the servomechanism would detonate the main charge, which, in turn, would trigger the subsidiary charges throughout the car. Little would remain of the Southwest Limited, its passengers and personnel.

With the train's lights low for the night, most of the passengers were asleep or dozing when the charges were set. Most of those awake had their eyes closed. When Jory West, the conductor, passed through, he saw only a few young people fussing with baggage or backpacks, probably readying to detrain at Kingman.

Only one passenger noticed the placement of the plastique. In Maxon's coach, one man, dressed in a long, swallowtail coat, a white ruffled shirt and string tie, the epitome of the old-time riverboat gambler, was wide awake and watching. He sat in the last seat near the exit, his bag at his feet beside him, ready for a quick exit. He was probably waiting for Kingman and the bus that would take him to Vegas and the green felt-covered tables that were his life.

A movement to his right made him look around. A huge black man, at least six feet three and two hundred and forty pounds, was kneading what appeared to be a long cigar-shaped loop of clay.

"What's that?" he asked.

The black man never blinked, never smiled. His eyes were dull, his face a mask. "Sausage, man."

The gambler turned away from the obviously hostile black man. It wasn't his affair. But further movement drew his gaze back across the aisle. The black youth had just molded the "sausage" to the underside of his seat. Now the material looked familiar.

"That's C4!" the gambler said, alarmed. "I handled enough in 'Nam to know. What the hell—"

The black drew a silenced Ruger .22-caliber automatic from his coat. The hole pointing at his eyes seemed like a tunnel to the gambler as his brain worked its way through its last thought. He opened his mouth to cry out, but had no time. A small hole appeared in the middle of his forehead. He was thrown back in his seat, slumped in the corner, eyes bulging hideously.

Maxon heard the soft splat as the hollow-point pushed its way through bone, then splintered into fragments to spread out and pulverize the brain. He shifted in his seat and turned his head to the rear.

P.J. was smiling. Maxon had seen that smile once before and knew the gambler was dead.

Maxon turned his head forward, bile rising in his throat. The shooting had been quick and efficient, exactly what the Raven would have expected. But Maxon wasn't the Raven. The killing bothered him. He looked back again. The expression on P.J.'s face hadn't changed. Doesn't that spade feel *anything*? he asked himself.

Las Vegas, Thursday, 12:45 A.M. *Pacific Daylight Time*

The Raven picked up his phone in his suite at Caesars Palace and dialed the Amtrak station in Kingman.

"The Southwest Limited," he said. "Will that be on time?"

"Two, maybe five minutes late," a disinterested voice said.

"Thanks much."

"Sure."

He replaced the phone and sat, reached down to the coffee table to retrieve a tumbler half filled with ice and Grand Marnier. He sipped it slowly, eyed the transceiver case open before him.

Approximately thirty minutes to go.

He wondered if all personnel had boarded the train at their assigned stations. He hoped so.

He wondered about Maxon. This was his first really big operation. Would he handle it without fucking up? He'd better. Maxon had been through the wars, but not the killing. He didn't have the killer instinct—nothing approaching the instincts of the Raven. But it didn't matter as long as he did his job.

The Raven had already heard via radio from Joyce and Merit in Kingman. Their van was parked a few miles out of town and the station wagon was ready.

Incredible! A really incredible adventure!

He smiled, a cruel, enigmatic smile. He sipped the Grand Marnier. It warmed his spirits. He could not suppress a giggle.

Incredible! So really well planned, so perfectly organized.

In his thirty-three years, the Raven had learned his work well, had become proficient and adept, shrewd and elusive.

He had not absorbed these arts at the four private schools and two colleges he had attended. His father had pushed him through school after school, without regard for what he himself wanted. No matter what he did to get thrown out.

The last prep school, St. Paul's, had been the worst

experience. He had fought a schoolmate in the gym's locker room. It had been the other boy's fault, witnesses would testify to that. But at some point the need to kill emerged from the depths where it always lay, ready to pounce. He had begun to see red—blind, furious, indelible, and everlasting red.

At that point in the scuffle, it had no longer been a matter of winning, but of killing. Having gained the advantage, he had taken hold of the boy's head, pounded and slammed it again and again against the locker door, not stopping, even when the boy was unconscious. He continued until blood dripped down the locker door, until his opponent's features were obliterated and a red stream ran thickly to the cement floor.

The witnesses, smaller and younger, had stood transfixed, not interfering until it was over.

"Don't you feel *any* remorse?" his pompous ass of a father had asked.

"Shit, Dad. It was him or me," he had said, shaking his head, confused at the question. For he felt no remorse, only a fury, hot as molten lead, at anyone who would challenge his position, his power, his physical being.

He still hated that boy to this day. He could not even remember his name, but he hated him.

He looked back on those school days with rancor and bitterness and in his mind spat on his schoolmates, laughed at their puny lives, their graceless efforts at success. He wondered what they would think of the awesome power that now emanated from his vengeful hands.

Graduating from the schools of weaklings to his present position had not been easy. Other, harder schools in far-flung places on the globe had shaped him, channeled his urge to kill, taught him to wipe out one or hundreds with ease, and, most important, without remorse. The learning had taken him to hell and back, but it was worth it. Kingman would be worth it.

That was the game being played in his mind. Power and death.

The power to move things, to change things. The power at the center that radiated in concentric rings making things rise and fall, disintegrate or explode, live or die. The power of manipulation and destruction. The power of money and position.

He loved money. He loved position.

But, of all things, he loved destruction, loved the sights, sounds, and smells of death.

When he'd been five, he had pulled the wings off a dragonfly and then placed it on the ground to watch gleefully as it struggled to fly. His father had discovered him and slapped him on the face. Dear old Dad and the local police had never found out who had killed the neighborhood pets—never suspected a small boy. He always wore plastic gloves and his rain gear when he sneaked out at night to kill. He washed off the blood with the hose behind the garage.

His father. When he thought of him, which was not often, a hotness filled him. It was part anger, part sorrow, part mystery.

He had not seen his father for some time. When he pictured him in his mind, the visage was obscured by the blind fury of the past, the lack of understanding, the studied absence of any real commitment.

He sometimes thought of his mother and would laugh. He saw her as an overfed cow, fat, short, frumpy, and thoughtless. He saw her eating chocolates all day, never out of bed, reading her newspapers and magazines with the devotion of a child. Then watching television, mindless, undirected, aging, embittered by life, disappointed her causes had come to nothing, helpless in the vortex of a whirlpool that pulled her into oblivion.

An unflattering scene, devoid of beauty, but flowing with decadence. Bourgeois. They had both been, and were, bourgeois.

His real education had begun when he had been twenty-five. It was after all the schools, after the communes, after the odd jobs, after the half-hearted effort to learn to play the guitar, after trading in drugs, wandering.

He had wandered into the radical left, not that he was ignorant of its aims and goals, but because in it he saw an outlet for his aggression and an opportunity to achieve what had become, through the years, a growing need within him—riches, power, and blood lust.

So his education had begun and he had covered a lot of territory. He had sweated his way through the Libyan desert camps, the dust-covered hills of Lebanon, the powder keg that was Cuba, and finally the ultimate teachings of Patrice Lumumba University in Moscow.

In these places he had relearned his lessons in Marxist theory and leftist politics. Here he had absorbed and polished his skills with high explosives, small arms, and urban guerrilla tactics. The training had been rigorous, harsh; sometimes it had been almost unendurable. He had started as a crude, impulsive killer, had emerged as a finely tuned instrument of death—a cold, unaffected, aloof, and merciless killer.

He was the terror of the late twentieth century. A terrorist. The ultimate terrorist.

Suddenly his thoughts were interrupted. The speaker of the transceiver came to life: "Blue to Raven." It was Merit's voice. "We see the light."

The light would be the oncoming train.

The Raven flipped the transmit switch. "Wagon set?"

"Set."

"Confirmed. That's a ten-four," the Raven replied as he switched off.

He sat again, sipping the Grand Marnier, the enigmatic smile again on his handsome face.

Incredible! A really incredible venture—the best yet!

Kingman, Arizona, Thursday, 12:50 A.M.
Mountain Standard Time

Kingman is the county seat of Mohave County, Arizona. It lies in the northwest corner of the state, just sixty-five miles east-southeast of Hoover Dam. The surrounding country is semidesert, hardpan as solid as cement, covered with a fine layer of dust, the only growth some dried mesquite and the lone yucca. For the most part, it was flat, but some rolling hills and outcroppings as high as fifty feet could be found to the west along the rail lines.

Approximately ninety-five miles to the northwest is the garish, scintillating neon-lit strip of Las Vegas, Nevada. For those who prefer to reach the tables of Vegas by train, the Las Vegas–Tonopah–Reno Stage Line operates a connecting bus service to the wide open Nevada gambling milieu.

With a population of about ten thousand, Kingman is a thriving little community devoted to the mining of gold, zinc, lead, and feldspar, with some livestock raising thrown in. It is a flag stop for the Southwest Limited. The elite train only stops on signal to take on or discharge passengers.

On this night, the Limited slowed as it approached the station.

In her double bedroom, Kate Kavanaugh lay nude in her berth under a thin blanket, the reading lamp on, a book by her side, unopened and unread. The room was comfortable, lined with veneers to be sure, but still looked luxurious. Fresh flowers stood proud in cut-glass vases clamped to the walls. They added color and gave off a freshness that masked the diesel smells common to other coaches.

Kate was gazing at her face in a small cosmetic mirror.

The handsome young man with the beard had been aloof and distant in the dome car, had resisted her subtle attempts at coquetry. He had withdrawn from her slowly, but with purpose.

At first, she thought he was embarrassed, as she sometimes felt in the circumstance. But, it had been more than that. She could not blame him. He had his reasons.

Studying her face in the mirror, she saw those reasons delineated in a tight closeup, no holds barred. The beauty, the classic beauty, was still there, but it was marred. Marred by aging, by the way she chose to live. The hair was still full and glorious in its copper red, the violet eyes were clear and sharp, bright and commanding. But crow's-feet were walking the beginning of dewlaps at the corners of the full, lush lips. A vein showed here and there, enough to bid the buyer beware. A loosening, a crinkling in the flesh of the neck. The first hint of another chin.

She did not feel rejected. She felt desolated. Damn it! she thought. Sometimes I play mothers now. Soon it will be grandmothers. She sighed, put the mirror aside. Well, why not? Davis and Hepburn did it. Why not me? After all, a part is a part. A check is a check. No money means no parties, no travel, no joy.

She turned off the lamp and stared upward at the ceiling. A full moon shone, and the reflections of light and dark above her changed patterns with the passing night.

She found herself thinking again about Philip Alden. He was more her style. And her age. But dammit! He loved those young broads. Had it been his fault? With all those young starlets so available? But he always insisted it was because of *her* peccadilloes.

Jesus! What a pair!

She laughed. They would fight, she knew that. The minute they got in the car in L.A. they would fight about something. Later, they would get drunk and laugh and have a good dinner. But the fight would still be there, between them, set-dressing but permanent, never to be struck and hauled away when the play was over.

That had been their downfall. The fights. Neither of them, with all their experience and intellect, would ever understand why. Would they go to bed before the next one? she wondered. She hoped. He was good. He had always been good.

The patterns reflected on the ceiling changed rhythm. The train was slowing. Must be approaching a station, she thought.

The Train, Thursday, 1:02 A.M. *Mountain Standard Time*

Three cars ahead of Kate Kavanaugh's sleeper, in the rear coach, adjacent to the lounge car, Gerald Maxon sat in his aisle seat gripping a fully loaded Browning automatic pistol in his hands. It was a G35 Hi-Power 9-mm, double-action weapon, with passive firing pin block safety and a decocking lever, but the technicalities meant little to him. He was not a weapons man, wasn't truly a killer terrorist. He held the gun in cold hands, hidden beneath a sloppily spread newspaper.

Behind him, P.J., dull-faced, eyes staring ahead, blank,

sat beside the body of the gambler. The dead man was
propped up in the corner, blood wiped from his face, hat
pulled down over his eyes. The smell of blood was camou-
flaged by the unwashed bodies confined in the coach for so
many hours.

Ahead of P.J., Maxon recognized another member of
the team casually going through his duffel bag. Another
was stationed on the upper deck.

The interior of the coach was comfortable and temper-
ate, but Maxon felt cold and hot at the same time. His
hands and feet were frigid, but he could feel sweat at his
armpits. His collar was soaked.

This was not his kind of work and he knew it. He was
more at home with a notebook or a typewriter, building a
better world through words and phrases, fighting injustice
and exploitation with metaphors and tropes.

Why he had let the Raven talk him into this he could not
comprehend. Sure, they'd had some pot and a few glasses
of wine, but he'd been that route before. It had to be the
Raven's will, his power of persuasion. But the Raven
wasn't here now. He was standing off somewhere, watching.

It was almost time!

He had to control himself. This was his operation. The
Raven had said so. He had sworn to do his part, and he
would do it.

It was almost time!

He *had* to do it. For ARM. For the movement. For the
future of mankind.

The forward door of the coach opened. A car attendant
pushed his head through it and announced sonorously,
"Kiiiinnngman! Kingman, Arizona. Kiiinnngman! Please
check overhead luggage racks and the area around your
seats for your personal belongings. Thank you for riding
Southwest. Kingman!"

The door closed.

Maxon's fingers tightened on the Browning. The safety
was on. The door opened again and Maxon's eyes flicked
up at Boros. Her ruined face looked buoyant, full of vigor.
Her eyes glittered. She came toward him and he moved
over.

"Beautiful!" she said. "Really beautiful!"

"Everybody in position?" To his own ears, Maxon's voice sounded hollow and far away.

"The two other coaches are covered by three each," she said, her voice rising. "I haven't been back to the diner, dome, or sleepers."

"Keep your voice down," he said, urgently. "It's okay. P.J. checked out the others."

"What about the stuff up front?" she asked.

"Don't worry about it."

"But—"

"I said, don't worry about it!"

She stared at him. "What are you nervous for?"

Maxon drew a silent breath. "Joyce and Merit will deal with the locomotive and the other cars up front. It's the rear of the train that counts—where the passengers are."

She looked puzzled. "I think we should cover the front cars."

Maxon's patience snapped. "Get your shit together, for Christ's sake!" he said, trying to keep his voice low. "That's Joyce's job. Do as you're told and don't ask too many damned questions!"

She glared at him. "Okay. Okay. So I'll do what I'm told, okay? But I have a question."

He glanced over at her.

"When do I set up the radio?" she asked.

"One minute after we pull out of Kingman."

"Okay. Where?"

"Here, for the time being. In this car. We can move it later. We'll probably set up our base in the dining car," he said, his tone less than civil. "Now get back to your seat. We're almost there."

She left, but not before glaring at him angrily, trying to stare him down, her mouth twisted in contempt.

This was one of the things he hated about his decision—serious games played by children. To them it was their first-grade fantasies played all over again, but this time deadly.

The Limited was slowing perceptibly now. It was almost down to a crawl. Maxon shifted in his seat, looked around the car. Most of the passengers were sleeping. The small ministerlike man was snoring loudly. The woman beside him had let her head roll on his shoulder. P.J.'s eyes were wide open, black, fathomless, pits of murky nothing. Maxon would never know what went on behind that shaved skull.

Ahead, the third member of the lower deck team was pulling his Uzi pistol from his duffel bag and into his lap. He pulled back the slide, clicked off the safety. Fool. Anyone could have seen it.

Maxon closed his eyes and began to breathe deeply, almost hyperventilating. His gut ached from the spasms it had gone through in the past half hour. As the time drew near, he was almost in a panic. The team leader was a fake.

Then he heard a small, child's voice. A voice singing off key, "*Vamos, vamos, vamos a ver . . .*"

The little one was singing.

"*. . . Vamos a ver al niño Manuel.*"

Jesus!

Thursday, 1:06 A.M. *Mountain Standard Time*

In an economy bedroom of the forward sleeping car directly below where Kate Kavanaugh slept, Ali Khan, a dark-skinned man, puffed lazily on a strong cigarette. He was short, wore a neatly pressed madras jacket, a turtleneck sweater, and immaculately pressed slacks. An Uzi automatic pistol, carefully wiped to remove surface oil, rested on his lap.

His partner, Chick, a big blond American youth dressed in jeans and a T-shirt, was busy chewing a wad of bubble gum as he pulled back the folding stock of an Armalite M16. He shoved the square cartridge case in place and cranked a round into the chamber. He worked with a face devoid of expression, as if he were picking up his lunch pail and setting off·for work. Neither man spoke. They were ready.

They had unwrapped their C4 plastic explosive, taped it to baggage racks, and molded it to the corners of the sleeper's washrooms. The main charge was in their own compartment, servomechanisms armed and tuned to the assigned frequency.

As the train jerked to a halt at the Kingman station, the Arab glanced out the window. He could see little in the blackness, a few vague shapes moving about as they detrained. No one got on.

A few minutes later, only minutes behind schedule, the train jerked again, moving forward slowly into the western night.

Thursday, 1:14 A.M. *Mountain Standard Time*

A few minutes out of Kingman and almost at maximum speed, the engineer leaned out of the cab and swore. "Christ Almighty! *Hit 'em!*"

The brakeman responded instantly and instinctively. Engines were cut. Brakes were applied. The wheels locked. Three million pounds of steel, wood, and plastic, eighty thousand pounds of flesh, blood, and bone resisted, sending a shrill, screaming voice into the night. Sparks flew from every wheel.

"My God! Did you ever see?" the engineer asked incredulously.

The brakeman didn't answer, too shaken by the sight to respond.

A station wagon loomed ahead of them, its body stretched across the tracks, its headlights poking lines of white into morning haze, its hazard signals blinking red.

No way the two would not meet. The juggernaut of steel loomed over the tiny shell from Detroit's factories and crushed it, pushing it down the track for a hundred yards in a cacophony of sound and fury.

Then all was still.

CHAPTER 8

The Train, Thursday, 1:15 A.M. *Mountain Standard Time*

Inside, the cars were in turmoil. In the sleeping cars, passengers were thrown from their berths. In the coaches, people were pitched forward into the resisting backs of the seats in front. Screams of fear, cries of surprise, curses. Everyone reacted as everything came to a shuddering halt and the inertia that had built up was suddenly shut off.

The engine crew had done their best. Except for minor cuts and contusions, the passengers had come through without major injuries. They seemed grateful as they picked themselves up.

They joked: "Musta been a cow on the tracks." "Ain't this trolley car got a cow catcher?" "Well, at least we're not wrecked."

Words of comfort and help: "You okay, miss? Let me help you up. You got a scratch there. I got a Band-Aid here someplace."

They were relieved, almost joyful. They looked at themselves, at the others near them, picked up possessions, brushed themselves off. Finally, one by one, they looked around. At both ends of their coach they saw grim-faced young people holding wicked-looking guns, blocking the exits.

In Maxon's coach, P.J. was the first to speak. "Now, all you muthuh-fuckahs siddown! You be good and ain't nobody get hurt. You be bad and you get dead."

Silence.

The train stood still in the night. It seemed as though time stood still.

A low, rich, contralto voice spoke in Spanish. It was the pregnant Chicano woman. She recited her prayers, rosary in hand, tears rolling down her face. She had fallen from her seat. She hurt deep inside.

The Train, Thursday, 1:16 A.M. Mountain Standard Time

The engineer signaled to the conductor to keep all doors closed until they had investigated. The passengers were in no immediate danger. He climbed from the cab, looked along the rail at the smoldering wreck. The gas tank had exploded on contact and rapidly burned itself out. The twisted, charred hulk had torn free and rested to one side of the tracks. When the police had investigated, they could get under way. No need for one of their rolling-stock cranes.

All this flashed through his mind first as he tried to get his shocked brain to think clearly. The brakeman stood silently beside him.

"Someone's there," he finally said.

"Where?" the engineer asked.

"Coming down the wayside. On the right, near the wreck."

Some twenty yards ahead, coming out of the swirling mist, two forms appeared out of the night, staggering, holding each other up.

"My God!" the engineer cried.

"Guy and a gal," the brakeman said. "Looks like they're hurt."

"Bloody miracle that they're alive!" the engineer blurted out, rushing forward.

A voice called, "We're hurt! Help us!" As the man spoke, he lost his grip on the girl. She dropped to the ground. "She's dead! Oh, Jesus! She's dead."

The engineer and brakeman both bent over the girl, exactly what Merit had intended. He took an iron bar from beneath his coat and swung with all his strength, once, then again quickly. The metal crunched bone through the railroaders' striped caps, the sound carrying into the night. Two blows like the pounding on a ripe melon, then two more.

Up above, in the locomotive, a metallic voice crackled from a speaker: "Kingman to Southwest. What's going on?"

The Train, Thursday, 1:30 A.M. Mountain Standard Time

Within minutes, the Limited had been secured. One announcement had blasted out of a bullhorn warning police to stay clear, that the passengers' lives were in danger. Fifteen hundred tons of railed fortress was under siege, locked in a battle of ego, ideology, and death.

Eighteen terrorists held sway.

Coach passengers sat hunched in their seats, frightened, tearful, thoughtful, or resigned. In the sleeping cars, men and women wept or stared out into the night, the desolate, mist-shrouded night of terror.

Police cars had raced to the scene, sirens screaming, then slid to a halt on desert hardpan. Domed lights flickered through the darkness; headlights beamed on the train; radios spouted messages of disbelief. Officers floundered about in dismay and confusion trying to make sense out of a situation that was an unreal and alien world. One more warning blasted from the bullhorn, loud and frightening, telling them to keep clear. They stood at a distance like confused Indian war parties ringed about a wagon train.

In Washington, the Department of Transportation called the Federal Bureau of Investigation. The FBI phoned the White House. By 5:00 A.M. eastern daylight time, Lucas J. Foreman, the president of the United States, sat at his desk in the Oval Office, calling aides from their sleep, drumming his fingers on the huge solid wood desk, thinking of the word he'd had, growing impatient with delays.

He was angry.

Aboard the Southwest Limited, Maxon had moved his command post to the dining car. Boros had set up the shortwave radio near him as he spoke through the bullhorn into the night.

"This is the voice of the American Revolutionary Mobilization!" he repeated over and over. "This train is ours and will remain ours until you meet our demands!" His voice was deep, hoarse, slightly tremulous. "All passengers aboard this train are now hostages. At the least provocation, they will be shot individually and thrown out for you to see! Explosives have been placed in every car. We warn you not to make a move against this train! If you meet our demands, most will go free. If not, they die! And we'll die with them, because we don't care. Do you understand that? We don't care!"

Maxon wiped sweat from his forehead. Boros was on the shortwave, turning to the agreed-upon frequency. "Blue to Raven," she said. "We got it!" Then she switched off and looked at Maxon. "Beautiful, Maxie! Really beautiful!" she said, her voice exultant, her pockmarked face one wide smile. "Give it to 'em again!"

Maxon picked up the bullhorn, but before he could depress the talk button, another amplified voice crackled through the night. "What are your demands?"

Maxon hesitated. He felt tired, disintegrated. "The Philadelphia Five will be set free," he said hoarsely. "They will be provided with transportation to Libya. An armored car will be brought here and a plane will be waiting in Las Vegas. We will take seven hostages with us. Those are our demands."

He switched off the bullhorn and sat back, sweat dripping down his back.

Outside, on the perimeter of police cars, a young officer swore. "Shit! What the hell are we supposed to do?"

"Nothing," his sergeant said. "Just hold. This is bigger than we are."

Ninety-five miles to the northwest, in his suite at Caesars Palace, the Raven finished his second Grand Marnier since one o'clock and slipped beneath the covers of his bed. His lips curled in a churlish smile.

Incredible! he thought. Incredible! They've got the great brute!

He closed his eyes. A few hours. A few hours and he would be ready again, refreshed, bright-eyed and bushy-tailed. He had learned this lesson in Lebanon and in the stark desert training grounds of Libya. A few hours and he would be ready to go down there, be with them, or at least be on the scene. He would do his duty "for God and country." He laughed at his own joke and corrected himself: "for love of blood, power, and money."

He laughed again, then rolled over to a sleep full of faces, the faces he'd removed from this earthly paradise.

To the southeast, where the action was, Merit scanned the controls in the locomotive. All seemed in order. Plenty of fuel, engine at full idle, alternators feeding electricity for light and heat to the cars behind.

He, too, had learned his lessons. He'd learned the hard way in Europe with Baader-Meinhof and in Asia with the Japanese Red Army. Railroads: trains, engines, consoles, the intricate machinery of a rapidly fading art in the Western world, had become his specialty. It was still a major means of transport in Europe and Asia. He had been carefully picked for this job and he was doing it well.

Joyce had skirted back through the dark to their wheels before the police had arrived and had pulled the blue van close to the cab where Merit worked. She handed up two Heckler & Koch G11 assault rifles and a box of caseless ammunition. Baader-Meinhof had stolen a half dozen of the prototypes from H&K's West German factory. They were the only ones in the world designed to fire caseless ammunition—a breakthrough—and the Raven had entrusted Merit and Joyce with them. Their job was to hold the power plant—they had no hostages. The police would be given a lesson in caution.

Joyce supported her piece on the frame of a cab opening, sighted on a set of headlights, and fired off a short burst. She checked the result with night glasses and saw the police scrabbling away from the cars. She switched to full auto and pounded a half-dozen vehicles until their tanks blew, lighting up the desert sky, creating updrafts that whorled out in circles to swirl down on distant onlookers, smelling of burning cordite and fuel.

The bullhorn sounded from the dining car. "Stay clear

of the train. If anyone approaches, they will be killed. If anyone tries to escape, they will be gunned down."

The message had been planned to follow Joyce's firing. The night was quiet again.

"What time is it?" Joyce stifled a yawn as she asked.

Merit looked at his watch and laughed. "Coming up to Armageddon."

When Kate had been thrown from her berth, her first reaction had been to stagger to the toilet and inspect her face.

Nothing. All was still perfect except for the natural deepening age lines and the early morning haggardness. But the back of her left hand had started to swell. It would bruise. She wrinkled up her face at the sight of it.

It was a blemish. She could not tolerate blemishes. To one who earned a living from perfection, flaws were abhorrent, an abomination. Whenever she had been hurt in any way or had been sick, she would see no one until she was whole again. Philip had chided her about it throughout their years of friendship.

Back in the double bedroom, right hand covering left, she gazed out the window, looking for a station.

No station. Nothing but the lights from some cars. She had not heard the crash. The bullhorn sounded like a radio out of tune. The gunfire had been indistinct, like the cooling of hot metal.

What the hell was going on?

A choking spasm filled her throat. An accident! Of course! We've been in an accident! Christ Almighty! I should have taken the plane!

She clutched her hands as though in prayer, still favoring the left. Nothing will happen! she repeated to herself three times, fast. She was scared. Was it over? Was she trapped in the wreck? Would it be an inferno? She thought back to the disaster pictures she'd starred in and knew how bad it could be. Nothing will happen! she repeated again and again, sometimes to herself and sometimes to the room.

Oh, God! Phil! I love you. Alicia. Will I see you again? Oh, God! Let me see them once again, *please*.

She dressed, pulling on panties, a blouse, and a skirt. Without hose, she slipped on comfortable slippers, then looked at herself in a mirror, fluffed out her hair.

Composed, aloof, superior, she opened the door and walked out into the corridor. She was confronted by a young blond giant.

"What's going on?" she asked haughtily.

"You're off limits, ma'am," the blond youth said. "Get back into your compartment."

Behind the gum-chewing blond, she saw another face, dark, almost olive. Might be Spanish, Italian, perhaps from the Middle East.

"An honor to meet you, Miss Kavanaugh," the dark face said.

Kate drew herself up haughtily. She loved to meet fans, but the circumstances had to be right. These were not. What were they doing ordering her around?

"I demand to see the conductor of this train," she said.

"*We* conduct this train, ma'am," the blond one said. "Get back to your compartment!"

For the first time she saw the Uzi, the small automatic pistol. Her first thought was of President Reagan's shooting and the gun his secret servicemen held while they tried to protect him, like those, not like anything she'd used in a film.

Now she was truly frightened. Terrorists, she thought. Oh, my God! No! Not in America!

But she retained her poise, standing erect and proud. When she spoke, it was as if she were looking down on the blond youth, not up. "I demand to see someone in authority," she said, coldly.

"I told you, ma'am. Go back to your room." The young blond waved the Uzi at her.

The Arab face behind him laughed. "Let her come. I will take her to Maxon. She may be important—the big-name star, you know?"

The blond looked back and shrugged. Turning to Kate, he said, "Okay, ma'am. Git along." He waved the gun at her again.

The Arab led her back through the first sleeper, where

two more men with guns stood at either end. Kate's alarm deepened, but she looked neither right nor left.

As they entered the dining car, she saw P.J., face expressionless, eyes dark pits, staring at her.

She shuddered inwardly.

Another youth, holding a long rifle with a telescopic sight, a Sauer SSG 2000 sniper rifle he'd taken from a downed SWAT man in Los Angeles, stood at the other end of the car. An ugly long-haired girl sat before a radio. Her face was hard and cruel, pockmarked from a long ago illness, her nose crooked from a more recent altercation. She couldn't have been more than twenty. She was slim, well proportioned, but ugly. Such women were the natural enemy of a Kate Kavanaugh. "Girls with ravaged faces," the song had said.

Kate's eyes scanned the car. It was comfortable, each table supplied with four straight-backed upholstered chairs. Ceiling fixtures bathed each table with subdued light. Vases along the walls held fresh flowers, their fragrance challenging the issue from nervous smokers. Most of the tables were empty. The few passengers who had been rounded up sat, stiff-backed, frightened. She could smell the fear.

A black waiter stood serenely, eyes dreamy, thoughtful, perhaps accustomed to hard treatment. The pregnant woman wept, kept crossing herself. A little man, open-faced, preacherlike, fidgeted with his hands, as if washing them over a sink. Two distinguished-looking men in Brooks Brothers suits sat immobile, their faces almost registering annoyance, but not quite. Unaccustomed to sitting with passengers, the conductor stood in a corner. One man sat alone, trying to keep his *Wall Street Journal* from shaking.

Then Kate's gaze settled on Maxon and her mouth widened into a broad smile. "Mr. Carpenter! My bright young man. Will you tell these people who I am, that they can't do this?"

Maxon looked up at her slowly, lifting his head as though it was a leaden weight. His stare was hard, yet it retained some softness. It was commanding yet shameful, as if he had strayed and been caught.

Behind Kate, the Arab broke the silence. "I bring you a present, Maxon. A most beautiful and important present.

One for the collection you have here.'' His words were pedantic, as if read from a script, his voice lilting, more Irish-sounding than Mideastern.

Kate saw the gun on the table and knew the Arab spoke to Carpenter—Maxon.

"You're one of them," she blurted out in disbelief. "The leader?"

He didn't speak, just averted his eyes and nodded.

"Oh, my God!" she murmured softly.

CHAPTER 9

Kingman, Thursday, 7:00 A.M. Mountain Standard Time

Thursday morning, as the sun hung low over the hard dust of Arizona and the desert mists burned away, the terrain took on a soft glow, light browns tinged with the purples of fossilized wood and the occasional craggy rock formation. It was desolate country, fit for grizzled prospectors and rattlesnakes.

The ring of police cars around the train had been augmented by two companies of the National Guard. These were a ragtag bunch, rousted hurriedly out of their beds, scurrying to find uniforms, wives calling the signals or complaining about another night out with the boys. They were mostly fat and rumpled, providing no confidence for the curious who had come from miles around.

A company of Rapid Deployment Force regulars, on maneuvers in a nearby canyon, had been called in and had taken up positions ordered by their officer. Captain John Marsh looked as fit as his men. Despite being on maneuvers and an overnight bivouac in pup tents, they were spit and polish, lean and alert. Unlike the National Guard, who did nothing but wait, lounging against their vehicles swapping stories, the RDF people knew what they had to do.

Charlie Beckwith had fought for the formation of such a force since he had been invited to spend a year with the 22nd Special Air Services Regiment in England back in 1962. It had taken more than twenty years of political in-fighting between the services and a lot of clout from high-ranking officers to create a force specifically trained to deal with terrorists. Now, in the Arizona desert, such a force was on site, but had to await high-level approval before moving in.

They had to wait in any case. They would never go in without complete intelligence on the situation. How many terrorists? Who were they? What was their background and training? What armaments did they have? Who was their leader? The RDF could act with lightning speed, knock out one or more terrorists in a crowd without harming the innocents. But they had to know the lay of the land. How strongly guarded were the exits? Did the cars have emergency repair exits or entrances?

Before Marsh took his people in, he had to know exactly what he was up against. Now he had men with telescopic lenses taking pictures of everything on or near the train. Some of his people had parabolic microphones trained on every car. He had sent for an Amtrak design engineer and the plans for each car, but the man wouldn't be here for another two or three hours.

Captain Marsh also knew he'd have jurisdictional problems. The FBI was on the scene, the local police, the state police, as well as the National Guard. He knew his force was the only one capable of taking the train, but the others didn't know that and were jealous of their authority. The decision would come from the White House—if it came at all.

In the low-lying hills surrounding the train, a few hundred yards from danger, hundreds of onlookers had gathered, peering down through telescopes, old opera glasses, binoculars. Their car radios crackled with news of what was taking place, not that the media knew any more than they.

Among the crowd was the dark-bearded man who had left Chicago as Seth Abelson, checked into Caesars Palace as Arnold Bayer, and who had just that morning rented a car under the name of John R. Mallory.

The pseudo-Nikon hung about his neck, and his coat bulged slightly with a new acquisition—a 22-mm Stoeger Luger that a former member of the Weathermen had passed on to him in Las Vegas. It wasn't a heavy caliber, but the hollow-point slugs would stop anyone not wearing Kelvar.

The Raven surveyed the scene below with a smile. This was his baby. The best yet. Not just for the Raven. The best for anyone.

Kingman, Thursday, 10:00 A.M. Mountain Standard Time

Just east of the train at the Kingman station, Allegro Stern looked on with resignation as reporters and television newsmen shouted and demanded a place in the sun as close to the train as possible. Police shouted back and Amtrak public-relations officials tried to act as mediators while insisting the passengers aboard the Limited were in no danger.

Allegro shuffled through the crowd, a tall, athletic woman in her early thirties, a natural blond with startling ice-blue eyes. Everyone wanted to get close to the train, to see the action, record the sights and sounds, interview anyone who knew anything—anything at all.

Allegro had been first on the scene and was furious with herself for not taking advantage. This was her bread and butter. The interview in Vegas had been for peanuts. She had to make this one work, to beat out the others no matter what it took.

She passed two old-timers from UPI and the *Washington Post*. She wasn't listening, but caught the drift of their conversation: "Think it's the Raven." "What's the difference?"

Allegro knew the difference. She, of all the people there, could recognize the Raven. She had interviewed him a few years back and would never forget the experience. He was the worst of a bad lot. If this was his work, they could expect anything. The Amtrak people didn't know what they were talking about. If the Raven was handling this, the people on the train might still be warm and breathing, but they were dead meat. They just didn't know it yet.

She had to get on that train—and off again. But how?

President Lucas J. Foreman sat in a comfortable chair in the Oval Office, surrounded by a team he'd pulled together hurriedly. He loved this room. Had loved it from the time he had been a junior senator and visited it for the first time. When he'd been sworn in, he'd had plans to put his own stamp on it, to make it reflect the character of a strong New Englander from Bar Harbor. But he hadn't. Once behind the huge desk with the flags at his back and tradition staring him in the face, he found he couldn't do it. Like many before him, he was inhibited by history.

President Foreman was Lincolnesque in appearance, tall and angular. He sat, legs crossed, at the head of a large glass table. To his right, the secretary of state, Jonas Price, a short, bald energetic man, fidgeted with papers, pulled at his tie, straightened his pants crease, looked around the table with ferretlike brown eyes. To Foreman's left, George Cash, the national security adviser, was the opposite of Price in every way—fat, calm, patient. He had blue eyes and a shock of unruly white hair. His pants needed pressing.

The secretary of defense, Horace Chance, a big man, neat, quick-witted and personable, was talking in whispers to General Forest Stone, the chairman of the Joint Chiefs of Staff. Stone was dressed in a gray pinstripe, but could never disguise his military bearing—short cropped hair, erect carriage, total concentration on whatever was at hand.

Howard "Dusty" Rhodes, the director of the Federal Bureau of Investigation, sat beside Chance. Opposite him, sitting calmly beside Stone, Prentice Tredwell, the director of the Central Intelligence Agency, had rushed in from Langley, where he'd conferred with the heads of all intelligence services before this meeting. The two men were a study in contrasts. Rhodes had been a field man, had the build of a wrestler, the cunning of a fox. Tredwell was thin and wiry, had been a political appointee, but was the best DCI Washington had ever had. Traditionally, the two men were bitter rivals, almost enemies.

Aides had drifted in and ringed the group, sitting quietly

in stiff-backed chairs. Coffee had been served. The steward and his staff had left, closing all doors. Tension filled the room, though no man or woman, all in positions of power, would ever admit to the tension, even to him- or herself. This was the inner circle—the place to be.

"All right," Foreman said quietly. "I want it known from the start—I won't give in to terrorist demands. So what do we do?"

"Mr. President." Price, the secretary of state, grabbed the floor. "More than four hundred people are being held. I don't have to remind you what happened in Germany and Milan. We have to go slow."

"Mr. President," Chance, the secretary of defense, broke in. "We have sat in this room and many others debating how to handle terrorists and we came to a conclusion." He crushed the paper he was holding. A shaking hand betrayed his tension. "We built the Rapid Deployment Force for just such acts as this. We have to let them do their job now."

"We've seen them in action in Iran," Rhodes jibed. The FBI director never let an opportunity go by to stick it to another service.

Margaret Brooks leaned forward and whispered in Foreman's ear. Brooks, though untitled in the White House hierarchy, was known to be Foreman's most trusted adviser. "I'd like to hear from General Stone." The president's tone brooked no argument. The men at the table relaxed momentarily.

General Forest Stone had been in or directed every battle the U.S. Army had been in since the mid-forties. He had been a strong proponent of a force to deal with terrorists since his visit to Bradbury Lines in England, where he had watched British SAS men in action. He had recommended the pioneers of the American force be sent to Bradbury Lines for a full year of extensive training. Nothing like it existed on the face of the earth at that time. Men who graduated the course there came away as supermen, a breed apart. He knew Captain John Marsh had been one of those men and was as capable as anyone in America to handle the Southwest Limited incident if anyone could. He stated his case clearly and convincingly, but, like those who had struggled through departmental jealousies before him, through twenty years, he met only disbelief and indecision.

"I believe General Stone stated the case very well," Foreman said, knowing half the men at the table didn't agree with him. "We are not going to release terrorists to satisfy this threat. To give in to terrorism is to surrender everything this office, this room, stands for." He picked up a yellowed corncob pipe and put a match to it. Gray and white smoke curled to the ceiling to be sucked away by voracious circulating fans, but not before the sweet smell of Lowlands tobacco mixed with some Kentucky Twist permeated the room.

"Mr. President," George Cash said. "I can't state strongly enough how much I oppose the use of a military force to free the hostages. I say let them have what they want and go after them when they are on their way."

"That would violate the principle I've already stated as my policy, George." Foreman turned snakelike eyes on him through a cloud of smoke. "If that's the best you can do as my national security adviser, I suggest you visit the Fort Bragg RDF camp again."

No man had reached this room without suffering the slings and arrows. George Cash's defeat wasn't going to stop them. "I agree with George, Mr. President," Tredwell spoke up. "I'm sure we can't take the train with force."

"The CIA can't, Prentice"—Foreman turned to his DCI— "but the RDF can." He looked around the group, setting his cold green eyes on Rhodes. "Do you agree with Prentice, Dusty?"

The president was known for his sense of humor during good times and bad. No one was laughing, but they all appreciated the situation. In five years as director of the FBI, Dusty Rhodes had not agreed with Prentice Tredwell once. But he was trapped. No way he could agree that Stone's people should have jurisdiction, but he didn't want to publicly agree with Tredwell.

"Let's hear from Stone again. I'd like to know how his people can do the job. If you insist on giving it to him, he'll have to accept the consequences of his actions." It was the best he could do under the circumstances.

"General?" the president said, puffing contentedly, looking at the four-star general. It was finally going the way he wanted.

"First," Stone said, leaning forward, his elbows on his knees, "the RDF must have time to gather intelligence. I agree with all of you. We can't endanger the lives of the hostages and we can't give in to terrorist threats." He looked from one man to the other, not forgetting to include some of the important aides, especially Margaret Brooks. "No force can move in without knowing every move they will make in advance," he went on. "They have to know where every terrorist is located on the train, how he or she is armed, where the best points of entry are, how strong these entry points are, what it will take to blow them. The train consists of thirteen pieces of rolling stock. They probably have more than twenty terrorists on board, spread out.

"We have to have time to gather this evidence and we're in the process. Standard procedure. If they don't give us time, we can't take them. They are experienced. They know how we operate. If they act fast, no one can take them."

"Do we know who their leader is?" the president asked.

"They're the American Revolutionary Mobilization, Mr. President," the DCI said, anxious to redeem himself. "We've heard the Raven is their leader."

"And who is the Raven?" Foreman asked, his tone cold.

"We don't know. Mr. President. No one knows. But if we're right and it's him, we do know something." Tredwell looked around the group. "Of all the inhuman killings, senseless bombings we've seen in the last few years, his have been the most cold-blooded. The Thirty-fourth Street job in New York last week was one of his."

The room was silent for a few seconds. "All right," Foreman finally said. "Despite the concerns of some of you, General Stone will handle this and will report to me every two hours, night and day. You will be kept informed. You will also cooperate with General Stone, will not hamper his operations by petty departmental jealousies or you will answer to me."

President Foreman knocked the old corncob pipe on a large glass ashtray and began to rise. "We will not capitulate to terrorism. Not while I'm president." On his feet, he turned to Stone. "Do the best you can, Forest. And god have mercy on their souls—all four hundred of them."

New York, 8:15 A.M. *Eastern Daylight Time*

In his paint-flecked little room, Grushenko awoke, fully clothed, his aged joints aching, his brain full of fuzz. The television was still on, but he paid little attention to the image or the voice that droned on incessantly. In the small bathroom, he removed his shirt and washed his upper torso, a flabby white mass of hairless skin. As he shaved, he peered at his parchmentlike face in the mirror and let thoughts of his son drift through his head. The age written for him to see and the son who worried him so were all part of the insidious change that had invaded the aged KGB man recently. He had been the toughest and the most cunning, and he was going soft. He had his job to do and he would do it, but he wasn't as coldly objective as he used to be. Pragmatism had gradually been replaced by traces of humanity—a fatal flaw in his line of work.

In the bedroom, the droning voice continued: ". . . just outside Kingman, Arizona. In a few minutes we expect a direct report from the scene by Milton Clark. Meanwhile, a late bulletin maintains the train was taken by ARM, the American Revolutionary Mobilization, lately led by one of the most violent of all terrorists, the Raven, a man about whom little is known. ARM, led by the Raven, has been responsible for the bombings of two restaurants here in New York, a television station in Phoenix . . ."

Grushenko stiffened momentarily. The razor scraped across his face in a steady rhythm, but his mind was busy, taking in the voice, assimilating details, sorting facts.

Kingman? Kingman, Arizona?

After toweling his face, he went to the bedroom and sat before the screen. The on-the-scene report had not yet come through. The voice continued. A middle-aged man with slicked-back silver hair looked out at the shirtless old agent, repeating what he had said before. His expression was serious, his tone grave.

Kingman? Where was that? Where was Arizona?

He pulled a clean shirt from his suitcase, thrust his arms through, and buttoned it hurriedly, knotting a polka-dot tie sloppily.

Outside, on Third Avenue, he stepped into a phone booth and dialed a safe house in the Riverdale section of the Bronx. The instructions given to him were brief and pointed.

Given an hour and a half to get to Penn Station, he entered an Irish tavern next to his hotel and ordered a breakfast of fried eggs with Irish bacon. Then he checked out of the hotel.

Near noon, he opened a baggage locker at Penn Station with a key passed to him quickly by one of the few redcaps on duty.

He took a small package from the locker and carried it to the nearest washroom. He opened it in a booth. It contained his own Smith & Wesson .38, brought in by diplomatic pouch, flown in by Aeroflot the previous night. It also held an airline ticket, nonstop to Las Vegas.

Someone else had been watching the news.

CHAPTER 10

Palos Verdes, Thursday, 8:00 A.M. Pacific Daylight Time

Philip Alden was having breakfast in his large, airy kitchen. It was his habit to begin the day with a good breakfast, from orange juice through eggs and toast to three cups of specially ground and brewed coffee. It made him feel normal, healthy. It took the edge off dissipation, returned the body to its soul, convinced him he couldn't really be an alcoholic.

He knew it was self-deception, but it was habit, and he persisted as he had since childhood.

He was thinking of Kate. She would arrive at the Amtrak station in less than two hours. He would meet the train, pick her up, take her to a good brunch at Monte's, or perhaps back at the house. He looked forward to the day. They would argue, of course, about everything and nothing. They would fight, then smile, make up, perhaps make love.

He smiled in remembrance. He was picturing her radiant red hair, the sharp, chiseled face, her slim body, her exuberance, enthusiasm, electric vitality.

I still love her, he thought. But it would never work out. Better to be divorced, friends, free to love from a distance—a love that encompassed understanding, free from the encumbrance of legalities.

When the phone rang, it startled him. It never rang before ten, rarely before noon.

"Phil . . ." The voice on the end was quiet, restrained.

"Harry? Isn't this a little early for you?" Alden laughed. "Don't tell me you sold *The Darkened Heart*?"

Silence.

"Harry?"

"Phil. Was Kate coming on the Southwest?"

"This morning. Yes."

"Phil." Zimmerman seemed almost unable to speak. "Have you turned on the news?"

"You know I never bother with that dribble in the morning. Why spoil the day?" He paused when Zimmerman said nothing. What was the matter with the man? "What's this all about, Harry?" he asked, the slightest bit of alarm tugging at him.

Zimmerman's voice was a low-pitched croak. "The train's been held up, Phil."

"Been what?"

"Held up."

"It'll be late?"

"I don't mean that. It's been held up. Taken over."

"What the *hell* are you talking about?" Now he was alarmed. Had the man gone mad? Kate? Was he saying Kate was in danger? His Kate?

"Turn on the news. Call me back later." Zimmerman hung up.

For a moment, Alden stood with the telephone in his hand, stunned, his mind groping for some reasonable explanation. He felt fear rising within him, a presentiment of doom.

When he clicked on the television, a voice filled the room: ". . . looking down now from a small rise about two hundred yards from the train. The soldiers in the foreground are part of a Rapid Deployment Force that had been on an exercise near Phoenix. If you look at the dining car on the right of your screen . . ."

The picture told the story. Alden was looking at the train in the western landscape, the troops surrounding it, the hordes of onlookers on a group of small hills in the distance.

". . . Jimmy, can you zoom in a little closer? See the top of the dining car where the terrorist leader is holding . . . put a loudspeaker on the roof last night . . ."

Alden was hearing it in bits and pieces, his confused brain unable to take it all in. They can't be talking about his Kate. God! He remembered the last time they'd made love—the white thighs, the silken skin.

". . . demanding the release of the Philadelphia Five, an armored car to take them, with their seven hostages, to McCarron Airport . . . One of them is believed to be Kate Kavanaugh, the . . ."

No! God, no! He fell to his knees, his fists balled over his eyes, unwilling to see any more. But he could not shut it out.

". . . Foreman's position on terrorist demands is known to be hard-line . . ."

No! You bastard, Foreman! You'll *kill* her! That's Kate! *My* Kate! He fell to the floor, curled in a fetal ball, willing himself not to cry. But, he cried. As sobs shook him, his thoughts were in a turmoil. A drink. No. Something else. Got to *do* something.

He got to his knees, weakly, then to his feet. He stumbled to the bar and held on. He could see Kate with the terrorists. God! She couldn't stand to have a splinter or a scratch. What were they doing to her? What was she going through? He reached for the scotch, poured one drink, and threw it back, straight.

He felt a little better. His hands had stopped shaking. A telephone was at the other end of the bar. He had to get there. He called the agency that booked most of his flights. The earliest flight had been fully booked, but he got a first-class seat on the second flight out of Long Beach Airport in two hours.

He dressed hurriedly, threw clothes into a bag, and headed out to the Mercedes. Traffic was light on both the Pacific Coast Highway and the San Diego Freeway. He had parked the car at the airport and was through the gate to his flight in what seemed like record time. The flight, an hourly shuttle, took off within minutes.

Now he had time to think. As he sat with clouds passing his window in wisps of fleecy white, his body was stiff and rigid, his gut churning. His mind was a clutter of emotions, a tangle of webs from the past.

I can do the part. I really can. Try me.

The voice, the rich, husky, commanding voice that could carry through walls in a whisper and reach the darkest heights of the balcony.

I can do the part. I really can.

He had tried her and her voice, her beauty, her radiance, had melted him to a state of adoration.

It had been his first play. It was her first part.

How young she had been! How beautiful! How full of fire, light, and talent!

Flash forward to the night they had made Alicia.

The night they had made Alicia. The night they had made Alicia. The night they had made Alicia . . .

Oh, God!

He rose from his seat, went forward to a lavatory, locked the door behind him, and threw up. Then he sat on the seat in the tiny cubicle and wept.

Six hundred miles to the west, another jet sailed like a silver bird toward Las Vegas, its contrail a white ribbon spreading like lost memories through a startlingly blue sky.

Grushenko was not concerned with memories now. His thoughts were on the nose of the plane, its destination, the future.

He knew little of Las Vegas except it had to do with gambling. It was, he'd been told, some hundred or so miles from Kingman, Arizona. And the Raven would be there. He *must* be there. But how to find him? Grushenko knew nothing about Las Vegas and less about Kingman.

He was traveling coach, pinned between a fat old woman on his left and a balding man of about thirty on his right. He saw little of the blue sky, but a lot of the flight attendants. They raced back and forth through the center aisle bearing drinks, food, and shallow smiles.

He ordered a vodka on the rocks, and as he sipped it, recalled that great, glorious day in Berlin when he and Dmitri Petrov had toasted victory until dawn the following morning. It had taken the two junior officers of military intelligence, the GRU, two days to come to their senses.

GRU, OGPU, NKVD, KGB—all the same, in essence, if not in the subtle Russian bureaucracy. Security police,

spies, spooks, and assassins if need be. Working for the
ideals of the Soviet state—what his own son had called a
police state.

He sighed. We need police. Without police we would
have no order, no plan, no scheme to delineate the lines of
civilization from those of chaos.

The Raven. His thoughts came back to the present and
the problem. We taught him. We trained him. We incul-
cated and programmed his mind like a computer. And now
the machine had rebelled, was going wild, was thinking
for itself. The revolt of the machines. Would it happen
throughout the world? Is madness the end of the game?

Not that the Raven's activities were unacceptable or
inimical to the interests of the Soviet Union. Any leftist
terrorism, unrest or revolution in any part of the world,
advanced its policies. Still, a man like the Raven might
become more of a detriment than an attribute. His sense of
independence, his lust for blood, for power and recognition, could become a negative factor in a scale of tradi-
tional values, upsetting the balance, disturbing an otherwise
peaceful war of nerves.

As Petrov had said, the Raven must be cautioned or
eliminated before he brought embarrassment to the Soviet
Union. Here, Grushenko thought, we are not dealing with
Libya, Cuba, or the Congo. This was the United States of
America, whose megatons and preemptive strike power
were awesome.

The Raven must be reasoned with and, if he did
not accept reason, eliminated. That was Grushenko's
mission—to evaluate, weigh, consider, then to decide.
It could go either way. It would not be easy, but it was
necessary.

The balding man to his right excused himself and while
he was gone, Grushenko moved over to the window seat
and gazed down at the terrain below.

He was amazed at the huge expanse of desert. It looked
like portions of the Gobi.

Where would he find the Raven in all this?

Again he wondered if he wasn't going soft. Was the job
getting to be too much for him? Was he feeling too much

empathy for the Raven's victims? Would he be able to evaluate the Raven's actions when the time came?

The coughing returned and the pain. Damn the pain! He had to keep going.

The Train, Thursday, 3:00 P.M. *Mountain Standard Time*

Miriam Boros's voice rang out across the western land in harsh, hate-filled tones.

"We want no phone lines! And we want no phony psychiatrists trying to talk us out of it. That kind of shit won't work. Hear that? We don't give a shit! We don't care! Hear that? We just don't goddamned care! Try getting a wire team up here and we'll blast 'em to hell, then blast the whole fuckin' train!"

Behind her, P.J. said, "That's the way, baby. Tell them muthuhs to go fuck 'emselves."

"Shut up, P.J.," Maxon said. "And you, too, Miriam. Cut the PA."

"All right. All right. So I'm cutting it," she said, flipping the switch.

Twelve people sat or fidgeted in the dining car—none calm: four terrorists, six passengers, the conductor, and a waiter, seven of them destined for Libya.

The tiny oilman, Chester Good, was terrified, but tried desperately to keep his fear from showing. He didn't succeed. He thought of his wife, Martha—whether he would ever see her again. His eyes were wide, like those of a cornered animal. He sat on the edge of his chair as if he were going to spring at any moment. In this time of danger, he thought kindly of his gargantuan wife, forgave her the years of domination.

The two vice-presidents of Litton, Hugh J. Fine and Fred H. Foley, played cards, appeared to be calm, cool, and reserved, never looking to the side, only at the cards and each other's faces. They had little choice. Both felt a show of strength or indifference was the best course to follow. Actually both were damp from sweat—the cold sweat of abject fear. Fred had soiled himself when he'd seen the dead gambler pulled from his seat and thrown from the car. He longed for a shower and a fresh pair of shorts.

The conductor, Jory West, was a rotund man who had been with the line for thirty-two years. He had dealt with every kind of hoodlum imaginable in that time, but never anything like this. Jory was the only one who was totally calm—a unique calmness that can only come from total resignation. He had lost his wife to cancer two years before. His children seldom called him. Last week the doctors had told him he had only two months to live. Death now or later meant little. He had been through the gut-wrenching "why me's," the days of hatred for a pitiless god, and the final state of acceptance. He had not told his boss, had opted to work out his last days.

Somehow, Jory West would get to these bastards. He never took his eyes from the gun on the table in front of the leader.

Bobby Elson, the average height, average weight, average broker, hid behind the *Wall Street Journal* as he had all his life. He had sat at his desk in the trading room, answered his phone, and talked with confidence, bought and sold, but never had been able to face the world of reality and all its ugliness. The trading room, his one-room bachelor apartment, and his mother's house for Sunday dinner had been his world. He had never seen a customer. Never wanted to. He couldn't deal with life. The words on the sheet in front of him were blurred, his eyes unfocused. Bobby Elson had gone totally and irrevocably mad in the past few hours.

Maria Gonzales, her abdomen swollen, her red cotton dress ridden up, revealing huge coffee-colored thighs, sat at a corner table, moaning softly to herself. She needed her family, couldn't stand the separation. She pulled a nail-bitten hand through straggly black hair at least once a minute, totally unconscious of the act. She wiped tears from her face with a frayed and grayed handkerchief. The child within her moved incessantly. Her time was near—she knew it, could feel it. But fear of death was closer than new life. She could smell death in this place.

Josh Amos, the waiter, filled his time fetching drinks and food or standing idly by, as he had all his adult life. Of all those in the dining car, he was the calmest. He feared no privation because he'd never had anything. He didn't fear the loss of freedom because he had never had real freedom from the day he'd been born. What could these muthuhs do to him that was so bad?

P.J. sat like a fat Buddha, his gun on his lap, his eyes slits of hate. Miriam Boros looked from one to the other, a sneer permanently etched on her face. The fourth terrorist, a short, fat reject from society they called Judd, leaned against an exit door, his sniper rifle held loosely in both hands.

Maxon gazed out the window at the surrounding troops, now and then glancing surreptitiously at Kate Kavanaugh.

Kate was held by one thought: Nothing will happen! Nothing will happen! Nothing will happen! Inside, she was a bundle of breaking twigs, splintered nerves, dead, falling leaves. Outside, she appeared reserved, cool, a mannequin of chin-high courage.

Act! she said to herself. Act! Perform! Command! Get them in your grip and sit them down stunned! Perform until their mouths open, their eyes moisten, their hands wring, and the rafters shake.

Christ! This is your greatest role. Do it! Do it from all the great parts you selected so carefully. Do it from the laundry list in your head. Who had said that? Ellen Terry? No. Older. Mrs. Fiske?

Forget the stage fright. Get the hell out there and *do it*! Or you'll never get off this stage alive.

She raised her head and looked at Maxon one table away. "May I sit with you?" she asked.

He seemed stunned and didn't answer. She had no way of knowing he was going through a thought process not too unlike her own.

She rose to her feet, dignified, poised, gliding easily, as though across a set, and settled herself at his table.

"Why?" she asked slowly. "Why?"

He looked at her for a moment, then dropped his gaze to the table. After a moment, he raised his eyes to hers. "Because it's necessary," he said, his voice expressionless.

"Necessary? For what?" Kate asked.

"To get rid of the shit. The deadwood, the garbage." As he spoke, his words were harsh, but his eyes were soft, looking at her as if through a screen. "The governments, the conglomerates, the multinationals who are all shaking us down, leaning on our shoulders, picking our pockets while their profits shoot through the roof."

"You're a Communist," she said.

Maxon shrugged. "Maybe. Maybe not. What's the difference? It's all the same to me. The system has to go."

"It's been good to me," Kate Kavanaugh said icily. "Do I look like a conglomerate? I had to do it the hard way, with my own hands, my own head. Alone."

Maxon didn't answer.

"That waiter, the conductor, the Chicano woman—do they look like multinational corporations?" Her eyes flashed with contempt. "And what about the others on this train? What are they? What have they done to you?"

"It's necessary," Maxon repeated.

"Necessary? Necessary to kill innocent people? To take innocent lives? Women and children, pregnant women who can't understand your language? Men who have families, men who take home just enough money to get by and support those families? Are they against you? Robbing you? Picking your pockets?" Her voice was deep, authoritative, throaty. It carried through the car.

Boros watched them from her place beside the radio. She didn't like the tall, haughty woman, and beneath the hatred was a seething envy, envy for what she was, had made of herself. But most of all, envy of her beauty.

"Tell her to fuck off!" she screamed.

"Shut your mouth!" Maxon said, then turned back to Kate. "You forget one thing, Miss Kavanaugh—"

"Miss Kavanaugh! You weren't so formal the other night."

His eyes flicked down. He looked ashamed. "I didn't think this would have to happen. I wasn't even thinking about it at all." He paused. "I'm sorry."

"I'm sure," she said scornfully. "What were you going to tell me, *Mr. Maxon*?" Her smile was disdainful, her eyes glittering.

"What Lenin said: 'The purpose of terrorism is to terrorize.' And that's precisely what we are doing."

Beneath the table, Kate Kavanaugh's knees were shaking. She smiled again. "Lenin was an awful playwright," she said.

CHAPTER 11

The Site, Thursday, 3:30 P.M. *Mountain Standard Time*

A hundred yards from the immobile train, in the heat of the desert afternoon, Captain March had set up a long table and was going over blueprints with the Amtrak design engineer who had finally arrived from the head office in Chicago. They had been at it for an hour, going over the whole structure of the train, bolt by bolt, steel sheet by steel sheet. In another hour, the captain would know as much about the structure of the train as the man who had brought the plans.

Another hundred yards behind the troops, an area had been marked off for television crews, newsmen, and reporters.

Allegro Stern snapped picture after picture of the train, the National Guard, and the RDF troops surrounding it. She had taken zoom shots of the small splotch that was a dead body lying outside the rear door of the third coach, attracting swarms of flies. Apparently he'd been a gambler on the way to Vegas. They had shot him and tossed his body out, announcing who he was and that he wouldn't cooperate, using him as an example of their intent.

Allegro had never believed in just reporting the news. She had gone in and found news, helped make news, had stirred it up and spit it out.

In the rucksack on her back she kept a variety of gadgets she seldom used. But when she did, they put her out in front of the competition. Now she wore a set of high-gain earphones that shut out the sounds of the disgruntled reporters around her. They were plugged into a gadget she held to her eye like a massive camera lens. It was a Double Farfoon Bionic Ear, DSD, distant sound detector, used by troops in the jungle and by deep-woods hunters. It had served her well in the Middle East and in Africa. She focused in on the RDF captain and his Amtrak visitor. She listened and she recorded.

". . . in the dining car. That's the third from the rear. Got about ten hostages with them." The captain was pointing to the blueprints, talking to the Amtrak person and his lieutenant. "Got to get in at several points without being seen. Can't blow our way in. Got to be something else . . ."

". . . washrooms. Two to each coach. Maintenance trap door in each. Got to get underneath, turn two butterfly screws, drop the hatch down. Double floor with plumbing connections underneath. Washroom floor hinges upward. Smallest men could squeeze through . . ."

The sound of the news team helicopters drowned out their discussion. Allegro packed away the bionic ear and put her zoom lens to her eye. The back of the train was guarded by the National Guard. They were sitting around, smoking. Their tents were set up in a depression several hundred feet behind their lines. They seemed unconcerned, anxious for their shift to end so they could get back to the tents and the cookhouse that had been set up. She remembered other days, or nights, she had crawled through similar lines to reach the real story. Bored troops were sometimes almost as bad as none at all.

As she knelt to get a shot from a low angle, she noticed movement beside her, the shuffle of an expensive shoe and a length of gray flannel trouser leg. Both struck her as out of place on a dusty desert knoll among a group of hard-working, underpaid reporters—unless it was Dan Rather or the Old Man himself. But they both knew better than to wear the best on location.

She eased up from the ground and, while rising, beheld what she had once or twice before in her life. Love at first sight. Love she knew would probably not be lasting love, the real love she craved. And, the first sight, the joy of discovery, might not last more than two days—if that.

She pulled a crumpled pack of cigarettes from her bush jacket and performed the subtle act of patting her pockets for a match. As expected, a lighter sparked in front of her face.

"Thanks," she said, blowing out the first satisfying lungful, looking up into his face.

What she had seen at first sight had been merely a fleeting wisp, but second sight was pure, solid, granite. He was tall, thin, gray, his body lean but hard. His eyes were expressive and beautiful, and the bones of his face were strong and well defined.

Oh, shit! she thought. She felt her pulse quicken.

An air of despair seemed to surround him. His strong shoulders were hunched, and his blue eyes, sad.

Allegro smiled. "From the look of the threads, you must be with *Fortune*."

Alden looked at her and saw honesty, directness. "I'm not with the press. I got in on my Screen Writers' card. The police don't know the difference apparently."

"Looking for a story?"

"More or less. I hope it has a happy ending."

Allegro's face grew serious. "So do I. But it's the Raven, you know."

Alden stared into the distance, toward the train. "The Raven? I think I've heard of him."

"You must if you've read the papers."

"I don't."

He was distant, aloof, within himself. She remained silent, staring at the Limited with him.

She knew he was thinking about her now, could feel his eyes turn to her, appraise what he saw. Her ice-blue eyes and long blond hair were what they usually commented on first. He would do so before the day was through. She wasn't an egoist, just used to adulation, used to fending it off. He would see her perfect complexion, dusted by desert brown, and the almost perfect body. He would wonder what she was doing in a place like this, the classic line.

She could feel the loss when he pulled his thoughts away from her and back to the train. He knew someone there. That was it—someone he loved. She could feel the vibes.

Damn! Why did it have to happen that way? Always did for her. Every man she truly wanted had someone else he cared about. She could feel the outcry from his tortured soul and wondered who it was he loved so.

"My wife is on that train," he said.

Allegro's head jerked around. "Oh. I'm so sorry."

She felt alone again. The cloak of his magic had been withdrawn and the cold of the desert night had descended on her in the afternoon.

Four hundred yards from the train, among the onlookers, the vicarious thrill seekers, sick minds who had come to watch the train explode and torn bodies fly through the air, the Raven looked down thoughtfully, hands in pockets, the ever present Nikon slung over one shoulder.

Things were going well. The shortwave interchange with his people had reassured him that all was under control and his comrades were in total command.

He had ordered them to keep the announcements going, to repeat the manifesto, reiterate the demands about every forty-five minutes. They should keep pounding away with the propaganda, make it clear through the media that this was not a charade but a serious battle of politics and power.

His fingers caressed the Nikon.

Thus far, the other side had reacted slowly. It had been sixteen hours, enough time for the other side to react. But he had no word from Washington, no offer to bargain, to retreat, to exchange.

His hands gripped the camera-radio tightly. He would blow the train if he must, without compunction, without guilt or remorse. The lives he would take meant nothing to him. They were pawns in a war of kings.

But the other victory would be more to his liking—to see the Philadelphia Five set free and his people on the train flown to Libya with their hostages.

He thought about the fat cats, the enemy in Washington. He spat upon the ground in disgust and turned toward his car.

He would contact the train again from somewhere to the east, where direction finder detection would have little chance of picking up his transmission. If he had to use the Nikon, his people should have a chance, not that they did, for the troops surrounding the train would be too much for them. But at least his warning would give them a chance to get out and fight.

He didn't really care. He could always find others, would always have an unending supply of angry, not too bright rebels.

As he slipped into the rental and turned the key, the Raven heard the PA system atop the train come to life again. It was Maxon. "This is the voice of the American Revolutionary Mobilization. This train is ours and will remain ours until you meet our demands. All passengers aboard this train are now hostages. At the least provocation, they will be shot individually and thrown out for you to see. Explosives have been placed . . ."

The Raven gunned the motor and drove off. The voice faded behind him. His lips were set tightly, but his eyes were dreamy.

He liked explosions.

Washington, D.C., Thursday, 5:00 P.M.
Eastern Daylight Time

In a walnut-lined den in his living quarters on the third floor of the White House, President Foreman stood looking out on Pennsylvania Avenue. The usual crowds stood at the metal fence gazing at the house. The long lines of the organized tours had disappeared in the past hour.

He never got used to the adulation of people. Day after day he faced his people, talked to them, shook their hands, kissed their kids. He wondered if he could be the strong man they expected. He had promised a strong hand against terrorists. He would not tolerate another Iranian situation anywhere in the world, and he had one on his own turf.

He turned from the window. "What do we know now, Forest?"

General Stone had come to the den at Foreman's request to brief him before the others met them at the Oval Office. "Captain Marsh has hundreds of pictures of the terrorists, but has only identified five," Stone said. "He made voice-prints of five others and is running them through Interpol now."

Foreman could see that the chairman of the Joint Chiefs of Staff was uncomfortable with the progress. "What is your best assessment of what we might expect at Kingman, Forest?" He was tired. It had been a long day of normal business with the constant stress of Kingman thrown in.

"Mr. President, dealing with terrorists is always slow. We want it that way. Our RDF people are the best in the world, but they need time. Before they can go in, they have to know where every terrorist will be at the moment of the strike, what his firepower is, what his or her reaction will be. If we don't have that, a lot of innocents might get in the way."

"You told me your people could pick out a target from many and kill selectively, day and night." Foreman paced nervously. The weight of four hundred possible deaths was beginning to tell. "Do they have everything they need?"

"They have portable laboratories on site: photo labs, sound rooms, chemical analysis facilities, worldwide communications linkups, a computer identification center. And they have the skills," General Stone said.

"But . . . ?"

"But I hate dealing with civilian casualties. Troops you train. They know the chances, sign up for the excitement, know what they are getting into. But the others—"

"You don't like our chances."

"The train cannot be approached for information. We have no one on the inside. That isn't going to change. No. I don't like it. If we have to go in, we may have to blow steel doors, then start blasting—always the worst choice. Surprise is the best solution and in this case—"

"I see." Foreman turned to the window again. "I'm not going to give in, General. At some time, your boys will have to handle it."

"Just one thing, Mr. President."

"Yes?"

"I need exclusive command. Any other force will just get in the way," Stone said. "Why not call off the FBI, CIA, and the National Guard?"

"You never were a politician, Forest, or you'd know how naïve that sounds. Come on. They're waiting for us downstairs."

Las Vegas, Thursday, 5:00 P.M. *Pacific Daylight Time*

When Grushenko touched down at McCarron Airport outside Las Vegas and sat through a seven-mile bus ride into the city, he had felt awed and totally out of his element in the passing scene.

The bland, stark desert, the dry plant life, then the vibrant colors and mammoth hotels that bordered the garish strip that was unique in the world. It was something his comrades at the Kremlin could never copy. He had seen pictures of Disneyland and thought it impossible. But this was even more impressive, and it was real, right in front of him. He had to believe what he was seeing. He could never find the Raven in a boiling pot like this. Hopefully, the Raven would be in Kingman. Where in hell was Kingman? How would he get to it?

Grushenko wandered into a hotel after the bus pulled away. Hundreds of slot machines filled the space where he expected to find a lobby. Men and women, young and old, slim and fat, all fed money in and pulled handles— incessantly. Scantily clad young women moved among the players serving drinks, but never stopping to collect for them. Uniformed security guards moved through the crowds, huge .45's in open display on their hips.

It was a sight to stun a Muscovite. The noise was at fever pitch. He had been told it never ceased, day and night, seven days a week.

At one end of the corridor that served as a lobby, shops sold clothes and jewelry. Next to them, he found a travel office. He was too late for the bus to Kingman, so he rented a car.

He drove out Route 93. On the way, he tuned in the radio to hear the latest news. He heard a voice, distant and hollow, that the announcer said was coming from the train. It was a terrorist asking America, in the name of ARM, to take up arms against their imperialist masters. The voice demanded freedom for its comrades and transport to Libya.

Grushenko smiled to himself. Effective propaganda, direct, forceful, fear-inspiring, well written and delivered. The Raven had apparently collected a talented group for this ARM organization of his.

Two hours later, as light began to fade, he turned from Route 93 to the hostage site, passing a red Volvo traveling west, toward Las Vegas.

The Raven sat behind the wheel of the Volvo.

The Train, Thursday, 7:00 P.M. *Mountain Standard Time*

The PA was blaring again into the fading light. It was the final message of the day, as ordered by the Raven in his last transmission to the train.

The voice of Miriam Boros rang out into the evening. "I'll repeat once more and that's it. You won't be hearing from us again until tomorrow morning at twelve. Twelve o'clock. If at that time our demands are not met, the hostages aboard this train will be shot one by one and thrown out for you to see. You've seen one. You'll see more. Twelve o'clock—that's it. Seventeen hours. Tell the fat cats in Washington to get off their asses."

Despite the cloying fear, the hostages in the dining car continued to order service from the sad-eyed waiter. The two Litton men ordered scotch; the stockbroker took the short bourbon he'd ordered in shaking hands; the oilman refused a drink, sat drumming his fingers on the table, his glazed eyes never leaving its surface.

Maria Gonzales muttered to herself, her lips never stopping. She passed rosary beads through calloused hands, shifted her weight as random pains crept through her abdomen. The conductor fretted, watched for an opportunity, ordered a Pepsi, and sat, sullenly, sipping through a straw.

The smell of marijuana hung in the air.

Kate sipped a dry martini, sitting at Maxon's table, eyeing him, feeling that within his shell could be a weakness, a remnant of humanity she could use, mold into semblance of rationality that might save them all.

Act, she told herself. Act, for God's sake!

"I don't understand," she said in an undertone. "You've got looks, talent, intelligence. You have so much to live for. Why you?"

Maxon's voice was hoarse. He had been on the PA most of the day, until he had turned it over to the woman. He had been arguing with his people constantly. They responded poorly to orders. "I explained all that before," he said with surprising patience. If he was going to shut her up, he would have done it long ago.

"I remember. 'The purpose of terrorism is to terrorize,' " Kate said, smiling derisively. "That doesn't explain anything. It's very bad writing. Redundant, don't you think?"

Maxon almost smiled, but was weary. "We'll talk about it later." His eyes began to close. "In the morning."

P.J. watched them all through murky eyes as if he wondered which one he would kill first. His speculation was wasted. Maxon would probably start with one from another car.

CHAPTER 12

On the perimeter, in the press area, a number of television cameras had shut down, although some continued to point their cyclopean eyes at the Limited. Newly appointed on-the-spot reporters continued to regale the nation with old news wrapped in different phrasing. Veterans of the network wars had packed it up for the time being.

"I'm going back to the hotel," Allegro said to Alden. "Nothing's going to happen tonight and I've been on my feet all day."

"What makes you so sure?" he asked.

"I've been through this scene before. In Europe, South America, the Middle East. These people mean what they say." She looked at him, through him, her gaze holding some mysterious secret only she could recognize. "It's been nice meeting you, Mr. Alden. Even under these circumstances."

He seemed not to hear. "What they said about killing them one by one. Do you think they mean that?" he asked, his voice uncertain, its former strength all but gone.

"Yes," she said levelly. "They always mean what they say." She turned and left him standing alone in the desert landscape, staring at the train.

He endured the cold for another half hour in the stillness, then turned toward his car and the motel.

Near the village of Chamonix, high in the French Alps and lying under the shadow of Mont Blanc, the tallest peak

119

in Europe, Alicia Alden drove rapidly through the fourteen miles of the Mont Blanc Tunnel toward its end in Courmayeur, Italy. From there she would continue to Milan and catch the earliest flight to the United States and Kingman, Arizona.

She had heard the news of the hostage taking and of her mother. Now, as she drove, she prayed for her and for her father, her eyes full of tears, making the already hazardous driving almost suicidal. She was full of anxiety, fear, love, and sadness.

Please, God, let nothing happen to her, she kept repeating as she drove.

Please, God, let her live!

I love her. I love them both.

She thought fleetingly of her half brother, Nicky, wherever he might be. He had never liked Kate and wouldn't show up in Kingman. He wouldn't show up even if the hostage was their father. She didn't like Nicky. He was strange, cruel, and uncaring.

Though neither knew it at the time, Allegro and Alden were booked into the same motel, not surprising in a town of only nine thousand souls. Later that evening, Allegro sat at a small cocktail table in the darkened corner of the bar near the entrance to an intimate dining room. The bar was shaped like a U, closed at one end by a serving area for floor waiters and a cash register. The room had only a dozen tables, plus a half-dozen booths down one side. Anyone sitting at the bar could see most of the tables. The lights were turned down low, to hide the hideous green flowered decor.

Allegro thought she might be overdressed in a cowl-neck black dress and silver necklace. She was weary of her work clothes, was trying to recapture some small semblance of femininity. Perhaps it was a return to civilized attire in a world gone back to the reasonless time of loincloths and spears.

As she sat, sipping a Campari and soda, her thoughts went back to the events of the day. She had clamored for adventure, for a new story tinged with a little danger. In her experiences on other continents, she had often been the first one on the scene, the only one to get close, to feel the hot breath of the enemy's anger. Somehow, she had to get closer to this one, to be with the hostages, to learn how they felt, to feel what they felt.

It was all here before her. Hers to cull, to keep and write home about, or to sell to any syndicate. Perhaps even a book could come out of it. But the image of Philip Alden marred the reverie, almost made it something she didn't want, a color out of place, out of harmony with the canvas.

Why couldn't he be a simple reporter, a television newsman, a stringer for some western newspaper, single, noninvolved, perhaps even divorced for years?

But no. He was married, and his wife was aboard the train.

What do you want out of life? she asked herself. What above all else? Right now?

I want him, she answered. I want him. But I will never have him.

Again, as she lifted her glass with care, she felt the gap, the void between what she was and what she longed for. She experienced the desolation, the bereftness she'd felt creeping up on her in the past few weeks, the defeat against the oncoming of age, an age she would experience alone.

In the north wing of the motel, far removed from the clatter of the bar room, but not far from the noises of cars and vans arriving and departing, Alden lay on his bed, fully clothed, trying to sleep.

He had had no alcohol, nothing to deaden the nerves and to dull the mind. He shouldn't be alone with his thoughts of Kate or his anger at her position. He shouldn't be alone or sober, but he was. How many times had she tried to get him to cut down on the booze? How often had he slept with a young piece when he should have been in his own bed with Kate?

In some distant, ill-perceived way, he wanted to save her. Not for himself, for the love that was dead, but for humanity, culture, and for the challenge. His personal

challenge to the hordes who now whored the earth. In
these thoughts, his mind built a fire fed with frenzy.

Because he knew he was weak and without honor,
without resolve, he wanted all the more to do it for her.
But he would fail. He knew he would fail. He was failing
to sleep, failing in his resolve to solve the problem—a
problem foreign to him, beyond his capabilities.

Io non mori, e non rimasi vivo.

I did not die, but nothing of life remained.

But, I will do something, he thought. I will do *something*.

He didn't sleep, but dozed fitfully, his dreams full of
Kate.

He came awake clutching for breath, life, and a new
direction for his tortured soul. He had no booze in the room
to deaden his fear, no warm young body to make him
forget. He reached for the cigarettes on the bedside table,
lit one, and inhaled like a man in a desert desperate for
water.

I need a drink, he thought. Not one, not two, not three.
Well, one or two, just to take the edge off.

He looked down at his trousers. They were wrinkled and
sloppy. But whose wouldn't be after a day like this? He
selected fresh slacks, pulled on a Dunhill camel blazer,
examined himself in the mirror, combed a lock of hair into
place. He caught himself as he staggered slightly, drunk
before he even got close to the booze.

One. Two. Maybe he'd have three at the bar downstairs.
With newsmen, journalists, reporters—people with whom,
in his adventurous mind, he had always identified. Not the
Hollywood writers he'd known, but the people who had
"been there." People who had been on the scene, writing
and reporting as it should be done. Men and women who
wrote the truth, not the fiction that mired him.

He had to be near those of his own ilk, to get his mind,
if not off the threat, at least a small distance from it. He
had to get operating again, working, absorbing, free to
choose action instead of remuneration and plastic thought.

She saw him first when he entered the bar, but gave no
hint of her presence—no uplift of eye, no move of shoulder, no smile or rise of eyebrow.

But she studied him as he took a stool at the bar. She watched him smile, watched his eyes grow in interest as he was drawn into conversation with the reporter at his side. But she could see the smile was weak and sad. His eyes, beneath the facade, were full of distant fear.

She wanted him. Oh, she wanted him. But this man was not for her. He was too far removed, too involved, too compassionate. And he was taken.

His eyes caught hers and her feeling of distance faded, replaced by interest and a feeling of hope, of two souls who might share. He crossed the room to her table and sat down.

"Mind?" he asked.

She tried to smile without giving away the pounding in her heart. "Of course not," she managed to get out.

She could see his eyes taking her in slowly, admiringly. "You look very different tonight."

"Does it surprise you?" she asked, letting herself smile for the first time.

"No. May I buy you a drink?"

"Thank you, Mr. Alden."

He was drinking white wine, ordered another Campari for her.

"What paper do you work for, Miss Stern?" he asked.

"I don't work for a newspaper," she replied, trying to keep her mind on the conversation. She had to have this man, the one she felt sure she'd waited for all her life. But it was impossible. Damn!

"I thought you were a reporter."

"Free-lance. Any paper or magazine that will buy my stuff. Call me a journalist. I like the word better anyway. It has a tinge of the old-fashioned about it." She paused. "And you? I imagine you write movies?"

"Screenplays. New-fashioned."

"Screenplays, movies, films." She shrugged. "What have you written?"

He named a few and her eyes lit up. "I liked them all," she said. "Especially *Train to Istanbul*."

Alden's eyes dulled and she knew she'd picked the wrong one. When he looked up, his expression was tight, strained. "This Raven," he said. "What's his background? What do you know about him?"

"I know very little about him and less about his background. But I've met him."

"You have?" Alden was suddenly tense. He leaned closer, ready to take in every word. "Where?"

"Rome. About three years ago. The article appeared in *The Atlantic*."

"What's he like?" He leaned even closer.

She could drink in the man smell of him and a hint of cologne. It wasn't fair. He was what she'd always dreamed of—someone she'd go after like a tigress. But, he was taken—and she had rules about that. She'd had too many of those already. No more. "An absolute egoist," she said. "Completely self-involved. No conscience. A sociopath. Psychopath might better describe him."

He had been looking at her face. Now he turned, stared over her shoulder as though contemplating some alien and futuristic landscape.

"You're a photographer, too?" he finally asked. "You took pictures for your articles?"

Allegro flicked ashes from the tip of the cigarette she'd lit while his mind had wandered. "I shot off two rolls of Triex 135–36. At the end of the interview, he had one of his guards rip the second roll from the camera, then burned both before my eyes, laughing." She lifted her drink and sipped. "He's a bastard."

"I don't understand people like that," Alden said, looking into the distance again. "I don't understand it at all. Four hundred people on that train. Innocent people."

Allegro hesitated. "I'm sorry about your wife," she said tenderly, touching his hand.

He looked at her sharply, questioningly. "Wife? Oh, you mean Kate. She's my ex-wife. Kate Kavanaugh. Maybe you've heard of her."

Allegro's throat went dry as joy washed over her, bringing color to her face and moisture to her loins. She tried to speak, but had to hesitate for a moment. "Of course I have," she was finally able to say. "But, you still love her." Her cheeks were aflame. Surely he must notice. The light. Was it too dark for him to see?

His smile was rueful "Love? What is love? If you mean constant bliss, happiness, exultation, no. If you mean romance, that fades." He lit another cigarette and continued. "But you're right, I guess. I did love her once, probably still do. But it's different now. From a distance, if you follow me."

She was following, avidly, and she knew exactly what he meant. He was better than she thought. He was defending a Hollywood marriage against all reason.

"We've been divorced for more than ten years," he went on. "But, yes, in a way I'll always love her—as I'll always love my first wife. Neither would work out again. They are over, but I still love them."

He seemed a bit stunned by his own candor, his freedom of thought with someone he'd just met, as if she had cast a spell to make him talk.

"Anyway," he said, drawing away and speaking formally. "I don't like to see this happen to her. I don't want to see it get worse."

He looked at her and tried to smile, but his lips remained tight. "Let's forget about it for tonight. As you said, nothing's going to happen. At least not tonight." He smiled with a little more warmth. "Shall we have dinner?" he asked.

For a minute, Allegro couldn't find the words. He had surprised her on two counts. Something *was* going to happen tonight—perhaps many things—and he had asked her to have dinner. He was walking into her web better than she could have planned. "You don't have to do that, Mr. Alden," she said, her voice tinged with a coyness normally foreign to her nature.

"Philip. Will you?"

"Yes," she said softly. "I'd love to."

Three tables away, a small, bald man with tightly drawn yellowish skin chain-smoked, eyed them mischievously while pondering the whereabouts of the Raven.

As they rose from their table and headed for the dining area, Allegro's heart was slightly off beat and the glimmer of hope in the darkness of her mind was brightening. She would polish it herself before the night was through. He would never forget Kate Kavanaugh, but he was not attached. Thank God, he was not attached.

It was midnight when Allegro let herself into her own room. The three hours since they had entered the dining room had been a whole new chapter of her life. She threw her evening bag on the bed and zipped herself out of her black dress for the second time that night.

The second time. The first had been for Philip. She thought of how she had undressed herself, then him, the hardness of him, his drive. As she relived the rapture, she sank to the floor, her knees unable to hold her erect.

The reverie lasted only a few seconds. She had no time to waste. She slipped out of the panties she'd pulled on only a few minutes before and headed for the shower. She turned it on and stood under it as hot as she could stand it for a few seconds, then switched the water to cold. Her heart pumped blood as fast as it had in his room. God! She had to get him out of her mind for a few hours.

Back in the room, she pulled a black jumpsuit out of the bottom of a duffel bag. She put it on over her underwear and tucked her hair under a black ski toque. A pair of black sneakers completed the outfit. She checked her camera bag for film, threw in a dozen rolls of high-speed color and made sure her 35–70 zoom lens and the strobe light were on the Nikon. She checked to see if her flashlight worked, then roped it around her neck. She found her plastic case of screwdrivers, put it in one breast pocket. In the other, she put a tube of axle grease and a tiny atomizer of Screwloose lubricant. She strapped the camera case to her back.

Allegro picked up the keys to the rented Camaro parked outside her door, slipped out the door, and started the low-slung car as quietly as possible.

The roads were almost deserted in Kingman. Most of the local police were on duty at the train. The whole area was eerie, lit by the lights from the military camps. The air was unnaturally damp for desert country. It smelled of the cookfires of the soldiers and the onlookers camped on the distant hills.

The train was partly in darkness and partly in light.

Allegro parked behind a cluster of yuccas she'd seen from the knoll earlier in the day and slipped, unseen, between dozing National Guardsmen and the bored sentries. By twelve-thirty, she was on her belly, crab-walking along the rail bed toward the last car of the train.

The Train, Friday, 1:30 A.M. Mountain Standard Time

In the early hours of Friday morning, Maxon sat at his table in the dining car, evaluating. He turned every aspect of the operation over in his mind, tilting the scale back and forth. For the first time in months, he was confused.

The woman sitting opposite him was persuasive. In some strange inimitable way, she was bringing back his ambitions of the past, his young idealism, his quest for quietude and peace.

"How can I put it to you?" Kate asked, half to herself. "What are you going to do when you grow up."

He glared at her angrily.

"You know what I mean," she said. Her expression softened. "Is this what you wanted? When you were young, you wanted to be a killer, a murderer? Is that what you started out to dedicate your life to?"

"It wasn't me," Maxon said, an edge to his voice. "It was society."

Kate shook her head, sadly. "I've heard that one before. Blame it on society, never on yourself." She lit a cigarette, blew the smoke to the ceiling of the car. "So blame it on society—that immutable force without a face. Society!" She laughed bitterly.

"You don't understand," he said, his eyes carrying little of the hostility in his voice.

They were talking in undertones, but Boros's ears were tuned in. Though she heard little, her suspicious nature parlayed one missing word into another and convinced her the talk was dangerous to the movement, to her own destructive impulses. What fueled her fire more, she hated the smart-ass bitch.

She rose from the radio and marched across to their

table, dumping herself angrily into a chair. "What's this?" she asked in her harsh, bitter way. "A private filibuster? Or some kind of fucking assignation?"

"Get back to the radio, Miriam," Maxon said calmly.

She bristled. "Don't give me orders!"

"I'm in command," Maxon said. "And you're smoking too much pot. Knock it off before you're so high you can't function."

"You friggin' bastard! Don't tell me I'm smoking too much!"

For a few seconds, Boros stared into his face, her eyes red and wet, then turned to Kate. "You!" she said. "Just who the hell do you think you are?"

"Excuse me," Kate said coldly. "I don't know you."

"But I know *you*!" Boros spat out. "You think you're an actress. Shit! Even Farrah Fawcett's better than you!"

Maxon had risen, pistol in hand. His voice was level, but cold. "Back to your station, Miriam."

Boros stared up at him sullenly for a moment, then pushed her chair back and stood. "Fuck both of you," she said, then lurched back to the radio.

Kate looked down at the table and crumpled an empty pack of cigarettes. "Do you think we can get another drink?" she asked. "And some cigarettes?"

Maxon motioned to the steward and ordered.

They talked for a few minutes, the theme always the same—Kate digging below the surface, Maxon defending his position.

"Is *that* your society?" she said, tilting her head slightly toward Boros.

At the radio, Boros made a show of checking switches. When they were preoccupied again, she took a small screwdriver and opened a panel. Inside, a small red lamp was wired into the transmit circuit. She unscrewed it.

From now on, they would be on permanent transmit and the red light wouldn't show.

CHAPTER 13

The Train, Friday, 2:00 A.M. Mountain Standard Time

The crab-walk along the track had been torture. Working beneath the railroad cars had been a bitch. The screwdrivers and cans of lubricant had bruised her breasts. She'd had to stop and transfer them to her pants pockets. And her hands would have been torn to shreds if she hadn't worn gloves. The railbed was of crushed stone and old cinders from the days of steam. Droppings—droppings of every conceivable kind—were all soaked into it. Sweat had poured from her, drenching her jumpsuit, making her gloves almost useless, turning her hands into slimy claws.

The butterfly nuts she'd overheard the Amtrak engineer discuss had been rusted to the emergency hatches, as she'd expected. She remembered her long-dead father's motto: "Nothing is ever easy." She had crawled along the railbed, from the last sleeper to the first coach, seven goddamned coaches in all, squirting every nut with Screwloose. Now she was back at the last sleeper, screwing off the first two nuts.

They turned easily, slowly, quietly. When the second nut was free, she inserted a screwdriver under the hatch and pried, praying it wouldn't make a noise.

All during the ordeal, she had thought about Alden—now her Alden. My God, he was a dear, and she was going to cleave to him like a leech. She had fed him wine through the meal, cocktails at the bar, and had led him to his room at about ten-thirty.

She had drunk little, had taken him to his bed, loved

129

him tenderly, and found he'd sobered as they thrashed about on the white sheets. He had been a wonderful lover and she'd matched him all the way. At one point, close to midnight, he had told her he loved her.

Then she had done the one thing that shamed her. She had fed him a knockout pill in a farewell drink and tucked him in for the night. If he knew what she was doing, that two women he loved were now in jeopardy, he might never forgive her, particularly if she survived and his Kate died.

The hatch came away with a slight popping noise. She shone her tiny flashlight through the maze of pipes to the hatch above. It was small, barely enough for her to slide through. She pulled herself up, put an ear to the upper hatch. Not a sound. She pushed upward. The hatch moved, making a grating noise. She poked her head through and looked around. The washroom was bathed in a dull night-light. The door was closed. She could hear muffled conversation on the other side of the door.

Captain Marsh had allowed himself two catnaps of about an hour each in the past twenty-four hours and hadn't slept for sixteen hours before that. It didn't bother him. The training he'd been through in the past ten years and the superb physical condition he always maintained sustained him. He had organized his people, had brought in all the technical and scientific help he could get, and had accumulated all the data he was likely to find. When the word came through from Washington, he would make his move.

Now he had a complication. For the past hour, he had been sitting on the ground, his back against a gnarled old yucca, one eye glued to an AN/PVS-4 night-vision sight set on a short tripod. It was new, second generation, equipped with ten-power magnification. He could see almost as well with it as he could with binoculars at twilight.

Someone had crawled through National Guard lines and had infiltrated the train. That someone other than his own people had done so galled him. He had planned to have one of his men do exactly the same within the next hour or two. Now he would have to await developments.

The intruder had used a small flashlight, had crawled

under the last seven cars, had been working on the hatches of the washrooms on each car, all fourteen of them. It seemed the intruder, whoever he might be, was intent on doing Marsh's job for him.

He had learned many things in the Army. One of the most important was patience. He would wait and see.

It was after two. Jory West sat in the dining car with the others, looking at Boros and Maxon with contempt. He slouched in his chair, his conductor's coat on backward to keep out the cool of the night. He had watched the Kavanaugh woman working on Maxon and was sure she was making some headway, but not enough to make any difference.

The Chicano woman was obviously uncomfortable. He could see she was terrified at being separated from her family. She grimaced with pain from time to time, as if she had come to term. He remembered how it had been when his kids were born, then shut it out of his mind. With the death sentence the doctors had given him, it didn't matter—nothing did.

He looked over at where Chester Good sat. The oilman had ceased talking to all and sundry, had even stopped talking to himself as he had through the evening. Now he sat rocking back and forth like an autistic child, his brain finally tortured beyond its limit.

The Litton men sat playing cards and drinking. On the surface, they appeared to be calm, but they dropped cards often, shouted at each other, and spilled drinks from shaking hands. They were probably more scared than the others, thinking in their own twisted corporate way they had more to lose.

The broker, Elson, was sleeping, his head back on the seat, his mouth open. Until about eleven, he had shaken like a child left out in the cold, arms grasped together, then his chin had dropped to his chest and he'd slept.

The Kavanaugh woman had fooled him. He'd thought she would be cold and standoffish, but when she paused to let Maxon think over her arguments, she cared for the others. She tried to comfort the Gonzales woman, pulled a blanket around her, made sure she had some water or juice. She had tried to comfort Elson and Good, but had little success.

Good old Josh just kept on working, serving food and drink as if it was a normal ride. He looked unafraid and probably wasn't. What could the terrorists do to him that society hadn't already done? Poor, deluded fool.

Jory was not deluded. He knew exactly what he had to do. He wasn't going to sit idly by and let the bastards kill all these people.

The nuts were finally loosened—all twenty-eight of them. Allegro shined her flashlight on her watch. It was two-thirty. Jesus! It didn't give her much time. She planned to make her exit about five, if they didn't kill her up there. She had loosed all fourteen hatches, one to each washroom at the end of each car. Fourteen hatches, fourteen escape routes. They had to let her go to the bathroom sometime, if, that is, they didn't kill her on the spot. No way she wanted to be confused when it was time to leave.

It had to be now. She had chosen the last sleeping car. Seemed to be less noise up there. She eased the inner hatch cover up and looked in the washroom, pulled herself up, and sat on the washroom floor. She reached over and latched the door.

She looked a mess in the tiny mirror. Couldn't be helped. She eased the hatch cover down and practiced opening it quickly. No problem.

Before she took the big step, Allegro combed her hair, checked her camera, slung it around her neck. She decided to use the facilities. You never knew what would happen. She didn't want to embarrass herself. She'd been scared under fire before and had filled her drawers.

She finally opened the door. She was in a small alcove at the extreme end of the train. No one was on guard. Strange. She had been sure they would protect their asses here of all places. She looked through a dust-covered window and found the answer. A terrorist sat on the floor on the other side of the door, head lolling to one side, an AK47 on his lap. She'd seen enough of them in Afghanistan to know a Russian rifle when she saw one. They were as distinctive as the heavy woolen suits the KGB sported.

She had time. Looking around, she saw the answer. She opened a side door, eased up the platform covering the steps, and let it drop outside. Then she eased the door almost closed.

When she turned, her hand still on the handle, the door behind her was open. The muzzle of the AK47 was stuck in her back.

She turned to face a tall blond youth with an acne-ravaged face. She raised her hands, smiled.

"Don't fire," she said, trying not to sound as terrified as she was. "Take me to your leader," she managed to get out through a mouth gone dry.

Alden tossed in the empty bed, disoriented, unsure, trying to ward off sleep and remember the vision who had spent the night with him. She had been everything he'd ever dreamed of—at dinner, in the bar, in bed. God only knew, he had tried out enough women to know the real thing when he found it.

His mind churned up a picture of Kate. God, he didn't want to lose her. God help her. But Allegro Stern was the one. His last chance. If he lost her, he didn't know what he would do. Already he felt she was a part of him— would forever be a part of his life.

He felt around the bed for her and found only cold white sheets. But the smell of her was there. The perfume of her clothes and the juices of her body. She had been real. He drifted off content they would have a life together.

Marsh had sent for his tunic and sat at the AN/PVS-4 night-vision sight hour after hour. He had first seen the intruder before he reached the train, crab-walking between the tracks to the last sleeping car. He had taken almost two hours to loosen all the hatches and had finally crept up one hatch at the rear of the train.

Why loosen all the hatches? Marsh needed them all loosened for his men, but why would the intruder do it? Insurance? Who was this person? What did he want? He could only think of one type that would do it. A reporter. He had seen them stick their heads up and get them blown

off from Hong Kong to Burma, from Thailand to Zaïre.
They would never learn.

Suddenly he sat up and the skin of his forehead fur-
rowed. The intruder had pulled himself up the hatch into
the last washroom. He could see movement through the
frosted glass of the tiny cubicle, then nothing.

He waited. After a minute or two, he saw movement to
the right of the washroom. In the poor light he saw the
intruder, hands over head, paraded through the two sleeping cars to the dining car, where the leaders of the group
were gathered.

Poor bastard. He was a dead man.

At two-thirty in Kingman, it was five-thirty in Washington. The principals were gathered in the president's favorite den, where he'd seen General Stone a few hours earlier.
Their aides had been excused. From here on in, the ses-
sions would be top level and behind closed doors.

They had made little headway. Foreman had seen Price
and Cash, separately and together, since their earlier meeting and had not been able to shake them. The secretary of
state and the national security adviser had not and would
not change their minds. They wanted the terrorist demands
to be met. They wanted no mass bloodshed on American
soil, no matter what the cost in prestige. They were both
completely ignorant of the remarkable skills of Captain
Marsh's men and nothing General Stone said would dis-
suade them.

Prentice Tredwell had not been consulted again on the
grounds that the matter was purely a domestic issue. Dusty
Rhodes had been included in the group, since the job
would have been his if the RDF hadn't existed. Unfortunately, like the first director of the Bureau, he was an
obstructionist.

"We have about four hours to sunup in Kingman,"
Stone was saying. "My men have enough intelligence to
go in now. They are dealing with eighteen terrorists in
eight locations. They have photos of most, have identified
most, know their weaponry."

Stone was weary of the civilian minds who blocked
him. He looked around the group. They were all in

shirtsleeves by now, drinking coffee, smoking foul cigars, eating Danish pastries, adding to their already gross waistlines. Sometimes he hated dealing with these oafs. He had offered to give them a crash course on the RDF, show them films. But the bigoted bastards had refused, pretending they knew it all without his input. It was beyond belief.

"How would your people get on board the train?" the president asked, taking off his glasses, rubbing the pressure marks on his nose.

"Each car has two washrooms. Each washroom has a trapdoor in the floor for maintenance," Stone said. He was the only one who still looked fresh. His shirt was still unsoiled, his tie straight and knotted. "Beneath these trapdoors, a lower hatch opens to service water pipes," he went on. He had just received the call, had not been told his men had not done the work, only that the work was completed. "These openings have been breached. It only remains for the men to crawl through and kill the hostages."

"And start a slaughter," Price insisted. "I am unalterably opposed to your men entering that train. I don't see how they can avoid killing our people."

"Can you imagine the headlines tomorrow?" Cash added. "AMERICAN TROOPS KILL AMERICAN CIVILIAN HOSTAGES."

"With all due respect, gentlemen, you don't know what you are talking about," General Stone said calmly.

Price and Cash both opened their mouths to speak. Foreman broke in to preempt them. "This meeting is adjourned, gentlemen. I will make the decision based on your input." He turned to Stone as they all started to leave. "Stick around, Forest. I'd like another word with you."

When they were alone, Foreman went to a cabinet hidden in one wall and extracted a decanter. He poured an inch in each of two snifters, handed one to the military man. "Forty-year-old brandy. Save it for special occasions."

Stone liked and respected Foreman but was disappointed in his performance in the past twenty-four hours. He sensed Foreman knew how he felt. Let him. If this thing went the wrong way, it wouldn't matter anyway.

"They're wrong, Forest. Damned fool wrong," Foreman said. "But I can't do a damned thing about it—not this time."

"Why?" Forest's snifter wasn't steady as he brought it to his lips. He had the steadiest hands in the Army, but tonight he couldn't control them.

"I need them, Forest. I need them on critical issues every day of my term. I can't fire them—couldn't find better men." He sighed. "They have a blind spot on this thing. Can you see my position?"

"Charlie Beckwith spent almost twenty years of his life fighting fools like those—men of power in the service who were as blind. He finally made some headway and was slapped down again. He began over and found support, found financing, made it work." Forest's voice was shrill, his hand so unsteady he put his drink down.

"We have the finest RDF in the world. Our men have worked their guts out for years, and I mean worked their guts out preparing for this day. We can save the people on the train. Your administration would never survive if all four hundred died because of two gutless men. We can prevent that." He leaned forward, looked the president straight in his tired eyes. "Give me the green light, Mr. President."

"I can't, Forest. They remember the Iranian foul-up, think you can't improve on that."

The general, weary from the futility of politics, finished his drink, pulled on his jacket, and turned to the door. "You'll have my resignation on your desk by nine. I want it to be effective immediately."

"Forest, don't do that. Don't ruin a brilliant career."

"Mr. President, I don't want my name associated with Kingman. I have a bad feeling about it. And I don't want to be associated with the Prices and Cashes of this world."

"And me?"

"I've always admired you, Mr. President. But you just lost me. You're as gutless as them. If you're going to let terrorists kick you around on American soil, you'll do it anywhere in the world. I don't want to be a part of that." He turned on his heel and left without invitation.

Allegro stood in front of a startled Maxon, her hands over her head. Everyone in the dining car was awake, interested in this new development. Here was someone from the outside, someone who was neither hostage nor terrorist.

"Put your hands down," Maxon told Allegro. "How did she get aboard?" Maxon, obviously annoyed, asked the tall blond kid.

"Forced open the last door, pulled up the steps. I caught her just as she was closing it," he said uncertainly.

"You had to be asleep. You fool!" Maxon screamed. He hadn't been as worked up since the whole thing began for him back in Chicago. "Who's guarding the rear now?" he asked, knowing the answer.

"I had to bring her—"

"Get the hell back there!" Maxon shouted. "P.J., go with him and check every door from one end to the other. Christ! If she'd been an RDF type, some of us would be dead."

When P.J. and the blond youth had left, Allegro took her Nikon from her neck, focused on Maxon and Kate, and took the shot before they could react.

Boros rushed from her corner, raised her gun to Allegro's head, and cocked the hammer. "Let me kill her. Throw her body off the train," she screamed.

Maxon waved her away. "For once you're right. She'll be the first to go when the time comes."

"And what the hell do we do with her in the meantime?" Boros asked. Then her ruined face was split in a huge grin. "Hey! Some of the guys got hot pants, you know? Why not let them have this bitch?" She laughed. "Serves her right. Came in all by herself, she did. No invitation or nothin'."

"There's your new society," Kate directed at Maxon without emotion.

"Leave her be," Maxon said. "What can she do? Let her talk to people, take her pictures. Then, in the morning, we'll shoot her and throw her out for the buzzards. You can personally destroy her film and put a bullet in her head, okay?''

''All right!'' Boros uncocked the hammer on her gun and went to sit by her radio.

''The new leader of the new society,'' Kate whispered to Maxon.

''Give me a break, will you? She would have killed the woman on the spot,'' he said, then turned to Allegro. ''Now, who the hell are you?''

Allegro was busy taking flash shots around the car. She was particularly interested in the pregnant woman and the little man who rocked back and forth. They both looked shell-shocked.

''Allegro Stern, free-lance journalist,'' she answered, taking another shot of Kate and Maxon.

''I know you. Didn't you interview the Raven a couple of years ago?'' Maxon asked. ''Lost your film then, too,'' he said, smiling for the first time in hours.

''Guilty,'' she said. ''He's running a poor ship this time.''

''I'm running this show,'' Maxon said.

''Sure. While he sits back and watches from a distance. His style, all right,'' Allegro said. ''He picks the most dedicated fools he can, points them at a suicide target in the name of ARM or some other equally fool organization, then sits back and watches them blow each other to oblivion.''

''That's dangerous talk,'' Maxon said.

''But exactly what I've been telling him,'' Kate broke in.

''You're Kate Kavanaugh, aren't you?'' Allegro asked, adjusting the zoom for a full face shot and correcting for light. She angled the strobe up for a bounce shot and pressed the shutter release.

''Yes,'' Kate said, adjusting her position for the shot as she'd done automatically for most of her life.

''I had dinner with Philip Alden a few hours ago. He's worried about you,'' Allegro said, ignoring Maxon.

''Philip!'' Kate exclaimed. ''My God! How is he? Must be worried sick.''

''He's surviving, but very worried.'' Allegro's feelings

were mixed. She wanted no harm to come to this woman, but she wanted no recurrence of her earlier romance with Alden.

"Who is this Philip?" Maxon asked.

The two women had been ignoring him. Now they were surprised at his question.

"A former husband, dear. Don't worry about it," Kate said. "A long-dead romance."

My God, this woman is working on their leader. The poor slob is infatuated with her, Allegro thought. "Look," she said. "How 'bout I leave you two alone? I'm going to take random shots around the train. If I'm to be shot at dawn, better do my best work now."

"I'm not sure all his people are literate, Miss Stern," Kate got in another dig. "But you can try. Be a hell of a story if it survives."

Allegro knew she would like Kate if they were ever allowed to become friends. And now, somehow, she knew Kate would never come between her and Philip—not while she lived. "Why don't you shake this guy for a while later, and we can have a chat?"

"Why not?" Kate smiled up at her. "The condemned shall have all last requests granted."

"Don't even kid about that, lady," Allegro said.

Boros laughed from her place at the radio and waved her gun in a salute.

CHAPTER 14

The Train, Friday, 4:00 A.M. *Mountain Standard Time*

Allegro roamed the train. She took pictures of Lois and Dunk in a front coach. Lois was the calm one, sat in a corner seat, her M16 across her lap. Dunk, a little man, sat at the other end, a bundle of nerves. His right foot was bandaged. As she took his picture, Allegro asked how he'd hurt himself. From the other end of the car, Lois shouted, almost in glee, "He shot himself. Someone moved quickly and he shot his own foot." She was almost hysterical with laughter. "Ask him about his underwear. Two-toned by now if I know the little cocksucker."

Allegro looked around the car, took pictures of frightened passengers. The place smelled somewhere between a football team locker room and a Manhattan sewer.

As she progressed from the front to the rear, two things were universal. The terrorists were kids, almost as frightened as the passengers, and the passengers were cowed, too afraid to move against terrorist guns. She couldn't decide which of the cars smelled worse.

In the sleeping cars, she came across the tall blond kid and an Arab. They had just backed out of a private car, leaving the door open. Inside, a woman lay on her back, naked, legs spread, her face covered with blood and bruises. Blood trickled from her crotch.

Allegro continued to take pictures of everything, asked the names of the two men as if the woman hadn't been raped. It was the only scenario that would work for her. The two men taunted her, asked if she wanted to be next,

140

but she didn't respond. If she'd come along an hour later, they might have been ready for seconds, but, for now, they had been satisfied.

In all, she counted sixteen terrorists, assumed more in the cab of the engine. She had what she came for. Now, could she get out?

Georgetown, Friday, 7:00 A.M. *Eastern Daylight Time*

General Forest Stone, a veteran, of four major wars and more skirmishes than he cared to remember, holder of four Purple Hearts, two Silver Stars, a military medal with cluster, sat at his desk in the book-lined study of the Georgetown mansion provided by the Army and slowly drank himself into oblivion.

On the desk in front of him, a letter of resignation was sealed and addressed to the secretary of defense. He had typed it himself before he had poured the first drink. His aide would see it at eight hundred hours, and no matter what the general's condition at the time, it would be delivered. He had left a note to that effect and his aide followed orders to the letter.

That was what he had always liked about the Army. Orders followed to the letter. He had followed orders from the day he joined the service as a buck private in World War II. He had been field-promoted to officer rank by the time he was twenty, had survived Germany, and had enrolled in West Point in 1945. From that day on, he had aimed at the top job—Chairman of the Joint Chiefs of Staff, CJCS.

Now he couldn't bear to be identified with it. Civilians ran the government and thus the military. No matter how you fought it, the civilians always won.

He thought about his friend Charlie Beckwith and the hell he'd gone through to bring the RDF, the Delta Force, to where it was today. And now the RDF would be hamstrung, left out to dry by a few lily-livered yokels who would shit in their pants if a gun was fired near them. God, how he'd like to wave a magic wand and put their asses on that train right now! Maybe they'd like to review the whole thing again while looking down the barrel of a terrorist rifle.

Bastards!

He poured his fifth scotch and looked at his watch. Seven hundred hours. That was five hundred hours in Kingman. No, four hundred hours, remembering that Arizona remained on standard time while elsewhere they switched to daylight savings time. Poor bastards! They wouldn't have a chance.

He thought about Captain Marsh. A good man. Trained to the hilt. Probably sitting on a hillock, his ass wet, his mind almost numb from lack of sleep, his eyes bloodshot from staring at the train.

Well, Marsh would never get an order to move. Damned if he was going to tell him or anyone. Be too damned drunk anyway.

Shit!

The Train, Friday, 4:15 A.M. *Mountain Standard Time*

Allegro had been on the train for nearly two hours. Time to think about getting off. What she needed was a diversion. A simple walk to a washroom and a disappearance down one of the trapdoors seemed too simple, but she might have to try it.

She had shot a dozen rolls of film, had memorized names and had connected them with faces. Miriam and Gerald, Lois and Dunk, Judd, P.J., Valasques, the Booth brothers, Chick and Ali Khan, and a half dozen others. She had taken picture after picture of them proudly holding their Uzis, AK47s, M16s. One, she thought it was Judd, had a SIG/Sauer SSG 2000 sniper rifle. He had shown it to her, given it a name, and showed her how to load and fire—not that she didn't know.

The passengers were in bad shape, some totally prostrate from fear, others hiding behind eyes tinged with insanity, most convinced they were dead already.

She'd had her chat with Kate, enough time to confirm

she liked the woman immensely. If they got out of this, they could be great friends. Allegro would have Alden, but they could share his friendship.

But they would not both get out. Allegro had taken her life in her hands and told Kate she had a way out, but the woman was stubborn, was sure she could convince Maxon to give it up. By now it was an obsession with her. She would not or could not stop trying to convert him.

Hugh Fine and Fred Foley, the Litton men, were maintaining a level of intoxication that dulled all thought. They were tuned into gin rummy, had tuned everything else out.

Bobby Elson, the broker, and Chester Good, the little oilman, were both in a state of shock it would take a panel of psychiatrists months to analyze.

The conductor, Jory West, was a strange one. He seemed to be sitting back waiting for the chance to spring at someone. Miriam Boros, a prime candidate for Bitch of the Month, laughed at him, poked her gun in his ribs every time she passed. He just seemed to smile and wait. What was he waiting for?

Good old Josh Amos kept everyone served as if nothing had happened. He walked among them serenely as if he had divine intervention. Allegro wondered if he knew something she didn't.

She had pictures of them all, had exhausted her film supply, had packed her camera away. The exposed film was distributed in the many zippered pockets of her jumpsuit. If anything was lost, it would be the camera, not the film.

Of all the people in the dining car, the Gonzales woman looked the worst. She seemed to be ready to pop, to give birth at any moment. As Allegro mused, Kate was bathing Maria's head with a damp cloth.

Suddenly, the woman screamed.

Kate shouted, "Her water has broken!"

Everyone crowded around. Maxon was frantic, tried to maintain order. Jory West took his chance, grabbed for Boros's gun, wrestled it from her hand. He waved the gun triumphantly. No one seemed to know what to do. Judd brought his sniper rifle around. Jory shot him, tearing away half his head, spreading blood and brain matter over the back wall of the car. The body spun around and fell in a corner by the door. Maxon aimed quickly, fired a gun for the first time in his life, and relieved the conductor of two months of horrendous pain. With the bullet hole in his head, Jory West would live about fifteen minutes and would never have to think of cancer again.

By the time Jory hit the floor, Allegro had closed the hatch, slipped to the gravel railbed, and was running to the back of the train, keeping low, praying no one from the military would mistake her for a terrorist. They had to have heard the shots.

When she reached the back of the train, she rounded the corner, slipped between the tracks, and started to crab-walk to safety. It was still pitch black. She was three-quarters of the way to safety when an obstruction stopped her. The cold muzzle of a gun was pressed against her temple.

Joyce and Merit had little to do in the cab of the locomotive. They had placed their explosives and sat, more vulnerable than the rest, waiting for the signal to depart. Joyce, the more adventuresome of the two, had crept from the cab, loaded down with C4, and had molded the deadly plastique and the servomechanisms to the undersides of the baggage car, the mail cars, and the crew car. It mattered little that she was observed. If she had been fired on, Maxon had instructions to kill two hostages and throw them out to the desert floor.

From time to time, Merit would adjust the power feed to the coaches, change the idle speed of the giant diesels. Joyce had no idea what he was doing. Her job was to place the explosives, maintain walkie-talkie contact with Maxon, and scan the cars behind for possible escape attempts.

Her Heckler & Koch rifle was equipped with a night scope. She could range the total perimeter keeping track of enemy activity, except for the track at the rear of the train. When Allegro was running down the port side of the train to the rear, Joyce was nervously trying to call in Maxon. She and Merit had heard the shots from the dining car and wanted to know what the hell was going on.

She got no answer. She would try again later. If they heard the shots, others would have heard. She knew men sat unguarded in the mail cars, two to a car, and at least three were in the crew car. It was her job to ensure they didn't run for it.

When she swung her night scope along the starboard side for the hundredth time, she noticed movement from the crew car: Someone had swung a foot out the door, was preparing to jump.

Her scope was centered on the dangling leg. She slipped off the safety. One round of the caseless ammunition was already in the firing chamber. The trigger was sensitive. She had to hold back or she would spray the car and scare off her game.

The foot was extended farther and a rump appeared and then the whole body. The man, or woman, hid under the car. He, or she, could go either way.

"We've got a live one," she screamed to Merit. "Cover the port side."

"What the hell's the port side?" he screamed back, picking up his rifle.

"You asshole landlubber! The right side looking back," she screamed back, her adrenaline pumping.

Joyce had enjoyed shooting up the police cars. The rifle had felt strange with no ammunition cases streaming from the breech. The action had been smooth, the rifle lighter, better for holding the target. She'd had her training in the hills of Lebanon like all the others. No. Not like all the others. As a woman, she had played a larger role, by choice. She had been the local whore through all the six weeks of training. She sometimes wondered who had learned most at the camp.

"I've got him," she screamed at Merit. "There he goes."

With cold deliberation, she tracked the runner as he left the car and headed for the military lines. She led him by ten yards, and on full automatic, sent a stream of lead into the night, letting him run into her line of fire.

The runner danced through the hail of lead, his body lifting and pitching forward into the circle of light from the National Guard posts. The body, sprayed by scores of rounds, stopped dancing, pirouetted twice, and landed within ten yards of a sentry post.

The chatter of gunfire was followed by total silence. Ten seconds passed, then twenty. With surprising speed, one of the overweight guards on duty raced out and pulled the body to his lines, leaving a track of boot marks and gore in the hardpan.

Then, all was quiet again.

The firing had started the moment the gun was pressed to her temple. Now Allegro was held down on the scum of the railbed, the cold steel of the muzzle at her head, praying the hand behind the gun wasn't shaking as much as she.

When all was still, her captor spoke. "Identify yourself." The voice was masculine, unemotional.

"Allegro Stern, reporter." She tried to sound confident, but her voice held a tremor she couldn't hide.

The hand released her. The muzzle of the gun disappeared. "Damned fool!" the voice said.

"Who are you?" Allegro asked, trying to look up.

"Captain Marsh of the RDF. I've had a glass on you since two o'clock—couldn't send anyone in after you," he said. "You'd better come with me." He hauled her to her feet and, holding her by one arm, marched her all the way to an RDF trailer.

At the back of the trailer, he had an office. He dragged her in and locked the door. "Strip," he said, his voice matter-of-fact.

"Go to hell!"

"Your press card." He held out his hand.

"I didn't take it with me."

"Strip."

Allegro was taller than average for a woman, thought for a moment about trying to take him on, going for the door. His eyes followed hers.

"Won't work," he said. "If you are Allegro Stern, you have nothing to fear. Nothing personal in this. Now, strip."

She knew she had lost, reached for the tab to the long zipper in front, pulled it down, and stepped out of the jumpsuit. She wore brief panties and bra underneath. She started to undo the bra.

Marsh stopped her with an open hand. "Won't be necessary. You don't seem to be hiding anything." The way he said it was so impersonal, she was almost insulted.

He piled the contents of her pockets on the table. Twelve exposed rolls of fast color film, four hundred and thirty-two shots. He piled her camera, flashlight, screwdrivers, and lubricant on the desk and sat back in wonder. "You ever thought of joining the Army, Miss Stern?" He smiled for the first time as he threw her jumpsuit back to her.

Maxon had been furious and scared at the same time. Kate had watched him closely, could see he was angry at himself for letting the Stern woman roam at will, never suspecting she had her escape route mapped out. She guessed he wasn't ready for the kind of press coverage Allegro could now provide. It could be detrimental to his cause. Kate wondered if she should have taken the woman up on her offer. She would have been clear of it by now.

It wouldn't have been the route for her. She had Maxon almost convinced the whole thing was wrong. If he could cancel it now, she would save all their lives. She looked at her watch, felt she'd been in this dining car for most of her life. The Gonzales woman had given birth to a little girl, seemed to be a different person. She was nursing the baby from ample breasts, grinning at everyone, telling them in Spanish and broken English she would call the girl Carmelita.

"Toss the conductor's body out with the other one," Maxon screamed at P.J., then watched as the body bounced off the gambler's. Coyotes and buzzards had fought over the body in the past few hours. It wasn't a very pretty sight.

"What the hell do we do with Judd?" Boros asked, looking at the mess that had once been a living, breathing, misguided youth.

"Leave him be," Maxon said.

"We tosses him out with the others," P.J. spoke up, a change for the usually silent warrior. "They thinks we offed two more. How they know he one of ours?" As he spoke, he took Judd by the ankles and dragged him to the door, leaving a trail of blood and brain matter.

"Go ahead," Maxon said, obviously no longer in complete control.

Kate began to wonder if she'd been wrong to stay, if any hope could be held out for Maxon's salvation, if any of them had a chance at all.

CHAPTER 15

The Site, Friday, 6:30 A.M. Mountain Standard Time

As the first light of dawn spread slowly across the landscape, the onlookers, the curious, the vicarious, had begun to assemble again. Some had remained through the night, sleeping in their cars, waiting for catastrophe, keeping the vigil of death. Some had made cynical bets on what time the train would blow up, but most stared in silent prayer, waiting for some miracle that would free the passengers and give them back their lives and loves.

Others gazed in anger, furious with the government for not taking the train, freeing the passengers and saving the face of the United States at the same time.

The press area had begun to fill again. Television cameras had been tested and aimed. Announcers for radio and television were already on the air reporting the shooting of the crewman, knowing nothing of Allegro's adventure.

Below, the troops surrounding the train held their positions, the National Guardsmen weary, the RDF men alert, ready, hungry for the action they knew would soon be theirs, would have to come.

Captain Marsh knew, or sensed, it would never come. He'd finished his interrogation of Allegro Stern before dawn, had gone over the pictures with her, attached names to the faces, confirmed the physical layout of each coach.

Now he was ready. He would have done better under cover of darkness, but he was ready. The remarkable Miss Stern had done most of his job, had even left all the trapdoors open. His call had gone in to the Pentagon nearly two hours ago, and he'd not heard from them yet. He suspected he had not heard because he would not hear. The civilians would block his move again, as they always had.

For the first time in his life, he felt ashamed to be an American.

At seven, Allegro had finished tucking the soiled jumpsuit in a plastic bag and stuffing it in the bottom of her suitcase. The RDF captain had given her all her negatives and a complete set of prints. She had been impressed he and his people could work so fast. She had told the captain all she could and they had exchanged commitments. She would not file her story until the crisis was over; he would never divulge she had been on the train unless she agreed.

Allegro had a very good reason for the deception. She loved Alden. She might never file the biggest story of her life if it meant losing him. It was a decision that could only be made later, when she had more facts.

She had showered, dressed in slacks and an open-neck shirt, and gone down to breakfast. Alden was waiting. They touched hands briefly, acknowledging the intimacy of the previous night. He was the same, but different. She knew he had meant what he'd said, but the light of day had sobered him, made him think again about the tragedy. It had to affect him, but she wasn't about to let him forget.

"I know you're hurting, worried. But we have to get it out in the open this morning." They had been seated alone at a table in the middle of the dining room. She leaned closer. "I love you. It has taken me a long time to find you," she said with passion. "When this is over, one way or the other, I'm going to pursue you."

He smiled wanly, put his hand over hers. "And I, you."

He didn't have to say more. She could see the love in his eyes. It was real. It was going to be permanent, but it would have to wait.

She thought about her deception and how he might take it. What were the scenarios? At worst, the Raven would blow the train and everyone on it to hell. Kate would be killed. Philip would never forgive her, particularly since she had been in a position to save Kate and had failed. And he would be furious she had jeopardized her life, too. At the very best, Kate would be saved, she would bless their marriage, and they would all live happily ever after.

She knew better. Life just didn't work that way. And she was sitting on the best story of her career. What about that?

In the split second these thoughts passed through her conscious stream of thought, their table was jarred by a figure walking past. Tea slopped on her slacks and Philip pulled back, trying to avoid having coffee spilled on his gray flannels.

"*Ach.* I am so sorry!" a guttural voice said. They looked up to see a smallish man with tight yellow skin hovering over them. He was bald and had the look about him of an aging lama.

"Please. Let me help," the man said. He sat by Alden, picked up a napkin, and began to sop the spilled liquid with the expertise of an incipient scullion.

"No need," Alden said. "The waitress—"

"Why wait for a waitress when I am here?" he asked. "Besides, it was my fault." He continued to wipe the table, lifting cups and saucers. "There. That's better," he said as he finished.

"Thanks," Alden said. "But you didn't have to."

"Your trousers need cleaning. I would be happy—"

"Just a spot. It will come out with Carbona."

The small man looked across the table at Allegro. He had large very blue and very alert eyes. He seemed to miss nothing. "And you, young lady. If—" He suddenly stopped, gazing at her in bewilderment. "You are Allegro Stern," he said softly.

She did not answer. Lit a cigarette.

"I have read your pieces," he said. "In many newspapers and periodicals. May I congratulate you?" He took her hand, kissed it in the European fashion. "You write well and your insight is deep. Your photographs—what can I say? Superb."

Flattery meant little to Allegro. She sensed something about this little man was wrong. Something was out of place.

"And you?" she asked.

"Allow me to introduce myself," he said in his guttural voice. "Eisenstadt. Ernst Eisenstadt."

She had guessed he was German. But the accent was not harsh. She took him for a Berliner. "You're with the press?" she asked.

"No. I am metallurgical engineer," he said in his sometimes imperfect English.

"Then you're in Kingman for the mining," Alden said.

Grushenko, alias Ernst Eisenstadt, let his eyes fall. His attitude changed completely. "No. I am here for the train."

An uncomfortable silence followed.

"I have a son aboard," he said. His mouth twitched nervously, his fists clenched. Inside, he wondered how he had learned to lie so well. It had not bothered him before.

He raised his eyes, looking from Alden to Allegro and back. "You two are with the press. Has any news been released? Will they be killing those people, my—my son?"

"I don't think so," Alden said softly. "It might all be a bluff." He felt sorry for the older man, but realized his attempt at reassurance was as much for himself.

Allegro peered at her watch. "We'd better be going."

"I wonder," Grushenko said, eyes suddenly bright, "if I may accompany you? I have no car and the special buses are crowded with journalists—"

Allegro threw Alden a warning look, but he was unaware.

"Of course," Alden said, "we can give you a lift. Let you off someplace. No trouble."

Jesus! Allegro thought. What naïveté! He gives everyone the benefit of the doubt. And somehow I doubt this little man. He's too smooth.

Alden paid the check and they headed for the door.

Washington, D. C., Friday, 10:00 A.M.
Eastern Daylight Time

After a sleepless night filled with doubt and anger, the president of the United States sat in his den, hands folded on the top of his head, thinking. He had calmed down, begun to think, to reason. Something he'd found difficult from the beginning. He had sought advice and had been put squarely in the middle. Now he was going to act. He picked up the phone and dialed his press secretary.

"Work up a statement, Frank," he said. "Tell the bastards we'll bargain. I mean *bargain*, not give in. Meet 'em halfway, something like that. Get it to me in half an hour and we'll go over it. But make it stiff, understand? Stiff, not soft."

In the Army town house in Georgetown not far from the White House, General Stone tried to raise his head from the pillow and remembered why he'd given up drinking years ago. He stumbled to the bathroom, threw cold water on his face, wiped it dry, and made his way through the house to his den.

The letter was gone. So it was done. He had made a statement against his government and for the first time in his life he had to consider what he would do this day, and for the rest of his life.

He looked at his watch. It was ten hundred hours. He had overslept. Another first. The horror of Kingman rushed back with the return of sobriety.

The Train, Friday, 8:45 A.M. Mountain Standard Time

The speaker on the top of the dining car squawked as it was turned on. All eyes turned to the train expectantly.

"We don't bargain, man, you hear?" It was P.J.'s voice this time, blasting out across the flat land. "What we want sticks! No percentages, man! No trades! You heard what we want and that's what we want! So take your bargains and shove them up your muthuh-fuckin' asses!"

A squeal rang through the air as the PA was shut off.

The CBS man was dumbfounded. For once, he didn't know what to say. "Well, you heard it," was all he could manage.

Closer to the train, Captain Marsh sat with his men. He knew they would not be in action. The signs were all there and he'd been through it before. The half-assed attempt to deal with the terrorists had failed. They would not back down and bodies would soon be thrown out the door. He was probably the only one, besides Miss Stern, who knew who the three were that lay by the train now. She had explained the conductor's action that had permitted her escape.

He thought about her as a woman now that his job had been scuttled—thought of her in her sheer panties and bra. She was one hell of a woman however you looked at her or thought about her. He had never thought about women in the RDF before. Not that he was a chauvinist—just that he never considered a woman could hack the pace. Allegro Stern could.

He looked again at the train. His men looked at him for orders, sensing something had gone wrong. He could give no orders—could not stand down—had to sit by and let it happen. It would be bad, very bad.

Standing with the press, between the curious on the hills in the distance and the troops, Alden's heart pounded. He could hear his pulse in his ears. Anger consumed him, anger at the rasping, hate-filled voices that erupted from the train. Anger that a handful of psychopaths could bring his nation to its knees—again. He was angry at the thought of Kate and the threat to her.

Most of all, he was angry with his own impotence, at his sense of alienation from a world he did not understand and could not deal with. He muttered something under his breath. Allegro glanced at him questioningly. "What did you say?"

"I said I'd like to kill them. Kill them all."

She reached for his hand, trying to offer some comfort.

The PA system squealed again. "It's nine o'clock." Boros's voice carried through the early light. "Nine o'clock. So synchronize your watches out there. You've got three hours. Tell your president that. Three hours until we start eliminating them one by one." She paused for effect. "If you meet our demands—all of them—nobody gets hurt. If we don't hear from you, we start shooting them. One every half hour. Believe it. I'll shoot the first one my-self." Her laughter rang out across the hills. "Any move

against this train and they all die—we all die. So make up
your minds. Three hours.''

Her mad laughter drifted across the hills and faded to
nothingness as the PA was turned off.

"Bastards!" Alden muttered.

Allegro regarded him thoughtfully. He has a temper,
too, she thought. But a positive one, directed at the right
channels. He was a complicated man. A man of many
passions.

Eisenstadt intruded on her thoughts. "They won't do
it," he said. He had attached himself to them, stuck like
glue right into the press area. He disappeared from time to
time, but always reappeared.

Allegro looked at him. He's wrong, she thought. They
will do it. They will surely do it. She'd seen it before.

But she kept her thoughts to herself.

Grushenko was looking for the Raven among the crowds
of onlookers, but he was pursuing an elusive fox. The
Raven kept his red Volvo moving continuously, driving
from place to place around the scene, exchanging brief
messages with Boros and Maxon, listening to the radio
news to catch the first signs of capitulation from Washington.

He had slept well in a town called Bullhead City. He
had seen no need to monitor the train through the night.
He knew nothing of Allegro's visit or the deaths of the
conductor and Judd. Boros and Maxon had not reported
the incident to him.

So far, the government had offered little. The armored
car, yes. But no more, not even the promise of a plane at
Las Vegas. Stupid. Why one without the other? They had
said the Philadelphia Five were convicted criminals and
would remain where they were, never to be set free.

Complete surrender was the Raven's objective. Anything less would be met with catastrophe. He had no
reservations about destroying the train. He could do it,
would do it. He didn't give a damn about the people, his
or theirs. Compliance by government was the thing. He
wanted that above all else. That would be the greater
victory—the revelation of greater power.

As he sat in his car on a low, sandy knoll overlooking

the train from a distance of a half mile, he was aware that
Boros's shortwave radio was on constant transmit. This
was contrary to his orders. He wondered if Boros was
trying to tell him something. She was a crude bitch, but
smart in her own way.

He started the car and drove closer to the scene, the
deadly radio-Nikon on the seat beside him.

The Train, Friday, 11:10 A.M. Mountain Standard Time

In the dining car of the Limited, Boros sat down at the
table where Maxon and Kate had been talking through most
of the night.

"Who goes first?" she asked.

Maxon stared at her.

"It's eleven A.M., Maxie. Do you know where your
hostages are?"

"What are you talking about?"

"An hour from now, twelve o'clock, we gotta kill and
dump one. You let that reporter bitch disappear, so who's
first now?" A nod of Boros's head indicated Kate. "This
one?"

Maxon's lip curled downward. "She goes with us to
Libya. Everyone in this car goes with us."

"If we ever see Libya," Boros said and giggled. "Okay.
Somebody from one of the other coaches. Okay."

"I'll let you know when," Maxon said. "We've got an
hour yet."

"Sure. You're in charge." She stood up and left.

At the end of the car, Boros conferred in a low voice
with P.J. "Keep your eyes on this bunch," she said. "I'm
going to round up our first card." She headed for the rear
coach.

The Litton men continued to deal cards and drink. They
were so bombed by now, they didn't know what they were
doing. They had given up on life. The cards, the drink—it
was all automatic for them.

The small oilman, hands clasped in his lap, his body
swaying back and forth, back and forth, was completely

out of it. He hadn't had food or drink in twelve hours, hadn't gone to the washroom.

The stockbroker was dozing or in a state of shock. The newspaper was crumpled in his lap. His eyes were half closed, glazed.

The black steward stared thoughtfully out the window or fetched drinks and sandwiches when asked. The death of the conductor had bothered him. He hadn't been a bad guy even if he'd been a whitey.

Mrs. Gonzales sat in a corner of the car on the floor, nursing her baby. She had seemed calmer since the birth, had accepted milk and sandwiches, had started to look around at the others for the first time.

Maxon looked directly into Kate's eyes, trying to fathom her, to analyze the power she had over him. Was he looking into her beauty, her radiance, or into her soul? She had convinced him. Now he lay under her gaze, limp and defeated, crushed beneath the heavy wheels of his own indecision.

She had, in her inimitable fashion, appealed to his sense of humanity, to his better instincts, his feelings for justice and fair play, and, most of all, to his lust for life so long dormant.

He dropped his eyes to the table. "We're not going to blow the train," he said softly. When he lifted his eyes again, he saw that Kate's were filled with tears.

Kate had been acting, playing her part for hours, using every nuance of emotion and word she had ever learned. But these tears were not play-acting. They sprung from joy, hope, and a feeling of triumph. She had given the performance of her life. This was the applause.

He held her eyes fixedly. "Don't look," he said in a low undertone, "but the new guy in back—the one with the blue metal gun—I've instructed him and he's alerted the rest of my people in the other cars. At eleven-thirty, we defuse the charges. At noon we try to make a break for it. None of you get hurt."

"You're going to fight your way out?"

"We're going to try."

Suddenly she felt pity for this young man, pity mixed

with a kind of love, an apprehension for his safety and future life. "Why not give yourselves up?" she asked.

He smiled cynically. "And spend twenty years in Leavenworth or some other dump?" He shook his head. "No."

"But if you surrender, they might go easy. They might even—"

"I said, no!" His voice was stonelike. "Listen," he said after a brief pause. "In case I don't make it, hold on to this."

He had written something in his blue notebook, torn out a small piece of paper, and moved it, under his palm, surreptitiously across the table to her.

Kate picked it up.

"Don't read it now," Maxon said anxiously.

She glanced quickly downward. "What does it mean?"

"I told you not to read it now. Hold on to it. Get it to the authorities."

The words on the scrap of paper were brief and meant nothing to her:

> *American Brandy 61*
> *Plastic boxes*

She looked at him questioningly.

Maxon whispered, his voice without inflection, "Get it to the police. Something's going to happen in England. I'm supposed to accompany—"

The Chicano woman screamed, her fear-filled wail rending the air, echoing throughout the car, driving terror deep into the hearts of the hearers. Her newborn picked up the wail, making it a duet.

The stockbroker jumped awake. The steward dropped his tray. The oilman continued to rock. The Litton men turned bloodshot eyes to the woman in wide surprise.

Kate and Maxon leaped to their feet. Kate clutched the small scrap of paper. Her heart beat wildly, almost bursting, filled now with horror instead of the hope it had held before.

At the end of the car, Boros was pulling at the arm of a young Chicano girl, her father pulling the other. P.J. jumped up and clubbed the Chicano with his pistol, splat-

tering the girl with blood as her father went down. Boros
was grinning, pointing her gun at the child's head. "Here's
our first card, Maxie. What do you say? After this one,
they'll give in, right?"

The Chicano mother's shriek was like splitting fire-
wood. "*No! No! Por favor!*" she cried. "*Por favor! No
Marguerita. Mi pequeña Marguerita. Por favor! No,
Marguerita!*" She fell to her knees, weeping, one arm
extended to the ten-year-old girl trembling in Boros's grasp,
the other clutching the baby.

"Let the kid go," Maxon said.

Boros shrugged and sat down before the shortwave radio. "Go to Mama," she said.

The child ran to her mother's arms. The Chicano woman
held her close.

The car was deathly still, the silence broken only by the
crooning of Maria Gonzales to her children.

Finally Boros's anger broke out. "Who the hell do you
think you are?" she screamed at Maxon.

"I'm the boss, remember?" He advanced on her.

"No. I'm brainless, remember?"

"You act like it too often."

Boros turned to P.J., a look of pure hate on her scarred
face. "What do you say, P.J.? At noon we dump the kid,
okay?"

P.J. nodded dumbly.

"The hell you will!" Maxon was shouting now. "Take
the kid back to the coach. Patch up her father and get the
rest of the family out of here, too."

Boros spat at his feet, turned to P.J. "Kill her, P.J."

P.J. raised his .22 Ruger pistol and pointed it at the
child's head.

The Gonzales woman screamed again and held the little
girl tightly against her. "*No! No, por Dios! Tenga
compassion!*"

"What's she talking about?" Boros spat out.

"*What's she talking about?*" Kate suddenly shouted
from behind Maxon. "She's asking for mercy! Can't you
understand mercy, you ugly bitch?" She had finally lost
control. After all the hours of steel nerves and iron control
she had blown it, and she felt like a fool.

Boros's bitter laughter boiled out through the car. "Now it comes out. Them versus us, good versus bad, the beautiful people against the ugly. What a piece of work! What shit!"

When Maxon spoke, his voice was a file over rough steel. "Take the girl back to the coach, Miriam. The mother and the baby, too. Leave the gun here."

With a hateful, death's-head smile, Boros turned to P.J. "Shoot the spic brat, P.J. Let's get this show on the road."

"Miriam!" Maxon shouted. "P.J.!"

But P.J. raised the pistol again, aiming it two-handed at the child.

"*Compassion!*" the mother cried. "*Por favor, compassion!*"

The shot was deafening in the confined car, the noise caroming like an avalanche off the steel walls.

The hollow-point slug ripped through P.J.'s head, tearing the back off and smashing it against the wall like a piece of ripe melon. The body, soaked in blood that cascaded down both shoulders, slumped to the floor.

"You shit!" Boros shouted. She was on her feet, lurching down the aisle, hands shaking as she lifted the awkward, too-big Steyr.

Maxon shot her through the chest, the hollow-point lifting her hundred-and-twenty-pound body off the floor, thrusting it back to the table where the two Litton men sat looking on in horror. They tried to jump out of the way, but ended up in a heap of arms and legs, all covered with blood from the saucer-shaped hole in the dead woman's back.

Maxon stood, shivering, breathing deeply, gun smoking. The first day he had fired a gun and he'd killed three people. After a moment, after fighting down the bile that threatened to send him running, he walked to the PA and flicked the switch.

"Now hear this! Now hear this!" his voice boomed out over the desert. "We're coming out! Read this clearly. We're coming out!" He paused for a few seconds. "Okay. We're going to defuse the charges and come out. The passengers will be safe. We're coming out."

The voice rolled out over the heads of disbelievers.

Cameramen reached for idle lenses. Newsmen listened carefully. Soldiers jumped to their feet and reached for weapons.

"We're coming out," Maxon's voice rolled out again, repeating so no one would misunderstand. "Some of us will come out with our hands on our heads, some will come out fighting. Understand this. We're coming out!"

He flipped off the PA system and turned to the youth holding the Mauser. He tried to sound authoritative, but he was shaking. He was scared. His gut churned as it had when he was a kid and scared.

"Start the defusing. Tell the others," he said. "Tell 'em to fight or give up—their choice. Everybody for himself."

The boy nodded and took off through the door to the sleeping cars.

Maxon remained standing, his body limp, swaying, his head down, the gun dangling loosely in his hand.

Kate walked over to him, held him, tightened her grip trying to bolster him. "Oh, God!" she said. "Oh, God!"

Then she rested her head on his chest and said, "Thank you. Oh, God, thank you for all of them." Then she began to weep.

These were not tears of acting. These were tears of gratitude for life, for hope. An expression of exultation and blessing.

CHAPTER 16

The Raven had heard it all—the shouting, the shooting, all of it. Now he sat in his car less than a mile from the Southwest Limited, his handsome face marred by the lines of grim hatred and repugnance. He pounded on the steering wheel in frustration.

He had listened to the Chicano woman's first wail for compassion. He had been stunned by the ensuing shouted exchange between Maxon and Boros.

Then the shots.

Then Maxon's surrender.

That shit! That shit never had his head together! I should have known!

He didn't hesitate. He drove closer to the hills near the site. Standing on a sandy knoll, all alone, he raised the Nikon and placed the viewfinder to his eye, focusing on a section of the rear coach at the dome. It didn't matter what part of the train he saw or if he pointed directly at the train at all.

But he wanted to see. After all the planning, he wanted to see it go.

The shutter release was a hair trigger. As he pressed it, his pulse throbbed and his body shook with excitement.

Everything went up at once: coaches, sleeping cars, dining and lounge cars—blown into thousands of splinters, shards of steel and glass. The locomotives, sturdier stuff, jumped into the air as if catapulted. They rolled lazily in circles and came down in two twisted heaps. Orange and red fireballs soared above each car, billowing smoke skyward in roiling circling masses of black, red, and yellow.

Then, pieces began to fall. Pieces of solid matter. Burned

162

clothing, pieces of bodies—an arm, a head, a torso. But nothing recognizable.

When he had seen it, the Raven felt no remorse or pity. It was a simple feeling, a flat, distant uncomfortable feeling, tinged with guilt, dirtiness, and disgust. The feeling that always came upon him after sex or masturbation.

Over thirty million people watching television witnessed the catastrophe in the safety of their own homes. Millions more heard the explosion and voice descriptions on radios— everything interrupted momentarily by the shockwave that knocked down cameramen and reporters.

They saw railway cars weighing a hundred and fifty thousand pounds each lift high in the air and splinter into pieces. Worse, they saw the carnage of human flesh—the charred bodies smoldering on desert sand, separated limbs and torsos stripped of clothing and partly roasted by the flames.

Among those close to the scene, Grushenko stood stock-still, rooted like a plant in the sand beneath his feet. Carnage, he thought. It was the only word he could find to describe it.

The explosion had shocked him, almost blown him from his feet, but he didn't run. He had seen it before and hadn't run. He hadn't run at Moscow or at Stalingrad. Now he was too old and tired to run. Carnage had been his education, but now it sickened him. This was not propaganda. This was not a show of political strength. To him, this was more than terrorism—this was murder.

It was the total, wasteful murder of hundreds of innocent people, the Raven's personal vendetta against mankind.

The Raven no longer served the Soviet Union. He served only himself, his perverted sense of power, his own madness.

Grushenko had to eliminate the Raven. But first he had to stalk him, to pick up his spoor, to corner him like a wild animal at bay. Then he had to kill him.

But how to start? He looked toward Alden and Stern standing, shocked, with the others. He smiled. His journey had already started. The Stern woman knew the Raven's face, his features, his habits, his person. She would not let this drop. She would follow this up.

*   *   *

The desert was a tumult of confusion, a frenzy of activity, a furor of smoke and shouting voices, cries of pain and suffering, a scene from the bowels of hell.

Many of the onlookers fled. Others spun through rolls of film or reels of tape in a frantic effort to record the truth.

The press area was a turmoil. Damaged cameras were frantically replaced with backups. Reporters wiped blood and gore from lined faces. Some lay where they fell, unable to move, too close to the purgatory they reported on with bland faces every day.

Alden ran straight into the inferno, the desert moonscape that had become a hell on earth. He tripped over objects, not realizing they were pieces of flesh, bits of bone. Smoke rose from the charred desert floor, carrying the stench of burned flesh mixed with the sheared-copper smell of blood, the odor of feces and human matter—a battlefield of death, the scene of shellfire, mortar, and flamethrower, the torn and shattered remains of those who had lost their fight with the grim reaper.

How would he find her? Oh, god! How she hated the slightest imperfection! He slipped and slid through the carnage without realizing his shoes were greased by human matter and the softness of the desert was human flesh. When he did, he cried for any piece of her he might have touched, violated.

Then he found her—what was left of her. Her head and torso, one arm and hand. He stood over her in disbelief, not able to move. Blood clotted her nose and mouth. God, the mouth he'd kissed a thousand times, had fed bits of food, had laughed with, caressed with his fingers. Her breasts were bare, those beautiful mounds he had worshiped. She would hate to have her breasts bared to the desert sun.

He stooped through rising wisps of smoke to gather her in his arms. He rocked her, kissed her cold cheeks, stared in disbelief at the bulging, sightless eyes. She was gone. The perfect woman, and she was gone. How could he have been such a fool to lose her in the first place?

He kissed the inside of her elbow and tried to kiss her palm as he had so often in the past. Her hand grasped a wisp of paper. He took the twisted scrap and shoved it in a pocket without conscious thought, then rocked her again.

That was how Allegro found him. She put her arms around him, rocking with him and the thing that had been Kate Kavanaugh, reluctant to tear him away from the human flesh that had once meant so much to him. While they both cried, she signaled to a passing paramedic.

"Are you all right, sir?" the young man asked, taking one of Philip's arms, disentangling him from the corpse and sitting him on the ground against a piece of wreckage.

The young man's eyes were soft, his face a mask of concern. "Maybe you'd like to sit here for a while," he said.

"You look like my son," Alden said. He was in shock, would probably not snap out of it for hours.

"Excuse me?" the young man asked, not understanding.

"You look like my son," Alden repeated. "My son, Nicky Alden." He looked up at the sky, tears rolling to his chin through smears of blood. "Oh, dear God!" he moaned, conscious of his loss.

The medic rolled up Alden's sleeve and took a syringe from his kit. "This won't hurt," he said. "It's just a mild sedative, Valium. Are you allergic to any sedative, Mr. Alden?"

Alden shook his head and didn't react as the needle went in.

In the distance, a random explosion rocked the scorched land. Someone screamed close by, not in pain, but in frustration and anger. Alden wept ceaselessly.

"I have to go, miss," the paramedic said. "Got to take care of some of the others. But I'll be back." He paused. "Will you two be okay?"

Allegro motioned for him to go. She held Alden close so he wouldn't fall back into the mess. Alden moved in Allegro's arms, looked around, saw the charred body of a child a few yards away.

"Rest for a minute and we'll get back to the motel," Allegro urged.

Suddenly, Alden's body shook like an overwound spring and she could not hold him. He sprang to his feet, stood rooted like a tree stump, waving his arms at the Hades

man had created. His eyes glowed with his inner fury
before the sedative took over. He gesticulated like a
madman.

"*Chaos!*" he screamed to the dead and dying. "*Chaos!*"
he screamed into the cameras and the ears of those weeping for the dead.

"*CHAOS!*"

Early Saturday morning, Allegro lay beside Alden, still
holding him, trying to counter the shakes he'd had for the
past twenty hours. A doctor had left a dozen pills, advised
she get him home to familiar surroundings.

She wasn't sure that was best for him. Kate had lived at
Palos Verdes with him. No. That would not be best for
him. The phone had rung incessantly. She had not answered, had asked the desk to hold all calls. His daughter,
Alicia, had sent a messenger to the room, and Allegro
called her. Alicia was in Kingman, would take charge of
her mother's remains, knew what her mother's last wishes
would have been, told Allegro where to bring her father.
Two days. They would bury what was left of Kate
Kavanaugh in East Hampton on Long Island in two days.

That gave her less than one day to get him on his feet
and on a plane. But she had a greater problem to solve,
greater for her. How was she going to tell him about her
visit to the train?

Was she going to file the story? If not, the problem was
simple. Don't tell him or not until he'd had a few months
to get over the shock of Kate's death. Not until she was
solidly established in his life.

Two things wrong with that. She hated falsehood, and
she couldn't sit on the best story she would probably ever
get in her life. She couldn't. If he loved her, he would
understand.

She slipped out of bed and looked at the huge stack of
pictures for the third or fourth time. They were some of
her best work. The ones of Kate talking to Maxon had
caught the action and intent perfectly. Few words would
have to be added. This was not for UPI or the daily sheets.
This was a *Life* spread.

She looked at Alden sleeping on his back, mouth wide

open, hair askew. He looked like a defenseless boy. She loved everything about him, but she was going to hurt him. Reporting was her job—the thing she did for a living. She was the best and this was her best ever. It couldn't be wasted.

She dressed, picked up the bundle, and went downstairs to the dining room. She asked for a light breakfast, a writing tablet, a couple of ballpoint pens, and some transparent tape. As she drank cup after cup of coffee, she sorted out the best fifty pictures, wrote captions for each, taped the captions to the positives, and set them aside.

In the lobby, she placed a collect call to a senior editor of Time-Life, a tall man in his fifties with gray hair, told him briefly what she had, accepted a generous offer, and was transferred to a rewrite woman, who recorded Allegro's lengthy description of her experience on tape. Allegro would not write the story but would get full credit. The package of pictures and negatives would be picked up by messenger service within the hour. She gave them carte blanche with the material.

That was it. Allegro wanted to be free to establish her life with Alden. Or to try.

She had been gone for two hours. When she put the key in the lock and opened the door, she heard running water. Alden came out of the bathroom toweling himself, looking better.

"Where have you been?" he asked.

"A little breakfast and some business. How do you feel?"

"Surprisingly, better. Can't believe what we can put ourselves through, and, you know . . ." He stopped, a tear forming in one eye. He brushed it away. "Any calls?"

"The desk has a stack of messages, I'm sure," she said. "I talked to Alicia. She's looking after things. The . . . funeral . . . is on Long Island, day after tomorrow. We'll have to fly out tonight."

He came to her, held her tight. "Thank God I found you. Thank God at any time, but now was a good time. I need you, my love."

"And I, you, Philip. But you don't know me, really.

God knows, I want you more than anything on earth, but you may not want me when you know what I am.''

She clung to him desperately, falling with him to the bed. He kissed here gently and lay with her, content.

''I filed my story while you were asleep,'' she said tentatively.

''I expected you would,'' he said into her ear, nibbling at one lobe, absently.

''Philip. Listen to me. I was with Kate on the train early Friday morning. Until about six hours before it blew.''

He stiffened in her arms, rolled away, sat up. He reached for his cigarettes, lit one, and blew smoke to the ceiling. ''Explain,'' he said.

''I'm a reporter. It's what I do. I overheard the RDF captain and the Amtrak person talking, heard something that would help me get on the train and off. I snuck on, talked to Kate and the terrorists, took pictures. She wouldn't come with me. I know what you're thinking, but she wouldn't come with me.''

''You bitch!''

''Philip! I pleaded with her to come. She was a heroine, almost saved all those people. I know. I was there. I saw how she worked on their leader.''

''Get out!'' He spat the words at her.

''What?''

''I said, get out! Are you deaf as well as stupid?'' he roared, tears coursing down his face. ''How dare you put yourself in that kind of danger? Knowing how I needed you, how I cared for you? What if you'd still been on that train? What if I'd lost you both—you and Kate. . . .'' He broke down completely. ''Oh, God!'' he screamed at her. ''Get the hell out of my life and stay out!''

Book Two

THE SEA

Religion, blushing, veils her secret fires,
And unawares, Mortality expires . . .
Lo! thy dread empire Chaos! is restored . . .
Light dies before thy uncreating word,
And universal darkness covers all.

—ALEXANDER POPE

CHAPTER 17

Why was he so stupid when it came to women? Barbara had beguiled him when he was too young to know better. She had produced a problem child and, instead of recognizing the young Alden's penchant for trouble, had fed him a steady diet of her wrong-wing politics. Kate had been Kate. He had loved her, had used and abused her, but had never felt that his life was irrevocably tied to hers. All the others—the long, tiresome, unending line of flesh on the hoof that had filled the in-between years—had been meaningless.

They had all been meaningless until Allegro. So why couldn't he forgive and forget? Why couldn't he accept what she was and live with it? She had scared the shit out of him and probably would do so again if he was to stick with her.

Thank God she was stubborn. He had thrown her out, but she had not gone far. She'd gone to the travel agent in the lobby and booked their flight to New York. She sat across the aisle from him in an almost empty first-class cabin, occasionally reaching for his hand. It wouldn't be easy to lose this one and he was grateful.

But he was not ready to forgive. Some unknown force was perversely keeping him from pulling her across the aisle and holding her close. He didn't understand it. He only knew it existed.

The Las Vegas–New York flight droned on. He looked

at her across the aisle. She smiled wanly, squeezed his
hand.

"Somebody told me Ethel Barrymore is buried there,"
Kate had often said, "and when I go, I want to share the
same ground."

So the burial of Kate Kavanaugh was held in a small
cemetery in East Hampton, Long Island, not far from the
rolling Atlantic, under a clear but cool sky early in May.
Kate had been misinformed. Ethel Barrymore did not occupy space in the cemetery. However, Kate had believed
it, so it had become the truth in her mind. She had liked
the quiet cemetery and had loved the sea.

A small group stood at the graveside—a few close
friends from stage and screen, Alden, Allegro, Alicia, and
Harry Zimmerman. Not far away, the small and delicate
figure of Vladislav Grushenko stood, his expression a
mixture of sadness and cunning.

Following the services, a quiet early dinner was served
before a crackling fire at the 1770 House, an old and
famous country inn on East Hampton's Main Street. It was
a refuge in aged wood and stone, dimly lit, intimate. The
talk was full of reminiscences, remembrances of things
past, of shared experience, of laughter, tears, and common ground.

"I remember," an aging actor said, "when Kate and I
played in *Idiot's Delight* together. I wasn't her co-star, of
course. Too old. Just one of the characters. I've forgotten
the role. We opened in New Haven to pans—ended up on
Broadway to raves." He paused, a mist filling his eyes.
"She pulled it all together, I always thought—not the
director, but Kate. What she taught me in those days,
instilled in me, I'll never forget. Well," he continued,
raising a glass and attempting a weak smile, "to Kate.
May she perform in heaven as she performed on earth."

More drinks were ordered, and the small, sad party
continued. But through it all, Alden remained apart, thoughtful, his mind dwelling on Kingman, Arizona.

And the Raven.

And where the others ordered scotch, bourbon, vodka,
and mixed drinks, Alden ordered a few white-wine spritz-

ers, cut those with water, slowly nursing his sadness, trying his best to smile.

Allegro was quiet, looking at him, studying him, concerned. She felt powerless to help him, the man she loved. She wondered whether her love would ever be returned, if he'd ever really forgive her.

Alicia was also quiet, sipping slowly at a glass of Burgundy, eating little, cool, distant, yet polite and responsive when spoken to. But inside, seething—seething over her mother's death, her father's despair, the thoughtless, insane barbarism of the terrorist groups.

A tall, gaunt raven-haired actress raised her glass and laughed boisterously. Her perfume was overdone, a challenge to the wood-smoke smell of the old room. "I played opposite Kate in an adaptation of Joyce's 'The Sisters,' " she said. "A road show, nothing much to speak of in money. I tried to upstage her. But every time I did, she did some little thing, some flutter of the hand, some sudden turn or inflection of voice—I don't know what. And you know? At the end of every performance, I felt like some wilting ingenue on stage with Sarah Bernhardt."

Laughter resounded around the table.

Harry Zimmerman chain-smoked throughout the meal, his face serious, his expression wistful. "She was a great actress," he said quietly. "And a great person."

A handsome young man seated close to the fireplace glanced up from abject sadness to look at the group. "I only worked with her once," he said. "In a film. But I'll never forget her—her talent or her person." And then with a wan smile, he added, "I loved her, too."

One by one, in couples or small groups, the guests departed the inn, leaving the table to Alden, Allegro, Alicia, and Harry Zimmerman.

"What are you going to do, Daddy?" Alicia asked, suddenly looking up. "What are your plans?"

Alden gazed into the dying embers of the fire. "Back to California, I guess."

Smoke drifted lazily from Harry Zimmerman's nostrils. "Why not take a vacation?" he asked. "Change of scene, a rest."

"You could come back to France with me," Alicia said. "To Chamonix. It's beautiful now, in the spring."

"I've never been there," Alden said. "Is that where you're working?"

"At the Richemond Hotel," Alicia said. "Not much of a job, but it's fun. I get to sunbathe and ski a lot."

"Or New York," Allegro Stern suggested. "You told me you haven't spent much time there in years."

He looked at Allegro with a wry smile and eyes full of reminiscence. "I was born there, and 'you can't go home again.' "

Zimmerman exhaled in exasperation. "Chamonix, New York, Acapulco, Hoboken! What the hell's the difference, Phil? You need a vacation, a getaway. One, two months. Chicago. Now there's a great town. The world's big, Phil. Full of beautiful places, out-of-the-way nooks, and different people."

But Alden's thoughts were on the whereabouts of the Raven. "I have a picture to write—a deadline," he said.

"Fuck the deadline," Zimmerman said, then looked at Alicia in apology.

"And Stackman?"

"Blow Stackman," Zimmerman said. "I'll take care of Warren. You know just as well as I do he's a good, understanding guy. Me—I'm off to Europe in a few days. Rome. Paris. Cannes. London. We could do it together."

"They're both right," Allegro said. "You need time, some R & R. You can't fight a war with your guts hanging out."

Alden turned to her, taking in her directness, her sense of honesty. She knew about his war, was probably the only one to know exactly what he intended. It was a war. Not like the Korean fiasco, where he'd served as an information officer. He'd never forgotten the hidden shame of that lousy desk job. No. This was another kind of war, and this time he'd see the blood.

"Maybe. We'll see," he said.

Before they all left the inn, Allegro and Alicia visited the ladies' room. Making up before the mirror, Alicia suddenly said, "I like you."

Startled, catching the younger woman's reflectioin in

the glass, Allegro said softly, "I like you, too, Alicia. I have every reason to like you, but what makes *you* like me?"

"Because," Alicia said, applying a line of light lipstick, "you're good for him. You know him, see into him, love him. I can tell. Take him to New York, Allegro. Get his mind off things. Help him to forget."

"You wanted Chamonix."

Alicia shrugged. "He's my father. I love him. But sometimes I think children and parents should keep apart, go their own way, be themselves."

"I've hurt him deeply. I don't know if he'll ever forgive me."

"For what? You've only known him for a few days."

Allegro sat silently for a moment, then decided to open up. She explained her job, what she'd done in Kingman, added the fact he'd ordered her out of his room.

The two women didn't speak for a few seconds.

"I appreciate what you tried to do for my mother," Alicia finally said. "Dad's not an easy man. Stubborn, willful, recalcitrant, always thinks he's right. Maybe he is. But he's also got a guilt complex a mile wide." Alicia's eyes misted ever so slightly. "He'll forgive you. He was hurt by the fear of losing you." She smiled wanly, started to rise. "Take care of him, Allegro." She leaned over and kissed her father's lover on the forehead.

Night was falling on the streets of East Hampton when they entered the limousine. Their route took them westward along Montauk Highway to the juncture of Route 24, then northward to the Long Island Expressway and New York. Behind them, weaving from lane to lane, sometimes passing, sometimes dropping behind, a gray Grenada trailed their steady track. Behind its wheel, chain-smoking even more than Harry Zimmerman, sat Vladislav Grushenko.

Alden wanted to grab hold of the past, the old haunts he'd loved when he and Kate had been young and struggling. When he and Allegro arrived in New York, he tried the Plaza first. It had always been his first choice. No rooms were available. Neither the Sherry Netherland nor the Pierre had a vacancy. Even the newer hotels—the New

York Hilton, the Park Lane, the Helmsley Palace—were all booked solid. New York had become a convention town. May was a busy month; rooms were expensive and at a premium.

They took a cab uptown to the Carlyle, off the beaten track, but the news was the same. As they lunched in the Bemelmans Bar, Alden sagged with a wry grin. "Well," he said, "California, here I come."

"That's not your answer," Allegro said. "You need a rest from the typewriter, from the business, from the pressure."

He looked across the table at her, not knowing what to do about her, knowing he couldn't get through the next few weeks without her. "Where?" he asked. "Not in this town. It's full of soot and sirens. Anyway, there's no place to stay, except maybe a bench in Central Park."

"You could stay at my place," Allegro said. "For a few days, a week, maybe. Until something opens up. It's not much, but it's cozy. And there's a pullout couch in the living room."

He looked at her, his thoughts jumbled. He hadn't been thinking clearly since Kingman.

Allegro stared back, her gaze level. "It's not far from here. Only a few blocks. And I have a couple of nice bottles of Château Carbonnieux. Why not take a look?"

He smiled, his eyes lighting up for the first time since the horror of Kingman. Maybe she was right. Deep down, he was thankful she was so stubborn. "What year is the Carbonnieux?" he asked.

She laughed. "Eighteen fifty-six."

Alden could feel the pressure ease. "Perhaps for a few days," he said, not yet ready to forgive and forget, but not willing to let go.

They hailed a cab and rode the few blocks. It was a cozy apartment, not what Alden had expected. Where he had pictured a three-room cell in a high-rise, he found a floor-through apartment in an old, neatly kept brownstone in the East Eighties.

It felt like home to him, like the old New York he'd known in younger days, full of warmth, quiet, and charm. The furnishings were comfortable and in good taste, all in browns and greens, blues and russets. The paintings on the walls were vivid with color. There was a working fireplace.

Within a few days, he had begun to loosen up, to smile, to laugh, to reminisce, to let himself relax. He slept on the convertible couch in the living room, for he still brooded about Kingman, the Southwest Limited, and Kate.

He had not forgiven Allegro, but they shared. They cooked together in the small but efficient kitchen. Allegro prepared her delicious chicken oregano and pan-broiled pepper steak. Alden tried out his complicated salads and cooked his infamous spaghetti marinara, loaded with spices.

They took long walks through Central Park, watching kite-flyers and softball games, resting before statues of characters from *Alice in Wonderland,* sauntering around the gravel walk that ringed the reservoir.

Sometimes, on these walks, they held hands, each convinced it was a grip of friendship. They were falling in love again, slower this time, the subtle and wonderful intertwining of souls like the blending of the sauces they had concocted . . . and, so wary were they of failure, they did not recognize success.

They did all the things new lovers do: visited art galleries and museums, took in plays and movies, ate in small, out-of-the-way restaurants, found little shops in the Village and Little Italy that sold the most outlandish foods either of them had ever tasted.

They laughed and cheered each other, began to truly know each other, and, finally, by the middle of May, realized they had fallen in love. But in that falling, each held a reserve, a constraint.

For Philip, it was the age difference, for this woman was not much older than his daughter. He would die long before she, leaving her alone with memories and pain.

For Allegro, it was the old fear foretold and never forgotten: the tall, thin, silver-haired man who never made the final commitment, who disappeared and disintegrated into the past. But they continued, each fearing the loss of the other, the loneliness that comes of loss.

It all came together about two weeks after they had been living in the same apartment but in separate beds. They had enjoyed a quiet meal in a nearby bistro, walked home, and entered laughing. The air was fresh. Stars lit the night sky. Pedestrians and traffic had seemed to fade, unimportant, not a part of their private reverie.

Inside the apartment, they had stood facing each other, hands clasped, basking in the warmth of their own awareness. They came together as naturally as they had the first night, searching for the warmth of mouths, the excitement of tongues. He picked her up and carried her to her bed.

The coming together was as slow and deliberate as the evening. They had been apart too long, had suffered deeply, needed the first embrace to be strong—strong enough to provide the foundation for a full life.

They undressed each other with a slow deliberation, mouthed their passion to a height they could not endure without complete fulfillment, then joined.

Again, there was no mad thrashing but a slow dance, every thrust and parry choreographed to full effect, the players eager, but restrained, the final curtain demanding the best of reviews.

Finally, a climax beyond their experience left them weak, grasping at each other, unwilling to move away. As their chests stopped heaving and breath came in even tempo, Alden gloried in the closeness of her, the feel of her head on his chest, her hands still holding him tightly. As they began to relax, he felt they had to talk, to clear the air, but he didn't know where to begin.

Allegro solved the problem for him. "Alicia and I had time to talk on Long Island," she said languorously. "She said something about you being a PIO. What did she mean?"

Alden laughed to himself. He wanted to talk, to clear the air, but this? Well, why not? It was a part of the problem. "Public information officer," he said. "Korean War. I was too young for the big war, but I wanted to do my part, make some contribution."

"You enlisted? She didn't tell me that."

He moved down, turned her head to his, looked into the ice-blue eyes. "I guess I'm one of those old-fashioned bastards," he said. "I believe in my country, the Declaration, the Constitution, the Bill of Rights . . . Washington, Jefferson, the founding fathers . . . all that shit."

He looked away, trying to gather his thoughts, to tell her exactly how he felt. "I don't know what I believe in now," he said. "Things have changed so much."

After a few seconds, he looked in those beautiful eyes once more, smiling. "I wasn't bad, you know? A good soldier. My body got tough, supple. I did my basic at Fort Benning, then went to officers' training school. I made Expert on the rifle range and mastered every weapon in the book. I looked forward to action, to becoming . . . what? A man?"

"A hero," Allegro said wryly. "And maybe a dead one."

Alden shrugged. "Better a dead hero than a live coward."

Allegro reached down to pull a cover over them, snuggled down again against his chest. "You're crazy."

"Crazy? Why?"

"All your talent, and you wanted to waste it on the desert air."

" 'Gray's Elegy.' You don't have to educate me."

She grinned. "Nobody could educate you. In certain ways—"

" 'The paths of glory lead but to the grave.' Same poem, right?" He held her close, needing her understanding, her respect. "The brass didn't see it my way. They saw the man with words, the PI officer. The man who tells the American public what they want to hear. Tell 'em we're making headway when we're going backward, that we're winning when we're losing. All the bullshit of lying with a smile."

Allegro's eyes were full of softness and pity. "Is that why you're so intent on the Raven?"

"Hmm?"

"To make up for your feelings of guilt, your feelings of impotence, for not being truly involved?"

"Maybe, deep down. But you forget Kate."

"No. I haven't. Nor will you. But it has to be accepted, redirected in a sense."

He laughed, a mirthless laugh. "So he goes free, murdering, assassinating, killing. He roams free while children bleed to death on the desert and people dining at outdoor cafés are blown to bits."

"He'll be caught," she said, shifting her weight, one hand on his chest.

Alden laughed again. "By whom? Interpol? The CIA? The local police?" His voice was bitter. He couldn't hide the hate and frustration.

"By somebody," Allegro said.

"Yes. By *me*." He began to shake and she held him close. "I won't shoot him," he said. "I won't kill him unless I have to. But I'll find him. I know I'll find him. And I'll bring him to justice, before a court of law."

"Where do you start?" Allegro asked.

"I don't know. But something will turn up. I've a feeling and a clue."

"What clue?"

"The note in Kate's fist: 'American Brandy 61. Plastic boxes.' "

"It could mean anything—or nothing."

"It means something. I know that. I have a feeling."

" 'Vengeance is mine, sayeth the Lord.' "

"Don't tell me you're a religious fanatic."

"Hardly," Allegro said. "I'm a realist. I believe in nothing and everything, if that makes any sense. But certain truths exist. 'The revenger revenges only himself, and suffers doubly.' "

"I used to believe that, too. But today? I don't know. I used to think I would die in wisdom, and now I feel ignorant."

After a long silence Allegro said, "You know, Philip, I respect you very deeply—your sense of honor, your talent, I admire your search for the truth, your respect for justice and civilization." She paused for a few seconds to make sure she would be clearly understood. "You've had no experience with the Ravens of this world. I've had some and I'll tell you honestly that I don't like the idea of you going after him. But if that's the way it's going to be, I'll be a part of it all the way."

When he looked at her again, a grim determination filled his gaze. He ran a hand over her silken flank, glorying in the possession of her. Whatever life held for them in the quest for a bloodthirsty terrorist, it was good to be together. Never again would he feel the emptiness of being alone.

CHAPTER 18

With each passing day, Alden wondered if he was ever going to solve the puzzle and find the monster who had killed Kate. He tried to keep the obsession from ruining his newfound love. One night as they got into bed and lay close, he said tenderly, "Allegro. That's a beautiful name."

"My father was a musician. Trombone. Nothing much to speak of. Never made the big time. But he always called me the joy of his life." She gave a wry smile. "Sometimes I wish I'd been named Andante or even Largo."

"Why?" he asked.

She shrugged. "There's a sadness in me—inside of me. I can't explain it. It's there. Deep. Desolate."

"You're anything but that," Philip said. "You're alive, vibrant, witty."

She looked at him thoughtfully, pulled him close, and took him in her hand. He was ready, had been ready for their union every night since he'd left the couch for her bed.

They had explored and had found familiarity. The movement of hands was familiar; the movement of bodies practiced. They found pleasures in each other never experienced before. This night was no different. It was full, it was brimming, it was beautiful.

When she cried out to him, "Look into my soul! Look into my soul!" it was awesome and frightening, even more so than Kate's, "Oh, God! Oh, God!"

Afterward, he contemplated their difference in age. This woman was young enough to be his daughter, he thought. But what is age difference—a few years measured against eternity?

He had not forgotten the Southwest Limited or the manner in which Kate had met her death. His obsession persisted. His vow persisted. He would find the Raven and deal with him.

"Please, Philip," Allegro begged, "try to forget it. Put it in the past, where it belongs. Bury the dead."

"No."

"I told you before. It's revenge. Pure revenge."

"It's not revenge."

"It *is*!"

"No, it's *not*!" He became sullen, as a little boy becomes sullen when he doesn't get his own way. "It's just that I want to see him behind bars, out of the way." He paused. Then in a trancelike way, he said, "Electrocuted, hanged, gassed."

Allegro looked at him in disbelief. "Isn't that revenge?"

He glanced at her sideways. "No one is perfect. You proved that at Kingman."

"*Don't!*" She held a hand out, palm toward him. "Don't bring it up again. We can't build on this if you won't let it drop."

"It's a two-way street. I'm going to get the Raven."

"I can't stop you. I know that. I'm just trying to make you play it smart."

He looked away from her in discomfort. "All right."

Allegro pushed herself up on one elbow, looked him in the eye. "It's not a question of being a coward. You just weren't built for this. The world of international terrorism is alien to you. You're not in Korea now. You're in the dirtiest war ever fought. People are killed for political ideology." Her eyes filled with tears. "I don't want to see you die in a cause you don't understand. You haven't been trained for this." She laughed. "Almost no one has."

She sat up, took his head in both hands. "Philip, you're a sensitive man and I happen to love you." She kissed him hungrily, pressing her lips to his in desperation. Then her body went tight, and she twisted her arms around his neck and dug her face into his shoulder, quivering, shaking.

As he held her tightly, staring beyond her, he was very aware of her plea, but other thoughts intruded. He was wondering: What did it mean—that note clutched in Kate's hand? What did it mean?

American Brandy 61
Plastic boxes

Whenever Allegro was out of the apartment, making the rounds of the editorial offices, shopping, or working one- or two-day assignments—donkey work, she called it—Alden would sit by the phone, calling state liquor authorities, the California vineyards in the Napa Valley, various wine associations. Everywhere he received the same answer: Brandy is made only in France or Spain.

One day he thought he had it. He was in touch with a distributor in South Carolina.

A slow, drawly voice said, "American Brandy? Yeah, ah think ah know what y'all mean. Now, lets see heah . . . uh . . . ." He riffled through some files. "Yeah, we got apple, peach, plum— "

"Apple! Peach! Plum! What good does that do me? I'm talking about real brandies! Cognac!"

"Now, listen heah! Ain't no sense gittin' yoah ass in an uproar! Ah'm trying to hep you!"

"You've been enough of a help!" Philip slammed down the phone.

One afternoon Allegro walked in the door just as Alden was hanging up.

"Who was that?" she asked.

He recovered quickly. She had decided to go along, but he didn't want his sleuthing to be obvious. "The studio," he said.

"Do they want you back?"

"No. Matter of fact, they want me to take another month or so."

"They called you to tell you that? The business must be in a bad way."

"No. I called them."

She turned and walked to the small kitchen and placed a bag of groceries down. Then she stared blindly ahead for a few seconds. He can't go back, she thought. At the sound of his step behind her, she turned, smiling. "We're having Poulet Picasso tonight. I've got all the ingredients."

She had to be strong. God in heaven, she had to be strong!

Toward the end of May, Allegro had to leave on a two-day assignment. The first day, Alden walked the streets, used the phone to poke at his "American Brandy" clue and gradually went stir-crazy. The second night, he went out on the town. New York bars were like old friends and he'd been on the wagon long enough. His nerves screamed for relief. He walked south on Central Park West to 67th Street, turned right, went to the middle of the block, and entered the Café des Artistes. He ordered scotch. No more vodka. It reminded him of Barbara and her politics. That bitch! Why had he married her when he might have had Kate from the beginning?

But Barbara had told him she was pregnant, and typical of the gentlemen of that time, he had offered to marry her.

They had married quickly, hastily, in order not to be ashamed in front of their families. It was only a month after the marriage that she had told him it had been a false alarm, the result of anxiety.

He had felt trapped, then relieved. Now he was free to marry Kate if Barbara would grant him a divorce. But she had become pregnant again, this time for real.

Nicky.

Again he felt trapped. Stupid! Stupid stud bastard! He tried to drown the memory—started pub crawling. He had not done it since California, had not done it for ten years before that.

This night he had an excuse—two excuses. One was Nicky. Nicky and the pregnancy that had trapped him. Nicky and all the pain. He had never understood his own son. Barbara had shielded the lad, had fed him her twisted doctrine, kept the young Alden's indiscretions from the world.

The other was the Raven, the murderous bastard who

had killed his Kate. And all the others, the hundreds who had died at his murderous hands all over the world.

Jesus! Jesus! The alcohol clouded his brain, but the ache would not go away. He had to do *something*. Allegro understood, finally. Ernst Eisenstadt understood. The little German had visited often, was as anxious as Alden to catch up with the Raven. Perhaps they would do it together.

Alden kept on the move, stopping at many taverns on the way uptown, always the last to leave when they began to upturn stools upon the bar.

He considered going back to Allegro's apartment, but it was blank without her, empty and cold. But he was approaching the talkative stage, when he needed companionship, the exchange of ideas. Deciding he was his own best companion, he headed for Allegro's.

Two blocks from the brownstone, it happened. The street was dark and no one was around. They stood in front of him, grinning, waiting for him to make the first move.

He stood on rubbery feet, knowing it was going to be bad. One was white, a tall, skinny kid about nineteen holding a length of pipe. The other was shorter, black, muscular.

Alden turned to run and tripped over his own feet. He heard them laugh, felt the pipe striking his neck and shoulders, the heavy boots working on his ribs.

"Stop! Take the money!" he screamed through the pain. He felt grimy hands going through his pockets, taking his wallet, then stripping off his watch and rings. The kicking went on—ribs . . . neck . . . face. He looked up through swollen eyes to the cold faces of the two who beat on him for pleasure. And he understood what made the Raven tick.

He did it for pleasure.

"No more!" he screamed into the night.

"Hey, man. We's got to get our kicks. Right?" The black man grinned as he leveled one more kick to Alden's head.

The beating stopped. He had survived, barely. Every muscle ached. His head felt like it was about to explode. He felt the blood run from his ruined face. He spat blood

from a lung he suspected was punctured by a broken rib.
He stank of blood and feces, and the garbage he lay upon.

Alden pulled himself to his feet and staggered down
the street, falling and getting up half a dozen times.

He found himself in front of Allegro's building. The
flight of steps to the door looked infinite, although there
were only five stairs. He inhaled deeply and started up,
holding on carefully to the stone banister.

Once inside the vestibule, he fumbled for the key to the
inner door, finally found it, and let himself in. The key to
the apartment gave him more trouble, taking him a full
five minutes to locate on the ring. Thank God they hadn't
taken his keys.

The apartment was empty. He headed for the bathroom,
placed his palms upon the edge of the sink, head lowered.
Slowly, he lifted it and gazed into the mirror. What stared
back was hideous, a bloodied mask, an alter ego, the
obverse side of the coin that was Philip Alden.

The man who had so recently been looking for a challenge, action, something to fight against, had found it—
and lost.

He began to weep, got control of himself, and undressed. He washed the blood from his face, the shit from
his legs, revealing cuts, contusions, and two shiners. He
patched himself as well as he could with Band-Aids, then,
leaving his clothes in a heap on the bathroom floor, made
his way to the bedroom and collapsed on the huge king-
size bed.

As he lay there aching, falling asleep in his hurt, he
remembered the eyes of the black man. That one had
enjoyed the hurting. For whatever reason, he had enjoyed
the tearing of flesh and breaking of bone.

Alden thought again about the Raven. They were the
same, though the Raven worked on a larger scale. He
enjoyed the killing. The money and the politics were
secondary to him. Alden understood that now. Instead of
feeling defeated, he felt his resolve harden. He would get
the bastard. Somehow, he would get the bastard who had
blown up the train.

*   *   *

At three o'clock Sunday afternoon the key turned in the lock and Allegro entered the apartment. Hearing no "Hello," she decided Philip was out. She walked through the living room, into her den, unslung the camera and lens case from her shoulder. She removed her safari jacket, yawned, and made her way to the kitchen, where she brewed herself a cup of tea. She stood sipping it, thinking of the weekend's work.

Another donkey-job assignment. She wished she could get her teeth into something, then thought of Philip and smiled. She felt weary, and crossed into the bedroom, unbuttoning her blouse as she walked.

When she saw him, she stiffened in shock. Panic shook her and a tight gasp escaped her throat. He lay sprawled on the bed, nude, the white sheets stained with his blood.

"Philip!" she screamed and ran to him. "Philip, what happened?"

Alden opened one blackened eye and regarded her without comprehension. He seemed to be looking beyond her.

Allegro shook him gently. "Philip, are you all right? What happened? For Christ's sake, what happened?"

The other eye opened. "Allegro."

She circled her arms around him and held him tightly. With a catch in her voice she said, "Tell me, Philip, tell me what happened! Were you in an accident? Oh, my God! Look at you!" She held him off, looking at his battle scars, then pulled him to her again.

He returned her hug forcefully, looking over her shoulder, ashamed, remorseful—and still angry. "I was mugged," he said. "Punks."

She loosened her grip and pushed him away, looking into his face. "Mugged?" Both his eyes were black and he was a mass of contusions. His left nostril and upper lip were a clot of blood.

He reached for a pack of cigarettes on the night table and winced as his lower left ribs throbbed. As he lit up, he said, "Mugged."

"Where?"

"A couple of blocks from here—an alley."

"Were you hurt?"

He pushed her away, looked down at his bloodied frame,

grinned at her foolishly, baring bloody teeth. "Not a scratch. They didn't lay a hand on me."

"I mean *seriously*. Were you unconscious? Do you have any broken bones?"

"No." He took a puff of his cigarette, wasn't about to complain about the ribs. He didn't like hospitals. The ribs would heal themselves. "Three of 'em," he said, stretching the truth a little. "Cowards. I could have taken 'em on one at a time."

"You mean three men jumped you?"

"Men?" He laughed bitterly. "Kids. In their late teens— early twenties. One of them big as a bull."

Her voice was quiet when she asked, "How did it happen?"

"Jumped me from an alley. Isn't that how it's done? Three against one. How do you like that? It's not fair."

"When are you going to learn the world isn't fair?" she asked.

She partially filled the tub with lukewarm water, helped him into it. "My God, you are a mess," she said. "Put the boots to you from the look of all these bruises."

When she finished, he did not look much better. Cleaner perhaps. When he coughed or laughed, the ribs hurt like hell, but he didn't let on. He no longer bled from the mouth, so he figured the ribs had not punctured anything after all.

He drank the rest of the afternoon, silent, sullen, brooding, turning the mugging and the reason over in his mind. When she spoke to him, he answered in monosyllables.

Allegro finally gave up, found a deck of cards, and began playing solitaire. Solitaire for the solitary, she thought. Aptly named.

Alden turned on a ball game, staring at the television screen but not reacting, hidden in his own thoughts, wrapped in a coil of nerves on the brink of explosion.

At last he rose from his chair, turned off the television set, and began to pace up and down the room, murmuring to himself.

"Philip, are you talking to yourself? Or am I included?"

He stopped his pacing suddenly, turned to her, eyes slits. "Terrorists! Those young bastards! That's what they are, terrorists! Total disregard for law and order! Institutions it's taken us more than two hundred years to build. They'd tear them down like that!'' He snapped his fingers. "No regard for the institutions, the people who built them, their elders, their parents! What kind of a civilization is that? It's *un*civilized!''

She did not answer for a moment. Then: "Terrorists? Kid muggers? You're reaching, Philip.''

He turned from the window, began pacing the room again. "Maybe I am. Getting paranoid in my old age. But dammit! They show no respect! They're like my son, Nicky.''

Allegro smiled wryly. "Is he a terrorist?''

"No,'' Alden said quietly.

"Am I a terrorist?''

He smiled. "Only in bed.'' Then the smile was replaced by a totally different mood. "You're different, Allegro. You understand life, have understood it for a long time. You know the difference between Bach and Beethoven and Gershwin, between Einstein and Newton. You're more like Alicia, but far beyond her.'' He reached for his glass, found it empty, went to the bar, splashed in three fingers of brown liquid. "You're nothing like Nicky. He's ungrateful, a useless parasite, interested only in himself, his guitar, his pot, his wanderings.''

He downed his drink, headed for the bar, again splashing himself a large dose of scotch, this time adding a little water, continuing to talk, his back to Allegro.

"I tried to give him direction, God knows, I tried. He was in Barbara's custody, but I made sure he had the best of everything. Do you know what opportunities I gave that boy?'' He turned suddenly, lurching drunkenly. "Do you?''

Allegro pondered for a moment. "Don't you realize what you're doing? You're so disappointed in Nicky, you're taking it out on all the rest of the kids.''

"Horseshit!'' He half rose from his chair, then fell back into it. "Horseshit! Nicky was a bloody *monster*.''

"That paramedic in Arizona. The one who helped you when we found . . .'' She paused for a moment, on dangerous ground. "He wasn't much over twenty. Would you call him a terrorist?''

"He was different. As you're different."

"Then *all* kids aren't stupid, inane, out for themselves?"

Alden remained silent. After a long pause, he said, "I guess I was drunk—still am. But what the hell, *three against one*!"

"You got mugged. It happens all the time." She looked at him intently. "But if you're serious about going after the Raven, you better sober up."

"I'll sober up," Alden said, and staggered over to the bar to pour another drink.

"That glass doesn't exactly look like it contains sobriety."

"It contains booze," he said, swilling it around. "Booo-ooo-ze." He gulped it down. Then he turned to her, unsteady on his feet. "I'll sober up. You watch. I was sober for ten years. When I say I'll sober up, I mean it. You watch."

She believed him. Yet, an alarm sounded within her. Drunk or sober, he was no match for the Raven.

"Let's go to bed," he said.

Allegro curled her lips. "I don't think you're up to it now."

"I don't mean for sex. I mean for rest."

In bed, they were silent for a long time, neither sleeping, the only sound the muted traffic on the street. When she thought he was asleep, and was about to kiss him, his voice broke the quiet. "Good and evil divide the world, Allegro. The Raven is evil. He must be expunged." He paused for a few seconds. "I've been thinking about it—a lot. My search for him is not vengeance, it's more like a latter-day quest for the Holy Grail, to obliterate evil. Though I know it will rise again, someplace else for others to kill."

"Give it a rest, dear heart," she said. "I'm getting a little tired of all this philosophy."

When she turned toward him for a response, he was sleeping.

CHAPTER 19

Grushenko spent a great deal of time alone in New York. He couldn't visit Alden and Allegro too often and arouse suspicion. He didn't want to rely on his people this time, but he kept Petrov informed.

In his last scrambled telephone conversation with Moscow from the embassy, Petrov had seemed distant, aloof, as he listened to Grushenko's report. At the end of it, Petrov had been silent and Grushenko had wondered whether his old friend was dissatisfied.

"Why the wait?" Petrov then asked. "Why not use our people and get at it faster?"

"No need. This way it will seem more natural. Trust me, Dima."

"If you say so," the man in Moscow said. Then Petrov cleared his throat in embarrassment. "I have personal news for you, Vladik. Not good." His voice cracked with emotion, compassion. The two men had known each other a long time. "Your son is in jail, just six floors below my office. He's in a cell here in Lubyanka."

"What!" Grushenko was shocked. "What is the charge? Drunkenness?" He knew better. It was his way of grasping at straws in the wind, hoping.

"The charge is dissent against the state," Dmitri Petrov said. Then more slowly: "I'm sorry, Vladik. But I'm sure you realize this does not reflect on you. Your service to the Soviet Union over the past forty years has been exemplary."

"I understand. Thank you, Dima," he'd said without emotion. He had cradled the phone as Petrov went on speaking. He tried to absorb the truth of it, to accept the certainty his son would end up in one of the gulags, lost to him forever.

He had sat very still at the desk, fighting back the tears that were forming in his eyes. Was it my fault? Did I do something wrong? Is there something I could have done that I omitted?

A few days later, the buzzer rang from the vestibule of the brownstone.

"Yes?" Allegro asked into the mouthpiece of the intercom.

"Ernst Eisenstadt," the filtered voice answered.

Oh, God, Allegro thought. Again?

"Who is it?" Philip asked, coming out of the bathroom toweling his face. He looked, and felt, much better.

"Ernst."

Alden's face brightened. "Tell him to come up."

"I was just about to," Allegro said with a half-hidden acerbity in her tone. She pressed the buzzer. "Your newfound friend certainly likes to talk."

"I like Ernst. Even if you don't."

"I didn't say I disliked him. I just think he's a bore, that's all." She slumped into a chair. "There's something odd about him—more than he seems. Can't put my finger on it."

"I find him odd but interesting," Alden said. "He makes a lot of sense. Philosophical sense, if you know what I mean? And I feel sorry for him, for the loss of his son."

"I do, too. But he's become the original Krazy Glue man."

Allegro was right. Two days after Alden had moved in with her, Ernst Eisenstadt had become a constant visitor, never more than an hour or two, but frequently, every two or three days. He never called—he just arrived.

He and Alden sat and talked about terrorism, the Raven, political philosophy, and social change. Ernst never talked about metallurgical engineering. Allegro had thrown a few questions to him on the subject, but he'd evaded them. She had felt suspicious of Ernst, ever since Arizona. She wondered what the hell he was doing in New York for so long—and why he clung to Philip.

"Sit down, Ernst," Alden said when the KGB man entered the apartment. "Vodka again?"

"Please."

Alden laughed shortly. "I always thought Germans drank schnapps."

"Brandy?" Grushenko smiled. "Vodka has the same effect. And I am not German. I am an American citizen and the most popular drink in America today is vodka."

When Alden went to the bar to mix the drinks, Grushenko looked directly at Allegro. "And how is my beauty today?"

"Fine, Ernst. Just fine."

"Tell me. Where did you get those beautiful ice-blue eyes? Father? Mother?"

Turning on the charm, Allegro thought. Well, Ernst, flattery will get you nowhere. "Liz Taylor," she said.

When Alden returned with the three drinks, his a light spritzer, he raised his own. "Skoal."

"*Prosit*," Grushenko said.

"Here's lookin' at ya," Allegro said as she gulped a third of her martini.

"You're wondering what happened to my face," Alden said.

Grushenko shrugged. "Truly my friend, I was."

"I was mugged," Alden stated. "Three punks did it, for pleasure. The way the Raven kills. For the joy of it."

"What can I believe?" Grushenko said. "To me it's rebellion, a rebellion against the established order. It's the same throughout the world—in Germany, the Scandinavian countries, France, Italy, even Russia." He dropped his eyes. He knew this too well.

The call to Petrov and the news about his son had affected Grushenko profoundly, made him all the more resolute about his quest to kill the Raven. He had been patient, had not used any of the facilities of his organization. But they were running out of time. "You must remember, these children grew up in fear," he said. "Fear of the bomb, the end of civilization as we know it. They don't look forward to a long life span."

Allegro leaned forward ever so slightly in her chair. Now he was making sense. She understood this.

"Well, for God's sake!" Alden said. "Who's not afraid of the bomb? I sure as hell am—I remember when the first one was made."

"He's right, Philip. You're older. You've lived a good part of your life. To you, it makes less difference than to a kid in his twenties. He looks forward. You look backward."

He ignored her and looked at Grushenko. "And what's this about the end of civilization? What civilization? An exploding population with not enough food to go around? Inflation and recession? Sirens in the street? Terrorists running amok, and nobody doing anything about it? Rock music, bizarre dress, drugs from pot to cocaine? And over it all, the shadow of the bomb?" He ground out a cigarette viciously. "Well, I say let it drop. The sooner the better."

Allegro had never seen him so bitter. "I'd rather live in this civilization and hope, rather than become a cinder," she said.

Alden jerked his head in her direction. "Hope for what?"

"For living, for loving. For marriage." And she looked at him peculiarly. "For children."

"Why bring children into this world?" he asked, making his way to the bar and mixing another spritzer. "What do they get for it, and what do you get for it in the end? They come down with a neurotic fear of the bomb, and you go crazy trying to please them. And the more you try to help, the more they hate you."

"Well," Allegro said, "this has been a pleasant conversation—repetitive, but interesting. I think I'll fix another drink. No, don't get up, Philip. Women's lib and all that."

As Allegro resumed her seat, Alden blurted, "I can't get my mind off the goddamned Raven. I wonder why nobody's caught up with him. You'd think the authorities— the FBI, the CIA—would have a lead by now!"

Grushenko looked up wearily. "And what about the Red Brigades, the Baader-Meinhof? They've arrested some of them, but others replace them."

"The FALN," Allegro said. "The PLO, the NFLP, not to mention the IRA."

"The IRA consider themselves patriots fighting the British," Grushenko said.

"They're terrorists just like the rest," Allegro said. "Mountbatten. Restaurants in London. Killing innocent men, women, and children. Don't tell me they're patriots."

"I think it's a conspiracy," Alden said.

"Conspiracy?" Grushenko looked puzzled.

"By the governments of the world. To create unrest and preserve what exists. These terrorist groups move around freely. A few years ago, two of the Baader-Meinhof were in New England. And nobody lifted a hand."

"And Carlos has never been captured," Allegro added.

Grushenko smiled to himself. Alden did not know how close he had come to the truth. Russia and the United States found it to be in their own interests to let the terrorists wreak havoc in order to direct their people's attention away from the real problems, like the quiet fight for oil in the Middle East. But the Raven was getting out of hand, creating his own scenarios. He must be found and killed.

"You have seen the Raven, my dear Allegro," Grushenko said. "And if you see him again, you can point him out. And we, Philip and I, will move in to avenge his wife's death and my son's."

The image of his son pacing a small cell in the Lubyanka caused Grushenko to clench his glass in anger at whatever the boy had done, and in sorrow and sadness.

"I have an old acquaintance at the CIA," Alden was saying as he squinted through the pane-glass window to the street below. "Maybe he has some answers. I'll go see him."

"In Washington?" Allegro asked.

"No. He's right here. In the New York field office."

Grushenko's eyes narrowed. He was thoughtful for a while, then he spoke his mind—finally. "Let me clarify something, my friends. I will never forget the sight at Kingman—the flesh spread across the desert." He paused to wipe a theatrical tear from his eye. "Some of that flesh was of my flesh. If you find out where the Raven is, I'm with you to the end."

"I'm going to have the last word here," Allegro said,

looking from one to the other. "I've met these men and women up close. They are killers. They don't think twice about taking human lives to further their cause." She stopped for a moment to force the strength of her will on these two men. "I think the Raven kills for pleasure. He's not political. He's twisted. Dangerous."

"And the point is?" Grushenko asked, his expression changing from the grieving father to the experienced agent.

"The point is, I'm tired of talk, of philosophy. Philip can't make up his mind if he wants to throttle the Raven or turn him over to the authorities. We're amateurs, but if we're going to do this, let's do it right." Again, she held them with the strength of her personality. "I don't want Philip hurt, but if he must crusade, if he and you are going after the Raven, Ernst, we do it right. We make up our minds, then we go in prepared with every ace we've got."

Walter Trask stood slightly more than six feet three, was thin, with deep grooves in his face, had a pronounced widow's peak and a Hitler-like mustache. He had two disconcerting habits: He was a starer, looking straight across the desk, never blinking an eye, and he cracked his knuckles incessantly. His smile, beneath the tuft of jet-black mustache, was a thin curling down of the lips. He was older than Alden; they'd met on campus, when Trask took advantage of the GI Bill to attend college.

But they had never been close friends. Something about Trask made him seem almost alien. Since graduation, they had seen each other rarely, usually accidentally.

After some small talk about the old days, Trask said, "What brings you here, Alden?" On campus he had always addressed him by his last name. A holdover from the military, Alden had guessed. "On the phone you said something about terrorism."

"Specifically, the Southwest Limited and the Raven."

"That's not exactly my end of things around here, but I'll do anything I can to help."

Alden took a breath. "My ex-wife Kate was on that train."

Trask never blinked an eye. "I didn't know that. I'm sorry."

"It was the Raven's work. What do you know about him?"

Trask shrugged. "Nothing. We have no picture. Nobody knows what he looks like."

Alden was becoming exasperated. "Well, what are you doing about it?"

Trask shrugged again. "Keeping our eyes peeled, our ears open, I suppose."

"You suppose?"

"As I said, Alden, those things—terrorist acts—are not included in my duties here. But I can ask around, if that will be of any help." Then he added, "Anything classified, of course, wouldn't be open to you."

Alden's face was red with anger. "It seems inconceivable to me that you, the FBI, and even Interpol itself haven't come up with anything on the Raven. He's operated here, he's operated in Europe for years. And no one has any clues, any evidence of where he is or what he looks like." He took out a pack of cigarettes, stuck one in his mouth, lit it, and blew smoke at the ceiling. "What are you guys getting paid for anyway? Keeping your eyes peeled, your ears open? If I were in your spot, Walter, I'd peel my eyes a little more and have my ears cleaned out!"

Trask's face flushed. "We're doing our best. It takes time. You've got to realize that terrorist groups are very secretive. They hit and run and nobody knows where they'll hit next."

Alden stood. "Thanks for the help."

"Wish I could be of more help."

Alden turned toward the door, then stopped. Facing Trask again, he said, in an even, flat voice, "I'll tell you one thing. If you and the others don't find the Raven, I will. Even if I have to go to the ends of the earth."

"I know how you feel," Trask said, and paused. "Sorry to hear about your wife, Alden."

When Alden had left his office, Trask closed his eyes as though it were an effort to keep them open. He rested his chin on his hands for a while, thinking. Then his eyes opened and he reached for the phone and dialed four digits.

"Trask here. Do we have a dossier on Philip Alden?"

He spelled it. "No middle initial. Lives in Palos Verdes, California. Call HQ if necessary. I want it on my desk pronto. I also want an eye kept on him. Right now he's living with Allegro Stern in the East Eighties. . . . No, not major surveillance. I just want to be kept informed of his movements. . . . Right." He hung up.

He looked at his watch. Quarter to four. He rose from the desk, took his topcoat from the rack, placed a hat on his neatly combed hair. He rang his secretary and said he was off for home.

In his apartment, he kicked off his loafers, mixed a drink, and sat down. No way Alden could locate the Raven. But the girl—she knows his face. If they somehow managed to trace him to England, it could mean trouble. The Raven might talk.

Trask had plenty to hide. He was cooperating with the Raven, ARM, the IRA, and other terrorists, providing sponsors, taking money from both ends, groups providing arms, supplies, and training. He could form a hit team at will; his cadre of mercenaries were tough, hardened.

For these services he received large amounts of money and covered his tracks carefully. No way he would end up like Wilson and Terpil, faces smeared in the newspapers and facing prison terms.

Finishing his drink, he got out of his chair, stretched, and entered the bedroom. He opened a closet, pulled out an electronic device, and began to scan his apartment. Satisfied it was clean, he replaced the gear.

He went to the phone and examined it carefully, taking earpiece and mouthpiece apart, listening intently on the line, tracing wires.

Certain it was not bugged, he began to dial. After all, who would bug Walter Trask, a loyal agent who had been with the CIA ever since its inception and had been a close and loyal friend of Wild Bill Donovan?

"May I help you?" came a voice.

"Overseas operator, please," Trask answered.

"Just a minute."

He spent the minute thinking about Alden. Amateurs. Damn them to hell!

"Overseas operator."

"I want Truro. That's in Cornwall, England."

Eventually, the connection was made and a British voice, full of charm and cheer, answered, "Royal Hotel."

"Mr. Blair, please."

"Mr. Blair? One moment."

He heard the ring to the room, or suite if Trask guessed correctly. Then another voice, a younger voice was on the phone. "Yes?"

"Mr. Blair?" Trask questioned.

"Speaking."

"Mr. Fawcett here."

The other voice paused. "Fawcett. Do I know you?"

"Indianapolis."

"Oh, yes. Mr. Fawcett. What can I do for you?"

"I was wondering, how is Coronet coming along?"

"Beautifully. But we're stalled. We need more supplies."

"They'll be on their way soon. Leaving June 1. Arriving in Liverpool, June 11."

"Good."

"Just thought I'd let you know," Trask said. "And Mr. Blair—"

"Yes."

Trask started to warn him about Alden, but decided against it. Why confuse matters? Alden and his amateurs might never find him at all. If they did, he'd know how to handle it. "Nothing," he said. "Unimportant. Good luck."

"Thanks."

Trask replaced the phone.

The Raven hung up the phone with a slight curl to his lips. He was satisfied Trask was holding up his end. He began to pace the living room of the suite, his smile broadening.

Operation Coronet!

He stopped at the bar, threw ice cubes in a glass, and covered them with Grand Marnier. He sat down in a comfortable chair, musing.

Everything was going well. Two of the IRA men had already arrived in England. The other two were on their way. They would meet in Penzance, where he would outline the plan and make sure every member knew his job.

The Raven relaxed back into his chair and raised his glass in salute.

To Operation Coronet!

What an incredible venture!

On the last day of May, a few days after Trask's call to the Raven, Grushenko was at Allegro's door again. Against her wishes she was beginning to like him, have respect for the old man. He knew so much about the world, had been to places even she had not seen, and his conversation was colorful, full of wonder and excitement, interspaced with descriptions of the people he'd met, their customs and mores.

She was listening intently to his description of the Amazon's rain forest and the habits of the men of Montaña.

Alden was off alone, in a corner, annoyed for once with Eisenstadt's prattle, trying to concentrate on the *New York Times*. He and Allegro had planned a day at the track for tomorrow, and he was checking the weather forecast.

"The trees, my dear," Grushenko was saying, "rise into the air over one hundred feet high, and their foliage blacks out the sun so that below, on the forest floor, there is only darkness."

Alden's eyes studied the isobars, the wind direction, and then he read the five-day forecast. It looked good. A fine day for the track. Warm but not hot, with a promising barometric pressure. The track would be dry, too, judging by the last few days. He hated a muddy track. Once he had seen a horse go down, throwing its rider. His sympathies had been with the horse.

His eyes wandered down the page and stopped suddenly, riveted. "Jesus!" he exclaimed. "Jesus!"

Allegro and Grushenko looked up, startled at his sudden outburst.

"Christ Almighty!" he said. "Why didn't I think!"

"What is it, Philip?" Allegro asked.

"*American Brandy!*"

"What?" Grushenko seemed confused.

"Right here!" And he slapped the page with his hand forcefully. "Read it!"

He catapulted out of his chair, strode over to them, still tapping the pages, pointing out where they should look. "Read it."

Allegro and Grushenko read it together:

> Shipping/Mails
> Outgoing
> Sailing Tomorrow 7 A.M.
> Trans-Atlantic
> AMERICAN BRANDY (Ameri-Panama Lines)
> Halifax June 4. Liverpool June 11, sails from Brooklyn Basin.

When she had read it, Allegro looked concerned. Grushenko's expression was one of perplexity. "I don't understand," he said.

"It's a freighter." He reached for his blazer. "Come on. I'll explain on the way to Brooklyn." He looked at Allegro. "Don't you see? The note: 'American Brandy 61.' What's the date today?"

"May 31."

"And tomorrow's June 1: 6/1."

They raced to the street. In a cab on the way to the Brooklyn Basin, a series of piers jutting out into the East River, Alden told Grushenko of the scribbled note he had found grasped in Kate's lifeless hand.

The old man nodded grimly. The others didn't notice his reaction to the clue. A clue he should have had earlier. A clue he could have followed. Why hadn't Alden told him?

Allegro sat stiffly, fighting a rising tightness in her chest, a fear that she had felt free of lately. Now Philip had inadvertently come upon the answer to "American Brandy" and was hot on the trail, obsessed, scenting the spoor of the Raven, the urge for revenge as strong as ever.

So be it. The waiting had been worse than the action. If he was going to war, she was with him.

CHAPTER 20

She was an old tramp, a whore of the high seas, and had seen many ports. She was worn, weary, her complexion scarred with rust and blisters. Below the Panamanian flag at her stern, her name, *American Brandy*, was gutted and hardly discernible.

Bow to stern, her length was four hundred and eighty feet, and she ran a beam of sixty-seven feet. She weighed in at sixteen thousand tons, and under full load drew twenty-eight feet of water.

She was not much to look at, but as Alden stood on the pier, he seemed fascinated.

Looking down at them, silhouetted against the sky, arms leaning on the rail, stood the squat figure of a man. He turned as Alden, Allegro, and Grushenko climbed the gangplank and boarded the ship.

His face was almost entirely covered by a long gray beard. Only his rheumy eyes showed beneath bushy eyebrows and a peaked cap, eyes full of experience, eyes that had seen everything and nothing by turning away, eyes that knew every human weakness and frailty, evil and good. The short, broad man seemed like the three monkeys— see no evil, hear no evil, and keep your mouth shut.

He smoked a pipe. The odor of his tobacco was strong and acrid. His uniform was a dark navy blue, almost black. The gold braid and buttons, like the ship itself, were tarnished with time.

He regarded them with watery green eyes. "Captain

Pierre Français," he said, rolling the *R*'s with a heavy French accent. "May I help you?"

"Do you have cabins aboard this ship?" Alden asked.

Français puffed on his pipe, and a gray swirl of smoke appeared from the tiny pink, fat lips buried beneath the coarse beard. He nodded.

"Are any available?"

"Where are you bound?"

"Liverpool," Grushenko said.

A glint appeared in the captain's rheumy eyes. "We have five cabins. But we're not licensed to take passengers." He paused. "Why would you want to book passage on this old hulk?"

Alden nodded toward Allegro. "My wife and I always thought it would be romantic to cross by freighter."

A low chuckle escaped the beard. "Have you ever been on the North Atlantic in June?"

"No," Alden answered hesitantly.

The squat figure turned to Grushenko. "And you?" he asked.

Grushenko shook his head.

"We are stopping at Halifax. Then out and northward behind Sable Island. It is cold, damp, foggy."

"Then you're willing to take us?" Alden said.

Français's mouth curled to the broadest grin it could manage. "I did not say that. The cabins are small, uncomfortable. Not your style, by the look of you." His eyes ran over Alden, from well-polished loafers to expensive blazer to open blue oxford collar. Allegro was wearing expensively cut jeans, a good safari jacket. She carried a leather pouch case that could have cost a fortune. Grushenko's attire was floppy, almost seedy. But clothes do not make the man, and the Captain saw money in the group. His mind began to figure.

"If you just want a freighter trip across, why not try Farrell Lines? They take the southern route. Much more comfortable."

"Farrell Lines?" asked Grushenko.

"Farrell Lines is booked a year in advance," Allegro said. She had made two or three trips on it, one of the last freight companies to carry passengers.

Français knew this, too, and grinned inwardly at his advantage. He puffed on his pipe and then turned away from them, looking out over the East River, contemplating. "As I said, we are not licensed to carry passengers. But—"

"How much?" Alden asked.

The captain figured in his mind. Farrell Lines was much neater, more comfortable, insured, and safer. He had a fair idea of what they charged, and equaled it. He turned from the rail. "Shall we agree on twelve hundred each?"

Alden hesitated, seemed to know he was being taken. But the quest for the Raven demanded any price. "Okay," he said, and reached into his blazer for his checkbook.

Captain Français raised his hand in admonition. "No checks. Cash."

"I'll make it out to cash," Alden said. "And endorse it."

"Cash. We sail before the banks open."

"Thirty-six hundred dollars?" It was Eisenstadt, slowly reaching for his wallet. He counted out the money in soiled bills, six five-hundreds and six one-hundreds.

Allegro looked at him in shock and surprise. "Are you making the crossing with us?" It was obvious she had hardly expected this, had wanted to be rid of the little man, be alone with Philip. "Why?" she asked.

He stared back at her. "You seem to forget my son."

Captain Français eyed the thin, drawn man skeptically. Something behind this he did not like. Where would this seedy little man get thirty-six hundred dollars? Yes, something was up here. They were too anxious. But Français could not care less. It was none of his business; he would turn his back and eyes away. For such an amount of money, he would do anything.

He accepted the money graciously, with a slight deferential bow and the hint of a twinkle in his watery eyes.

"Would you mind if we looked over the ship?" Alden asked.

"Be my guest," the captain said. As they turned and walked aft, he called after them, "The *American Brandy* has seen better days, but she is still seaworthy."

*   *   *

The cabins were small, cramped, dingy, an upper and lower bunk for sleeping, a settee against the wall. Two people would find it hard to move around each other.

"Maybe we ought to take three," Allegro said, frowning.

Alden smiled. "And miss the fun of making love like monkeys in the trees?"

Grushenko laughed. "I shall be more comfortable. But not much."

Each cabin contained a sink. Between it and the next cabin, an adjoining head, also small, with shower and commode.

"Well, it's not the QE2," Alden said.

"More like the *African Queen*," Allegro offered.

Grushenko was looking about. "What size would you say this room is?"

"My mental tape measure would put it close to nine by ten," Alden said.

"Not much living space for an eleven-day voyage," Grushenko said.

"You don't *live* in here," Allegro said. "Only sleep—if you can. The *living* is done in the salon."

"Let's go see it," Alden said.

The salon, too, was small. It contained a dozen or so small rectangular dining tables. It was paneled in dulled mahogany that, in its day, must have been attractive. Here, after the dinner dishes had been cleared away, the crew would play cards, drink, and talk. But it had a certain charming ambience, more so than the cabins.

In his mind, Alden was wondering what this old hulk could have to do with the Raven. "Let's go topside," he said.

"Topside?" Allegro grinned. "I thought you were Army, not Navy."

"You forget. Between here and Korea there's a lot of water. I went by boat. You pick up the terms."

On the weather deck, Alden's eyes narrowed as he surveyed the scene. Not much activity here. A few members of the crew lolled about, spitting over the rail into the water. A motley crew, he thought, but those who sailed under the Panamanian flag were the dregs of the sea. The

flag was one of convenience. Anybody or any group could
own this vessel, and avoid safety regulations.

The two aft hatches were covered; the way the ship rode
in the water, high above the Plimsoll line, there could be
little below the covers.

Walking forward, along the narrow lane between the
ship's outer rail and the superstructure, they headed for the
bow. Number two hatch was open and Alden suddenly
stopped, eyes wary.

"Wait!" he whispered to Allegro and Grushenko.

They stopped, looking at him queerly.

"What is it, Philip?" Allegro said.

He did not answer, but kept his gaze fixed on the number
two hatch. It was open. The carrier gear of the king post
was lifting long wooden crates on pallets from the dock,
slowly stowing them in the hold. The corner and seams of
the crates leaked a greasy substance. On the pier waiting to
be loaded were other boxes, square, bearing markings
Alden remembered from his war days.

Grushenko remained silent. He, too, recognized the import of the crates and boxes.

The clue found in Kate's hand had to connect to the
Raven. The ship was carrying arms. *The connection to the
Raven had been made.*

Allegro glanced from one to the other, her expression
one of puzzlement. "What's got into you two?"

"Tell you later," Alden said, and walked toward the
gangplank.

Captain Français was still puffing lazily on his pipe as
they passed him. "See you in the morning," he said. "Seven
A.M. sharp. Don't be late."

He waved. Allegro waved back. Alden's face was set in
hard lines. Grushenko was hunched over.

"And wear warm clothing," Français called after them.
"It's cold out there." And a small, silent chuckle issued
from his lips.

At the bottom of the gangplank, they passed a tall,
clean-shaven, sandy-haired man of about thirty-five boarding the ship. He wore tattered jeans, a worn pea jacket,
work shoes. He looked at the three descending people with

suspicion. A crew member, Alden thought, who did not like casual passengers.

But the sandy-haired man was not a member of the crew. He was also a passenger. Bound for Liverpool.

They had to walk five blocks before finding a cab. No one spoke. On the way back to Manhattan, Allegro sat stiffly between the two men. Alden stared directly ahead through the front windshield, his lips grim, eyes set. Grushenko glanced out the window to his left.

After a while, crossing the Manhattan Bridge, Allegro broke the silence. "All right, you two sphinxes, what's the big secret?"

Alden turned to her. "Did you notice those crates and boxes being stowed in hold number two?"

"Yes."

"Do you know what they contained?"

"No idea," she said.

"The crates were leaking."

"Grease?" she guessed.

"Not exactly grease," Alden said. "But something like it. Cosmoline—used to protect rifles. And the crates were the right length." He paused. "And the boxes—explosives. Plastic explosives. Probably C4."

"How do you know this?" Allegro asked.

"From my Army days," he said. "I used to watch them off-load ships at Pusan."

Grushenko nodded. "Philip's right. I spent four years with the Wehrmacht. I recognized them also."

"Obviously," Alden said, "the *American Brandy* is running guns and explosives—to Halifax or Liverpool, I don't know which. But we'll soon find out."

Allegro felt a rising tightness in her throat, a constriction, and her heart began to hammer. It was all coming together now. That sandy-haired man on the gangplank. She was almost certain she had seen him before, that ill-defined feeling from the past.

He reminded her of one of the group around the Raven when she had interviewed him. But perhaps not. For Philip's sake, she hoped not.

She decided to say nothing.

*   *   *

It was warm the following morning, June 1. As Alden, Allegro, and Grushenko climbed the gangplank, the sun in the eastern sky cast a glow over what promised to be a bright and cloudless day.

Finding the small cabins dark and stuffy, they did not unpack but decided to sit out on the deck and watch the ship slip from her berth.

Crewmen were busy on the weather deck, running lines, winching, talking to one another. Some stood at the rail, smoking lazily until it was time for them to do their job.

The two aft hatches were still closed, battened down, and as Alden had climbed the gangplank, he had noticed that the *American Brandy* still rode high in the water, her Plimsoll line well above the waters of the East River.

She was traveling empty—except for the guns and explosives in hold number two.

They found three tattered deck chairs and set them up between hatches one and two. From this vantage point they could look up the ship's house, the superstructure; first, the cabin deck, containing the officers' cabins and salon; next, the boat deck with cabins for the passengers and the captain; and finally, the bridge deck, from which all of the ship's operations were directed and which housed the radio operator's shack, which also served as his cabin.

The strong scent of tobacco assailed Alden's nostrils. The wide, squat little captain stood beside them, hands clasped behind his back, pipe jutting from his barely visible lips, smoke rising in coils about his head.

"Morning," Alden said.

Français nodded. "*Bon jour,*" he said, his accent Parisian.

"It promises to be a beautiful trip," Allegro said.

Français managed a small smile. "Promises are made to be broken. Do not count on it."

"Captain Français," Alden said, and hesitated. "From the looks of things, you're going up empty."

Français puffed on his pipe. "No real traffic between the United States and Canada," he said. "At Halifax, we pick up flour, farm machinery, crates of toys, odds and ends bound for England."

"You're taking nothing up?" Alden asked, knowing number two hold was not empty.

"A few minor things, small."

"I thought you said seven A.M. sharp for departure time yesterday, Captain. It's already seven-twenty."

"The best-laid plans . . ." Français raised his hands, palms, and shoulders upward in a gesture of resignation. "We developed turbine trouble, but it should be fixed shortly."

Grushenko turned his head. "These few *minor* things? They are to be off-loaded at Halifax, then?"

The captain's expression remained as it had been. "No. They are bound for Liverpool." Then he looked at his watch. "Excuse me, but I must go and see how the turbine repair is coming." Then he chuckled. "As I said, promises are made to be broken, but I promise you we shall be slipping the berth by eight o'clock." Then he walked forward.

"Interesting man," Grushenko murmured.

"Yes," Alden said. "I find all men of the sea interesting. Wise, philosophical. Most are well read. I once met a seaman who could quote Chaucer."

"What else can a man do on a long trip?" Allegro interjected. "When you're not on watch, you're in your berth, reading."

"If it weren't for his heavy French accent, you'd think he was American," Alden said.

Every muscle in Allegro's body tightened. Rounding the superstructure, a man approached. He wore a pea jacket, frayed jeans, and work shoes. He was sandy-haired, about thirty-five, and he walked with his hands in his pockets, chin on chest, eyes lowered.

The same man she had seen on the gangplank the day before. No. It was her imagination. He had not been in the group when she had interviewed the Raven. He merely bore a resemblance. But she thought of the contents of hold number two, and her fists clenched.

"Morning." Alden nodded as the young man passed them, hugging the wall.

The sandy-haired man glanced at Alden without raising his head, muttered something incoherent and unintelligible, and continued his walk toward the bow area.

"Loquacious, isn't he?" Alden said, and smiled wryly.

The sandy-haired man circumvented the ship's rail three more times, never raising his head, eyes fixed on the deck. And each time the expression on Allegro's face grew more worried.

Grushenko had been studying her. "What is it, my dear? You seem pale."

"Nothing. Nothing really. I just feel a little . . . queasy."

Philip laughed. "Seasick already and we're not even off." He hugged her.

She gazed at him, her lips breaking into a weak smile. "I'm a better sailor than you are, Sinbad. You watch when we get under way."

At eight-twenty, bells sounded on the bridge, levers clanked, a deep rumble came from the innards of the ship, and the *American Brandy* shuddered. When a head of steam had been worked up and the engines were in neutral, the heavy hawsers were freed and the ship stood unfettered in her berth. The engines were put in reverse with a heavy jolt, and the old hulk began her slow, smooth exit from the pier. Once clear of the bollards, in deep water, the engines were slipped into neutral again while the rudder was kicked. The passengers felt another jolt as the engines were put into forward drive and the bow of the *American Brandy* headed into the East River.

They slipped through the Narrows into the lower bay, turned in the direction of Ambrose Lightship, rounding it smoothly then turning east toward Montauk Point. At Montauk, they stayed well off the shoals and rocks as they headed northeast.

Their journey had begun—the pursuit of the Raven. Grushenko was introspective; Alden's feelings were a combination of exuberance and grim determination; Allegro was sensible enough to feel fear, but put it aside in her determination to help.

The schedule had indicated the trip to Halifax took four days. As the *American Brandy* worked her way northward, the weather became cooler. Alden was glad he had brought a sweater and a light windbreaker. Allegro stood the increasing cold as long as she could in her light safari jacket;

on the second morning out, she appeared on deck with a
Swiss sweater beneath the jacket.

Alden smiled. "I was wondering when you were going
to notice we're not headed for the equator."

"Me, Jane," she said.

"Me, no Tarzan," Alden answered. "It's getting as
cold as a well digger's ass up here."

Grushenko laughed behind them and they turned. He
was dressed in an overcoat, fur hat, and gloves. " 'Well
digger's ass.' An apt analogy. But I always thought we
Americans said 'cold as a witch's tit.' "

"Sometimes," Alden said.

" 'Well digger's ass.' I like that one better." And he
laughed again.

On the second night out, they were all invited to dine at
the captain's table. The tables were quite small, and three
of the crew had to be pushed together to accommodate
Alden, Allegro, and Grushenko, in addition to Captain
Français and the purser, a man named Gordon.

Other tables were filled with off-watch members of the
crew, officers, and seamen. At a table in a corner, the
sandy-haired man ate a solitary meal.

Allegro could not take her eyes off him. He in turn
looked up from his plate now and then to cast a furtive
glance at her. She was certain now she had seen him when
she had interviewed the Raven. Once sure, she concentrated on her meal, paying the man no attention, joining in
conversation with the others at her table, acting as though
he did not exist.

The food was abominable, but the wine the captain had
served was from his own private stock, an excellent Bor-
deaux, and they drank it in quantity to overcome the taste
of the cooking.

Alden was in high spirits after the first bottle. His
questions were sharp, incisive, and he seemed not to care
about revealing his ignorance of the sea.

"What's a purser?" he asked. "What does he do? I've
heard and read the term all my life and I'm still not sure
what his job is aboard ship." He was looking at Gordon.

Gordon laughed, a rattle in the throat that emerged from

his scrawny neck in a titter. "Ask Captain Français. He knows."

Alden turned his head to the captain, who suddenly looked uncomfortable. "He does the paperwork. Like a ship's secretary, *non*?" His watery green eyes had taken on a sharpness that threw daggers across the table at Gordon.

Gordon smiled. "I also keep the captain honest."

"I *am* honest. You have nothing to fear with me in command of this vessel."

Gordon did not answer. But his eyes pierced.

It was obvious Alden had touched on a delicate matter, so he changed the subject. "Where was the *American Brandy* built, Captain?"

"In Belfast. At the Harlan-Wolfe yards."

"What's your complement?" Allegro asked.

Français raised his wine in an elegant toast. "For such a beautiful mademoiselle, I will answer in detail. We have nine officers. Myself, the purser, or spy for the company—"

"Spy?" Gordon looked hurt. "Just because I'm the owner's nephew? Not so. I'm the company's agent on board."

Français ignored him. "Then we have the chief mate, the second mate, and the third mate, *mon cher*. Then the chief engineer, and three assistant engineers. And twenty-one seamen. Thirty in all." He was looking at Alden's light windbreaker draped over the back of his chair, and at Allegro's bush jacket. "Is that all the clothing you brought?"

"Yes," Alden said. "You said to bring warm clothes. My sweater and the windbreaker are warm enough."

Français moved his head from side to side. "Not on the great circle route. Once we round Sable Island, you'll need something. But we'll fix you up."

Allegro leaned toward the captain and asked, almost in a whisper, "That man over there in the corner—what's his job?"

The captain glanced shortly to the sandy-haired man, then back to Allegro. "Him? He is not a member of the crew. He, like you, is a passenger."

"Any more passengers?" Allegro asked.

The captain shook his head. "Only the four of you."

Allegro waited for a moment. "What's his name?"

"O'Rourke, I think." He glared across the table at Gordon. "Is that right, Purser?"

Gordon nodded his prematurely bald head. "That's correct. Patrick O'Rourke. Which reminds me—we have something to discuss. In private."

Alden had been listening. Allegro could sense he was drawing his own conclusions: the arms shipment, the sandy-haired man as the courier, the Raven. You put them together and you have . . .

She watched him raise his wine to his lips, then apparently change his mind, returning the glass to the table. She knew what he was thinking. He would have to have a clear head from now on.

A chill went through Allegro. He knows, she thought.

Later, on the weather deck, Alden and Allegro took their nightly constitutional, his arm around her shoulders. The weather was turning cold, no longer merely cool, and it was damp with fog. They had been issued heavy oiled sweaters and foul-weather gear by a member of the crew. Through the fog, they looked like fat extraterrestrial beings.

As they neared the bow, they heard low voices, and could distinguish two blurred figures leaning over the rail. They stopped, listening. Even though the men were speaking *sotto voce,* every word was clear.

"How much did you charge those three passengers?" Gordon asked.

"What business is it of yours?" Français growled.

"Plenty. I could have you fired. You wouldn't have command of a ship for the rest of your life."

Français laughed. Then after a hesitation he said, "Five hundred apiece."

"I don't believe a word of it."

The captain's shoulders went up. "What do you think this is, Farrell Lines? *Merde!*"

"And O'Rourke," the purser said. "Five hundred, too?"

"*Oui.*"

"I still don't believe a word of it, but I'll take fifty percent."

"Thirty."

"Fifty!"

"Forty," Français said. "After all, who's in command of this tub, the captain or the purser? We must keep those lines clearly demarcated."

After a few seconds of silence, Gordon said, "All right, *Captain Chiseler!*"

They heard Français laugh as the purser turned and walked away. He had made a good bargain.

The purser strode past Alden and Allegro, seated near number two hatch, invisible in the mist. The captain followed a few minutes later, walking slowly, puffing on his pipe. He mounted the stairs to the bridge.

Alden lit two cigarettes and handed one to Allegro. "Chisel, chisel, chisel," he said. "Gyp, gyp, gyp."

Allegro puffed and said, "Life's a big rip-off, Philip. One big rip-off. Everybody out for what he can get."

"Yes, I guess you're right. It took me a long time to learn." He rose. "Shall we continue our walk?"

She took his arm and they walked toward the bow. The mist hung over it like a shroud. The swells of the black sea had deepened.

"Things have changed," Alden said.

"They've always been the same. We just didn't notice."

"But everything happens so fast now. Events fly by. You turn your head one way and before you can turn it back, something else has happened, a new change. And as they say any change is for the worse."

"You're a cynic," she said.

They turned to each other, age and youth, disparate in their past experiences. They studied each other. Then Alden put an arm around her and led her along the deck.

"Let's go to bed," he said.

Two cabins astern of Grushenko, Patrick Xavier O'Rourke lay in his berth, smoking, staring at the bottom of the upper berth. It was her of course. No mistaking it. Who could forget those startling ice-blue eyes.

He rose and put out his cigarette in an ashtray. He shrugged into his pea jacket, buttoned it. He strolled out onto the cabin desk and climbed the stairs to the bridge deck, entering the radio shack.

The radioman looked up.

"I'd like to place a call to Truro in England. The Royal Hotel. That's in Cornwall."

"It'll take a few minutes."

"I'll wait," O'Rourke said.

He sat down while the radioman tried to make contact. In about fifteen minutes, he was through. He handed O'Rourke the instrument and went out to the rail for a smoke.

"Royal Hotel," came a pleasant English voice.

"I'd like to speak to Mr. Blair, please."

A ring. A moment's pause. Then: "Blair here."

"O'Rourke."

A longer pause, then an edgy tone. "Where are you?"

"At sea. On the way."

An audible sigh of relief. "Why the call?"

"You remember that girl? The photographer? The one who interviewed you?" O'Rourke fidgeted in his chair, picked at nonexistent fingernails, at bloody hangnails.

"How could I forget?"

"She's aboard."

A long silence. "Did you talk to her?"

"No."

"Did she talk to you?"

"No, maybe it's coincidence."

"Maybe. Anybody with her?"

"Two men. One an old geezer with a foreign accent. The other's an American. Mid-fifties. I don't recognize them."

"Yeah, maybe a coincidence," the Raven said, "maybe not. You need help?"

"Is Corrigan there?"

"He'll meet you with the truck."

"We can handle it, if it's serious, which I doubt."

"Okay. I'll see that you're equipped."

The Raven hung up and sauntered over to the bar. He had found a new drink, Armagnac, and he poured liberally. Then he sat, brooding, a frown knitting his brows.

That O'Rourke. How stupid can you get? Telephoning from sea for everybody to hear. But they couldn't make much out of the conversation. It had been ordinary. No threats, nothing given away.

And if it were pursuit, not coincidence, O'Rourke and Corrigan knew how to take care of it.

The two men. They could be anybody. Her assistants on a photographic assignment. Or CIA?

The thought disturbed him, but not for long. Nobody knew his real name. If anything happened to them, he was out of it. Nobody could point the finger. But nothing would go wrong. He'd made it work in New York and Arizona and he'd make it work here. Luck was with him. The gods were on his side. Not that he prayed to them.

He sipped the Armagnac, rolling the glass in his hands. Nothing would go wrong with Operation Coronet either. It was too well planned.

He raised his glass and toasted. To Operation Coronet!

CHAPTER 21

When the *American Brandy* put into Halifax, Nova Scotia, Canada's largest port, Alden had positioned himself on the rail where he had a clear view of number two hatch, in the event Captain Français or the purser was lying. He stared out at the city, its skyline a mixture of old and new—the preserved forts of early settlers still on Signal Hill overlooking the buildings and spaghetti junctions built by new generations.

Patrick O'Rourke was making his rounds of the deck again, head bent, never looking up. When Alden said hello, he grumbled something and kept his eyes down.

The three aft hatches had been opened and were being loaded with flour and farm machinery. The second mate was directing operations while the captain looked on from the bridge.

It was a cacophony of creaking wood and squealing metal, loud voices and soft thuds as the giant king posts worked to fill hatches. The air was filled with diesel exhaust and the smell of rotting flesh. It took a number of hours to complete the job. Alden could feel the ship becoming heavier, settling close to its Plimsoll line.

When it was done, the aft hatches had been battened down. Number two hatch had been opened briefly. Four huge crates had been lowered below, set aside the arms crates, together with a few bundles of lumber. The original cargo, as Captain Français had said, was headed for Liverpool.

*   *   *

On the second day out from Canada, in a relatively calm
sea, the hatch to number two hold was opened and hammering could be heard from above. Captain Français kept
a scrub crew busy around the hatch, making it impossible
for anyone to look below. The operation took all day, and
the hatch was then resecured.

Grushenko asked Alden and Allegro to meet him in his
cabin before dinner. When they entered, he was finishing a
search for listening devices. He had found none.

"A little cloak and dagger, Ernst?" Allegro chided.

"I'm not used to this game, but it seems to me they
could bug our cabins," he said, trying to appear amateurish.

Alden sat on the lower bunk, Grushenko on the settee,
while Allegro tossed a cushion to the floor, sat with her
back against the wall. Cigarette packs were opened. They
all lit up and the room filled with smoke. Grushenko
opened a porthole and cautioned them to whisper.

"What do you think they were doing?" Alden asked.

"The crates they put in with the arms were labeled
toys," Allegro offered.

Alden had his own ideas. "Hammering all day and a
load of lumber down there. Adds up," he said. "They're
disguising the arms shipment." He took a drag of his
cigarette, watched the smoke curl out the porthole. "If
they mix the toys with the arms, what about the crate
markings? What about the manifests?"

"We've got to find out. When we get to Liverpool, it's
essential we know what cargo to follow," Grushenko
offered.

"Something else bothers me," Allegro said. "Captain
Français has to be in on the switch. No one plays with
cargo at sea. Too dangerous—and illegal." She looked
from one to the other, dragging on her cigarette. "Puts us
in the minority. Captains have unlimited authority at sea."

"So what do we do?" Alden asked.

"I think we should call ahead now before they suspect
us of spying on their cargo," Grushenko said. "I have
friends in England, could call for a hired car, maybe a
launch to take us off at sea."

"First we have to know what they've done. I'm going into that hold tonight," Allegro said.

"You are like hell!" Alden almost screamed at her.

"Keep your voice down!" Grushenko said, then stayed out of it as they argued. He couldn't reveal his hand.

"I know ships better than either of you. And I'm used to sneaking around."

"I'm going with you," Alden insisted.

"Go ahead," Grushenko said. "I'll cover your backs. But first, I want a little reconnoiter of my own. About two in the morning would be best for your work. Might even be better if we left it until the last night out."

"No way. I want it over with," Allegro said.

Grushenko lit a second cigarette from the first, tossed the butt out the porthole. "All right, I'll go to the radio room before dinner. Any objections?"

Allegro and Alden exchanged glances. They had no argument to offer.

Grushenko moved off the settee, slipped from the room. When he'd gone, Allegro got up, walked noiselessly to the door, and peeked out. The corridor was empty.

"What are you doing?" Alden asked. "He'll be back in a few minutes."

"Don't you feel the least bit suspicious?"

"Of Ernst? Why should I be?"

"Why is he following us?"

He threw his butt out the porthole, stood looking at the wash slide by. "You're paranoid. He's in it for the same reason I am."

"Are you carrying a gun?" she asked, joining him at the porthole, tossing out the end of her cigarette.

"You know I'm not."

"Ernst is. Looks like a .38 caliber. A shoulder holster. If I spotted it, so did the captain."

Alden was silent for a minute, went back to the bunk, lit another cigarette. "Proves nothing," he said. "One out of every five people in America has a gun registered with the police—maybe more."

"I don't trust him, and if you added it all up, you wouldn't either. He's stuck to us like glue since Kingman. It's not natural."

"Let's drop it, okay? I like Ernst and he's going to be a help." Alden turned to the door. "I'm getting claustrophobia from these cabins." He touched a wall with one arm and could almost touch the other when he stretched. "Let's take a walk before supper. We'll catch up with Ernst later."

Grushenko made his way to the radio shack and found it empty. He knew it wouldn't be left unattended long, so he wasted no time. He started with the cabinets nearest the door and went through every drawer in the place. He found what he sought—two flashlights and a battery lantern. He opened the door cautiously, peeked out, and hurriedly hid the stolen articles behind a lifeboat. He had just finished and was standing outside the door when the radioman returned.

"What can I do for you, sir?" the man asked politely.

"A call to London. Any problems?"

"Take a few minutes. Do you want me to call you?"

"I'll wait."

Grushenko stood behind the man, lit a cigarette, offered one to the radioman, who refused politely.

In ten minutes of pacing, Grushenko smoked two cigarettes, filling the room with smoke. He had noted that the man slept here, that it would be difficult to sneak in, place a call in an emergency.

"Your call, sir." The man handed the phone to Grushenko and left as he had when O'Rourke made his call.

"Don't talk. Just listen," Grushenko said in Russian when he was sure he had the right party. "In four days a freighter named *American Brandy* is due at Liverpool." He stopped for a few seconds as the sharp pain he'd been suffering attacked his chest. "I want a fast boat to take three people off about forty miles out. I don't want weapons to be obvious, but you should have a couple of automatic weapons, AK47's. Keep them concealed. Your men should speak English, appear to be local fishermen. Have you got that?"

"Yes, comrade."

Asshole! The man had been trained not to use the familiar "comrade." The new ones were all fools. "I want a fast car at the dock with the keys under the driver's seat,'' he said. "Make sure it's red so I can spot it quickly.''

"Petrov wants to talk to you.''

Double assholes! "Tell him I have a pipeline to the Raven. It will take time. I have to do it my way.'' He hung up in the middle of a protest. No matter. They would do as they were told.

The radioman was leaning on the rail smoking. Grushenko nodded as he passed. Back in his cabin, he was alone. He hadn't expected to see them now. Dinnertime would do as well.

In the captain's cabin, O'Rourke was handing over a thick package of bank notes. Captain Français smiled, his beard parting to allow for the expansion. Blackened teeth showed momentarily and were again hidden by the wealth of gray hair.

"The crates are sealed, marked with red emblems—doll faces. The others are green,'' he said to the sandy-haired man. "The new manifests will work. You will have no trouble.''

O'Rourke didn't return the smile. "That part of the job doesn't worry me. You took on three passengers who do. I'm sure they are more than they seem.''

"Let me give you some advice,'' Français said, his face passive. "I don't want trouble with this. If you start trouble, you will not have me with you. I'll have the stuff dumped overboard first.''

"We had a deal. They could screw it up,'' O'Rourke shouted.

"Get this straight, *jeune fou*. This is my ship. I give the orders. I want no trouble between you and those three. If they step out of line, I will deal with them.''

"But—''

"No buts. I'll protect *mon derrière* as the Americans say. You keep your nose out.''

O'Rourke left feeling vulnerable, not knowing how much sleep he'd get in the next four days.

*　　*　　*

At dinner, Captain Français again insisted they sit with him. He invited O'Rourke, who declined, his expression telling the story.

Later, the Americans met in Grushenko's cabin again.

"I have arranged for a car at Liverpool and a launch to take us off before we land," he said.

"Isn't that being a little melodramatic?" Alden asked.

"I'm not expert at this," Grushenko lied. "But it seems to me we'd be better ashore before this old tub docks. We can observe and have transport handy."

"That presumes we know what we're looking for," Allegro said.

Again, they all lit cigarettes. Again, Grushenko opened the port and cautioned against loud talk. "I trust you will find out when you go below," he said. "I obtained flashlights for you. I also looked over the layout, found a companionway that leads to all holds."

He pulled a rumpled piece of paper from a pocket and spread it on the floor. They all hunkered down to look.

"On the cabin deck, forward of the salon, a door marked CREW ONLY leads to a long catwalk over the holds. No one will see you in the early hours."

"You learned all this when you went to send a message ashore?" Allegro asked.

"Yes. Why?"

Allegro looked sideways at Alden. "Nothing. You did very well."

"I suggest we get some sleep," Grushenko said. "If you start out at two, you should be fresh."

Allegro agreed with alacrity. She took Alden by the arm and guided him to the door. "We'll come to your cabin at three when it's over," she said.

"No. I'll come to yours at one-thirty. I'll have the flashlights, a crowbar of some kind, and a hammer."

When they had gone, Grushenko lay back on his bunk, exhausted. He didn't know what was wrong with him, but it wasn't good. The pain in his chest persisted. He tried to ignore it. He had enough problems.

Amateurs. He couldn't do it all himself without arousing too much suspicion. As it was, the woman suspected him.

She was a sharp one. Maybe . . . just maybe . . . with her they might pull it off.

He wasn't going to take a chance. He would provide the tools at one-thirty, then he would follow at two. If they got into trouble, he would have to bail them out. It was too important for them to blow it now.

It was still early, about nine. Back in their cabin, Alden sat on the bunk, set his trusty travel alarm for one. Allegro's face wore a distant, grim, almost scornful expression, and Alden knew she was angry at something. He watched her undress.

"You've got a lovely body," he said. "Sexy."

"Hmmm."

"And your breasts. I love them. And your hips and thighs."

"Hmmm."

"Not to speak of your slim waist and tapering calves." He was smiling.

"Hmmm."

"Look," he said.

She did not turn. "I know," she said. "You've got an erection."

"How right you are."

"Hmmm." She was getting into her woolen pajamas.

"What are we going to do about it?"

"Not tonight, Casanova."

"Why?"

"I'm tired."

"Tired of me?"

"I just think we should get some sleep if we're going to play at spy tonight." Then she started to giggle. For he was looking up at her like a child. And his erection had gone down, his penis limp between his legs. "And you think you're impotent," she said, laughing. "And you are." Her eyes focused on his member.

"But not that way. I *know*."

"I'm impotent in the world, Allegro," he said softly, resignedly. "That's why I'm after the Raven. I've got to do something important before I die. I've got to make something happen." He bent his head. "And I feel weak."

"You're not weak, Philip. You're the strongest man I've ever known. To carry your guilt about the Korean War and your need to strike out for Kate takes a strong back."

He looked up at her, as though he were asking, Do you mean it? Do you really mean it?

"Oh, Philip." She rushed to him, clasped him to her.

"I'll be all right," he said in a strong, even voice. "I'll be all right once this is over."

"Maybe we should reconsider," Allegro said.

"No." His tone was firm.

She hugged him tighter. "All right. If you have to, I'm with you."

He responded to the warmth of her body, melting into her embrace. His penis began to stiffen again. He cupped one breast, and then the other. He kissed her, and their tongues brushed and swirled. Slowly, he undid the buttons of her nightclothes, bending to gently kiss each nipple as it came into view. Then his hand was between her legs, feeling her moisture rising. Her breathing came faster. She bit her lower lip and moaned. When his tongue was between her thighs, she screamed. She did the same for him, gently rolling the tip of her tongue around the top of his penis, making it rise and jerk, sipping his precoital syrup.

Hands roving, pinching, squeezing, tracing patterns. Lips searching, sucking, biting. Limbs entwining. Legs, thighs, bellies, pressed together.

Faster, faster.

Bodies writhing, riding, smashing.

"Look into my soul! Look into my soul!" she screamed.

And again, Alden was afraid at the moment he came.

Then the quivering, the relaxing, the soft breathing punctuated by short gasps. The closeness.

Sleep.

The alarm was close to Alden's pillow, could not be heard outside the cabin. He turned it off and stirred. Allegro was stretching like a sated jungle cat, content after a satisfying meal. She had slept through Grushenko's knock when he'd delivered the tools they'd need. Now she was awake and starting to dress.

They had talked about it and decided on dark slacks and windbreakers. They didn't expect to run into anyone, but if they did, they didn't want to be caught with camouflage makeup.

Grushenko had supplied two black knit caps to cover their hair. On deck, they didn't look out of place.

The steel-grated stairs to the deck below was deserted. They had no trouble finding the door Grushenko had pointed out. It opened silently. They slipped inside. Alden had a flashlight in one hand and and a heavy wrecking bar hooked down his pants. Allegro also held a flashlight. A hammer was hidden under her jacket, the night-vision goggles weighted one of her pocket.

A dull bulb lit the steel-grated landing at the top of the catwalk. It was surprisingly quiet, but the ghostly light over the huge holds below was eerie. Their footfalls echoed throughout the huge cavern of the ship's interior. If anyone was below, he would hear them for sure.

Alden led the way, shining his light in the places where dim bulbs left deep shadows. They had to walk down a long flight of steps to the floor of the holds, then along a narrow passage to the door of hold number two.

It was not locked. Inside, it was pitch black. Two pencils of light from their flashlights showed eight crates and no lumber. The four ammunition crates had disappeared.

"Where are they?" Allegro whispered, her voice echoing through the hold.

"They've got to be here," Alden said, shining his light on one crate and pulling out the wrecking bar.

He pried open the first crate.

As the plank screeched loose, Allegro's flashlight flickered and went out.

Alden looked up from his work, but couldn't see her. He heard an object move through the air, a thud and a grunt as a body hit the steel deck.

His flashlight rolled away, taking the little remaining light with it. In the dark, he fell to his knees, feeling around for Allegro, calling her name.

The swish of a moving object broke the silence of the hold again. The pain was fleeting as the object crashed down on his skull.

CHAPTER 22

A light hurt his eyes. After the dark of the tunnel he'd descended, the light was like the brightness of heaven, the shining purity of the pearly gates with the angels attending to the work of Peter.

Instead, a monster stood over him, a club in one hand. He cringed, holding an arm over his head.

"It's all right," the voice echoed in the huge chamber. It was Grushenko. He held a lantern in one hand, an iron bar in the other.

"What happened?" Alden asked, gingerly feeling the lump on the top of his head.

"That's what happened," Grushenko said, shining the light on an unconscious O'Rourke.

"Allegro! I heard her go down first," Alden wailed.

"She's all right."

Grushenko shone the light on her. She was sitting against a crate, rubbing her head.

"Is he dead?" Alden asked.

"No. He'll be out for a few minutes."

"Let's get the hell out of here," Alden said, making his way over to Allegro, touching the egg on her head tenderly.

"We're here. We do the job now," Grushenko said, taking charge. "Are you strong enough to pry a few boards?"

"I think so," Alden said. He struggled to his feet and grabbed the fallen wrecking bar.

He'd had one board loose from the new outer shell before he was hit. He pried another loose.

Grushenko pulled out a few packaged dolls before his hand came away soaked in the residue from the gun wrappings.

"They've packed dolls around the munitions crates and built a second wood shell around them. New stencils," Grushenko said. He shone the light on the red doll insignia.

"I'm going to inspect the whole place. You wait here," he ordered. He found Alden's flashlight and left him talking to Allegro.

It took about five minutes. The ship rolled from swells not evident earlier. Crates creaked and shifted. Alden shone his light on O'Rourke. The Irishman had not moved. A trickle of blood ran from his temple to his chin.

The place was scary—a black and stinking cargo hold in the mid-Atlantic, surrounded by men who could kill them with impunity.

Grushenko returned. He was calm, seemed to be taking the whole thing in stride. Strange for an old, weak metallurgist.

"Eight crates," he said. "Four have red emblems; four have green. If we open one more red and one green, I'm sure we'll have what we want."

"I think I should get Allegro back to the cabin," Alden said.

"Won't take more than a few minutes," Grushenko said, shoving the crowbar at Alden. "Let's get it done."

Alden pried two boards loose from a red crate and two from a green. Grushenko pulled out dolls, found residue in the second red crate and none in the green.

"As I suspected. Four crates are the disguised armaments and four are genuine. We follow the red ones," the small man said. He handed the hammer to Alden and held the lantern. "Okay. Nail them closed. They can't be sure we've been into them."

Alden hammered away, doing a fair job. He put the hammer and the crowbar inside his jacket and started to help Allegro to her feet.

"What about him?" he asked.

"He'll live. I didn't hit him hard enough to kill,"

Grushenko said without emotion. ''Where's Miss Stern's flashlight?''

''Couldn't care less,'' Alden said as he started to lead Allegro to the door.

''We can't leave it. You start back. I'll clean up here. If they can't find anything, it's our word against his.''

When the two had disappeared up the stairway, Grushenko moved over to the fallen Irishman and rolled him over. He had a slight cut on his forehead and a lump the size of a small egg. When he came around, he would remember following Alden and Allegro, and the captain would be told. They had to avoid the captain's wrath at all costs.

He put the lantern on the floor next to the fallen man and took a small leather case from his jacket. Three syringes and a half-dozen small vials were packed neatly in its velvet interior.

Grushenko selected a green vial, gently eased a clean syringe through the vial's diaphragm, pressed the plunger to clean out the trapped air, then injected the whole vial into the Irishman's arm. It was not a killing drug or a debilitating one. O'Rourke would simply be confused for a few days. He dragged the prostrate man from the hold to the foot of the stairs. It was almost impossible and the pain in his chest seemed almost too much to bear, but he did it. Afterward, he had to sit beside the body for a few minutes, the light from his lantern a dull glow against the walls and growing dimmer.

He had little time left.

With a great effort, he pulled himself up and looked around. The scrape marks where he had dragged O'Rourke were plainly visible. He found some excelsior and, on his knees, cleaned the floor where he and Alden had worked and the whole area from the crates to where O'Rourke lay. During the cleaning, he found Allegro's flashlight. When he was finished, he was exhausted. Again, he sat beside the body as the light faded to black.

Now it was dark and he was fifty feet below the deck. He was old. He was tired. And his chest was on fire again. He desperately needed a cigarette.

One other thing left to do in the blackness of the hold.

He had to search the sandy-haired man. He knelt beside the body, felt in the pockets, looked over each item by the light of a match, carefully putting each burned match in a coat pocket. He was about to leave when one last idea occurred to him. He turned the body over and felt around the belt of the pants. His hand closed over cold steel. A gun.

He pulled himself to his feet again. Lit one more match. Found the steps, and labored to the top.

Alden led the way out of the hold and to the bottom of the long stairway. Allegro was wobbly, but gained strength as they reached the top. He opened the door cautiously and peered out. No one was around.

They dragged themselves to their cabin, helped each other with cold compresses on throbbing heads, and sat, smoking cigarettes, not talking.

"So now you know what it's like." Allegro grinned through her pain.

"What's that supposed to mean?" he asked. His head throbbed. He was in no mood for humor.

"I mean it isn't going to get any easier. Going after the Raven is for professionals. We could get killed."

"Speaking of professionals—our friend Ernst handled himself like a professional if I'm any judge."

"So you're beginning to catch on. I'm not going to say I told you so," she said.

"I can't believe a man his age backed us up, got what we needed to know, and is right now cleaning up after us." He pulled deeply on his cigarette. "It's just not natural."

"If he's not Ernst Eisenstadt, metallurgical engineer, what and who is he?"

"You know? I don't give a shit. If he's on our side, it's enough," Alden said.

They were interrupted by a soft knock on the door. Alden glanced at his watch in the glow of the one bed light they had lit. It was after three. Ernst had finished and wanted to see them. Alden moved to the door and opened it a crack.

It was Eisenstadt. He pushed his way in and closed the door quickly. He lit a cigarette and sat on the lower bunk.

His parchmentlike face was more of a death mask than ever. In the soft glow, he looked like something dragged from an open grave.

"Are you all right?" he asked.

"We'll survive," Allegro said. "How are you?"

"I'm all right. Do your wounds show?" he asked.

They shook their heads.

"Good. It's important we show absolutely no sign that anything happened tonight. We have to survive for the next three days—our word against O'Rourke's."

"But how can we? If Français is in on it, we'll be suspect immediately," Allegro said.

"I don't think so," Grushenko said. "I'm almost sure O'Rourke will have amnesia for the next few days."

Alden and Allegro exchanged glances. This man was proving to be a complete stranger, very different from the Ernst Eisenstadt who had been the garrulous old man in New York. The desire to avenge a son doesn't provide skills like these for the asking.

"Give me your tools and the flashlight," he commanded. He opened the porthole and one by one consigned them to the deep.

He turned, took a 9-mm Luger from his belt. "Either of you know how to use this?"

"I do," Allegro said without hesitation.

"O'Rourke's?" Alden asked.

"Yes." Grushenko had finished his first cigarette and, in characteristic fashion, lit a second from the first.

"This doesn't fit with your penchant for neatness," Allegro said.

"Can't be helped. I left him at the bottom of the stairs. He's supposed to think he fell. Won't remember what happened to his gun. Besides, we will need it more than he." He tossed it to Allegro. "Hide it in a safe place outside this cabin before you go to sleep," he said. "Somewhere you can get your hands on it in a hurry."

"Where's yours?" she asked.

"You noticed?"

"I noticed," she said.

"It's under a tarpaulin on lifeboat number one. It's close to the portside docking ramp the pilot will use to board. If we need the guns, it will be just after he comes aboard.''

He turned to leave, noting his friends were speechless. "Can you both swim?'' he asked.

They nodded.

"One last thing. Act natural for the next three days. Do what you normally would, okay?''

Again, they nodded.

He grinned, a grin of triumph they'd never seen before, and as quickly as he'd come, he left.

The next morning Alden woke to find Allegro had left the cabin early. Her woolen pajamas were draped over the back of the settee, and her outdoor clothes were not in the small closet.

Looking through the porthole, he saw a misty but bright day, the sun struggling to break through the fog, making the sea and sky dazzle with whiteness.

He dressed hurriedly, and climbed down to the weather deck, looking right and left. She was nowhere to be seen. He finally came upon her on the starboard side braced against the rail, eye to viewfinder, camera fitted with a zoom lens.

He crept up silently behind her, placed his hands on her slim waist, and nuzzled her neck.

Startled, she jerked and turned. "Philip! You spoiled my shot!''

"Shot of what? I don't see anything.''

"It's a berg. The lens cuts through the fog. Here, take a look.'' She gave the camera to him.

He peered through the viewfinder. Everything became sharp, and a huge mass of ice loomed before him, possibly a mile away but well defined.

"This is a good lens,'' he said. "Damned if it isn't an iceberg. Big, too. I hope the captain knows what he's doing.''

"And as they say''—Allegro laughed—"that's just the tip of it.''

A rasping clunk sounded along the side of the ship, and looking down over the rail, they beheld a chunk of ice

measuring about three feet. It bounced and jigged along
the hull and disappeared into the wake.

"Bergy Bit," Allegro said. "The language seamen have.
Colorful. And very descriptive."

"So," an approaching voice said, "we're taking snap-
shots this morning? Of what? I don't see anything but a
Siberian sky." It was Grushenko, clapping his gloved
hands together. He liked this kind of weather. It was
Russian.

"Morning, Ernst," Philip said. "You seem to enjoy
this weather."

"Brisk," Grushenko said. "Like the Bavarian Alps."
He thought he'd covered his tracks well, let them understand he'd been to many places in the world. Seen many
things.

"An iceberg is ahead of us, Ernst. Here, take a look."
Alden handed him the camera.

Grushenko made a show of understanding cameras, but
Allegro had to teach him, looping the strap about his neck,
fitting the viewfinder to his eye, aiming it, and focusing
for him. Grushenko knew cameras very well, but he said
in an awed tone, "An iceberg. A real iceberg. I've never
seen anything like this." He held the camera for a long
time.

While Grushenko peered through the lens, Allegro heard
footsteps approach from the bow. Through the haze, a
looming shadow appeared, like a ghost, a silent banshee.

It was O'Rourke, hands in pockets, head bent.

After the previous night's work, a shiver of fear went
through Allegro. Alden played the game well, seemed
unperturbed. He looked the man in the eye and said,"Good
morning."

For the first time, O'Rourke did not mumble incoher-
ently. He stopped and, looking straight at Alden, said,
"And the top o' the mornin' to you, sir," his Irish brogue
pronounced. A half smirk crossed his face, he nodded to
Grushenko and Allegro, stared for a moment, seemed to
be disoriented, and then went on, continuing his bent-head
walk into the haze.

When his steps had receded and he was rounding the
stern, Alden, leaning on the rail, hands clasped, chuckled.

"You see? He does have a tongue. He *can* speak. After last night, I find that rather odd."

"He's a banshee," Allegro said.

"Banshee?" Alden smiled. "In Irish folklore a banshee is a *woman* who appears in front of a house when death is near."

"That's what I mean," she said. "All right, a male banshee, then. He gives me the creeps."

Alden was silent, and when he spoke, looking out over the rolling sea, his tone was serious. "I know what you mean."

Grushenko looked at Allegro. "You are suggesting we will not leave this ship alive?"

Allegro did not answer. They'd been through a bad time the night before and didn't know what to expect.

A bell sounded.

Alden looked at his watch. "Time for breakfast. I wonder what we're in for this time. Thin oatmeal, overdone scrambled eggs? Tough sausage and burnt toast? Does that suit you?"

"You forgot the watery coffee," Allegro said. "But let's try it. I'm famished."

The sausage was not tough. Sausage was replaced by bacon, a strange kind of bacon, a quarter of an inch thick, hard as bone, knife- and fork-bending bacon.

They all gave up after a ten-minute struggle.

"This food's lousy," Alden said.

"That's what we bargained for," Grushenko said. "Remember we are sailing under the Panamanian flag. This ship could be owned by anybody, probably avoids most of the regular safety precautions. The crew—men who for one reason or another can't find a better job—are undoubtedly unhappy because the food is, as you put it, lousy. They're paid miserable wages. None of them are unionized." Grushenko grinned. "And the captain is probably taking a cut of everything, as is the purser."

"Cut of what?" Philip asked.

Grushenko shrugged. "The stores, the crew's pay—and *us*. Probably sixty percent to the captain, forty percent to the purser."

"Exactly right," Allegro said.

Alden wondered why he was aboard this ship in the first place. Smoking, he looked around the salon. O'Rourke was at his usual table in the corner, wolfing down his food, even the bacon.

O'Rourke was one of the reasons for his being on board. The note: "American Brandy 61." The loading of the rifles, and boxes of plastic explosives. And O'Rourke as the casual courier.

Alden continued to stare at the sandy-haired man, but O'Rourke was too busy gulping his food to notice. He gave no indication he'd found them last night, nor did he show any sign of injury.

The conversation at the table had turned to politics. "Do you think we'll have a war?" Allegro was addressing Grushenko.

The Russian hesitated and a frown creased the pale yellow forehead. "Eventually, yes."

Alden turned from watching O'Rourke. "And what side will your country take?"

"Germany?" The small man raised his shoulders in a shrug. "It's split. East and West. Who knows, the East Germans may bolt to the side of the West Germans. They've been climbing the wall for years. But what does it matter? In a nuclear war, the whole of Germany will be flattened, incinerated."

"We'll all be flattened and incinerated," Allegro said grimly.

"Who do you think will push the button?" Alden asked.

"Does it matter?" Grushenko replied. "The preemptive strike is in the hands of the preemptors, I'm sure."

"If a terrorist nation ever got hold of a bomb or two," Alden said, "they'd be the preemptors, I'm sure."

"A terrorist nation?" Grushenko frowned. "What are you thinking about?"

"I was thinking about Iraq, Iran, Pakistan, Libya."

Grushenko nodded. "Three of them I can believe. But Iran? They're too far behind the times since the revolution."

"The Russians could show them how," Allegro said. "They're next door in Afghanistan now."

Grushenko chuckled. "Who could deal with that crazy Khomeini?"

"The Russians," Allegro said. "They'd kick him out."

Grushenko knew this was exactly what his country would do.

"But it's a long shot." He smiled. "Is that the way you say it in English? 'A long shot'?"

"It's a short shot for the oilfields and the Gulf," Allegro said levelly.

"Speaking of terrorist nations and terrorists in general," Alden said, "I don't like the feel of that man." He was staring at O'Rourke again.

Without turning his head, taking a sip of coffee, Grushenko said, "He won't give us any more trouble."

"I'm sure he's the courier for the arms shipment. And I wonder where those arms will end up and what they'll be used for?" Alden mused.

"The IRA from the looks of it," Allegro said. She was thinking of O'Rourke's brogue.

"Would the Raven supply the IRA?" Grushenko looked surprised.

"He's helped other groups in Europe. Baader-Meinhof, the Red Army Faction, the Red Brigades in Italy. It's all one. International terrorism," she said.

"But the Irish have had a grievance against the British for hundreds of years," Grushenko said. "And I for one believe it to be a genuine grievance. Why are the British in Ireland in the first place?"

"To keep the peace," Allegro said and, looking straight at him, added, "And if they were successful in kicking the British out, the Prods and the Provos would continue to slaughter each other. I despise nothing more than a head-breaking Irishman full of macho ideas."

Alden had been silent, thinking. Now he said, "Liverpool is just across the Irish Sea from Dublin. But I wonder, are the arms to be used in Ireland or in England?"

Allegro turned her head to him. Grushenko had his cup halfway to his lips and stopped, staring.

Alden did not speak for a moment. Then he said, "Like the Minister of Something—I've forgotten his name—who was shot down in front of his home while his wife and children watched." He paused. "And Louis Mountbatten."

"That was in Ireland," Grushenko said.

"Yes," Alden answered.

Allegro spoke softly, but with definite feeling. "That was a tragedy. Mountbatten was a man I admired and respected. To end up that way was despicable." She stared across the salon lost in thought. Then she said, "There's no reason for it. To kill innocent people. To bomb restaurants and theaters, and kill women and children in England. And as far as the Prods and the Provos are concerned, a plague on both their houses. And I'm half Irish on my mother's side." She savaged a cigarette in a dirty ashtray.

"Have you been to Ireland?" Grushenko asked.

"Oh, yes. I did a photo essay about the *trouble* in Belfast. I saw it all. And if you ask me, the people of Northern Ireland are disgusted. It's the head breakers who are at the soul of it."

"You are a brave woman," Grushenko said, and he meant it.

"I do my job, that's all."

"I think," Alden said, "the rental car you wired ahead for should be the answer. We'll follow the arms shipment to wherever it's going." He paused. "And I think we'll find the Raven there."

Allegro looked at Alden coolly, but inside, her stomach fluttered, her muscles tensed, and there was a pounding in her ears.

CHAPTER 23

Walter Trask sat behind his desk, hands cupped behind his head, rocking back and forth in his swivel chair. Alden had meant what he said. If the CIA did not find the Raven, or Interpol, or any police force in the world, then Alden himself would look for him. And now the amateur bastard was getting too close. Trask had asked for reports on his major movements, and a major movement had been his boarding the *American Brandy*. He must know something. He must have somehow got wind of the arms shipment. Or O'Rourke.

And the girl, Allegro Stern, knew the Raven, had taken his picture, although the negatives had been ripped from her camera. And . . .

Trask sighed and picked up the phone. He put in a call to the Royal Hotel, to Mr. Blair. The circuits were busy, but they would call him back just as soon as a trunk line was open.

He sat back, musing. The arms shipment was going straight to the Raven's people. For Operation Coronet.

The phone rang and Trask picked it up.

"We're ready with your call to Truro," a brassy voice announced in Brooklynese.

"Thank you."

A pause. A ring. An English voice announced the Royal Hotel. Trask asked for Mr. Blair. When the Raven picked up the phone, Trask said, "I'm calling from the office."

"Oh? How are you?"

"Pretty good. Yourself?"

"Not bad."

"There's a woman coming your way."

"Yes. The photographer."

"Then you know," Trask said.

"O'Rourke alerted me."

"I see." A pause. "Do you foresee anything?"

The Raven laughed. "She'll be taken care of. Don't worry."

"I wish I could be with you."

"You could be. If you had the guts." And then the Raven hung up abruptly.

Fresh bastard, Trask thought. Talks about guts. He's miles away when the action starts—pressing buttons. But Trask breathed a sigh of relief as he smiled. You've got to hand it to the Raven. Tough son of a bitch. Trask admired him.

Alden and Allegro sat in deck chairs, out of the wind, congratulating themselves on their success. The sun was bright, its rays warm and welcome. The crossing had become rough, the biting cold of the northern winds almost more than the borrowed clothing could withstand. They enjoyed the respite.

Grushenko had been to breakfast, looking old and worn out, and had retired to his cabin to rest. They had three days to sit it out before Liverpool. They agreed his bunk was the best place for him right now. His actions had puzzled them.

"Who do you think he is?" Allegro asked. "Do you still believe he's our innocent Ernst Eisenstadt?"

"He may be Ernst Eisenstadt, but he's not innocent. He's an agent of some kind. He's after the Raven, but not because of a dead son."

"He's not my idea of an agent. I've met countless CIA men, Mossad, and the rest. I've never seen one like him."

"Next. Is he German?" Alden asked. "If he is, would you guess East or West?"

They were interrupted by a seaman who approached and in broken English asked them to follow him to the captain's cabin. Before they entered, he patted them down for weapons.

Captain Français sat behind a huge oak desk in an equally huge executive chair. The office didn't fit the image of the old boat. It was modern, lined with expensive wood veneers, furnished with plush chairs and glass-topped tables, all secured to the lush carpeted floor. Beyond a half-open door, a stateroom of equal splendor was visible.

Captain Français was not smiling. Grushenko sat in front of the desk facing him. Français waved Allegro and Alden to chairs on either side of Grushenko.

Grushenko had been talking when they entered and, after a cursory nod, continued, "As I was telling you, we are private citizens of the United States. I resent your questions, Captain. And I warn you. My company knows where I am and expects to see me at the dock in Liverpool."

He had given them the lead. But what was their excuse for being on the boat in the first place? Alden and Allegro could be on a romantic interlude. But they could have chosen hundreds of places more romantic. And why would Grushenko have paid for all three? No. They had no plausible explanation.

"I'm going to make it easy for you," Français said. "O'Rourke is a passenger. You are passengers. All four of you paid what I asked—no questions. So you all have ulterior motives." He picked up a huge carved pipe, fingered it, but didn't light it. "My motive is money," he went on. "I suspect O'Rourke's is revolutionary."

He looked from one to the other. "I know you were in hold number two last night. I don't think you saw the cargo and you won't." He looked at the three sternly. "O'Rourke is like a zombie today. That means one of you got to him. And that makes you professionals."

The two Americans knew enough to keep a straight face. It might be a standoff. Grushenko lit a cigarette from a butt and ground out the first in a large glass ashtray.

"I'll tell you what I think," Captain Français said. "I think you're here because of O'Rourke and what he plans. I don't want to know." He held the huge pipe in his right hand, gesturing. "But I don't want trouble on my ship. I'm going to post guards at cargo doors, protect the holds from your prying, and confine you to your cabins at night. When we land, you'll be free to go.''

"Thank you, Captain," Grushenko said, rising. He motioned to the others and all three left without comment.

Back in Grushenko's cabin, he went through the usual search for listening devices. When he was finished, he announced, "They've made a very thorough search of this cabin."

"How do you know?" Allegro asked.

"I know. I left a few traps for them to fall into."

"Who the hell are you?" Alden asked.

"Ernst Eisenstadt, sometime metallurgical engineer, sometime Interpol agent."

Alden scowled, furious that he had been taken in by an old pro. The man could have made a life for himself in Hollywood as a character actor.

"Don't Interpol agents retire—you know—earlier?" Allegro asked.

"A lot earlier. My son wanted to follow in my footsteps. Damned fool. I decided to stick around and show him the ropes," he lied.

No one spoke for a few seconds. The Americans didn't want to bring it up again, but finally Allegro asked, "Your son was really on the train?"

Feeling his son was already dead to him, on the way to the gulags thousands of miles from Moscow in the frozen wastes of Siberia, Grushenko merely nodded. It was a small lie. One story hurt as much as the other and showed as clearly on his face.

"We will be model citizens of this scow for the next few days." He raised a grieving face to theirs, knowing their actions for the next few days were important. "They have searched our cabins and know we have no weapons. Did they search you before you entered the captain's cabin?" he asked.

"I wasn't overjoyed about that," Allegro said.

"Part of the business, dear girl." Grushenko allowed himself the beginning of a smile, then his face took on a hardness they hadn't seen before. "They will take on a pilot just before we sight land. When we see the pilot boat approach, we will collect one small bag each and retrieve our guns." He looked from Allegro on the settee to Alden on the lower bunk, holding their attention. "Everyone will be occupied. We can act natural, stash our bags in a lifeboat, keep our guns handy. As soon as the pilot boat pulls away, it will be our turn."

"To do what?" Alden asked.

"They will have lowered a landing deck for the pilot boat. Before they can haul it aboard again, we will take it and hold it," the KGB man replied.

"For our boat," Allegro finished it for him. "How will they know when to come? Who are they?" she asked.

Grushenko had been standing. He looked frail and weak. Allegro slid to the floor, motioned him to the settee.

"They will be standing out a few miles with powerful glasses. When the pilot boat docks, they will start in. By the time we are in position, they will only be a minute or two away," Grushenko explained. "They are my people— Interpol. They will be heavily armed, but will show no weapons unless we need help."

"You say you're German, Ernst," Alden said. "East or West?"

The old man looked at them from the settee and for the first time in a long career was uncertain how to answer. He had come to like these people. He had spent too many years in the West, had absorbed too much of their attitudes, was hurting too much from his son's detention.

"Does it matter?" he asked. "Accept me for what I am. The Raven has to be stopped." He clutched his chest for a moment, waited for the pain to dissipate. "We all share the same convictions. Let's leave it at that."

"I think you need to lie down for a while," Allegro said, concerned for his health, despite her doubts about his motives.

"One last word before you leave," Grushenko said. "Our lives may depend on each other. For the next three days, act normally, and when the pilot boat arrives, remember what I said."

They both nodded and headed for the door.

"Whatever you represent, Ernst," Alden said. "If you're after the Raven, we're with you. But if you are lying, if you have other motives, we'll look out for ourselves."

The old agent allowed himself a smile as he closed the door after them. Amateurs.

Three days later, at 8:10 A.M., the *American Brandy* came to a standstill with no land in sight. Anchor chains ripped, and the heavy sea anchors caught bottom.

The Americans played their roles to the hilt, conscious of the fact that someone might be listening. Allegro turned to Alden. "Are we near Liverpool? Why are we stopping?"

"I don't know," Alden said. Then he saw the captain standing at the rail about twenty-five feet astern. "Let's go find out."

As they approached, Français looked up, a smile half hidden behind his beard. "We're waiting for the river pilot," he said before they could ask anything. He was used to the question.

"I don't see any land," Allegro said. "How far are we from Liverpool?"

"To the Mersey estuary, about forty miles. Then up the river. We stay here until the pilot arrives. He will tell us when we can enter the dock area, and how long it will take." Français looked down at the water. "We may have a long wait."

"Wait? How long a wait?" Alden asked.

Français shrugged. "Five, perhaps six hours. The pilot will let us know when we can lock in when he gets here. They are all dry docks, you know, down in Liverpool on the Mersey River. It all depends on the tides. If the tide is low, we'll have to wait or arrange a slow speed across the bay to the Mersey estuary. When we are there, we might have to wait until a ship of our draft is able to get out of its lock. We may be lucky. The port may be inactive."

"Dry docks," Alden said. "I didn't know. Are they large?"

Français smiled. "The Titanic was fitted out in Liverpool."

"The Beatles came from Liverpool." It was Grushenko. He had just arrived on deck.

"Good morning, Ernst," Allegro said.

"It is a good morning, isn't it?" he said, looking about. "Clear, warm. What the English would call balmy."

Alden laughed. "We'll ask the natives when we dock."
He looked at Captain Français. "Or lock in."

Allegro pointed. "Is that the pilot?" A motor launch
was approaching swiftly.

"Yes, that's the pilot boat," Français said.

Suddenly his mood changed. "I have been satisfied with
your behavior since our talk," he said. "If you get through
the next few hours the same way, we will have no problems." He turned from them without further comment.

They weren't concerned with his problems. They moved
to their cabins, returned, stashed their carryalls near the
landing area, and retrieved their guns.

The crew members were busy hoisting a metal gangplank and docking platform over the side. Ten minutes
later, when the pilot climbed aboard, there was a short,
crisp conversation at the rail.

"Français, you bloody old pirate," the pilot said. "*Comment allez-vous?*"

Français laughed. "*Pas trop mal, mon vieux.* Not too
bad."

The "old friend" greeting was purely from habit. The
pilot was a middle-aged man with black hair and blue
eyes.

"Look, old boy," he said. "The tide's at its lowest and
Liverpool is full up. You want to take it easy getting up
there, or would you rather be in irons for a while?"

"What time?" Français asked.

"Oh, I'd say two o'clock or a little before."

Français turned and shouted to one of his mates. "Weigh
anchors!"

He turned back to the pilot. "She is all yours. But treat
her tenderly."

"What, this old hulk?" the pilot said, mounting the
stairs to the bridge deck.

"That's what I mean!" Français shouted after him.
"She may fall apart!"

Before the crew could react, a twin-screw racing launch
appeared from astern at fifty knots and was at the docking
steps within seconds.

Grushenko pointed his .38 between the captain and the

pilot. "Don't do anything foolish. We'll be leaving you here."

As planned, Allegro scrambled down the steps and stood with her Luger pointed at the men above. Alden followed slowly, making sure Grushenko made it without trouble. Before anyone above could draw their weapons, they were in the launch and had cast off.

The run to Liverpool took less than an hour.

"They'll radio ahead," Allegro screamed into the wind.

"No, they won't," Grushenko said. "Their radio doesn't work."

"How did you get in the radio room?" Alden asked, shouting into the old man's ear.

"Didn't have to. Cut their antennae," Grushenko said, smiling enigmatically.

For the first time, Alden knew the old man enjoyed what he did. He enjoyed it because, whatever or whoever he was, he was the best. He had been through it all. Alden's problem was not whether he and Allegro could go on with him, but the reverse—whether they could succeed without him.

"How do we get ashore without immigration problems?" he asked.

"Interpol doesn't bother much with immigration people," Grushenko answered. "We will land far from where the *American Brandy* will dock. I have a car ready. We will have a comfortable meal, learn where the old tub will dock, and be waiting."

Their conversation came in spurts as they alternately viewed the sights of the port and dreamed up new questions. By the time they had finished with one and the other, the launch was well up the Mersey, had slowed, was turning into a nondescript dock far from the huge dry docks.

CHAPTER 24

A board the *American Brandy*, Captain Français was furious, cursing himself for a fool, cursing the crew for useless idiots, cursing O'Rourke and his bloody shipment.

O'Rourke was the only one who had acted. He knew what the escape might mean to them, and headed straight for the radio room. It was then they discovered the antennae were sabotaged.

The pilot was unaware that the power-boat episode had been unplanned. Immigration and customs were not in his line. The anchors were hauled, the engines resonated in a deep rumble, and the *American Brandy* was on her way again. The ship seemed hardly to move at all, its wake a ripple as it steamed from Anglesey, where they had taken on the pilot, to Liverpool Bay, and into the Mersey estuary, where they turned south into the river itself.

Traffic on the Mersey River was considerable. Ships heading north to the estuary went faster than incoming craft, which had to wait for a lock of the proper depth.

"Ever been to Liverpool, lad?" the pilot asked O'Rourke, who stood nearby, and gestured to the docks and landing stages where large ships lay.

The pilot's name was Clifford Franklin Fry. He had sailed the seas for years and was now content to pilot his beloved Mersey. He never missed the chance to sing her praises.

"In the year 1200," Fry said, "Liverpool was a small fishing village. Much later, during the trade with the West

245

Indies, it became part of the slave trade." Before he could explain further to the preoccupied O'Rourke, word came of an open lock. The radioman had repaired his equipment. Under Fry's orders, the ship began a slow turn.

Farther inland, at a smaller berthing area, the boat carrying Alden, Allegro, and Grushenko had dropped off its passengers. The two men had pulled away without a word.

"That must be the car I ordered," Grushenko said, pointing to a nondescript red Austin sedan.

"Our friends won't dock for hours, if we can believe Captain Français," Alden said. "What do you suggest we do until then?"

"My people should have left a map in the car." Grushenko said. "We have to drive along the estuary until we spot the ship, then follow her to her berth."

"How about provisioning first?" Allegro asked. "We could be stuck without food or water once we pick them up."

The Austin was gassed and ready to go. On the front seat, a map of the Mersey area was folded to reveal the area they would be searching. A pair of binoculars lay under the map.

"Your people are efficient," Allegro commented.

Grushenko turned to Alden. "Have you driven a right-hand drive?"

"Not for years, but I'll manage."

They piled in. Grushenko sat in front and acted as navigator. They turned onto A561 toward the sea. Alden had to concentrate to keep on the left side of the road. Every time he came to a roundabout, an intersection with a traffic circle in the middle, he had to steel himself not to revert to the right side of the road.

After a half hour, they were approaching Aigburth Road, leading to the docks. Allegro spotted a grocery, suggested they stop.

"Has anyone got English money?" she asked.

Grushenko and Alden shook their heads. She took off and was back in a few minutes with a brown paper bag. It was filled with fresh fruit, bottled water, and cans of juice. "They took my money," she said. "One for one."

"Good. Let's get after them," Grushenko said. "I'm not going to feel right until we have that old tub in sight."

Alden wheeled the red car into traffic and headed west. At St. James Street, Grushenko suggested they turn down Parliament Street to Sefton Street and head west again. Within another half hour Sefton had become Wapping Chaloner Street, then Strand Street, and finally New Quay. At the Pier Head, where the towers of the Royal Liver Building stretched to the sky, they spotted the *American Brandy* heading for the far shore.

The day was cloudless, had warmed to a balmy seventy. The Mersey was running an outward tide carrying debris and pollution to the sea. The smell of diesel fuel, rotting garbage, and fish demanded the recognition a seaport deserves.

"They're going to dock on the other side. It'll take us hours to go around," Allegro said.

"I'm sure I saw a tunnel on this map," Grushenko said. "Here. We passed it a block back."

Alden pulled into a parking lot to make the turn. He found the tunnel entrance and joined the line of cars heading into the darkness.

"Can you still see her?" Grushenko asked, straining to see.

"We'll pick her up soon, Ernst. Don't worry," Allegro said. "Take them at least two hours to dock, clear customs, unload and all that."

At the toll booth, Alden handed the attendant an American dollar.

"That all you got, mate?" she asked.

"Sorry. Haven't got to the bank yet."

"Bloody Yanks! Have to do then, won't it?" She waved them on.

On the other shore, Alden concentrated on keeping to the left. Grushenko scanned the map, while Allegro searched between old red brick warehouses for signs of dock areas. The fish smell here was worse, drowning out the smells of refuse and fuel oil. They had to be near a fish-processing plant.

"Turn right at the next street," Grushenko said. "Corporation Street runs parallel to the docks."

Within a half mile they saw a sign: VICTORIA DOCK. They pulled up to the quayside, parked, and looked back toward the opening into the dock. They could see the superstructure of a ship heading through the gap. Grushenko put the glasses on her and waited for the hull to show as she passed the fish plants.

"That's her," he said. "Pull back to an alley until we see where she docks."

Customs and immigration men boarded when the hawsers had the old ship secured to the weathered cement dock. While they were aboard, the three watchers opened their bag, munched on fruit, drank some water, and waited, their car parked in an alley out of sight. In less than an hour, the officials trooped down the gangway and the cranes started emptying the holds, beginning with hold number two. O'Rourke skipped down the gangway to talk to a lorry driver who had pulled his two-ton lorry close alongside.

When the lorry had received the four crates emblazoned with red dolls' heads, O'Rourke and his partner climbed into the cab, O'Rourke behind the wheel. The truck moved out onto Wapping Street and headed north to the intersection of Hanover, where it turned right.

Alden started the Austin, let in the clutch, slipped out of the alley, and screeched down to Hanover just as another car made a right turn into the street. The truck was just ahead of the other car. Alden decided to keep it that way, one car between the Austin and the panel truck, hoping O'Rourke would not realize he was being followed.

At John Street, the truck turned left, followed it to Victoria Street, and made a right turn. The other car had turned right, so Alden let another take its place.

After several turns right and left, the truck entered a tunnel.

"Is this tunnel on your map? Where is he headed?" Allegro asked.

Grushenko scanned his map for a few seconds, then

said, "There are two tunnels. The north one goes from Wallesey, the other from Birkenhead."

They exited the tunnel at Wallesey, paralleled the river on the east side, south to the Birkenhead tunnel they had used earlier, and queued up again, the lorry two cars ahead.

"What the hell's he doing?" Alden asked, his nerves frayed by the wrong-side driving in heavy traffic.

"Making sure he's not being followed," Grushenko offered.

"Think they've spotted us?" Allegro asked.

"No. They'd have continued south if they had, tried to lose us in the residential area," a tired Grushenko replied.

The woman took another dollar from Alden, making a remark about "funny money."

"Now where?" Alden muttered.

Their target provided the answer. It turned south onto Route A41.

"Beautiful day for a motor trip," Allegro said. She puffed lazily on a cigarette, but her pulse was racing. This was her kind of action.

In the lorry, O'Rourke said, "We're being followed."

Corrigan turned to him in surprise. "Are we, now?"

"You didn't notice? All the way from Wapping Street."

Corrigan looked into the side-view mirror. "By what?"

"That red Austin back of the Ford."

"Well now, I wonder who's in it?"

"Three passengers from the *American Brandy*," O'Rourke said.

"Who are they?"

"One's a free-lance writer-photographer—a woman. The other two I don't know. The girl interviewed the Raven a while back. She knows what he looks like."

Corrigan stared through the windshield for a few seconds. "Now, I wonder how they got a whiff of the whiskey?"

"I don't know," O'Rourke said. "But we'll have to do something."

"Give 'em the slip?"

O'Rourke was thoughtful for a moment. "More than that, I think."

Corrigan smiled at him and patted his shoulder holster. "I see your meaning."

A41 passes through the town of Whitchurch, about forty miles south of Birkenhead. A mile or two below Whitchurch a side road, B5467, branches off south. The truck continued along that road.

The traffic on A41 had been heavy, but there were few if any cars along route B5467. Alden found himself tailing the panel truck with no car in between.

"I don't like this road," Allegro said.

"Why not?" Alden asked. "The sky is blue, the grass is green, the birds sing." But he was trying to keep the rising sense of danger out of his voice.

"It's lonely," Allegro said. "Not a car in sight. And it'll be getting dark soon."

"They know they are being followed," Grushenko said.

"I agree," Allegro said. She sat forward in the backseat, her face between the two in front. She turned to look at Grushenko. He'd drawn his .38.

"Time for the artillery?" she asked, taking the Luger from her pocket. She slid out the clip, counted the 9-mm bullets. "I've only got three rounds," she said.

"Whatever or whoever you are, I'm glad you're with us, Ernst," Alden said. "If they start shooting, we're not exactly sitting ducks."

Grushenko was silent. He was sorry he'd had to lie to them. He was sorry for Alden's ex-wife, and for Alden himself. He was sorry about his own son. He was sorry about his life. The chest pain was getting worse. Nothing seemed to be going right. Maybe life was like that when you got old.

O'Rourke's lorry passed through the quiet town of Tilstock to a lonely stretch of road. No car, wagon, or human was in sight.

"Now," O'Rourke said.

Corrigan smiled and removed a Coonan .357-caliber pistol from his holster. He opened the window on his side all the way, leaned out, and looked back. Holding the gun in his left hand and steadying it with his right, he sighted along the barrel.

"Just a wee bit more to your left, Patrick," he screamed through the wind.

O'Rourke carefully edged the lorry to the left-hand side of the road, bordering a ditch. Most of the Austin came into Corrigan's range.

"Ah, sweet, now. Sweet." He squeezed off a shot.

A slug tore through the windshield of the Austin. Allegro screamed. Alden swerved to the other side of the road. Another shot bounced off the hood and ricocheted. A third smashed a headlight.

"Whoever the marksman is, he's damned good. Let me get a shot!" Grushenko cried hoarsely. "Bring the car more to the left! The left side!" He leaned out the window, Smith & Wesson in hand. "More! More to the left!"

At that moment a bullet tore into the left front tire. The Austin slipped and slid from one side of the road to the other with Alden trying his best to bring it under control. Grushenko's shot went wild as the Austin turned completely around, flipped over twice, and tumbled into the ditch.

In the lorry, Corrigan turned to O'Rourke. "Now there. That's done. Shall we go back and have a look-see?"

"No," O'Rourke said. "Even if they are not all dead they can't follow us. We'd best get to Shrewsbury as fast as we can and transfer the goods to the other lorry."

"Then on to London," Corrigan said. "And Operation Coronet." A thin, almost grim smile spread to his lips.

Twenty minutes later, as the skies had begun to darken, a lone cyclist on his way from Tilstock to Edstaston came across the Austin.

"Blimey! What have we here?" Carefully propping his bicycle on its stand, he approached the car. "Anybody in there?" he shouted.

"Yes." Alden's voice was feeble, muffled. "Get us out."

"Just stay as you are, mate. I've a cycle here and I'll ride to the nearest phone for an ambulance and the police."

A low moan came from the car as the cyclist rode off, pumping the pedals as hard as he could.

                        *   *   *

Dr. Ashton was a stocky man with a mustache and an almost hidden twinkle in his eye, although he seldom smiled. At Liverpool General, he had seen too much human misery, too much suffering.

"I'm afraid she's had a slight concussion," he said to Alden. "Her level of consciousness is diminished, her reflexes asymmetrical. A CAT scan will tell us if it's more than that."

"May I see her?" Alden asked.

"By all means." He led Alden to the emergency room.

"The CAT scan sounds ominous. When will she be able to leave the hospital?"

"Barring a positive scan, tomorrow morning, I'd say. But I rather think no real problems will be found."

"What about Mr. Eisenstadt?"

The doctor stopped his walk for a moment. "Now, that's more serious. Nothing fatal, but he's suffered a slight fracture to the tibia, needs a leg splint. He's got a more severe concussion than your lady friend. He was sitting in the front seat, wasn't he?"

"Yes."

"Without a fastened seat belt. Dangerous, dangerous."

"How long will he be in?"

"Oh, I'd say a week to ten days. Well, here we are. Don't be too long. She's scheduled for the CAT scan prep in fifteen minutes." He opened the door and left.

Alden walked over to her and stared down. She met his gaze and managed a weak smile. "Philip."

He was subdued, quiet. "You'll be all right. The doctor just told me. The CAT scan you're to go through is just a precaution."

"How is Ernst?"

"Worse than you, but he'll live. I'll take you out in the morning."

I almost killed her, he thought. I almost killed her. He forced a smile. "I'm glad you're alive."

Her smile broadened. "So am I."

Two attendants wheeled in a gurney and, as Alden watched, moved her onto it.

"CAT scan time, miss," one of them said. He looked up at Alden. "She'll be back before too long."

"Don't wait, darling," Allegro said, her eyes looking back as they wheeled her out. "I feel so sleepy. Just come for me in the morning."

"I will." He was forcing back tears, crying inside. He had been afraid for her on the boat, but until this—this near thing—he hadn't realized how much she meant to him.

Before he'd met her, he'd been sick of life. Now he had something to live for. And she had given it to him—given back his sense of enjoyment, enthusiasm, love of life. And in his foolishness he had almost killed her.

He inquired at the emergency station about Ernst, was told he was in another treatment room. He could see him for only a few minutes. The old man had his leg in a cast. He seemed to be in a daze.

"Hello, Ernst."

Grushenko turned to him and said in a faint voice, "Alden?" He was looking beyond him with a vacant stare.

"Do you feel up to talking?"

"Go ahead. How is Allegro?"

"Fine. She can probably check out tomorrow morning."

Grushenko smiled. "That is good."

"You'll be here for a week or so."

The old man nodded.

"We'll be staying at the Savoy in London. In case you want to get in touch."

"The Savoy," Grushenko repeated, his voice becoming weaker. Then his eyes closed in sleep.

Alden waited a few seconds before he turned and left.

When Alden picked her up the following morning, Allegro was bright and cheerful. "The CAT scan was negative," she said with a happy note in her voice as they embraced.

"I knew it would be," Alden laughed. "Dr. Ashton told me."

"Do you have a car?"

"Uh-huh. The Swan people found me a silver-colored 450 SL."

"Hollywood Alden and his passion for Mercedes."

"Why not? I take full collision insurance."

"You're a wastrel," she scolded, but her eyes brightened. "Where shall we go?"

"How about London? The Savoy? Buckingham Palace? The Houses of Parliament? The Inns of Court? The—"

"Sounds great." A look of sudden concern crossed her face. "My camera!"

"It's in the car. Not a scratch."

"Excuse me, sir." It was the constable from Edstaston who had been on hand the night before. "They found the lorry you described. Abandoned at Shrewsbury."

Alden turned to him, his eyes steady. "The arms?"

"Gone. Transferred to another vehicle by the looks of it. We called Hotchkiss & Sons in London. One of their lorries was stolen two days ago. It checks with the one we found, sir."

"Then we don't know where the arms are going."

"Afraid not, sir. But your descriptions of the two men— that's a plus, sir. We'll catch up with them."

"It's a long shot. But let me know if you do. I'll be at the Savoy in London."

Allegro's heart had begun to sink. She had made up her mind to help him no matter where it led. Now it looked like a dead end. In her work, she'd seen it happen so often before. Philip would be no different from others. He would enjoy London for a few days and would become restless. Nothing would make him settle down now until he'd met and dealt with the Raven.

The village of Penzance lies near Land's End at the southernmost tip of Britain, about thirty miles south of Truro. It is a resort town, its warm climate making it the getaway for the thousands of Britons and others who flock to it every summer. Even in the winter palm trees flourish and subtropical plants abound in the Trengwainton Gardens.

It was to Penzance that the Raven drove the same morning Allegro was released from the hospital. He enjoyed the drive along route A30 to a pub near the intersection of Route A394, close to Truro, for his meeting with four members of the IRA.

He was dressed for the occasion in old baggy slacks, a turtleneck, and worn shoes. He wore a peaked cap. The Raven was a chameleon, changing his appearance to suit the background.

He entered the pub and glanced around. They were there, at a table in a corner, each with a pint of bitters before him. They had left a vacant chair for the Raven at the head of the table. It was an old pub, low-ceilinged, heavily beamed, smelling of burned wood and stale ale.

He sat and looked around. He knew O'Rourke and Corrigan, but the other two were unfamiliar faces. One wore what appeared to be an expensive sweater.

"What's your name?" the Raven asked.

"Flaherty. Liam Flaherty."

"Where did you get that sweater?"

The young man's chest swelled with pride. "Me mother knitted it special. I'm from the Aran Isles off Galway."

"What's that got to do with it?"

"Well now, in the Aran Isles, each family has its own personalized stitch, so's when the bodies of the fishermen are washed up from sea, they can be identified."

"That sweater wouldn't last two days in the sea, man. Are you trying to kid me?"

The young blue-eyed man, who could not have been over twenty-five, gave the Raven an icy look. "For the fishermen, they're oiled. I be not a fisherman!" The Irish brogue rolled smoothly off his tongue.

"What are you then?"

Liam Flaherty's chest swelled again, and it was accompanied by fierce anger in his eyes. "I'm a loyal member of the Irish Republican Army. That's what I am!"

"Willing to die for it?" The Raven's question was quick, dartlike.

"I am!"

The Raven was silent, eyeing Flaherty's sweater. "It's a shame what's going to happen to that sweater. It would bring at least one hundred fifty dollars in the States."

"It's not up for sale, Mr. Raven! Me mother made it and I'll die in it!"

Their eyes locked for a moment, then the Raven shifted his gaze to the fourth man. "And you? What's your name?"

"Tyrone," the man mumbled, not lifting his eyes from his beer. "John Tyrone." He was the oldest of the lot, in his forties, the Raven guessed.

"And what do you think, Tyrone?" the Raven asked.

The man shrugged, looked up. "I'll do anything against the British. That's why I'm here." He drank from his pint.

The Raven looked around the table, directed his eyes at O'Rourke.

"What about you, O'Rourke?"

"I'm thirty-five. Seen it all, been through it all. What's left to live for?"

"And I'm a bit off twenty-seven and feel the same way," Corrigan said. "After all, man, I've seen it all, too. I've had me a piece of ass, and good food. I've seen the sky, the sun, the trees, and the moon. What's left? I'd rather be out of it before the old-age sickness falls upon me."

The Raven took his elbows from the table and leaned back in his chair, smiling. A waitress came over for his order and he thought of asking for Armagnac, but felt it would be out of place.

"I'll have a pint," he said.

When his drink was on the table, the Raven leaned forward again and lifted it, taking a long swallow and wiping his lips. "Now here's the plan," he said. "This coming Saturday, the queen will leave Buckingham Palace for Trooping the Colour. I guess you're all familiar with the ceremony?"

The others nodded.

"The route will be up the Mall from Buckingham Palace almost to Admiralty Arch, where she'll turn right to Horse Guards Parade. We'll get her before she reaches Horse Guards Parade or even near Admiralty Arch. Now, here's what we'll do. . . ."

The king was in his counting house, counting out his money. The queen was in the parlor, eating bread and honey. And outside, on the Mall, four members of the IRA stood waiting at the intersection of the Mall and Marlborough Road, two on either side, in front of the jamming throng, their bodies beneath their jackets enveloped with plastic explosives.

The Raven held his Nikon camera-radio in readiness on a knoll in St. James's Park.

Actually, the queen was not in the parlor, nor was she eating bread and honey. She was in a dressing room, putting the finishing touches to the clothing she would wear for this occasion, tilting the tam just so, as she always had.

Prince Philip, her consort, fully dressed in his uniform, was awaiting the queen in one of the huge libraries of the palace, conversing jovially with a close friend.

Satisfied that she looked her best to review the Coldstream, Welsh, Irish, and Scots Guards and the Grenadiers, she sent word to the prince.

They met in one of the courtyards of the palace, mounted their horses amid the queen's personal bodyguard, waited for the correct time, and then exited the palace grounds.

In St. James's Park, the Raven heard the mounting cheers, the shouts, the cries of joy as the queen and her entourage entered the Mall. He smiled gleefully.

Soon, through the zoom lens attached to the Nikon, he could see the queen herself, riding slowly, holding the horse almost to a walk.

As she approached Marlborough Road, the cheering grew in intensity. The Raven swung his camera to the intersection of Marlborough Road and the Mall. He saw Corrigan and O'Rourke on the far side. On the park side, he could make out Flaherty and Tyrone, their backs to him.

The queen came on. He had measured the distance to Marlborough Road and the Queen Victoria Memorial as three hundred and fifty yards. She was near, the shouting increased, the throngs waved. Inch by inch, she came on. Then Marlborough Road . . . three hundred yards . . . two hundred . . . and he depressed the shutter release.

A terrific explosion shook the Mall.

The queen, bloodied, was thrown from her horse and smashed head-first onto the pavement. Her horse reared for a moment, then fell dead.

The prince pitched forward to the ground, a look of utter surprise on a face already dead.

The queen's bodyguard was blown to bits.

Seventy-two people in the crowd lining the Mall were killed. Many others were injured.

Cries, sobs, curses, filled the air.

The smell of powder and blood was overpowering.

Chaos.

Again.

Book Three

THE MOUNTAIN

For he being dead, with him is beauty
   slain,
And, beauty dead, black Chaos comes
   again.

—WILLIAM SHAKESPEARE

CHAPTER 25

"So that's it. Operation Coronet." The Raven looked about the table, measuring reactions from the four members of the IRA suicide team.

They were silent, sipping or looking down into their bitters.

"Any questions?" the Raven asked.

"What about the queen's personal bodyguard?" It was the oldest of the group, John Tyrone.

"Don't worry about them. The crowds will be too much for them to worry about you. They'll be looking for guns. Just don't act suspicious and you're safe. What I meant was," the Raven went on, "do we have any cold feet here, any second thoughts?"

"I told you before," Tyrone said without lifting his head, "I'll do anything against the Brits."

"And I've seen it all," O'Rourke mumbled.

Corrigan said, "I think I'll get me a piece of ass tonight and tomorrow night. Ha! Me last fling!"

They all turned to the youngest man, Liam Flaherty, wearing the sweater his mother had knitted for him on the Aran Isles.

He had a fierce, determined look on his face. "Count me in, boys. I hate the British as much as you. And me father was shot down in Belfast. Shot down like a dog, he was."

Satisfied, the Raven leaned back in his chair and ordered another pint.

When the barmaid had left, he said, "I don't want any no-shows. If any of you fail to show, you'll have a slow death."

The four stared at him and believed him.

The Raven scanned his well-manicured fingernails and thought of ordering Armagnac. Even Grand Marnier would do. He wanted to be finished with this meeting and back in Truro. He would like to screw a beautiful broad—not the kind Corrigan was used to. He said, "The C4 is in London. We'll meet there this Friday night, about nine o'clock. And the next morning . . ."

"Operation Coronet." Corrigan raised his glass, his eyes gleaming.

That afternoon, Alden and Allegro were unpacking their things in a suite at the Savoy Hotel overlooking the River Thames in London.

"We were lucky to get this suite," Allegro said. "What with Trooping the Colour coming up on Saturday."

"They know me here. I always stay at the Savoy when I'm in London. Have you ever been to London?"

"Many times. But I never put up in a fancy place like this."

"I wonder," Alden mused. "Harry Zimmerman is in Europe. He never misses Trooping the Colour if he can make it. Or the Derby. He usually puts up at Claridges." Alden laughed. "Can you imagine that? Hollywood Harry at Claridges?"

"I've never been to Claridges," Allegro said. "Too rich for my blood."

"I wonder," Alden said again, and reached for the phone. When the connection was complete, he said, "Would you have a Harry Zimmerman registered?" A wait. Then: "You do? Put me through." He grinned and looked at Allegro. "He's there. Hello, Harry? Harry from Hollywood? This is one of your clients, Phil Alden. I'm at the Savoy."

"Well, for Christ's sake," Harry Zimmerman said. "What the hell are you doing here?"

"It's a long story. I'll tell you when I see you. You here for Trooping the Colour?"

"You bet. Is Allegro with you?"

"Yeah."

"Good. Let's get together for dinner or something."

"When?"

"How about tonight?"

"Fine. Here at the Savoy?"

"Sure. Listen, are you two going to the ceremony on Saturday?"

"I don't think so, Harry. The Mall will be mobbed."

"I have a ticket for Horse Guards Parade. Maybe I can rustle up two more."

"You're a hustler, Harry. Rustle up two more tickets and we'll be delighted to join you."

"I'll let you know tonight. What time shall we meet?"

"Oh, eightish." He looked over at Allegro for confirmation. She nodded.

"Good show!" Harry said.

"You Flatbush Britisher." Alden laughed and hung up. When he turned back to Allegro, he noticed the concerned expression on her face.

He frowned. "What's the matter? Don't you like Harry?"

"No, quite the opposite," she said quickly. "He's warm, gentle, kind."

"Then what's the matter?"

"Have we given up on the Raven?" she asked. "Are we on holiday now?"

He did not say anything for a moment, just sat, staring at his clenched hands, head lowered. Then he rose and crossed to where she sat on the sofa. He put his arms around her, held her tightly.

When she returned his pressure, eyes moist, he knew what he had to say. "I don't want to die and I don't want you to die. I've found something to live for now—you. Before we met, I was jaded," he went on. "I thought I'd seen it all, been through it all. Two unsuccessful marriages, two kids who never pay much attention to me, and a world gone mad."

"Not much you can do about it alone, Philip," Allegro said.

He looked at her steadily. "I really love you, Allegro."

She felt happy, content, knowing she was loved. She tightened her grip on him, holding him closer.

"I'm glad, Philip," she said. "I'm glad."

His face buried in her neck, he forced the words out. "But you've got to remember one thing, my love." His face had lost its softness. "I haven't forgotten Kate, or all those other passengers on the train. If I ever do get the smell of the Raven, from a distance, and can't get at him myself, I'll notify the authorities. If it gets to be more than that, I'm still going after him and I want you out of the way." He breathed heavily. "I almost lost you at Kingman and came close to getting you killed just now. I don't want to do it again."

For a moment she shuddered. He had not given up after all. But he had promised not to actively pursue the Raven. He was no longer obsessed.

"Promise?" he asked.

"Yes," she said. "Of course."

It was enough. If it happened, it happened, and she would be with him. But he was no longer on a crusade.

In Liverpool, Vladislav Grushenko lay on the bed staring at the hospital-room ceiling. He felt trapped, powerless. Alden was out there on his own, with no good clues to the Raven's whereabouts. Maybe Allegro had persuaded him to give up the hunt. Grushenko knew that Allegro had ambivalent feelings toward him, and did not trust him, ever since she had seen the gun. She did not believe he was with Interpol, of that he was certain.

It was imperative he call his embassy in London, get more information, set up his next move. He could not risk calling through the hospital's switchboard.

"How long do you think I'll be here?" he asked Dr. Ashton.

Ashton slumped into a chair at the side of his bed. He looked overtired. His expression was bleak. "I have some bad news."

Grushenko didn't need bad news. What he needed was to get out and after the Raven. "What is it?" he asked impatiently, reaching for a cigarette.

"Those," Ashton pointed to the crumpled pack, "have

killed you. Why in hell people smoke like you do I'll never understand.''

"So they will kill me. We all have to die.'' Grushenko lit one up and blew smoke away from the medic.

"We do routine tests on everyone we admit, Mr. Eisenstadt. I don't like what we've found. Have you been suffering from chest pains?'' he asked.

"Spit it out, Doctor.''

"Your X-rays show lung cancer. I'm sorry. We'll do a biopsy, of course, but the result will be the same.'' Dr. Ashton tried to look the old man in the eyes, but could not. Eisenstadt seemed to have aged years in the little time he'd been with them. "Advanced lung cancer—both lungs,'' he finally said. "We can't understand how you could walk around so long with the pain.''

"I have things to do.''

"You'd better get them done, Mr. Eisenstadt. I'm sorry,'' Dr. Ashton said. He drew one hand over his forehead. He was tired, tired of death and the futility of life. This was one of the days when he wondered why he had become a doctor.

"You don't have more than a few weeks to live—perhaps four or five if you take care of yourself,'' he went on. His sad eyes met those of the older man. "You should remain in hospital for the time being.''

"How soon can I walk? I'm not staying, Doctor. Sorry.'' Grushenko could feel the panic rise within him. He needed to be alone to absorb the news.

"We'll aim for Saturday to practice with a walker.''

"Saturday,'' the old Russian said as he thought about the job he had to do. He couldn't stand the waiting. "Forget the other—the cancer. When can I walk, get out of here?''

"We'll see. Perhaps ten days. But your bones are old. That slight fracture could become more serious with any strain on it.''

Dr. Ashton backed out of the room, his expression bleak. He was looking at a dead man and counted the loss in his own plus and minus columns. The net result was moving toward zero as drugs and unemployment ravaged Liverpool. He'd have had a happier life as a plumber.

Grushenko lay in deep thought for a few minutes. Then he reached for the phone and asked for the Savoy Hotel in London.

Alden was not in his suite. Grushenko felt frustrated, blocked. He waited for nightfall. Carefully easing himself out of bed, he started toward the closet where his clothes hung. Just two feet from the closet door, he felt a stabbing pain shoot up his leg, and then it buckled under him and he fell to the floor.

He could not stifle the scream of pain.

A nurse ran in from the corridor. "Now just where do you think you're going? To the films?"

The next morning, Dr. Ashton looked grim. "You've really done it, old boy. It'll be at least another two weeks now." He was thoughtful for a moment. "What made you get out of bed? Isn't it comfortable enough?"

Grushenko did not answer. He was thinking of the futility of his life, of the loss of his son, of the bastard Raven walking the face of the earth while he was being ravaged by cancer.

The tables would turn. He would kill the Raven if it took the last ounce of his strength.

The Raven arrived in London on Thursday evening with a reservation at the London Hilton. He liked the hotel. More Americans put up there and more international operators, wheeler-dealers. It was his element.

He had ordered a bottle of Armagnac and as soon as he was in his suite, he opened it and poured. His hands were trembling.

The Raven was nervous, and did not know why. Was it because Operation Coronet was the most ambitious project of his career to date? Or was it because he feared something would go wrong? That the IRA men would not show up on Friday night?

He sipped from his glass of Armagnac again, and his lips curled in disgust. It wasn't fear; it was his distrust of the IRA. He had worked with them before and found they were all talk. They had kissed the Blarney Stone and were full of high speech and no action, most of them, and the group he was working with now had not a brain among them.

He paced the room, then sat down again and lifted his drink. His hands were still trembling. He frowned. What was it?

Perhaps it was the dreams. The dreams shook him. Before, he had dreamed only of faces—faces of the people he had killed—and they did not bother him.

But lately he was having the old dream again, the one that went back to his childhood. His father chased him across a wide field. He was filled with fear, because his father was holding a hunting rifle and was screaming at him, cursing him. He ran as fast as he could, but his father was gaining on him, shooting at him. He was sobbing, "No, no, don't!" but his father would not give up the pursuit. I wish I were a bird, I wish I were a bird. His arms became wings, and he became a great black bird, soaring, rising into the sky, circling his father, who diminished in the field below. He was safe. But then his father also turned into a bird and rose into the sky to chase him again, still holding the rifle.

"You stinking crow!" his father shouted, and gripping the rifle in his talons, raised it to his beady eye and sighted along the barrel. "You stinking crow! I'll kill you!" he said, and began to squeeze the trigger. And the crow, the Raven, awoke screaming.

He was screaming now, inside his skull, and his grip on the glass of Armagnac was painful. His forehead was beaded with sweat, and his hands shook.

He sighed and drank from his glass, then filled it again. Goddamn! It was only a dream. Why did it upset him so?

Shit! Fuckshit!

He drained his Armagnac in one swallow, then rose from the chair, rubbing his hands. They were clammy.

Only one way to deal with this, he thought. Get a broad. He hadn't had a broad in weeks. Fuckshit, get a broad. Treat her nice. Take her to dinner and then fuck the hell out of her. He needed release.

Release!

He slipped on his jacket, adjusted his tie, ran a comb through his hair. Satisfied with his appearance, he smiled

at his reflection in the mirror and then slipped out the
door. He found a bar downstairs. It was jammed. He had
to stand for his first drink, but then a couple left and he
took a stool.

He did not have to wait long. His handsome looks drew
them like a magnet. The first to take the bait was blond,
full-chested, and tall. Pretty in an English way. He offered
her his seat.

She hesitated. "No," she said in a clipped English
voice. "You just got it. I saw you."

He flashed his handsome smile. "Go ahead. I was lying
in bed all day anyway."

She sat and asked, "American?"

"Yeah."

Her name was Nan and she came from Essex. He gave
his name as Charles Morley. He had registered at the hotel
under that alias and he had the credit cards and driver's
license to go with it. A chameleon.

After some small talk, he found out she was not expecting to meet anybody and was free for dinner.

"Where shall we go?" he asked.

"Do you like French cooking?"

"Real French cooking? Yes."

"Le Gavroche," she said. "Just around the corner from
the American Embassy."

"Let's go," the Raven said.

When they were seated at a table in Le Gavroche, he let
his eyes scan the menu. This is going to be expensive, he
thought. At least one hundred and fifty dollars for two
with wine. But she was not the ordinary tart, and later she
would prove it. If you wanted the best, you had to pay a
high price.

He lowered the menu and looked into her eyes and
smiled. He was already beginning to feel relaxed, had
found the release he sorely needed.

While the girl and the Raven were enjoying Le Gavroche,
Alden, Allegro, and Harry Zimmerman were dining at the
Savoy Grill.

Harry chain-smoked and listened with a concerned expression on his face as Alden and Allegro outlined their

trip to Liverpool on the *American Brandy,* the loading of the lorry with plastic explosives and rifles, and the experience on the back road.

When they had finished, Harry inhaled deeply on his cigarette, mashed out the butt in an ashtray, and let an angry stream of smoke issue from his nostrils.

He glared at them both. "Do you know what you are?" Receiving only stares, he went on, "A couple of goddamn fools, if you ask me. You might've both been killed."

"Don't count me in on that," Allegro said. "I tried to talk him out of it back in New York."

"I know," Zimmerman said softly. Then his hard gaze shifted back to Alden. "Tell me, Phil, just who and what you are. Have you *found* yourself yet?"

Alden was furious. His own eyes met Harry's with defiance. "You tell me, Harry. What and who do you think I am?"

"All right! You're a writer, and a goddamned good one," Zimmerman said. "But writers deal in fantasy, the unreal."

"I never denied that!" Alden said angrily.

"You're denying it now!" Zimmerman said. "You've been acting out a part, and you're not the author, so you don't know how it's going to turn out. You're no spy! Stick to what you know!"

"I know how Kate died!" Alden said. "I saw it! And I saw others die, too! I loved Kate! Don't you understand? I loved her!"

Zimmerman lit another cigarette, inhaled slowly, and let the smoke drift from his nostrils. His voice was subdued. "Then why did the two of you fight all the time?" he asked. "I was there the night she threw the candelabrum at you and you took a swing at her, remember?"

Alden lowered his eyes. The fire had gone out.

"Is that a marriage?" Zimmerman asked. "To love and to cherish? In sickness and in health? Is that what you and Kate had?"

Alden said nothing.

"Maybe you did love her," Zimmerman went on. "And maybe she loved you. I don't know. All I know is you weren't meant for each other. As friends, maybe. As marriage partners, definitely no.''

Silence descended on the table.

''You're the last romantic, Phil, remembering the good things and not the bad, acting out a part you have no training for.'' He paused. ''I suggest you get back to the Coast. Finish the script. Warren has patience, but he can't wait forever.''

''Yeah,'' Alden said. ''Just a couple of more weeks. I want to visit Alicia in Chamonix.''

''Sure. Okay,'' Zimmerman said.

Alden raised his eyes and looked at Harry. ''Still friends?''

Zimmerman smiled slowly. ''Didn't I get two extra tickets for VIP seats at Trooping the Colour?''

Alden laughed. ''You did?''

''Sure. And it wasn't easy.''

''You're a hustler, Harry.''

''That's why I'm an agent.'' He smiled.

Allegro breathed a sigh of relief. ''Well, now that's over, shall we order? I'm starved. I think I could eat a horse.''

''How would you like it done?'' Alden asked, beckoning for a waiter.

Later, lying in bed, side by side, staring at the ceiling, smoking, satisfied with their lovemaking, Allegro said, ''You never told me much about your marriages.''

''Nothing much to tell,'' Alden said.

''Not according to Harry. Did Kate actually throw a candelabrum at you? And did you take a swing at her?''

Alden was reflective. ''Many times. The marriage was a Pier Six brawl most of the time. Harry was right. We weren't meant for each other. But there was *something*. A mutual respect, a deep understanding of theater. But it didn't work out—couldn't, I guess.''

''Did she have any extramarital affairs?''

''Many.''

''Did you?''

''Yes. And I was jealous, angry with Kate—all the time.''

Allegro was thoughtful for a moment. "It wasn't made in heaven, was it? Sounds more like purgatory."

After a pause, he said, "I wonder how Ernst is doing."

"Why do you worry about Ernst? He's in good hands." Her voice had an edge to it.

"I'm not worried, just curious."

"I've been wondering about him for a long time. Since Arizona. I don't trust him," she said, "and I don't think his name is Ernst, any more than I think yours is Alexander Hamilton."

"I agree with you."

"But—"

"I began to suspect him when he conveniently paid our passage on the *American Brandy*," Alden said. "He seemed too eager. And where did he get thirty-six hundred dollars in cash?"

"I don't know."

"And I don't think he's Interpol either," Alden went on. "That's why I took his gun when we had the car wreck. Before the police found it. Couldn't find the one you had."

"You have his gun?"

"In a box. In the trunk of the new car."

"Philip Alden, you amaze me."

"He's a nice old man." He drew in smoke, exhaled. "I wonder who he really is. And whether he can lead us to the Raven."

Allegro put her arms about him, pulled him closer. Her face was in his neck and shoulder, and her tears slid down his naked torso. He could feel her trembling with the sobs.

He gripped her hands. "I'm not going to forget the Raven," he said softly. "I'll not be as obsessed, but I'll not forget him. I promise."

Her arms tightened around him. "I can live with that. If we find him, fine. If not, we forget—not forgive and forget, just forget." She squeezed him to her breast. "I'd hate to lose you," she said.

CHAPTER 26

By Friday, Grushenko was becoming slightly paranoid. He had called Alden at the Savoy any number of times, leaving his name, "Ernst Eisenstadt." None of the calls had been returned. He was also feeling claustrophobic, cooped up in the Liverpool hospital room. The news of his illness had shocked him more than he'd admit to anyone. He needed to get on with the kill, to talk to someone outside the medical staff.

Reluctantly he reached for the phone again and asked for the Savoy Hotel in London. After a long wait, the phone was picked up in Alden's room.

"Hello?"

"Philip?"

"Yes."

Grushenko forced elation to his voice, though he did not feel it. "Ernst Eisenstadt, Philip. At last I find you in."

"How are you, Ernst?"

Grushenko could sense the wariness in Alden's tone.

"Coming along," he said. "But I won't be out as soon as expected. I had a little accident." Grushenko forced a chuckle. "But nothing serious. I tried to walk too soon." He tried to sound hurt. "Why haven't you returned my calls?"

Alden was evasive. "To tell you the truth, Ernst, Allegro and I have been out of London most of the time. Touring the countryside, you know."

Grushenko let it slide by. He said, "Tell me. What

272

do you hear of our *mutual friend*? You know who I mean."

After a long pause, Alden said, "I hear nothing. The lorry was found abandoned in Shrewsbury. Everything missing." Alden's voice was firm. "I've lost the trail. I'm going to visit my daughter in Chamonix, and then return to the States and pick up my work."

Grushenko did not acknowledge what Alden had said, but only clutched the phone more tightly. "Philip, I lost a valuable item in the crash. You have kept it for me?"

"Yes. When you get out, come to the Savoy and I'll return it to you. If we're gone by then, I'll leave it at the desk, or in the vault. It's in a cardboard box."

After a long pause at both ends of the line, Grushenko said, "Good luck, Philip."

"Good luck to you, Ernst."

That evening the Raven was in a foul mood. The English girl had not put out the night before. Over coffee and dessert, she had smiled at him and excused herself for the ladies' room. He had smiled back and, while waiting for her return, had felt the familiar hardening in his groin, the tingling. After thirty minutes, the tingling had disappeared, replaced by a furious anger.

She had had no intention of coming back, but had walked out another exit, thwarting his designs, frustrating him.

Bitch! When he had bedded down afterward, alone, he did not have the nightmare, but only his usual dreams, the faces. And her face was foremost.

That evening he went back to the bar, but she was not there nor did he really expect she would be. She probably played her game at every bar and pub in London.

He had to smile at her ploy. After all, a girl has to eat. And she had taste.

He ordered a drink. Seconds later, a young woman took the stool next to him. She was attractive, well built. But beyond his handsome winning smile, he had no time for her. Not now. It was Friday, and he must meet with the four IRA men.

The Raven played chameleon again that night. He left

the Hilton dressed to the nines, but in the car he had a suitcase with a change of clothing. He stopped along the road and changed and when he appeared at the broken-down working man's pub on Lovat's Lane, he was wearing jeans, rough-worn shoes, and a sweater.

They were all there, waiting for him: O'Rourke, Corrigan, Tyrone, and the young man from the Aran Isles, still wearing the sweater the Raven envied.

A churlish smile spread on the Raven's lips. "I see we have the luck of the Irish with us tonight."

"What's the matter?" asked O'Rourke. "Didn't you think we would show?"

"Never entered my mind," the Raven answered. He left them, walked to the bar, ordered a pint of bitters, and returned, looking around the group. "It's tomorrow I'm thinking about."

Liam Flaherty's chest swelled and a frown creased his brow. "You take us all for cowards, do you? Well, we're not! I'm willing to give my life for Ireland, and the others, too! Am I right, boys?"

The others nodded, a look of contempt on their features as they glared at the Raven.

"You have our word," Tyrone said. "And where I come from, that word is a promise. A promise broken shames a man."

The others nodded agreement.

The Raven knew when to stop. These men were his tools. And not a brain among them. He cleared his throat, forcing back a smile of victory. He said, "The C4 is in a warehouse nearby. We'll pick it up after we've finished here." He looked at them, but no change of expression showed on their features. They only stared.

"Now, here's the thing," he said. "The Trooping of the Colour is at about eleven A.M. The—"

"Trooping the Colour," Tyrone corrected him. "It has no 'of' in it."

"All right. Trooping the Colour," he said. "Scheduled for eleven A.M. But the Mall will be mobbed hours before. I want you to strap on the explosives early in the morning and be in the vicinity of the Mall by seven, eight at the latest. If you see people lining up at the intersection of

Marlborough Road, get in front. I want you there early.
Got it?''

They shuffled uneasily. Tyrone stared down into his
beer. Flaherty was reflective. O'Rourke scowled. Even the
ever cheerful Corrigan wore a blank expression.

The Raven raised his glass. ''Well, here's to the luck of
the Irish. And the IRA.'' He smiled.

They raised their glasses and turned their faces to him
with set, tightened lips. Nobody returned his smile.

They would all be dead in the morning.

Grushenko hardly slept at all that night. He lay in his
bed, eyes open, staring at the dim outlines of the ceiling,
softly lit by the lights from the corridor.

A tear dripped from one eye. Here he was, a Hero of the
Soviet Union, dying, powerless, unable to move, made
impotent from a stupid accident—and his own foolish
years of neglect.

And he had lost a friend, had been abandoned. It was
his job alone now to find the Raven. And all clues to his
whereabouts had vanished. But he, Vladislav Grushenko,
Hero of the Soviet Union, would find the Raven. It would
be, he knew, the final covert operation of his career.

His shortened future haunted him. If he had time, he
would resign from the KGB, retire to his dacha, fifty
miles outside of Moscow, and await death. He would try
to help his son, that misguided fool.

The boy was a fool, but he was flesh of his own flesh,
seed of his own seed. Another tear formed at the corner of
Grushenko's left eye. He closed his eyes and a shudder ran
through his body.

Then he slept.

Saturday morning dawned dreary, drizzly, and foreboding. The Raven was on site at 6:00 A.M., walking the Mall,
prowling St. James's Park. Even at that hour, tourists fed
the ducks, Londoners read their morning papers on benches,
men and women in colored track suits jogged along the
dirt paths.

Flowers bloomed in profusion in well-kept beds, their
fragrance brightening the early morning hours, but the

Raven was unaffected, was like a stalking tiger, his Nikon camera slung about his neck, the scent of prey strong in his nostrils, his adrenaline running like a riptide. Small groups of people had begun to assemble from Buckingham Palace to Admiralty Arch.

The Raven could not resist the temptation of raising the Nikon to his eye and sighting through the lens to Marlborough Road. His pulse quickened, his impulse toward destruction rose, his sense of power became pervasive.

In a few hours, he would kill the queen of England . . . destroy the monarchical symbol of authority the people of England so lovingly respected . . . defy the world.

He would be famous, he thought, and smiled. Or infamous.

He giggled. Two joints of pot had already saturated his brain. An hour passed in wandering and watching. As he stood on a knoll looking out over the Mall, the camera to his eye, a hand suddenly reached, gripped him by the shoulder. A bright, surprised voice cried, "Nicky! For Christ's sake, Nicky Alden!"

Nicky Alden, the Raven, turned to stare into the smiling face of Harry Zimmerman, dressed in jogging clothes.

In turning, the Raven's finger inadvertently depressed the shutter release of the Nikon.

Early strollers in St. James's Park witnessed a strange and horrible occurrence. A young, handsome blue-eyed man, wearing a beautiful hand-knit sweater, exploded, body parts flying in all directions, his sweater becoming no more than blackened patches of charred wool.

Tyrone, walking south on Marlborough Road, burst into noise and flame just as he was passing St. James's Palace, blowing in a door on his right and shattering windows along the street.

O'Rourke and Corrigan were just locking the door to their cheap hotel room in Soho when they heard the explosions and retreated inside to pull off the webbing and the C4. They removed the servomechanisms that would explode the plastique and stood looking at each other, stunned.

Operation Coronet was finished before it started, its perpetrators the only victims.

*   *   *

Zimmerman looked at Nicky Alden in puzzlement. The simultaneous explosions had shattered the early morning quietness.

"What was that?" he asked.

The Raven shrugged. "Probably some dynamiting at a construction site. Come on, let's walk."

They were near an exit from St. James's Park, facing away from the area where Liam Flaherty had been blown to bits. They did not see the people running to the site of the catastrophe.

The Raven was shaking, appalled. This Zimmerman, this smiling, friendly face, this *asshole*, this *idiot*, had totally annihilated the greatest plan, the most incredible act of his life.

He despised the man.

He seethed, but he smiled.

"Your father's in London," Zimmerman said, a frown clouding his face. For he knew of the acrimony between Alden and his son.

"He is? No shit!" the Raven replied.

"Yes, at the Savoy."

"Where are you staying."

"Claridges."

"Well, for Christ's sake," the Raven said. "I've never been to that stuffy old hole. What say we go there? Have a drink, and I'll call the old man and surprise him?"

"A deal," Zimmerman said.

They crossed the Mall, entered the Queen's Walk, heading toward Piccadilly. When they turned into Berkeley Street, sirens sounded behind them.

"That must have been quite a blast," Zimmerman said.

The Raven nodded in agreement. "Where is Claridges?"

"Just up the road. We skirt Berkeley Square, find Davies Street, and it's just a few blocks up."

"You jog every morning this early?"

"Yeah. Never miss it."

The Raven's fury peaked. Of all the goddamned fucking luck! A jogger, an asshole, fuckshit jogger had to ruin his operation.

The old asshole would pay.

When they reached his suite at Claridges, Zimmerman excused himself to take a shower. "These jogging clothes are sweaty."

"Go ahead," the Raven said, and sat in a chair.

Zimmerman was not long. Inside of twelve minutes he returned, dressed in an expensive suit, shoes, shirt, and tie.

The Raven grinned. "You look different."

"Savile Row," Zimmerman said. "You like it?"

"Yeah, I like it."

Zimmerman crossed to the bar, his back to the Raven. "I don't usually drink this time of the morning, but today's a special day. Trooping the Colour. You ever seen it?"

"No," the Raven said, festering inside. He could have seen it. He could have blown it sky-high. Except for this bastard, this asshole. Little did he know.

"What'll it be?" Zimmerman said, his back still to Nicky.

"What've you got?"

"The usual." Zimmerman peered at the bottles, then opened the cabinet below. "Scotch, malt whiskey, gin . . ."

"Armagnac?"

"No."

"How about Grand Marnier?"

"No, but I see some cognac. That okay?"

"Sure," the Raven said.

As Zimmerman poured the drinks, he said, "Look, Nicky, I know the situation between you and your father. I know how you feel about each other. But a time comes in life when fathers and sons must make peace, try to understand each other. Are you willing?" Harry was mopping at a pool of cognac that he had spilled.

"Sure. Anytime." Nicky reached into his blazer and felt the butt of the .22-caliber Ruger automatic.

"Then here's to peace between fathers and sons," Zimmerman said, turning. "And here's to Trooping the Colour."

He held aloft the two drinks, and then saw the pistol in Nicky's hand. A shocked expression crossed his features. "Nicky?" he said quietly.

A shot reverberated through the room and a small hole appeared in Zimmerman's forehead. It began to ooze blood. Another shot shook the silence as a bullet tore through the old man's heart.

The Raven, a handsome, wide grin on his face, sat in a thin cloud of smoke, permeated with the smell of cordite.

A look of puzzlement spread over Zimmerman's face as he slid silently to the floor, his back against the bar, the two drinks still clutched tightly in his hands. When he was in a sitting position, his fingers went loose, and the liquid spilled on the carpet.

The Raven sat for a moment, watching, then got up from the chair and approached the body.

He held the muzzle of the Ruger close to Zimmerman's right temple and squeezed the trigger.

Zimmerman's head jumped.

"Bastard!" the Raven said through clenched teeth. "*Asshole!*"

As he stepped across the body and walked toward the door, he was in a blind rage, but an insane, perverse thought made him stop.

Turning quickly, he walked to the bathroom and, taking a piece of dry soap, began to scrawl on the mirror. He decided to let the world know that he, the Raven, was responsible.

When he had finished scrawling, he looked with glee at what he had written, an insane look in his eyes. He giggled.

> *The Raven did this!*
> *And fuck you all!*

CHAPTER 27

The blast that killed the two IRA men echoed and re-echoed throughout St. James's Park and the surrounding area, but by the time it reached the Savoy Hotel, it was muffled and distant.

However, it awoke Allegro, curled into the curve of Philip's back, and she said sleepily, "What was that?"

"Huh? What was what?"

"Sounded like an explosion," she said.

"Probably a backfire," Alden said with a yawn. "Go to sleep, love. It's only seven and I left a call for eight."

"Hmmm," she murmured, and cuddled into him.

It seemed only seconds later that the phone jangled with the wake-up call. Alden checked the bedside travel alarm and mumbled his thanks.

They were showered and dressed within an hour, had a quick breakfast of toast and coffee in the suite. By 9:30, they were at the Savoy entrance, hailing a cab. They were to meet Harry Zimmerman at Horse Guards Parade at 10:00 A.M.

"Horse Guards Parade," Alden said to the cabbie, who nodded and tipped his cap.

They drove for a while in silence, until the cabbie said, "You a government man, sir?"

"No. Why do you ask?"

The driver shrugged. "I only have it by word of mouth, you might say, guv'ner. But I hear there's been an attempt on the queen's life and everything's been closed off. Only police and government men allowed in that area now. I could tell you were on your way to see Trooping the Colour. But I thought you would have heard by now."

A pained expression had come over Allegro's face. She was thinking of terrorism again and when it would stop, if ever.

Alden looked out the window. "Jesus!" he said, and his mind was full of the Raven.

"You say an 'attempt,' " Allegro said. "Then she's all right."

"Oh. Her Majesty's okay, as you Americans say. I could tell you were American soon as I picked you up. The bombs went before she and the prince'd left Buckingham Palace. Early in the morning, they say. But people were killed. IRA, they say, did it, or so they suspect. Ask me, I say take all them head-busters and line 'em up against a wall. That's what I'd do."

They had been driving south along The Victoria Embankment, and were now at Northumberland Avenue, where they turned right toward Trafalgar Square and Admiralty Arch.

The traffic was light, no surprise to Alden on this day. As they neared the Mall, neither he nor Allegro heard the usual cheering of the throngs. A sinister silenced filled the air.

When they reached Trafalgar Square, they saw the first barrier. A policeman wearing a rain poncho stepped out and held his hand up in a signal to stop. "Where are you headed, sir?"

Alden leaned forward. "Horse Guards. But I hear Trooping the Colour has been called off."

The policeman's expression never changed. "Yes, I'm afraid it's been cancelled, sir."

"Are the streets to Claridges clear?"

"I think so, sir."

"Thank you."

The cabbie looked back. "Claridges?"

Alden nodded.

The cabbie nodded back, gunned the engine, and headed toward Regent Street, where they made a right. At Hanover, he turned left, and within a few more blocks they were in front of the entrance of Claridges, thronged with limousines, Rolls-Royces, Aston-Martins, and expensive foreign cars.

Alden paid the driver, who smiled at the large tip. "Too bad about Trooping the Colour being cancelled, sir. Seen it myself many times from beside the Mall. Colorful, it is, right colorful. Well, that's the way it goes, I guess. Have a good time in London, guv." And he drove off.

Alden and Allegro entered the lobby, which was half full of people speaking in hushed whispers. Every once in a while they would pick up a phrase: "The second attempt against the queen." "Glad the prince wasn't killed. He's so handsome!" "IRA buggers. Oughta be drawn and quartered." "The UK should get out of Ireland entirely."

Alden headed for the house phones. He asked for Mr. Zimmerman's suite. He let it ring ten times, then hung up.

"He's not in," Alden said when he returned to Allegro. He took the chair beside her, placed a cigarette between his lips, flicked his Dunhill lighter.

"Maybe he started for Horse Guards and met the same situation we did. Maybe he's walking back."

"Maybe," Alden said. "We'll wait."

They waited for almost an hour, keeping their eyes on the entrance, Alden now and then getting up to try Harry's suite again, then going to the public phones to call the Savoy and ask if a Mr. Zimmerman had left any messages. Nothing.

Each time he returned, the lines of concern, of worry, deepened on his face.

While they waited, Allegro looked around the lobby of Claridges, at the grand sweeping central staircase, at the wrought-iron balconies, at the people—hushed people who seemed to speak in whispers.

Alden stood up abruptly.

"Phones again?" Allegro queried.

"No. I'm going to see the manager."

"Why?"

He stopped his forward motion and turned to her. "Harry's had two coronaries already. Maybe he's up there and . . ." He left the remark unfinished and walked off.

In the manager's office, it took Alden but a few minutes to explain his relationship to Harry.

The manager smiled. "We've known Mr. Zimmerman for years. Always a gentleman."

After Alden had finished describing the circumstances that had brought him to Claridges and Zimmerman's history of heart condition problems, the manager, his face serious, sat a moment with steepled forefingers before his lips, then rose from his desk. "We'll look into this, Mr. Alden." He held the door to his office open for Alden.

Allegro was standing just outside. Alden introduced her as his wife, and the manager mumbled something like "Mrs. Alden" and smiled.

In the elevator, on the way to Zimmerman's suite, the manager stared at the ceiling, then suddenly shifted his gaze to Alden. "You know why Trooping the Colour was called off?"

"We heard—but not the details."

"An attempt on the queen's life," the manager said. "Went off prematurely. Two men wearing plastique beneath their clothes were blown to bits. Others are dead or injured."

"Did you say plastique?" Alden asked in a strained voice.

"Yes. Why do you ask? Do you have experience with plastique?"

Alden did not answer.

But Allegro read his thoughts. He was back in Arizona. With Kate. And the Raven. She shuddered. Please. Please, God!

"If Mr. Zimmerman were in the vicinity he might be among the injured. Have you called any of the hospitals?"

Alden shook his head. "No."

The elevator had stopped. They headed for the suite.

"Perhaps that should be your next step, Mr. Alden," the manager said.

But when the door swung open, Alden saw Harry at once.

"Call a doctor!" Alden said as he stepped into the room.

The manager picked up the phone and spoke crisply into the mouthpiece.

Alden knelt beside Harry. He noticed the small hole in Harry's forehead, the one in his temple, found a third in his chest. Blood stained Harry's lips and clothes.

"Never mind the doctor," Alden said. His voice was thick, croaking. "Call the police."

Allegro and the manager stared at the blood on Alden's hands. The manager picked up the phone again slowly.

Alden looked down at Zimmerman's body. "Harry!" he sobbed. "Harry, for Christ's sake! What the hell happened? Jesus!"

Allegro had seen death scores of times, but she was profoundly affected every time. Death could not be shrugged off, even by hardened reporters. She rushed to the bathroom, splashed her face with cold water. When she was finished, she raised her head to the mirror.

Oh, my God, she thought. Oh, my God, no!

In his suite at the London Hilton, the Raven lay on his bed in a fevered sweat. He was shaking. He had had breakfast after Zimmerman's murder, and a few minutes later had run for the bathroom and vomited.

His fever was 101. But he could not fathom whether it was his body or his soul that was sick.

That clown! That fucking clown Harry Zimmerman! He had spoiled the greatest adventure of his career!

Nicky! For Christ's sake, Nicky Alden! The smiling prick! Asshole!

Your father's in London.

He is? No shit!

Yes, at the Savoy.

Just that near. He thought he was going to retch again, but he quelled it. He was burning up, his handsome face contorted into a grotesque mask, eyes hollow and sunken.

He had to get away. Far away. They were looking for him anyway. Although they had no photograph of him, they knew his *modus operandi*.

To the mountains, the high, clear mountains. The Alps, maybe. Yes, the Alps. London was stifling and he knew they were already looking for him.

He dressed hurriedly. But he needed money, a lot of money.

Trask. Trask had never let him down. He would phone him today, Saturday, at the private number in his apartment. He'd be in. Weekends off.

As he was knotting his tie, he thought, the Savoy. Father. He felt as if he was going to heave again, but controlled it, concentrating on his half Windsor.

He had to change hotels. They knew his habits—the Metropolitan Police, Scotland Yard, Special Branch, MI6, and the rest. They knew he enjoyed the best, knew his taste for the good things in life.

He would find a cheap hotel, somewhere on the other side of the Thames, maybe even Soho, to hole up and call Trask later. It was five hours earlier in New York.

He would go to Paris. Anyplace to be far away from the scene of the crime—and from his father.

He must get away from him, to the ends of the earth if need be. But he must go.

He shuddered at the thought of his father. The image, the remembrance of his father filled him with a terrible awe, a sense of impending doom.

He packed his bags hastily, slung the Nikon over his shoulder, and checked out of the Hilton.

At the Eros Hotel on Shaftesbury Avenue, O'Rourke sat in a chair near the window, watching the street, idly picking at curls of loose wallpaper with bloodied fingernails.

The C4 was nowhere in evidence in the nondescript room. It had been dumped in dust bins behind a restaurant on Curzon Street.

Corrigan lay on the bed, a cigar sending a curl of smoke to the stained ceiling.

"What in hell do you suppose happened to John and young Liam?" he asked as much to himself as O'Rourke.

"Dead," O'Rourke said, smashing a fist against the flowered wallpaper. "That bloody Raven sits back and pushes buttons and the likes of us die. Our mates just died for nothing."

"Do you know where he stashed the arms he was supposed to ship for us?" Corrigan asked.

"No. I traveled on that bloody tramp from New York to Liverpool with those fuckin' crates, and that bloody Raven's blown the whole deal for us." He stopped picking at the wallpaper to pick at a pimple on his nose. "I'd bet a hundred quid he never sent them to our people."

"We should blow the bloody Raven. Somebody should," Corrigan said. "What the hell do we tell Liam's mum, eh? That he was blown to bits for nothing? I say we blow the bloody Raven. He's a bloody menace."

"How do we find the bastard?"

"Trask. He'd know where the bastard is."

"What do we use for money?"

"Ask Trask for an advance," Corrigan offered. "Hell, he's getting bloody rich while we bloody die for the cause."

"I know him best. I'll call. What the hell time is it in New York?"

CHAPTER 28

The inspector from Scotland Yard was tall, thin, and balding. His smile was warm and patient. He sat in a chair. The other man from Special Branch, named Grey, was as tall, but heftier, broad, all bulging muscle. He was leaning casually against the bar.

They were in Harry Zimmerman's suite. The body had been removed and the forensic team had finished.

"As I understand it, Mr. Alden," the Scotland Yard man said, "you were one of Mr. Zimmerman's clients. Had known each other for thirty years. You were both in London at the same time, and were to meet at Horse Guards. When he didn't arrive, you came back here."

Alden raised his head. "Of course. Horse Guards was closed off."

The inspector nodded.

"How long had you known Zimmerman?" Grey asked, looking at Allegro, his voice husky.

"Not long," she answered. "Only since Kate Kavanaugh's funeral."

"Kate Kavanaugh was your ex-wife," the inspector said.

"Yes," Alden said. "She was killed on the Southwest Limited."

"The Raven's work," Grey said.

"Yes," Alden said angrily. "And *this* was the Raven's work!" He popped a cigarette from his pack, lit it with a shaking hand. "But why?" he asked. "Kate was one of a

287

hundred or more passengers on that train. Why Harry? What's the connection?''

Grey examined his fingernails. Then said, ''Maybe they knew each other.''

''You're implying that Harry Zimmerman was part of the Raven's organization?''

''Let me tell you something, Mr. Alden,'' Grey said. ''We know you're after the Raven. We know about your little accident outside Liverpool. Let me give you a bit of advice. Don't put your nose in this. Leave it to us professionals to track down the Raven. Otherwise, your nose may be blown off!''

''Professionals!'' Alden's voice was bitter. ''The Raven's been operating for years now. All over the world. And what have you done? What have you so-called professionals accomplished? You don't even know what he looks like!'' He dragged on his cigarette fiercely.

''Which reminds me,'' the inspector said to Allegro. ''Miss Stern knows what he looks like. She photographed him.''

''But the negatives were destroyed,'' Allegro said.

''Don't talk to me about pictures,'' Alden said. ''You and every police department and antiterrorism group in the world have had a photograph of Carlos for years now. And he still runs free.''

Neither the inspector nor the man from Special Branch had an answer for that.

The inspector rose from his chair. ''If I were you, Mr. Alden,'' he said, ''I'd take Grey's advice. Keep your nose out of this.''

''After Kate? After Harry?''

''You're an amateur, Mr. Alden. You've read too many spy stories. Mark my words, Mr. Alden, you're no match for the Raven. If you do find him, you're a dead man.''

Walter Trask was watching the midday news, a disgruntled look on his face, a scotch sour in his hand. The cocky bastard sure screwed that one up, he thought.

The images on the TV screen flashed by, the devastation of St. James's Palace, the carnage in St. James's Park, the bodies, the blood. And the queen not among them.

The announcer babbled on: ". . . prematurely, about two hours before the queen and her entourage were to leave Buckingham Palace on a route up the Mall to Horse Guards Parade. It is believed to be the work of the Raven, in association with the IRA, whose bodies, wrapped in plastic explosive, went off like bombs early in the morning. The Raven is thought to be responsible for the blowing up of the Southwest Limited here in the United States in May, in the name of ARM, the American Revolutionary Mobilization."

That idiot, Trask thought. Squeezed the trigger before the target was in sight.

"But that was not the entire extent of the Raven's operations in London this day. We take you now to Herb Andrews at Claridges Hotel in London."

The scene changed. A trench-coated reporter holding a microphone was standing before the entrance to Claridges.

"This is Herb Andrews. In London's most distinguished hotel, host for royalty, heads of state, and people of affluence, an American was murdered early this morning. Harry Zimmerman, Hollywood agent for many well-known writers, was shot down in his suite . . ."

Trask leaned forward swiftly. His body stiffened and he spilled part of his drink on the carpet. Harry Zimmerman! Goddammit, he thought. His father's agent! If they ever ran the Raven to ground, Trask's whole network would be put in jeopardy! Idiot! Fuckup!

". . . and he left a note, written in soap on the bathroom mirror announcing, 'The Raven did this.' There was more, but it is too scabrous to repeat on the air . . ."

Trask turned off the set in a frenzy, mixed another scotch sour, and began to pace the room.

He'd have to find him. But where was he? London? No. He'd probably flown the country by now. He could be anyplace.

As if in answer to a prayer came the soft ring of the telephone from where he kept it in a night-table drawer, his unlisted, bug-free telephone.

He opened the drawer and lifted the receiver carefully, his heart thumping. "Hello?"

"It's me, man."

He recognized the voice immediately. "Where are you?"

"In a phone booth in Soho."

Trask could here the traffic outside. He nodded into the phone. "Okay. Keep going."

"I tried you four times today, but the trunks were tied up."

Trask smirked. "Why wouldn't they be? All I can say is you certainly botched that one."

"It was an accident. A freak accident out of a clear blue sky. I never expected it."

"I'll bet."

"But I've got a few other things lined up. Three scenarios that'll stand the audience's hair on end. All on the same day. Even you'll like it. I'm telling you, man, it'll turn the world upside down."

"Scenarios?" Trask was puzzled.

"Films, man, films. But it'll take a lot of money. A lot of money." The Raven was talking fast. "I'm going to Paris. You come over. I'll be staying at the Paris Hilton. I'm telling you, man, what I'll have to say will blow your mind!"

Trask could sense the frenzy in the Raven's voice. "Okay," he said. "I'll be over the first flight I can get. Sounds interesting."

"The Paris Hilton. I'll be registered under the name of R. Butcher."

Apt, Trask thought.

Phones were hung up on either end. Trask sat on the edge of the bed for a long time, thinking. He was beginning to worry about Nicky Alden. He had sounded as though he were going crazy.

If he was, he would have to be eliminated. And Trask had to keep his hands clean. Get someone else to do it.

In the cab, on the way back to the Savoy, they had been silent, Allegro introspective, Alden with his hands clutched, head down, a puzzled frown between his eyes. In the suite, the silence continued, Alden sitting stock-still in a chair, staring at some point in space others could not see, Allegro curled up in a loveseat, her face buried in a magazine that she was not reading.

Finally, she broke the silence. "Do you want something to eat?"

"No. I'm not hungry."

"You've got to eat."

"I know. Fuel and all that. But I'm not hungry."

Allegro understood. She herself was not hungry. Who could be under the circumstances? But she persisted. "We could go down to the Grill. Or order something light up here."

"No. I'm not hungry, darling. I couldn't eat a thing, believe me. But thanks."

The silence continued, until Alden broke it by saying with a bitter chuckle, "Where shall we bury him? In Westminster Abbey? A lot of kings and poets are buried there." A sob came to his voice, an uncontrollable shaking in his vocal cords. "And he was a king—and a poet."

He stood up and began to pace restlessly. "I'm going for a walk, love. Do you mind? I have to think."

"No," she said. "I don't mind." She understood his need for solitude.

He bent, kissed her lightly, and left the suite.

Don't get drunk, she thought. Don't get drunk, Philip.

She waited for over an hour, her mind filled with images. Philip. The Arizona desert where she had first seen his shoe, his trouser leg, then his face. New York following the catastrophe. The places they visited, the restaurants they had eaten in, their long walks through Central Park, their times in bed—they were all priceless.

Harry. The first time she had met him at Kate's funeral, she had recognized the bond, the deep, indestructible friendship between him and Philip. The second time she had met him, at dinner in the Grill. And the third and last time she had seen him. She shuddered.

Alden entered the suite.

He had not gone out to get drunk, thank God, but he had a look of determination on his face. He carried a cardboard box.

"What's that?" She smiled. "A present?"

He proceeded to open the box. "Ernst's gun," he said without inflection in his voice. "I'm going after the Raven."

She was aware of the affirmative, the imperative tone in his voice. She rose from the loveseat, crept up behind him.

She watched him take the Smith & Wesson apart, barrel, cylinder, butt, trigger guard. She placed her hands on his shoulders. "You don't know where he is."

"I'll find him. And shoot him." He stopped cleaning the revolver and turned to her. "You stay here. Out of the way. I don't want you involved in this."

"I'm already involved," Allegro said softly.

"I don't want you killed."

"I don't want to die, and I don't want you to die, Philip. But if worst comes to worst, if our numbers are up, I want to die with you, Philip, by your side. The world means nothing without you."

A hesitation, then he pulled her to him, burying his face in her hair. "Allegro!"

She drew her fingers through his hair, gently, caressingly.

"I can't talk you out of it?"

"No, love," Allegro said. "No."

"You make me feel like an idiot."

"No, you're not an idiot. You've got a reason, a commitment. The others—they're only professionals. I'm on your side now, Philip."

They remained in that position for a long time. His hands found her buttocks, began to smoothly caress. She shivered.

She pushed him away against her will. "Later, love. Later."

He looked at her with an impish smile. "Why later? I'd say now's the time."

"No. We've got to find the Raven first. And I think I know where to look."

He became serious again. "Where? Here in London?"

"I don't think so. They're probably right—he's skipped by now. But I have connections among the terrorist underground. Right here in London. But it will cost."

"How much?"

"Five hundred should do."

Alden rose from the chair quickly, dug into his blazer pocket for his wallet, gave her the equivalent of five hundred dollars in British notes. "'Where do we meet these people?''

"Person, not people. And not we, me. He knows me. You he might be suspicious of.''

"Where?''

"I'll find him.'' She went into the bedroom. He sat at the desk again, warily looking at the pieces of the Smith & Wesson. Five bullets. That's all he had. He would have to make them count.

Then his thoughts turned to Allegro. Beautiful, lovable Allegro. She was with him, for better or for worse. But he was ambivalent about it. He did not want to see her killed. Moisture came to his eyes.

Allegro returned from the bedroom dressed in Wallabys, tattered jeans, her safari jacket and dark glasses, huge dark glasses. Her hair was tied in a pigtail.

"You look beautiful,'' he said.

"Where I'm going, this is the look.''

"Where? I wish you'd tell me.''

"None of your business,'' she said. "Anyway, there's no danger.''

"Still, I'll worry.''

"Not to worry. I mean it.'' And she left the suite, the five hundred tucked in a wallet in the upper left-hand pocket of the jacket.

The Raven had checked out of the hotel in Soho, and now, feeling the need of a long walk to limber himself up and to think, he turned into Charing Cross Road in the direction of the Strand, then north toward Waterloo Bridge. He carried his two light bags and the Nikon slung from his neck. In his pocket was a small brown paper sack. Reaching the bridge, he turned into it and crossed to the center, where he rested his elbows on the rail and looked down into the River Thames.

Glancing carefully in all directions, he decided he was not under surveillance and, taking the brown paper sack from his pocket, held it over the side of the bridge and let it drop. He watched it disappear beneath the rolling waters.

It contained the .22-caliber Ruger pistol he'd used to kill Harry Zimmerman.

The Raven could always pick up another gun in Paris. He had already booked a flight and a room at the Paris Hilton. He waited a few seconds, then walked to the end of the bridge and hailed a cab for Heathrow Airport.

Dr. Ashton smiled down at Vladislav Grushenko. "Expect you'll be a free man by Wednesday."

Grushenko glared moodily at him.

"Wednesday, Thursday at the latest," Ashton said. "If things continue to improve as they have. You're a tough old boy," and he gave Grushenko an encouraging nudge on the shoulder before he backed out of the room, smiling.

Grushenko glared at the closed door. Butcher, he thought. But in the back of his mind, he knew it had been his own fault.

Sarafian. He'd had a first name but that had been long ago.

He was inordinately fat, loved good food and women, good times. He was cheerful to the point of a twinkle in his eye. He was also shrewd. He had come from Armenia fifty years ago, when he was six. He had been a member of an international terrorist group, but had given it up seven years ago, because he felt he could make much more money by setting up his own network—a network of informers, spies, spying upon spies and terrorists.

He was gorging in a Persian restaurant when Allegro approached his table. He smiled up at her with his large teeth. "Sit down."

Allegro sat.

"What brings you here, my headstrong beauty?" Sarafian asked.

"Business."

"What kind of business?" he asked, and without breaking his sentence, he said, "Dolma?" and offered her a piece on the end of a fork.

Allegro shook her head.

"Shish kebab?"

She shook her head again.

"What's this business you came here to see me about?"

"I want to know where the Raven is."

A low chuckle issued from the fat belly. "Why ask me?"

"Don't kid me, Sarafian. You know everything."

"I know nothing," he said, mouthing another dolma.

"You just don't remember."

"I have a good memory," he said, chewing.

Allegro unbuttoned her pocket and extracted her wallet. From it she took half of what Alden had given her—two hundred and fifty dollars. "Maybe this will jog it," she said.

Sarafian looked at the money on the table and then at her wallet, where he saw more. He went on eating, nodding. "It jogs it. But not at any great speed. Sure you won't have a dolma? They're delicious."

Allegro sighed with a hint of disgust and took the remainder of the bills from her wallet. "You drive a hard bargain, Sarafian. That's all I have."

"Who tried to drive the hard bargain?" he said. "You knew what you had. Why didn't you let it all hang out?"

"Where's the Raven?"

"Like you, he came to me for information. Where's Wollman of Baader-Meinhof? Where's Spinelli of the Red Brigades, Villefranche of the French underground?"

"Why?"

Sarafian shrugged. "Says he's mounting a new venture. You know the Raven. He's conceited. One plan goes wrong, he tries another. Truthfully, I think he's mad. He doesn't look well. Said he was thinking of taking a vacation in the French Alps to think things through." He laughed. "He needs it."

"Did you tell him where these people are?" Allegro asked.

Sarafian nodded. "He paid."

"Then he may be anyplace: France, Italy, Germany."

Sarafian picked at a salad of cucumber and yogurt. "Try Paris first," he said in a low voice. "He said he was to meet a man there. A very important man who owed him money."

Allegro hesitated. "Sarafian, is this a bum steer?"

"Bum steer?" He looked at her, surprised, and a loud laugh issued from his belly. "Never!"

Allegro rose and left under the barrage of his laughter.

"Paris," she said.

"Are you sure he's right?" Alden said.

"Sarafian's not usually wrong. And he's honest."

"Where in Paris?"

"He didn't say. Doesn't know."

Alden was thoughtful. "It's a big city," he said. "And from what I've read about the Raven, he likes the best. There's the Ritz, Bristol, George V, Meurice, and others. We'll have to try them all. You know his face. Paris it is then."

"Where are we staying?" Allegro asked.

"George V."

"Won't that be booked solid?"

"I always stay there when I'm in Paris. The manager knows me." He grinned at her. "Somebody's going to be bumped."

He had reassembled the Smith & Wesson. Now he lifted it, hefted it, sighted along the barrel.

"You taking that to Paris?" Allegro asked.

"Why not?" Alden said.

"How are you going to get aboard a plane with it?"

"I never thought of that." A frown creased Alden's forehead. "We won't take a plane. We'll take the car ferry from Dover to Calais."

"They have electronic detectors there, too. And customs."

Alden's frown deepened. "I've got to have a gun."

"Leave it here. For Ernst, or whatever his name is, when he gets out of the hospital. I'll get us guns."

"How?"

"Sarafian. All he has to do is make a phone call to Paris."

"Are you sure?"

"Positive."

"Okay," he said, and then peered at her. "You said guns—plural."

After a long pause, Allegro said, "I'm in this with you, Philip."

He stared at her, his face filled with fear. Then he rose

from the chair, and they embraced, hugging each other tightly.

Corrigan stood at the window of their room at the Eros looking down on Shaftesbury Avenue. It was raining. The surviving IRA men had waited twenty-four hours for Trask's answer, were stranded, couldn't risk being recognized. Their world was four walls of peeling wallpaper and a cloud of smoke, its smell fighting a losing battle with the stale smell of cooking that wafted up the service-elevator shaft down the hall.

Corrigan turned suddenly, his eyes wild. He picked up a lamp and threw it at the far wall. The pink silk shade buckled as the frame folded. The glass base shattered, sending shards over the bed and the floor.

"Damn!" Corrigan shouted. "What's taking so fuckin' long?" He slumped into a chair. "That bloody Trask has plenty of mouth and no action. Bastard!"

The sandy-haired O'Rourke raised his head from the pillow. "Won't do any bloody good shouting. Take it easy, mate."

Corrigan paced, went to the window again. The rain was beginning to let up.

A knock sounded on their door. Both men reached for their guns.

"Who is it?" Corrigan called out.

"Hall porter, sir."

"Think it's all right?" Corrigan whispered.

O'Rourke nodded.

Corrigan took the chain off the door and opened it a crack. The hall porter, a wizened old man, stood with an envelope in his hand.

"Cable for Mr. Patrick O'Rourke," he said.

"I'll take it," Corrigan said, slipping his gun under his belt and opening the door wider.

The porter handed over the envelope. "Sign here, sir."

Corrigan scribbled his name and closed the door.

"Give it here," O'Rourke said, holding out his hand.

Corrigan already had one end of the envelope ripped open. He read the cable aloud: " 'Your friend Paris Hilton. Two thousand pounds· at American Express office, Haymarket Street name of O'Rourke. Good hunting.' "

It was signed, "New York Hunt Club."

"That better, man," Corrigan said, slapping his partner on the back.

"Let's get it," O'Rourke said, reaching for his knapsack. He pulled open the door, scraping its lower edge over broken glass.

Corrigan reached for his bag and, smiling grimly, led the way. "Let's get the bastard," he said.

CHAPTER 29

At 18 Avenue de Suffren the Paris Hilton rises, looking out over the Seine, a marvel of modern glass and plastic, five hundred rooms, each with its own balcony. One of its restaurants, Le Western, features Texas T-bone steaks and apple pie à la mode.

On one of the higher balconies sat the Raven, nursing a Grand Marnier and himself. He was feeling ill. Although he relished T-bone steaks and apple pie, he had tried a meal and it had all come up within half an hour.

Now he sat, staring off at the nearby Eiffel Tower, feeling empty and weak. His complexion was sallow. There were dark circles under his eyes. He was still running a fever.

His father. What had the old man been doing in London? Fuck it. *Fuck it!* His father had nothing to do with his sickness! He had a bug, that was all. All he needed was a little rest, clean air, the mountains. All cities stank! They were putrid all over the world!

But in order to have his holiday, he needed money. He needed help—and Moscow was out. The KGB was probably looking for him. Trask would supply him, but where the hell was he?

Trask. He wouldn't cop out on him now. Or would he?

He took another sip of his drink and shuddered. He was back on Grand Marnier now, thinking that perhaps the Armagnac had brought on his illness.

He kept staring at the Eiffel Tower. In his mind it became a huge phallus, a penis.

His father . . .

Goddammit, why did his thoughts persist on returning to his father?

I can't escape him, I can't escape him! Why is he following me!

He stood up, trembling, smashing the glass of Grand Marnier on the balcony floor.

Fuck you, father! Fuck you, old man!

You stinking crow! I'll kill you!

The Raven took a few steps and found he was reeling. He made it to the bedroom and lay down, stomach heaving, pulse hard and fast.

Was he really following him? Impossible! He had no idea!

Trask. Trask, come soon. Save me.

He felt sick and ran to the toilet, where he retched, but nothing came up. He rode out the dry heaves, then returned to the bed, closed his eyes, and tried to sleep. He had the dream again.

You stinking crow! I'll kill you!

Alden sighed heavily. "I just called Harry's son, made arrangements to have the body shipped to California. You didn't know Harry had a son and two daughters." He paused. "Christ, I hope they don't choose Forest Lawn."

"You wanted Westminster Abbey," she said softly.

"Anyplace but Forest Lane. Even underneath his tennis court, so they'd think of him while they play."

"Bitter this morning, aren't we?" she said. "How did it go with his son?"

His voice choked. "It went badly. He'd heard it on the news. The boy loved his father." Visions of Nicky and Alicia came to mind. He could die, and they'd never know, never care. His mind jolted back to the present. "I'm sorry. What thought got into your head?"

Allegro was removing her safari jacket. "Just this. We're probably being watched. By Scotland Yard, Special Branch, MI6, Interpol, and God knows who else. If we check out of the hotel, we'll be followed."

Fingers steepled before his lips, Alden became pensive for a few moments. Then he said, "We won't check out of the hotel."

She peered at him questioningly.

"We'll keep the suite. Take the car and as little as possible. One or two small bags, a picnic basket." He looked at her and grinned. "You *do* wear wash and wear panties, don't you?"

She smiled. "And bras. Learned that a long time ago, traveling about."

"We'll pick up what we need in Paris."

"And how do we get to Paris? If I'm right, they'll have the airports covered."

He was still thinking, and said slowly, "We go by car. From here to Dover, where we get on the British Rail hovercraft."

"Hovercraft? Do they take on cars?"

"Yes." He was still working things out in his mind. "It's about two hours from London to Dover. We'll give it three. If we have a tail, we'll head toward Surrey. I know the roads there. We can lose them in Surrey."

"What about the other side? Calais?"

"It's six to seven hours by car from Calais to Paris. If we can't lose them in that time, we are amateurs, as the man from Scotland Yard said. What do you say?"

"I say let's try it. When do we leave?"

"Now. Sunday is a somnolent day. Maybe they won't expect it. I'll call the desk and have the car brought around. I'll tell them to keep the suite—that we'll be back after a few days of touring the countryside. You go pack, love. Just the essentials."

They were ready within half an hour, two small bags packed neatly in a picnic hamper. The Mercedes was just outside the lobby entrance. Philip left the cardboard box containing the Smith & Wesson at the desk with the name "Ernst Eisenstadt" penned on it. They exited the lobby, entered the car, and began to worm their way through the London traffic.

For a while, Alden suspected they were being tailed, but when he turned toward Surrey, the car behind them, a tan Volvo, continued on straight. Still, he took no chances. He might have dropped to another tail. But when he had passed through the suburban parts of Surrey and entered the broad stretches of green fields, he chose a narrow, winding road and slowed down. Not a car behind him, not a helicopter chopping the clear, blue sky, not a light plane droning.

He smiled, as though in victory. "Did it."

"Seems so," she said.

"Road map. Glove compartment."

She gave it to him.

He looked at it quickly, jerking his head up and down while he was driving. " 'Ere we go!" he said in a broad British accent.

"Didn't know you could speak English," she said, imitating as best she could.

He made a hard left turn. "Didn't you, though? I'm a descendant of old John Alden. Came over on the *Mayflower* as keeper of the beers and strong waters. Ended his life on a scaffold. Hung—hanged."

"You're kidding!" Allegro said, and laughed.

"Not about his end, poor bugger. But descendant? I've often thought about it."

"This the road to Dover?" Allegro asked.

"Yes. Plus a few others."

They drove for fifteen minutes in silence. Then his head lifted, and his deep voice bellowed out in song.

> "Put on your old gray bonnet,
>   With the blue ribbons on it,
>   And we'll hitch old Dobbin to the shay,
>   And through the fields of clover,
>   We'll ride down to Dover
>   On our Golden Wedding Day!"

Allegro laughed as he looked over at her. She had never seen him so happy. Then she joined in.

"We'll ride down to Dover
On our Golden Wedding Day!"

She wondered whether there would ever be one. Fifty years. He was in his fifties now. An icy fear took hold of her, and her hands clenched. How would he go? Cancer, heart? When? If only he would die of old age, just plain old age. Eighty-five, ninety.

It would be simple. She would take her own life soon after he was gone. There was nothing after him.

Nothing.

Walter Trask's flight via Pan American touched down at Charles de Gaulle Airport in the early hours of Sunday. His CIA identification and arrogant attitude had intimidated the young reservations clerk, and a passenger holding a first-class ticket had been bumped.

A cab pulled up. He threw his bag in the back, settled himself in, then said to the driver, in heavily American accented French, "Ten Cassette Street."

Preferring to keep a low profile, he had chosen a small hotel on a quiet street. The Abbaye Saint-Germain had once been a monastery and the prices were moderate. He checked in at the front desk, picked up his key, and made his way to his room. Once inside, he removed his jacket, kicked off his shoes, and flopped into an easy chair, his feet propped on an ottoman.

He had been up for almost twenty-four hours and was exhausted. The flight across had not helped. It had been turbulent.

The Raven could wait until tomorrow.

In any event, aside from getting some rest, he had to make some plans. Alden had accompanied the IRA arms shipment to Liverpool, lost the truck, and then had gone on to London to put up at the Savoy. That much Trask knew from his man in London.

Where was he now? He had to know. Yawning, he rose from the chair and crossed to the telephone. He put in a call to his partner in London.

"Hello?"

"Are you swept?" Trask asked.

"You know my apartment is always swept."

"I'm in Paris. Is he still at the Savoy?"

"Left. On his way to Dover by car, and the ferry or hovercraft to Calais. He'll be in Paris sometime this evening. Staying at the George V."

Trask smiled. "How do you know all this?"

"I made the walls of his suite have ears," the man said. "Good luck with him."

"Thanks," Trask said and hung up.

He stretched and lay down on the bed, studying the ceiling. So far it was working. He'd see the son first, Monday, tomorrow. Then the father, sometime later in the week. Between Alden and the IRA crazies, he should see the Raven in his grave.

He yawned again and closed his eyes. Soon he was sleeping peacefully.

The hovercraft slipped across the English Channel like a powder puff. Behind them, the white cliffs receded, Dover Castle stood out in sharp relief against the sky, and the Roman lighthouse, Pharos, rose like a sentinel.

Allegro leaned forward, hair flying in the wind, wearing dark glasses to protect her eyes. Alden was beside her.

"It's thrilling" she said.

"Haven't you ever been on a hovercraft before?"

"No. Have you?"

"Many times," he said.

"When will we be in Calais?"

"About thirty-five minutes."

Allegro looked behind her. She sang:

> "There'll be blue birds over
> The white cliffs of Dover,
> Tomorrow, just you wait and see."

When they reached Calais, it was just beginning to
turn to dusk. As they approached customs, Allegro gripped
Alden's hand tightly.

"Don't be nervous," he said. "I left the gun for Ernst
at the Savoy. Remember?"

The French customs inspector was a bored-looking indi-
vidual. "Passport, monsieur?"

Alden dug inside his blazer pocket. The customs man
glanced at it briefly and returned it.

"Madame?"

As he poked his nose through Allegro's passport he
glanced up, eyed both of them, and tried to smile. "*Merci,*"
he said, giving the passport back to Allegro.

The customs inspector let his eyes drift the length of
the Mercedes. He seemed on the verge of asking Alden
to open the trunk, but then his eyes caught the Hertz
sticker.

He turned back to them, tried another smile, which
appeared as a grimace. "*Vacances?*" he asked.

Alden looked puzzled. "Oh. Vacation. Yes." Alden
smiled back. "A few days," he lied.

"*Bon chance,*" the customs man said, and waved
them on.

Allegro let forth a long breath as Alden slowly inched
forward to the road.

"What are you so nervous about?" Alden asked.

"I don't know, love. Just nervous, that's all."

"We have every right to be here," he said. "I'm not
carrying contraband."

"I know. It's just—everything." She looked back through
the rear window.

"Are we being followed?"

"I don't know yet."

"If we are, we'll lose them between here and Paris. It's
a six- to seven-hour drive," he said.

Allegro slumped in her seat.

Later, on the *route nationale*, as they were passing
through Saint Omer, Alden said, "It was easy, wasn't it? I
mean immigration. He didn't even stamp the passports."

Allegro shrugged. "They're usually easy on Americans. Especially in a rented car. Hundreds of people make the trip across the channel every day. Especially this time of year. I shouldn't have been so nervous." She hesitated. "But I still have an awful feeling we're being tailed, Philip."

"We'll see," he said.

When they reached Arras, Alden executed a number of sharp left and right turns, parked, started up again, drove down dark, deserted streets.

"I don't see any car following us," he said. "Who'd be tailing us anyway?"

"The Sûreté, the Deuxième Bureau, Interpol. Who knows?"

"The hell with them!" Alden said angrily. "Let them follow!" He stepped on the accelerator, making his way to Autoroute A1, the main highway from Lille to Paris.

Walter Trask phoned the Raven that evening at the Paris Hilton. He asked for Mr. Butcher.

"I'm in Paris," he said when the Raven answered.

"Good to hear your voice, man. Where are you staying?"

Trask did not answer the question. "How about dinner tonight?"

"Sounds great. Let's make it Le Gourmet in Montmartre."

"All right."

"You got money?" the Raven asked.

"Yes, I've got money."

"Good. You know where I am."

When he hung up, Trask asked the operator for a number he had for his CIA Paris station contact.

"Did you pick them up?" he asked.

"Piece of cake. They're at the Hotel Frémicourt. Name of O'Reilly and Carson."

"Not very original. Thanks."

Before he called the Frémicourt, Trask lit a cigarette and pondered the situation. If all went well, he would be able to stay in the background, let the IRA people do his dirty work . . . or Alden.

He picked up the telephone again, asked for the Frémicourt.

When it was answered, he wasted no time. "Trask. Your friend will be having dinner with me tonight at Le Gourmet in Montmartre. Let me get clear before you move in."

"How the hell did you . . . ?" O'Rourke spoke into a dead line.

Trask wondered why he didn't just give it up. He was too old for this.

But if not this, what? He had done nothing else all his adult life.

CHAPTER 30

The George V is elegant, luxurious, and ostentatious in the French manner. It has a magnificent lobby furnished with Louise Quinze chairs and sofas, statuary, huge paintings, and arras. The rooms echo the lobby. Some have working fireplaces. It is the meeting place of film people, tycoons, and others rich enough to afford it.

Alden and Allegro checked in late Sunday night, the drive from Calais having taken not the six or seven hours Alden anticipated, but between eight and nine.

Before following the bellhop to their suite, Alden guided Allegro across the lobby to one of the most chic bars in town.

"Need a drink," he said.

They ordered martinis. The drinks were strong. The lovers smiled wearily at each other, sipping.

Alden looked into his drink. "Is this a wild goose chase?"

"I don't know. Is it?" Allegro said.

Alden sighed and let his head rest on the back of the plush booth. "It's a big city out there. Almost three million people. How do we find the Raven?"

"Simple. It's only a one in three million chance."

Alden laughed, a bigger laugh than necessary, one arising from exhaustion and weariness.

Allegro's eyes glowed. "I'm feeling the martini. Whew!"

"Come on. Let's go to bed," Alden suggested.

Upstairs, in the suite overlooking the Champs-Élysées,

they undressed and went to bed nude in each other's arms. Allegro was asleep within minutes but Alden stayed awake, smoking, thinking.

A montage of images passed upon the screen in his mind. Like a series of clips from a motion picture, they flickered and flashed before him—scenes with Kate, with Harry Zimmerman. It was a poorly edited film of disconnected scenes that nonetheless told a story—a sad, cheerful, funny story of times together, of sharing, of hope and despair, of good times and bad, until the climax, the final two scenes interwoven, superimposed upon each other: Kingman, Arizona, and Claridges.

He exhaled angrily, and the smoke spelled hate.

One chance in three million. But he would take on the odds.

He could understand about Kate. She had been one passenger among hundreds on a train. But Harry—Harry had been one man, in one hotel suite, on a solitary trip.

Why? Why Harry?

Why did the Raven kill Harry?

Or did he? Perhaps it was someone else, someone who wanted to shift the blame on the Raven after what had happened in St. James's Park.

He mashed out his cigarette in utter frustration and sat up in bed, fist clenched. One chance in three million or one in five billion. It didn't matter. He would find the Raven, track him down, follow him to his lair—and kill him.

Their table was in a corner, far from the center of the restaurant. They had agreed to meet far from their hotels, in neutral territory. The place was small, served only French cuisine, was usually the haunt of Parisians.

Trask, smoking lazily, listened as the Raven outlined his plans.

"Did you hear me, man? Or am I talking to a brick wall?"

Trask nodded. "I heard you."

"The president of the United States, the chancellor of West Germany, and the president of France. All on the same day!"

Trask nodded again. "Go on. How are you going to arrange it?"

The Raven gestured impatiently. "No sweat. I've got ARM in the States, Baader-Meinhof in Germany, and in France, the New Underground. All it needs is organization, and that I can do. Organize. To the second." He giggled. "Can you imagine, man? Can you picture it? How the world will react?"

The Raven's eyes were full of fire and fury, and as Walter Trask stared into them, he thought he was looking into the soul of insanity, the essence of madness.

The Raven pulled out a cigarette and Trask leaned over the table with a lighter.

"Thanks," the Raven said. He did not know that the lighter was a miniature camera or that Trask had already snapped his picture three times. Whether the Raven lived or died this night, Trask wanted a clear picture of him at last.

The Raven leaned back in his chair, smiling, blowing smoke, looking straight at Trask. "Well? What do you think?"

Trask paused before answering. "Do you think you're up to it, Nicky?"

The Raven lunged forward. "What do you mean, am I up to it? Of course I'm up to it! Why do you ask, shithead! I could kill God if I had to!"

Trask was cool. "You don't look well."

"I feel great!" he lied. "Caught some kind of bug in London, that's all." He shifted uncomfortably in his chair, then mumbled, "I need a short R & R, a vacation. Think things through, come up with a schedule."

Trask said nothing, only stared, as was his habit.

"Shit. Take those eyes off me," the Raven almost shouted. "Don't you ever smile?"

Trask tried a smile, but it didn't come through. Just a small flashing of teeth. Then his lips compressed again.

They were silent until the Raven said, "You bring money?"

Trask reached inside his suit pocket and brought out an envelope. He placed it on the table between them. The Raven looked at it. "How much?"

"Twenty-five," Trask said.

The Raven smiled. "Twenty-five thousand?"

Trask nodded.

The Raven reached for the envelope, pocketed it, smiled. "Thanks."

Trask stared. "That represents your commission for the introduction to Qaddafi. He's bought a lot of stuff. You can't say I don't pay my debts." Then he said, "Yes, you should take a little vacation, Nicky. You need it. Think things over and plan this latest venture of yours carefully." He stood up. "By the way. Where are you going?"

"I don't know yet." The Raven grinned. "But thanks. I'll keep in touch."

Trask left the restaurant. He has to go, he thought. He has to be wasted.

He's crazy.

Across the street from the restaurant, two men lounged in a store front. One was tall and sandy-haired; the other, short, dark, and stocky. O'Rourke and Corrigan had flown from London on the first flight, had followed Trask's instructions. They had seen the Raven enter the restaurant, had watched Trask enter and greet the killer.

Waiting for the men to leave, the IRA men had been plagued by women plying their trade. Gendarmes had eyed them with suspicion. Each time an officer showed up on the narrow street in Montmartre the two would split up, wander around the block, but always with one pair of eyes on the restaurant.

The women left trails of heady perfume in their wake— almost but not quite strong enough to drown out the smell of garbage piled in dark alleys along the street. Streetlights were dim. Cars were parked on both sides of the street, almost blocking it. Few cars came through.

Time passed slowly. Every ten or fifteen minutes, one of the men would check his gun with nervous hands. Corrigan would pull out the clip, look at the rounds, slide it back, shove the gun under his belt in the small of his back. O'Rourke would flip the cylinder, look at the six rounds in his revolver, and with a flick of the wrist, slam the cylinder home.

It was something to do.

Finally, Trask left alone, looked over his shoulder at the dark street suspiciously, and walked away briskly. The Raven, that bloody animal who had killed young Liam and their friend John, still sat. They could see him through the window.

After casually finishing his wine, he rose, moved toward the door. The Irishmen knew what they had to do. It would be no accident. If he hailed a cab, they would rush him and kill him on the spot. If he decided to walk, they would take him on another quiet street, preferably far from the restaurant.

He decided to walk.

The Paris Hilton was a long way from Rue Saint Marc, where the two had eaten. The Raven walked west toward the hotel, kept to the larger streets, was seldom far from a streetlight.

O'Rourke kept to the same side as the Raven. Corrigan took the other side. They signaled often, hanging back, blending in with the few pedestrians on the streets.

Along the Boulevard Haussmann, not far from L'Arc de Triomphe, the Raven turned off onto Rue de Berri and then into a dismal little street with no street sign in evidence.

Corrigan kept to the shadows, ran ahead, pulled his gun. No one was around.

O'Rourke crept up behind. "That's far enough."

The Raven half turned, moved with his back to the wall. He could see O'Rourke now in the shadows to his left. Corrigan was farther away to his right and coming fast.

"What do we say, gentlemen? Is it 'top of the evening to ya'?" he asked, mimicking the brogue with a sneer on his face.

"You bastard. You killed our mates for no reason," Corrigan spat. He had come up from the right, stood out in the road, his gun level.

"An accident." The Raven's voice was cold. "I don't waste anyone who can help me."

"Accidents don't win wars, Raven. This time you lost and you're going to pay," O'Rourke said, his face a mask of hate in the dim light of the street.

"You talk too much. All IRA bunglers talk when they

should be fighting," the Raven said, baiting them. He had his gun in hand under the coat. The small-caliber Mauser was deadly at close range. This time he had soft-nosed slugs in the clip. They would tear a hole the size of a man's fist as they exited human flesh. The gun was aimed at O'Rourke.

"You bastard!" Corrigan shouted, rushing headlong, forgetting he held a gun in his mad dash to get his hands on the man he hated.

The Raven shot O'Rourke and ducked under Corrigan's charge. When the short Irishman rolled over the Raven's back, landing on garbage-strewn asphalt, the Raven shot him in the head.

O'Rourke lay on his back, holding onto a shattered arm, his eyes wild. The Raven put his gun to the sandy-haired head and, with the smile of a madman, spoke into his ear. "You're a dead man, just like Corrigan and the other two useless Irish bastards. How did you know where to find me?"

"Stuff it."

The Raven rammed the gun into the man's ear until blood ran down the blond sideburns. In the dim light it was black, just like the fluid pouring from the shattered arm.

"It was Trask," the wounded man blurted out.

"You just bought your life," the Raven whispered into his ear, his voice cold as steel. "Tell that bastard Trask he's a dead man, then crawl back into your hole in your precious Ireland."

The Raven had been kneeling over the prostrate man. As he started to rise, he clubbed the blond head once and watched the pupils roll up until only the whites showed.

"Goddamned amateur Irish bastards," he said as he walked away.

Alden slept late the next morning. He had not had an easy night. It had been full of visions. Allegro dead, himself dead, and the Raven smiling above them. Still at large. The thought of Allegro dead chilled him. She was so young, so beautiful, had so much before her, a life to give, to share.

Nor did he want to leave life just when he had found its meaning. And he questioned his own courage. Could he kill a man? Even the Raven?

He thought about it, eyes still closed. He thought about Kate and Harry Zimmerman and decided that yes, he could kill.

He opened his eyes and found himself in an empty bed. Allegro was in the living room, slipping into her bush jacket.

"What's the matter, darling?" she said. "You look frightened."

"Just a bad dream," he said, and let his breath out slowly. "Where you off to?"

"To get the guns. I called Sarafian while you were sleeping. He told me where to pick them up."

"I'll go with you," Alden said.

"No, love, you stay here. You look tired." As he was about to protest, she added, "Tell you what. Why don't we meet for lunch?"

Alden hesitated, then sat down. He was tired after a night with little sleep. "All right. You name it."

"How about Le Bar des Théâtres? It's a sidewalk café."

"Where is it?"

"On the Avenue Montaigne," she said. "Near Place de l'Alma."

"What time?"

"About one."

"See you there," he said. As she opened the door, he blew her a kiss. "Be careful," he said softly.

After she had gone, he sat very still, hands gripping the arms of the chair, as the pendulum swung the other way, as love left his soul and hatred took over.

He hoped they would be good pistols, accurate and powerful.

He had to kill the Raven.

But Alden had no plan, no place to go, nowhere to turn. How does one go about finding a man who could be anyplace in the world? Once again he felt powerless, impotent in the face of God and reality. One man alone, up against a mountain that seemed insurmountable.

*   *   *

That same morning, Vladislav Grushenko was released from the hospital, against medical advice. He wore a cast on his leg and his progress was slow.

In the lobby of the hospital he found a public telephone and immediately called the Savoy in London. "Is Mr. Alden still registered?" he asked.

"Yes, he is," said the front-desk clerk.

"Would you ring his suite for me?"

"Of course. But I'll have to give you back to the main operator."

He could hear voices, conversation at the other end.

"Oh. I'm afraid he's not here. He's gone off for a few days to tour the countryside."

Grushenko cursed inwardly. "When do you expect him back?"

"I can't say. Perhaps tomorrow or the next day. Any message?"

"Yes. Tell him Ernst Eisenstadt called."

"Oh, Mr. Eisenstadt," the voice said, brightly. "He left a package for you at the desk."

"Thank you," Grushenko said. "I'll pick it up."

After the phone call, he trudged outside to a waiting cab. The pain in his leg nagged at him, but was no match for the tearing pain in his chest. He had to force himself to go on.

"The railroad station," he said. It would be a long ride by train. He didn't know if he was up to it.

The package would contain the gun, the Smith & Wesson he treasured. He had felt lost without it.

If Alden had not returned the next day, Grushenko would call the embassy, speak to his own people. It was Allegro he had to keep in view. She knew the Raven's face, and had connections with terrorists. Alden also knew his face, although he was not aware of it.

Poor decadent Western bastard. Was he so different from an ancient KGB man? Neither had a son to be proud of. He wept for himself and for Alden.

CHAPTER 31

Alden was seated at a table at Le Bar des Théâtres, waiting for Allegro. He had ordered a half bottle of wine and a pitcher of water, which he mixed, three to one. He noticed the waiter shrug and look skyward.

To hell with him. Alden had been drinking lightly since his last binge in New York. He felt that he must stay in shape for his confrontation with the Raven.

He watched the passing scene. The Parisians, he thought, were so cool, so urbane, so supercilious, so eccentric: that old man crossing the street, white beard flowing, beret rakishly perched atop his head; the beautiful model or aspiring actress a few tables away, fastidiously applying lipstick and eye shadow while looking into a small compact mirror; the tall, thin gentleman eyeing her; the passersby, chins up, aloof, dignified, strutting toward their destined appointments; that man with the beard who . . .

"Nicky!" he gasped.

Nicky Alden froze. I know that voice! he thought. But it can't be! First London, now Paris! *It can't be*.

The Raven turned slowly, an expression of sheer horror on his face.

Alden had risen, was motioning toward a chair, smiling, his eyes moist. "Nicky! Nicky, sit down, son."

The Raven's handsome features suddenly broke into a wide winning smile. "Pops! For Christ's sake!" He walked to the table and sat. "Pops! What the hell are you doing in Paris?"

Alden smiled. He felt a sudden warmth for the boy, his son, his seed. "Nothing," he said. "Just traveling. Research, you know?" He was surprised, full of the gladness of happenstance, the fortunate chance of this meeting, full of love, tolerance, and forgiveness.

"It's good to see you, son. What've you been up to?"

"Oh, this and that, this and that. You know." Nicky's heart had begun to pound at the sound of his father's voice, and was still pounding. He was full of fear. Before him sat the man he despised and hated, loved and revered.

Alden suddenly let forth a loud laugh, a great guffaw. "They've always told me that truth was stranger than fiction," he said. "Here I am, sitting on the sidewalk in Paris, and who should pass by but my own son, whom I haven't seen in five years."

The Raven did not return the laugh. He said, "Yeah, I guess it has been five years or so."

"We've got some catching up to do, son," Alden said. "I guess I haven't been a very good father, have I?"

"I dunno," the Raven said without enthusiasm. In his heart he thought, The bastard. If I told him the truth, he'd be at me, defending himself; it would lead to another argument.

And the Raven felt too weak to argue.

"Remember that time you caught your first fish?" Alden said. "Remember?"

The Raven was silent.

"It was at Lake Mary, up in the Sierras. You—" Noticing the blank look on Nicky's face, Alden cut himself off. "Well," he said, and shook his head, staring at his drink. He realized that his son was in no mood to talk about the past they had shared together. Maybe it was just as well. The past was the past, and so much had happened since. Alden did not want to fight, either. Let bygones be bygones, he thought. Don't spoil the moment.

Alden lifted his drink and sipped. He said, "What'll you have?"

"Nothing," the Raven said. He looked at his watch. "I've got an appointment."

The barrier was up, the stone wall still sturdy and unapproachable, the barbed wire strung bitterly.

Alden sat back in his chair, twirling his drink on the table. "What are you doing in Paris, son?"

"Just passing through."

"Where are you staying?"

The Raven thought quickly. "No place. Just passing through, y'know, like I'm on vacation, y'know?"

"Seen Alicia?" Alden asked.

"Not for a year or so."

"She's in Chamonix," Alden said. "On some kind of a hotel job. Why don't you take your vacation down there?"

"We don't get along too well," Nicky said. "But I'll think about it. I'll think about it," he mused. "The French Alps. That might be good."

Across the street, Allegro stood stunned. It was like a dream, a terrible nightmare. There, at a table at Le Bar des Théâtres, sat Philip and the Raven. Philip was smiling.

Allegro's lips trembled, her entire body felt weak. She stepped back into a doorway and watched.

At the table, Alden looked into the distance. "Kate's dead, you know."

"No, I didn't," the Raven lied.

"She died on the Southwest Limited. You must have read about it."

He had, but only looking for references to himself. He had not been interested in the casualty lists or the article about Kate. He had known her only slightly, had met her rarely. "Sorry to hear that," he said. He knew what was coming next.

"And Harry. Harry Zimmerman. You remember Harry?"

"Sure. Sure, I remember old Harry. He was a nice old guy." *I hit him where it hurts. I hit him where it really hurts!*

"The Raven," Alden muttered into the distance, then turned to look at his son. "You've heard of the Raven."

"Yeah. Here and there. I've heard of him."

"He killed them both," Alden said. "He was responsible for both Kate and Harry."

The Raven looked at his watch again. "Look, Pops, I gotta go."

Alden was perturbed. "Not yet, Nicky," he pleaded. "I

want you to meet someone. She'll be along soon. Why don't you have a drink?"

The Raven stood. "Sorry, Pops, it's important. I've got to go."

"But, Nicky," Alden said, rising. "It's been five years. Over five years." His voice choked.

"It's been nice, Pops. Maybe some other time."

Suddenly, Alden reached out, took his son by the arm, held him close, eyes moist. "I love you, son."

"Shit!"

"I love you. I really do!"

"I'll keep in touch, Pops." The Raven's heart was thumping again. In anger. Why couldn't he fight this man?

Alden, in a rare show of emotion, embraced his son, kissed him on the left cheek.

The Raven tensed. Body rigid. Goddammit! In a public place.

"See you, Pops," he said as he twisted away and walked off.

Alden watched him go, heart heavy, shoulders stooped. He let himself drop back into the chair and picked up his drink.

Why can't I bridge the gap? What does he have against me? I did my best, didn't I?

His thoughts were interrupted by Allegro as she sat down in the chair the Raven had just vacated.

She had waited until he was out of sight, rounding a corner. "Hi," she said, and hoped her voice was steady and controlled.

Alden looked up at her. "You just missed my son."

"Was that your son? I saw him as I was crossing the street. What's he doing in Paris?"

"I don't know. He didn't tell me. He doesn't look well."

A knot had formed in Allegro's stomach. A chill raced down her spine. "Got the guns," she said in a steady voice. It was what he expected her to talk about.

"What kind?" Alden asked automatically.

"I think they're Swedish Army issue. Automatics, 7.65 mm."

Alden was silent for a moment.

"You've never said much about your son," she said.

Alden looked up, a trace of moisture still in his eyes. He smiled. "We don't get along. Why, I don't know."

How can I tell him his son is the Raven? Allegro thought. I can't, I just can't! It would destroy him!

Alden looked in the direction Nicky had disappeared. "Basically he's a good kid. Maybe a few problems." He paused. "At least he's not a terrorist."

Allegro turned away as bile rose in her throat.

At the Paris Hilton, the Raven packed his things as though he were being pursued, throwing clothes haphazardly into his two bags, jamming toiletries on top of them.

He had to get away! He had to get as far away from that man, that supreme being, that god, as possible.

The Alps. The Himalayas. The South Seas. Anyplace! Anyplace away from that man!

After he had finished packing, he poured a Grand Marnier with trembling hands, the bottle clinking against the rim of the glass, some of the liquor spilling on the bar. He sat, lifted the glass to his lips. More spilled on his lap. He shuddered. He could not face any of his terrorist cohorts like this! They would think he had gone bananas!

He did this to me, he thought. He did this to me!

You stinking crow! I'll kill you!

Murderer! Murderer of souls!

After a few large swallows of the Grand Marnier, he went into the bathroom to brush his teeth, then remembered he had already packed his toothbrush and toothpaste. He caught his reflection in the mirror and saw something gaunt, a death's-head with a stick body.

Christ, I'm dying, he thought. You did this to me, you high-handed, haughty shit! You, with your morals and bourgeois mores, your disapproving looks and your disgusted manner. All my life you've haunted me, hands clasped as though you were a priest.

You murdered me! You killed me when I was young! You shit!

He punched the mirror with his fist, breaking the glass and bringing blood to his knuckles.

He held his head for a moment, breathing heavily, then

walked back into the living room and sat beside his glass and the bottle of Grand Marnier. He lit a joint, inhaled, and held it until he was forced to let go.

Shit, I'm having a nervous breakdown, he thought. Too much booze and grass and not enough food.

He could not eat. Everything he ate came right back up. He was having the dream every night, every day if he dozed, and sometimes while he was awake.

You stinking crow! I'll kill you!

After four tokes of good Colombian pot, the Raven's mood changed. He giggled.

I'll go to Chamonix, he thought. Why not? They have a casino there—and Alicia.

This time I'll hit the bastard where it really hurts.

He took another drag on the marijuana and lifted his glass.

Here's to you, Pops!

Up yours!

Across the street from the Hilton, O'Rourke had been parked in a rented Peugeot for hours. His right arm had been crudely bandaged. Two oversized pieces of gummed tape had been plastered over a wad of gauze on his forehead; his ear was similarly swathed. He had bought the items in a *pharmacie* and had taken care of his own wounds with great difficulty.

The woman at the automobile rental agency had doubts about leasing a car to him. It was only after he had slipped a hundred-franc note into her grasping hand that she changed her mind.

The Peugeot was not new, but was heavy and fast, exactly what he needed. He had no idea how he was going to get the Raven, but he was going to do it. The gun he had yet to use was under the seat behind his left heel. It wasn't going to help him now. He wasn't much of a shot with his right hand, and with the left, he suspected he could hit nothing, even at close range. His style was hit and run, spraying with automatic weapons or bombing from a distance.

The waiting finally paid off.

The Raven walked into the hotel like he was in a great

hurry. Ten minutes later, a red sports car pulled up in front. He knew it was a rental. They had been delivered all afternoon by youths with small motorbikes in tow. The delivery man parked the car and took off on his bike.

Ten minutes later, the Raven walked out of the hotel, threw a bag in the back. He drove away, leaving a trail of rubber.

The determined IRA man pulled in behind.

Grushenko had no time for self-pity. After he left the hotel, he took a cab to the Russian Embassy in Belgravia and for the first time in weeks conversed in his own language, sat down to a dinner of borscht and chilled vodka. For an hour or two he felt almost human, could almost forget he was a walking dead man with a son on the way to the gulags.

But he couldn't waste time. While he ate, he talked to both KGB and GRU station chiefs. His reputation was legendary. They had done all they could for him.

"Philip Alden has gone to France, comrade," the GRU man revealed. "We assume he has driven to Paris. As far as we know, the Raven is already in Paris."

"We are sure he will not stay there long, Comrade Grushenko," the KGB man said.

"You will have to get me into France secretly. I want to take my own firearm."

"No problem," the KGB man said. "We still have Colonial Charter. We'll fly you to a small airfield outside Paris. No customs. No immigration."

"Transport?" Grushenko asked, enjoying the power he could wield on home soil.

"Our limousine to the Colonial aircraft. In France, an agency car will take you to our embassy," the GRU man added.

"I want complete information on the Raven's movements, and on Alden and the woman."

"It will be done, comrade," the KGB man answered. He was trying to make an impression on the older man, the legend of the KGB, but he had not been heard. Grushenko was looking around the luxurious paneled dining room with its original oils and Persian rugs.

He memorized the square lines of the Slavic faces at the other tables, the rounded flank of a young waitress. This was a piece of home. Not typical, but home nonetheless.

He knew it might be his last sight of home.

"One other thing I might need," he said.

"What is it, comrade?" the KGB man asked.

"A helicopter standing by at the airport in France," the old warrior said, trying not to wince from the pain. "I think I might have to pick up the trail in a hurry."

"It will be done."

Again, Grushenko didn't hear the response. He was operating on reserves, on nerve and a will not to feel pain or accept failure.

CHAPTER 32

On Wednesday morning, Alden was awakened by the jangle of the telephone. "Jesus Christ! Seven o'clock in the morning! Who calls anybody at seven o'clock in the morning?" He lifted the phone from its cradle. "Hello?"

"Hope I didn't get you up, Alden."

"Who is this?"

"Walter Trask."

"Walter Trask?" He paused for a few seconds trying to figure out why Trask would be calling him. "Christ! Where are you and why so early?"

Trask answered the second question first. "I thought we might have breakfast."

"You're in Paris?"

"That's right, Alden. And I have something I think might interest you. Something on the Raven."

"Who?" Alden was not quite awake, couldn't believe someone had come up with something at last, if that's what it was. He was still half asleep.

"The Raven," Trask said.

Alden's head suddenly cleared. "What is it?"

"Not on the phone. I'd like to see you. For breakfast."

"Where?"

"I can come over to George V," Trask said.

"All right. Give me half an hour. Downstairs." He picked up the cigarette pack on his night table and lit his first for the day.

They hung up.

"Who was that?" Allegro asked, yawning.

"Walter Trask." Alden was perched on the side of the bed, thinking, idly blowing smoke to the ceiling.

"Trask? Do I know him?"

"I mentioned him," Alden said. "Maybe you don't remember. I called him in New York. CIA."

Allegro sat up abruptly. "What did he want?"

Alden exhaled smoke. "Wants to have breakfast. Says he has information about the Raven. Took him long enough."

The familiar feeling of dread, of impending disaster, took hold of Allegro, the wrenching of the stomach, the tingling of nerve ends she had experienced ever since she had seen Nicky sitting at a table with Alden.

The Raven with his father.

Christ! First she had convinced herself she had to help if Philip insisted on his bull-headed quest. Then they lost track of the shipment and it was over—they had no way to track the Raven. Poor Harry's death had changed it all, and despite her misgivings, she was again resolved to support Alden.

"Where are you meeting him?" she asked.

"Downstairs. I'd better get a move on." He rose from the bed, headed for the bathroom.

"I'd like to go with you," Allegro said.

Alden stopped at the door. "No." He smiled. "You wouldn't like Trask. Anyway, I'll tell you everything when I get back."

Alden ordered coffee and croissants, and after the waiter had taken Trask's order, he looked across the table. "You sure pick the times, Walter. Seven o'clock in the morning. Christ!"

Trask raised his eyebrows. "I thought you were after the Raven."

"What made you think that?"

"You told me. Back in New York. And you followed the IRA arms shipment aboard the *American Brandy* to Liverpool." He sat across the table looking straight into Alden's eyes in his disconcerting way. The waiter had brought *café au lait* and had gone back for the croissants.

Trask took a sip from his cup and continued. "Then you went to London, where those bastards came within minutes of wasting the queen." He looked away for a second. "And you lost Harry Zimmerman."

Alden was aghast, holding his cup in midair. "How do you know all this?"

"We have our sources," Trask said.

Alden leaned forward. "Don't tell me you've picked him up?"

"No. Unfortunately."

"Then why this breakfast?"

Trask sighed, reached into his inside pocket, and pulled out a manila envelope. Inside was a photograph, one of several Trask had taken of the Raven on Sunday with his lighter-camera. He'd had them developed and blown up to five by seven.

"We finally have a picture," he said.

Alden looked hard at the envelope. "When was it taken?"

"Sunday."

Alden felt his skin go cold. He could sense they were close. "Where?" he asked. "Was it near here?"

"Here in Paris."

"Who saw him, took the picture? Who?" he asked. He was starting to rise from the table, his face suffused with blood.

"One of our informants," Trask said. He paused, again staring across the table. "He's dead now. The Raven killed him," he said, deliberately lying to add drama. "But he overlooked the camera. A miniature, in the form of a cigarette lighter." He nodded at his own lighter, which lay on the table between them. "Like that one."

"May I see it?" Alden asked.

Trask had been holding the envelope close to his chest. Now he handed it to Alden.

Alden opened the envelope quickly and removed the photograph. It was upside down. He turned it over. A handsome man in his thirties. A striking man.

Nicky. His own son.

Alden's hands began to shake. His face paled. With tears half formed in the corners of his eyes, he looked across the table at Trask. "Are you sure?" he asked.

Trask's blank stare never changed. "I'm sure. Why would I lie to you, Alden?" He paused. "Do you know him?"

Alden's voice choked as he lied. "No. This was taken in Paris? Sunday?"

Trask nodded. But he was laughing inside. Amateurs. They were like windows. Some you could see through clearly; others were dirty and not as transparent. But they were all weak and easily maneuvered.

"Then he's still in Paris?" Alden said.

"Who knows? He could be anyplace. Anyplace in the world," Trask said. "The Alps, Spain, Germany. Anyplace."

Alden felt sick. His stomach was churning, and sweat beaded his brow. He looked up at Trask and only saw what he had seen before, a man staring. Not a feature out of the ordinary or out of place.

"May I keep this?"

Trask nodded. "That's why I asked you to breakfast. We need your help, Alden. If you should by any chance see him."

"Why should I see him?" Alden blasted.

Trask shrugged. "We're not stupid men. You're after him yourself. You've got to have strong hatred for him after Kavanaugh and Zimmerman."

Alden rose. "Excuse me. I'm not feeling well."

He left the table.

Trask watched as Alden lurched across the dining room, staggering like a drunken man, weaving between tables, clutching chairs for support, making for the exit.

Trask smiled his little smile, a bare showing of teeth. He was convinced that Alden, betrayed and hurt, would kill his own son.

If it did not work out, he would have to devise another plan and keep his hands clean, let O'Rourke or Alden do the wet work. Nobody in the international terrorist organization would deal with him if they learned he had done in the Raven personally.

But he would if he had to—if he could do it without detection.

Trask decided to stay in Paris for a week and keep his

ears open. If it all panned out as expected, he would head
back to the States. If nothing happened, he would stay
another week; he would get into the wet work himself.
You had to be flexible to survive.

Allegro had just stepped out of the shower and was
toweling herself dry when she heard the door to the suite
open and close.

"Is that you, Philip?" she called.

She heard nothing.

"Philip?"

Still no response.

With the towel wrapped around her body, she came out
of the bathroom, crossed the bedroom, and peeked through
the open door to the living room.

Alden was seated on a couch, head down, a photograph
dangling from his hands.

"Philip?" she whispered as she walked over to him.
"What is it?"

He looked at her, his features torn with pain, a haunted,
haggard expression in his eyes. She had never seen him
like this.

"What's the matter, love?" she asked.

He lifted the photograph, held it out to her.

She took it, looked at it, hands trembling. "Where did
you get this?"

"Trask." Alden's voice was flat. "It's the Raven."

"I know," she said, her heart going out to him.

He answered as if he hadn't heard her reply. "My son,"
he said. He bit his lip tightly. "My own son."

"I know, Philip. I knew when I saw you together at Le
Bar des Théâtres," Allegro said. "But what could I do?
How could I tell you?" She knelt, grasped his knees,
letting the towel drop to the floor.

"Philip, it's *his* guilt, not your own," she insisted.

He raised his head and stared at her vacantly. "It's my
guilt, too. I fathered him. He's my seed."

"Why did Trask give this to you?"

"He says they need help. That if I see Nicky, I—" He
stopped, his face full of anguish. "He's my seed," he said
again. "And my guilt. I brought him into this world. Now

I have to destroy the plant that grew from that seed." He pounded a fist on one knee. "I must!"

"You're talking nonsense!" Allegro was on her feet again, wrapping the towel about her.

Alden looked up at her. "Why?"

"You can't kill your own son! No matter what he's done!"

Alden remained silent. He was remembering the locker room at the private school and the other boy in a coma after Nicky had beaten his head against the metal of the locker.

"He's dirt," he said evenly, without emotion.

"Philip!"

"He's always been dirt."

Allegro was on her knees again. "Why not call it off now?" she pleaded. "Let Trask find him or the Deuxième Bureau or Interpol or MI6. Leave it to the professionals."

Alden smiled wanly. "The professionals." His tone left no doubt about his conviction. The professionals had blown it for years.

Allegro was on her feet again. "All right! Have it your way! But *your* way isn't *my* way. I don't want to be witness to patricide or filicide!" She had started for the bedroom, but whirled on him again. "I was with you when it was just the Raven, a terrorist bastard who deserved to die. But this . . . Count me out, Philip. I'm going back to the States."

Alden glanced up at her. He said softly, "Go back to the States then. I wouldn't want you to see it either. I love you too much. You've given me something to live for."

Allegro broke into sobs. "Philip, for God's sake! You know I love you."

He held his arms out to her and she fell into them, kneeling again, weeping into his shoulder. He grasped her to him.

"Please, Philip," she sobbed into his shoulder, "please give it up. I was with you before, but I can't let you do this. Not to your son. Terrorism will always be a fact of life. We've had the terrorist disease through eight thousand years of history. It's not going to go away."

"It has no justification, no reason. Not for sane men," Alden said quietly.

"Damn the reason!" Allegro said, pulling away from him. "You'll never find a reason, except man's inhumanity to man. They have to fight, to be macho, to say 'Cross that line, I dare you.' It's a sorry world, Philip, and one man's not going to change it overnight."

Her sobbing stopped. "I love you so," she said, her face still streaked with tears, and kissed him. She tried to smile. It came forth tremulous and quivering. "Look, love, we're in France. Beautiful, wonderful France. Why don't we see it, go every place?"

Alden gazed at her thoughtfully, distantly, but said nothing.

"We'll do everything," she said, trying to work up his enthusiasm, endeavoring to bring him out of his dismal preoccupied state. "The wine country, Nice, St. Tropez, the Midi." She pressed against him, looked straight into his eyes. "It will give you time to think. After all, you can't expect to find the Raven soon. He's a needle in a haystack."

Alden continued to gaze at her, unshaken in his resolve.

"Chamonix," she said. "We'll visit Alicia!"

At the mention of Chamonix and Alicia, Alden felt a sudden terror rip at his gut. *He could be anyplace*, Trask had said. *The Alps*.

Alicia. *We don't get along too well*, Nicky had said.

Alden was gripped by a frigid fear. He couldn't, he thought. He couldn't!

The Raven could well have headed for Chamonix.

"All right," he said without inflection. "We'll do that. We'll do it your way."

"Call her now," Allegro said. "Call her right now." Her voice was eager. She thought she had won him over again.

"I'll do that. But," he added, "don't forget. It's only a time for thinking things through."

"I know."

He smiled tightly. "Get dressed. You're a distraction that way."

Allegro rose, smiling again, and started for the bedroom. At the door she stopped, turned. "You couldn't kill your own son, could you?"

He thought for several seconds before answering. "I don't know," he finally said. "Go get dressed."

When Allegro closed the bedroom door, Alden picked up the phone and put in a call to the Richemond Hotel in Chamonix. He asked for Alicia Alden. The call went through quickly.

"Allo," she answered in the French way.

"It's me, Alicia. Dad."

"Daddy!"

"I'm in Paris."

"Paris! Fantastic!" she exclaimed, then paused. "What brought you to Paris?"

He paused before he spoke, his mind clicking. "Research," he said. "But it doesn't take all my time. We thought we'd visit you before heading back."

"Great! Just great! Who's the we?"

"Allegro and me."

"Wonderful! I like Allegro. When will you be arriving?"

"Soon as possible. Tonight if that suits you."

She sounded excited. It was a welcome change from the events of the past two weeks and the bad news about Nicky.

"Sure. The work's easy and the whole place is laid back. Love to see you." The delight in her voice was obvious. "Daddy, take the TGV. It's a thrill, really, and a beautiful trip. From Lyon you can get another train or hire a car."

"Alicia," he lowered his voice. "Have you seen Nicky?"

"Nicky? Why should I see that creep?"

Alden's chest tightened. "Just wondering. You haven't heard from him?"

"Daddy," Alicia said impatiently, "he goes his way and I go mine. Never the twain should meet."

"Okay, sweetheart," Alden said. "See you tonight."

CHAPTER 33

The Train à grande vitesse, or TGV as it is known, is one of the fastest trains in the world. It cruises at a hundred and sixty-five miles per hour and can attain a top speed of close to two hundred and forty miles per hour. It covers the distance from Paris to Lyon in two hours.

Allegro found the trip through the beautiful countryside a joy. "Look!" she kept saying to Alden. "Look, look, look," while she pointed out farms and pastures, villages and vineyards, tunnels, bridges, and churches.

But Alden was preoccupied, and she had to nudge him every so often to have him take notice.

"Yes, that's pretty," he would say. Or, "Very nice."

She understood, and her heart filled with pity for him.

"What did Alicia say on the phone?" she asked.

"Alicia?" He seemed to be searching for words. "She said she'd be glad to see us, I told you that."

"Nothing else?"

"She likes you. That's about all." He sank again into silence. After a while he said, "I didn't tell her about Nicky."

"You shouldn't. It would upset her," Allegro said.

Alden fell again to musing.

We don't get along, we don't get along, we don't get along. It took on the rhythm of the wheels of the tracks. *We don't get along, we don't get along.*

Alden's anger rose; his fear for Alicia nearly strangled

him. He looked at Allegro. Did she notice? Could she see it? He stretched his lips into a false smile.

When they reached Lyon, Allegro suggested a rental car for the trip to Chamonix.

"That's over two hundred miles!" Alden said. "And over mountains!"

"You're a good driver. Besides, the country is so beautiful." She wanted him to relax, enjoy the scenic views, come out of his funk. She wanted him to be like he was before . . . before the meeting with Nicky at Le Bar des Théâtres. She wanted him to love her again, free from his obsessions and preoccupations . . . to pay attention to her.

"Christ!" Alden complained.

But they hired a car.

Trask learned that the IRA men had failed soon after he arrived back at his hotel. He had checked in with the Paris station chief, who had all the details. The Deuxième Bureau had their noses in it now. They had taken Corrigan's body to their own coroner for examination and had an all points out on the Raven.

"How did they figure the Raven?" Trask asked.

"The thing in London—the explosion on the Mall? Interpol has sent word out," the station chief said. "They're sure it was the IRA and the Raven doing a job together. Corrigan is IRA. They're just adding it up."

"That the way you see it?" Trask asked.

"Pretty much."

"What about the man I asked you to watch at the Hilton?"

"Checked out. Rented a car and headed south."

"Somehow I feel you are going to give me some bad news. What is it?" Trask asked.

"Our man was in an accident. We've lost him."

"Great. Just great." Trask wasn't as displeased as he sounded, but wasn't about to let the man off the hook. "What about Alden? You lose him, too?"

"Alden took the train partway and is driving the rest of way. He has a daughter working at a hotel in Chamonix."

"That gets you off the hook, my friend," Trask said. He alone knew the Raven and Alden were father and son.

If Alden was heading for Chamonix, it followed the Raven was, too. But why? "You can pull your man off Alden," he said. "I'll take it from here."

"You should take it easy, Mr. Trask. If the Raven's close by, it could get messy."

"When I want your advice, I'll ask for it," Trask screamed at the man. "And keep your goons clear. From here on, it's mine. Got that?" Trask slammed the receiver down. Every time he decided to go into the field, one of the young bucks reminded him he was getting old. Fuck them.

He was slipping an arm through the webbing of his shoulder holster when the phone rang again. "Yeah," he shouted into the receiver.

"Listen carefully, Trask. Corrigan bought it doing your dirty work and I may, too," O'Rourke said. "But I wanted to tell you the Raven is heading south through the mountains. I'm on his tail."

"How the hell did you know my ho—"

"Shut up and listen!" O'Rourke interrupted. "You're not the only one with contacts. I want to make sure that if I miss, you'll be backing me up. You got that?"

"Sure. Where is he now?"

"Buying gas. We're at"—he leaned out the booth to look—"Villeneuve."

"He's heading for Chamonix," Trask said, his voice picking up enthusiasm as he went along. "That's past Lyon. He won't want to cross over into Switzerland, so he'll pass through Chambéry and take Route 525 through the mountains. You got that?"

"Yes. Hurry. He's getting in his car."

"No problem. You pass him and wait in the mountains on Route 525. Don't let him spot you."

"Are you sure, Trask?"

"Absolutely. You got a map?"

"Yes."

"Okay. Wait for him just past Albertville. Good luck."

"Thanks. If he gets to Chamonix, get him for me . . . for all of us."

"You can bet on it."

*   *   *

The so-called charter airline that took Grushenko to Paris that night consisted of three small jets—two British and one American. The KGB ownership was unknown to MI6 or the CIA. It filed procedural flight plans and all was seemingly in order.

It landed at a small airport outside Paris, again manned by KGB agents, so Grushenko had no trouble with his Smith & Wesson revolver.

He went straight to the Hotel George V and approached the front desk. "Is Mr. Philip Alden registered?" he asked in French.

The desk clerk looked through the files. "No," he finally said. "He checked out today."

"Any forwarding address?"

"*Non.* Sorry, monsieur."

"*Merci,*" Grushenko said, and turned.

He took a seat in the lobby, pulled out a pack of cigarettes, and started to chain-smoke, thinking. He had never quite believed that Alden had given up pursuit of the Raven, and since he had read about the death of Alden's agent, Harry Zimmerman, he was sure that the hurt continued.

Grushenko lit his second cigarette and pondered, remembering. Alden had said something to him on the phone about visiting his daughter somewhere in the south of France. Where? Then it came to him. Chamonix, a resort in the French Alps. It had hotels, swimming pools, Mont Blanc to the south. It had . . .

He stopped, his thought on one word: gambling.

Of course. Chamonix had a gambling casino. And the Raven loved to gamble. That was one of the few things in the Raven's dossier Grushenko could depend on. The man would plan his action near a casino if he had a choice.

Grushenko rose from his chair and left the hotel. He got into a cab outside the George V and told the driver to take him to the Soviet Embassy.

No one he knew worked at the Paris KGB station. But they all knew of the great Vladislav Grushenko. Being a legend had its advantages.

While he was talking to the bureau chief, the pain

grabbed him so fiercely he fell to his knees, bringing on a searing pain in his broken leg.

They carried him upstairs to a bed, sent for the doctor. He was given two painkillers and a cup of hot tea.

"I will rest," he told them. "But first, have you anything for me?"

"A young man answering the Raven's description rented a car and was seen to take the autoroute to the southern provinces," the station chief, seated by his bed, told him. "Another report placed Philip Alden and Allegro Stern on the train to Lyon, where he then hired a car."

Chamonix. Grushenko was sure of it now.

"I will sleep tonight, but I will need the helicopter in the morning."

"Are you sure you can do it alone, comrade?" the station chief asked.

Grushenko knew he must look like hell. If he were the station chief, he would insist on taking over. But he was Grushenko and the station chief would keep his mouth closed.

Alden and Allegro arrived in Chamonix late that evening and registered at the Richemond. When Alicia saw them, her lips broke into a wide grin.

"Daddy! Allegro! Wow!"

"Hi, Alicia." Allegro smiled.

Alden took his daughter in his arms, hugged her tightly. Alicia noticed tears in his eyes. This was unlike him.

"Hungry?" Alicia asked.

"Famished," Allegro said.

The dining room was still open and they seated themselves at a table in the corner. "This is my bailiwick," Alicia announced. "I was promoted to assistant banquet manager last week."

"Well, congratulations," Allegro said.

Alden only smiled, engaging his daughter's eyes with his own, staring at her as though she were a possession, a treasure that he feared would suddenly disappear.

They chatted, they laughed, they exchanged experiences. But Alden was preoccupied, as though on the other side of a pane of glass looking in.

At length, he excused himself for the rest room.

Alicia paused, then asked. "What's the matter with him? Aren't you two getting along?"

Allegro took a drag of her cigarette, letting the smoke drift from her nostrils. "We get along all right."

"Is it Nicky?"

Allegro's eyes flicked upward at Alicia. "Why do you ask?"

"I don't now. When he phoned from Paris, Daddy asked me if I'd seen him or heard from him." Alicia sighed. "Maybe I'm just warped, imagining things. But I think he's worried about Nicky."

Allegro said nothing.

The old Peugeot was tucked in behind a snowbank just west of Beaufort. O'Rourke had scouted the road ahead and then doubled back. He knew exactly where he was going to do it. Between his position and the outskirts of Beaufort ten miles ahead, he had spotted three dropoffs where a car could be forced off the road.

While he thought about it, the red sports car flashed by. He had been expecting it, but the car was upon him and past in a split second. No matter. He could catch it. He could catch it and put it over the side.

That was the best way. No more relying on guns and bombs. No hand-to-hand stuff. He had the bigger car and he would have the advantage. The red Porsche could go faster than his Peugeot—but not on this mountain road.

He engaged the clutch awkwardly into first gear, and pulled out of his hiding place. He shifted to second, then bypassed to fourth on the next shift. This wasn't a race. He would gain quickly enough, and when he did, it would be time to avenge his friends.

The miles slipped by as he drove. The Raven thrilled to the curves of the mountain roads, kept the revs as high as he could without skidding off the edge.

Traffic had not been heavy since he'd passed Chambéry. He hadn't seen a car in the past ten minutes or more. Then he saw it. At first he just got a flash of it as it turned into the same straightaway as he. Then he saw it every time a new turn came up.

Finally, it was on his tail and he had to decide whether to let it pass or to floor the gas pedal and leave the car behind.

What the hell? He hadn't been feeling his best. For once, he would let the car pass and keep his cool.

They approached a long straightaway. The mountain was on their right. The car could pass on the left, with the dropoff on its left.

But it held back, riding in his draft.

On the next straightaway the mountain was on the left, and the dropoff, on his right. Again the car held back.

This didn't smell right.

Nicky pressed the accelerator to the floor, but it gained him nothing. The bigger car handled the packed snow better. It slowly pulled alongside, on his left.

The driver had bandages on his head and arm, sandy-colored hair, and a wide grin on his face.

O'Rourke! Damn! He knew he'd made a mistake back in Paris. He should have killed the damned fool.

The grinning O'Rourke pulled his steering wheel to the right. The two cars bumped. The Raven swung his wheel toward the bigger car, trying to compensate, but he didn't have enough weight. After the second bump, his front wheel cut through the snow and sent gravel flying over the edge.

The Raven watched the road disappear in front of him as he slipped off the edge. He had no time to watch for traffic ahead, but became aware that the larger car had pulled back and was letting an oncoming vehicle pass.

The Raven pulled free of the edge, tried to speed up, to use the opportunity to slip away. He failed. On the next straightaway, the same conditions prevailed, and for the first time the Raven felt he was going to lose, was going to pay the price at last.

Again, O'Rourke gained on him and tried to come alongside. The Raven swung his car out, blocking the larger vehicle. They bumped. The Raven had to steer wildly to hold the road.

They bumped again, this time much harder. The Raven's Porsche fishtailed wildly, but he managed to hold his position until they came to the bend. They would be at the next town soon. He couldn't stop until then.

They flashed around the bend, ignoring the possibility of other traffic. O'Rourke held his position all the way around, managed to gain as they hit the straightaway.

Again that grinning face. Again the crunch of metal on metal as the bigger car pushed the Raven toward oblivion.

The Raven didn't trust himself to brake since the tires didn't have good traction on the snow. But he had few options. As O'Rourke pulled the steering wheel in his direction, a satisfied grin on his face, the Raven braked and prayed . . . prayed he wouldn't just skid straight off the edge.

The brakes put him into a controlled skid. O'Rourke slid past, but immediately slammed on the brakes and started a slow circle in the middle of the road.

They were running out of straightaway. The Porsche had dropped back about fifty feet. The Peugeot continued to slide in a long, slow turn.

Everything seemed to be happening in slow motion to the Raven. He could see O'Rourke wasn't going to make it and was no longer concerned about him. His problem was how to avoid following the bigger car down.

He eased his foot off the brake, turned the steering wheel slightly to the left, gave the car some speed. He shot past the Peugeot and into the next turn.

As he hit the next straightaway, he looked in his rear mirror and saw nothing. At the next curve he continued watching the mirror, but saw nothing.

A mile farther on, the Raven brought the Porsche to a stop, made a U-turn, and slowly retraced the last few miles. Around the second bend, a blue car stood at the side of the road. The passengers were standing, pointing to something below.

He slowed, made another turn, and rolled down the window. He didn't have to get out. He could smell the burning fuel. In the clear mountain air the smell was unmistakable.

O'Rourke had bought it.

As he put the Porsche in first gear and pulled away, he wondered how many others were after him.

CHAPTER 34

The encounter with O'Rourke had shaken the Raven. It was so unexpected and so vicious. What the hell had the Irish madman wanted from him? It wasn't his fault that prick Zimmerman spoiled the plan. Did they think he didn't care it hadn't gone down? Had they expected an apology, for God's sake?

In the hours since O'Rourke's car had plunged over the cliff and burst into flames, the Raven had been on the run, moving quicker than planned. He had to stop often to vomit. His nerves were shot. What if O'Rourke wasn't dead? No. There was no way the damned IRA man could have survived. He was becoming paranoid. What had happened to the cool and collected Raven?

Damn!

He had decided to rent a car and drive from Paris to Chamonix at a leisurely pace, stopping along the way, gambling where he could find a casino, picking up broads. He'd been in no hurry.

He'd wanted to go slow, to try to get his health back. He had been feeling ill for too long. He wanted to be what he once was, hale and hearty, strong, sinewy, macho.

But he was still shaken. His hands trembled at everything, the minutest chore—pouring a drink, holding a newspaper, buttoning his shirt. With the few women he had met recently, his erection was limp. He blamed it on the women and became angry.

He wondered what he would find in Chamonix. Alicia,

341

for one. She worked at a hotel. It was a small resort town, had only a few hotels.

Alicia. Pop's favorite.

If his father showed up there, he would kill him, too!

He would kill them all!

Another spasm gripped the Raven's stomach, and the car veered across the oncoming lane and back. He steered onto the shoulder and brought it to a halt. He opened the door and leaned out, vomited a thin stream onto the road.

He got out and stood looking at the magnificent vista spread out before him, at the deep cleft in the earth covered with evergreens from valley floor to a line along the ranging peaks, magnificent growth as far as the altitude would allow, pure white snow above the treeline. At any other time he would have gloried in the scene.

He looked back at the car, at the scrape along the side where O'Rourke had played his games.

He felt like hell. He had not been eating well, had been drinking too much, hitting the pot too hard, and once had mainlined.

That's all it is, he thought. Garden-variety dissipation. I have to eat more, stay off the booze and drugs, he told himself. Get my body and head back together.

He stood still for a few minutes, taking deep breaths of mountain air, then returned to the car, turned the ignition key, and went on with his life.

The Raven arrived in Chamonix Friday morning and registered under an assumed name at the Mont-Blanc, one of the more expensive hotels.

In his room, he flopped on the bed.

Alicia could wait.

The department of Haute-Savoie in France is bounded on the north by Lake Geneva and in the south by Mont Blanc and its range of smaller peaks and glaciers. To the east lies Switzerland, with just a wedge of Italy sharing the Mont Blanc area.

The village of Chamonix is in the south, just about twelve miles northeast of Mont Blanc, which dominates the scene with its 15,771-foot elevation. The village itself shares a valley with the Arve River, its left bank in the shadow of Mont Brévent, a mountain rising over 8,000 feet above sea level. Chamonix is on the right bank of the Arve, at an elevation of approximately 3,300 feet, nestling close to a range of mountains named Aigulles, the Needles.

Up, up, almost vertically straight up behind Chamonix, about another 6,000 feet, the Mer de Glace runs majestically, a sea of ice, four and a half miles long.

Flowing year by year, century by century, it has inched its way along for over sixty million years, ever since the Cenozoic Era. It hangs like a frozen monster over the village.

The shining sea of ice is approached by a cog railroad not far from the Gare Central, which rises to Montenvers. A restaurant is perched on the crags of Montenvers, commanding a magnificent view of the surrounding peaks and valleys—Mont Blanc, Pic du Midi, Mer de Glace—and the village of Chamonix.

It was here that the Raven intended to spend the first few days of his visit. He did not stay at the restaurant with its crowds of people, but walked the glacier, making his way along the rocky moraines at its sides, wandering far and wide, exploring both the geography and the hard-to-reach crannies of his troubled mind.

The morning after he arrived, he sat on a rock, chin in hands, and surveyed the awesome beauty of the Mer de Glace, its changing multitudinous colors—the shades of blue, the hues of purple. At times, as the sun coursed through its arc overhead, the panorama would be bathed in reds, browns, oranges . . . a kaleidoscope . . . a rainbow.

Here he sat for hours, in a lonely spot far from any human being. He brooded about his life, his twisted world, his sins.

Suppose it had been different, he thought. Suppose he had followed in his father's footsteps and had become a writer. A small, bitter laugh came from his throat. A writer! Pops certainly hadn't encouraged that. He had written a short story when he was twelve, while visiting his father on the Coast, and the man had criticized it, torn it to pieces.

His mother had encouraged him in everything, indulged

him. But that fucker with his high standards of morality and perfection had left him empty.

Power, money, status—those were the important things, he thought. Power, money, status, and the things they brought.

Looking out across the glacier, he turned his thoughts to death. For it looked like death. The oranges, reds, and ambers were gone. Now the icy landscape reflected only varying hues of blues and purples. It was a domain of death.

Even the silence was deathlike.

I'm dead and I don't know it! he thought. Goddamn you, old man! Goddamn you, God! You've murdered me and you won't even let me know it!

He slapped himself, flung snow into his face. The sting brought him to his senses. Death had no pain. Nothing in death. Nothing. Just a long sleep, without pain, without anguish, without a conscience nagging him. Total oblivion.

Pain meant he was alive.

He stood up as though to prove it. He started back toward Montenvers and Chamonix.

And Alicia.

He had learned where she worked. At the Richemond. He would kill her. He would take away from that god the thing he adored most. He would get him where it hurt.

And if his father were in Chamonix, the Raven would kill him, too.

He would kill God!

He laughed, and his laughter echoed across the glacier in a mocking voice. He would rape Alicia before he killed her. He'd always been infatuated with her.

Why not?

He laughed again. He had regained some strength in the mountain air, had limited his Grand Marnier to two a day, and had not taken a toke of grass or anything else, had eaten—and kept the food down.

He would kill Alicia.

He would kill them all.

He would kill God!

* * *

That same morning, Allegro awoke to find Alden nude on the floor at the foot of the bed, doing push-ups, sit-ups, leg exercises, and Yoga stretches.

"What are you doing?" she asked sleepily.

"Got to keep in shape," he said panting.

"Shape? What kind of shape? You'll kill yourself."

He murmured something unintelligible.

She watched, fascinated, taking in his broad shoulders, rippling muscles, narrow waist, strong legs and biceps. She felt a tingling between her thighs.

"I can think of better ways to exercise," she said.

He stopped, breathing heavily, looking up at her. "And just what would that be?"

"Come up here, and I'll tell you."

Alden lunged up from the floor, already hard.

This time they needed no foreplay. A few kisses and they cleaved together, on their sides, facing each other, eyes open. Panting, grasping for a few minutes, plunging, and then they came as one.

Alden remained inside her, his penis still half erect. Soon he was fully tumescent again; he rolled her onto her back, loomed above her, took her in long, slow strokes. Allegro's head moved from side to side. She bit his wrist. She screamed.

When it was done, when they were both spent, Allegro said softly, "You're strong. I like that."

He grunted. He was gone from her. His mind was with Nicky.

Allegro did not try to break through. He'll work it out for himself, she thought.

She lit a cigarette, but after two puffs it tasted rancid and she crushed the burning tip in the night-table ashtray. She rose from the bed and crossed to the clothes closet.

"Yes, get dressed," she heard Alden say from the bed. "We'll go for a drive."

The small airport at Chamonix was not built for jets. You arrived at Chamonix by car, small aircraft, or helicopter. Grushenko stepped from the helicopter, grimaced as his bad leg hit the frozen ground.

Bright sun attacked his watery eyes. A fierce wind whipped

in from the mountains, rocking the helicopter behind him. As a car pulled up for him, another helicopter came in out of the sun. He didn't see it. He was too involved with the pain and his inner thoughts.

The Raven had to die. He didn't want Alden to do it. The man would have to live with it for the rest of his life. No. It was his job. He had helped create the monster and he would destroy him.

If he had the strength to do it. He could feel it leak from him hour by hour. He was having trouble walking. His hands shook.

He talked constantly to a god he'd never known. To the unfamiliar god, he prayed for strength.

Trask was filled by the memories of all the crazy jobs he'd taken on for Uncle Sam. Since the days of Wild Bill Donovan, he'd put his life on the line scores of times. One day, if you challenged the odds too often, you would come up empty. He knew that.

Trask was so preoccupied, he didn't see anything but the glare of sun off the ice below. He had no interest in the wonders of nature, the town. He thought only about the people: Alden, Allegro, and Alden's daughter, Alicia. They were probably in danger. He'd have to get to the Raven first.

He'd had a report about a car going off the road about fifty miles south of Chamonix. The charred wreck was the same model that O'Rourke had been driving. O'Rourke had failed. Nothing stood between the Raven and his victims now but an old agent, a man truly out in the cold.

But he was going to succeed. He *had* to succeed. He needed absolution, even if he had to provide it himself.

During the drive, Alden and Allegro spoke little, Alden looking ahead at the twisting road, Allegro smoking. Every now and again, she glanced at Alden, but he did not notice. His eyes were fixed on the road. His face was set in grim lines.

"Where are we going?" she asked.

"Just a drive," he mumbled.

They drove for ten or twelve minutes, then turned into a

side road that led through a dense stand of forest. The road
was rough and bumpy. It narrowed to a dead end. Alden
stopped the car, turned off the ignition, and got out.
Allegro followed him, wondering what he had in mind. He
seemed to be searching for something.

At last he stopped, looking ahead. "Wait here," he
said, and walked toward a large tree about thirty feet
away.

She watched as he halted before the tree and withdrew
two sheets of paper from his pocket. Targets, with
bull's-eyes.

He walked back to her, the 7.65-mm automatic in his
hand. "Target practice," he said flatly.

Then he turned from her and, half squatting, legs apart,
held the gun in two hands and squeezed off a full clip. He
hit the bull's-eye with one, kept the rest within a five-inch
circle.

He had not touched a drop of liquor since the day he had
met Trask in Paris. He was exercising, getting into shape.
Now he was practicing with a gun. And the paper target
represented his own son. Nicky.

Allegro realized they had come down the final stretch of
road. No turning back now. He had told her in Paris, when
they sat at a table at Le Bar des Théâtres, that Nicky was
planning a vacation in the French Alps. And his sister, or
half sister, Alicia, was here. Alden was getting ready to
kill his son. Or be killed by his son.

The last stretch of road.

His voice brought her out of her reverie. "Well? You
want to try?"

She looked at Alden and the blur became a face. He was
smiling grimly. She forced herself to be strong for him.
She resumed control. Play it cool, she said to herself. Play
it cool.

She removed her gun from the lens case cum purse and
took her stance, her body at a right angle to the target. She
raised the gun above her head, straight up toward the sky.
Slowly, her arm began to descend.

She squeezed off three shots in rapid succession. Two
hit the outer rim. The third nicked the bull's-eye.

*   *   *

The Raven was restless. He went to the casino that evening. He gambled, but indifferently, accepting his wins and losses without interest. He didn't know whether he had come out a winner or loser in the end, and he didn't care. He didn't even try to pick up a girl, and many at the tables had been stunning.

He went to his room early, had a nightcap, and got into bed, his mind spinning in anticipation of the next day. He'd had enough of a holiday. It was time for action.

Trask checked into a small *pension*, a kind of guest house, then roamed the town, ending up at the casino. As he walked up the steps, he had no way of knowing that the Raven had left only minutes before and was not more than fifty feet away.

Trask entered the casino, walked from one room to another, searched every face at the blackjack tables, at the craps table, and the chemin de fer room. No Raven.

He thought about asking the pit bosses if they had seen a man fitting the Raven's description, but too many men in the room had the same general appearance.

He would have to keep looking.

As Trask walked down the steps of the casino, a car pulled up. A crippled old man stepped out. The light from a street lamp illuminated Trask's face.

Grushenko moved back momentarily. He knew the man. Who was he? The old Russian searched his brain. A series of files he'd studied in Moscow started to come clear in his mind. Trask. Walter Trask. The man was as old as he. What the hell was he doing in Chamonix?

Then it came to him. The CIA had finally got a line on the Raven. Perhaps they traced him to his family and were keeping an eye on them hoping he'd make contact.

The Agency would want the Raven alive. Grushenko had to get to him before they did. They couldn't learn who had set him up in the business of terrorism.

Pain tore at his chest, almost bringing him to his knees. He felt weak. He felt so damned weak!

*   *   *

The Raven tossed and turned, couldn't get to sleep. His eyes, half open, scanned the darkened room. His confused mind thought he could see the spirit of O'Rourke standing over him. He waved his hands to shake off the hallucination, as he always did when his victims came to torment him at night. He fought O'Rourke off with waving arms and mumbled entreaties to leave him in peace.

"Why should you have peace, you devil?" a voice said.

O'Rourke seemed so real, standing there. In the dim light the Raven could see the bandages, now blackened with smoke. The sandy hair was disheveled. The hand that held the gun shook.

Gun? The Raven shook his head, sat up in bed, and shook his head again.

"It's me, right enough," O'Rourke said. "This is your third strike, Yank. You missed me twice and this is your last time at the wicket."

"O'Rourke!" the Raven moaned. His face took on a ghostly pallor as he pushed against the back of the bed.

"I hope you're ready to die, you filthy bastard," O'Rourke croaked hoarsely. "Never have I seen a devil like you. And I've seen a few." He stopped for a few seconds. The gun shook in his hand. "I've got six bullets. I'm going to shoot you six times. I have plenty of time."

He fired. The bullet almost grazed the Raven's skull. He pulled the blankets higher, begging for mercy.

"You'll get no mercy from me," O'Rourke said, coming around the bed to stand closer.

The Raven had panicked for a moment. Where was the man who had always been cool under fire? he asked himself. He looked at the Irishman. The sandy-haired giant was hovering over him, grinning, his bandaged arm close to the bed.

The Raven lashed out with a foot, caught the blood-soaked bandage full on.

O'Rourke screamed. The gun fired again, sending a slug into the pillow next to the Raven's head. The Raven grabbed the gun as the IRA man slid to the floor. The Raven was in charge again. He laughed like a madman, leaned over the wounded man, pointed the gun. "This time you are dead, you fucking nuisance." He started to pull the trigger and thought about the noise the shots would make. It was a miracle no one had investigated the first two. He turned the gun in his hand and brought it down on the sandy-colored head. Once . . . twice . . . a third time. Each time he struck with more force. Blood splattered on his nightclothes and the sheets.

O'Rourke was off his back at last. The Raven slumped to the floor beside the body. Blood had poured from the wounds. O'Rourke's eyes were rolled upward and his tongue lolled out of his mouth. Not a pretty sight.

He had to get rid of the body. He walked to the balcony doors, opened them, stepped out, and looked over the side. A huge trash container stood below and to one side. He was on the sixth floor. His room faced a dark and gloomy mountain. Maybe he could toss the body down.

Back inside, he rolled O'Rourke's body in a bloodied sheet and carried it to the balcony. It wasn't easy. He lacked the strength he'd had only weeks ago. He hoisted the body over the balcony rail, aimed it for the container below, and shoved.

He watched with horror as the body hit the inner lip of the container, and hung, half in and half out.

God Almighty! He would have to go down there.

The Raven moved fast. He pulled on his clothes haphazardly, his heart beating wildly in his chest. It had never been like this. It had always been cool, controlled. He was the Raven. It had never been like this.

He rolled up the other sheet together with his pajamas. The hallway was clear. He went down the back stairs two at a time. A door led out to the rear service area. As he opened it, he prayed that no one would be around, that no one had seen the corpse tumble down.

No one was in sight. He reached up, past the pulpy skull to the shoulder, and pushed hard. The body moved slowly upward until it finally fell inside, out of sight. The Raven wiped the blood from his hands and tossed the other sheet over the side into the container.

Back in his room, the Raven knelt over the toilet bowl and retched for a few minutes, then sat down to think. It had never been like this. Usually he planned ahead. Finally, he sneaked out to the hall, took fresh linen from the maids' closet, and made his bed again, rumpling the sheets.

He lit a cigarette and slumped into a chair, then jumped up suddenly, and packed his bags. He would move to another hotel to give himself time. All he needed was about twelve hours and it would be over.

He would kill Alicia. After that, he didn't know. He wasn't sure if he cared after that.

CHAPTER 35

While his son fought for his soul and for his life, Alden snored. Allegro lay awake, her ears pounding, staring into an enveloping darkness. Should she do something to forestall the hideous confrontation? Someone would be killed, and she was sure it would be Philip.

But Nicky might contact Alicia, or he might not. He might be in Chamonix, or he could be anywhere. Sh̲ ̲ad only suspicions—and dread.

Would the police place any credence in her suspicio ̲ ̲
They would laugh at her.

Or would they? She was a photojournalist with many credits to her name. She had met the Raven and other terrorists. They might take heed.

The next morning, the Raven awoke refreshed. After the horror show with O'Rourke, he should have been wrung out, but his new regimen of abstention was paying off. At ten-thirty, he called Alicia.

"Morning, sis," the Raven said jovially.

"Nicky!"

"Surprise!"

"Where are you?" Alicia asked, the hand that held the telephone trembling.

"Here. In Chamonix. Great place. Thought we might have lunch together."

For a moment Alicia hesitated. She had promised Alle-

352

gro. But if she could reunite the family, she would be a heroine.

"I usually eat here," she said.

"The Richemond's a rathole."

"I happen to be assistant banquet manager!"

The Raven laughed. "Okay, Assistant Banquet Manager, how about taking a vacation from that dump? I know a little bistro near the Central Station that has great food. It's called Le Coq d'Or. How about one o'clock?"

"Okay. But make it twelve-thirty."

"Right. See you there."

After hanging up, Alicia pondered a moment. Allegro had said not to tell Daddy. But she could tell Allegro. She rang their suite, but after nine rings, she gave up. They were probably out on one of their drives.

She sighed. She might as well see Nicky and learn his side of the misunderstanding.

Grushenko awoke with a fever. Every bone in his body ached. His broken leg hurt more than ever. The searing pain in his lungs was almost more than he could bear. Since leaving Liverpool, the old Russian had taken no painkillers. He had to keep alert, couldn't afford a clouded mind.

He looked at his clothes, hanging over a stuffed chair across the room. He felt so weak. The clothes seemed so far away. As he struggled for control, a pain like he'd never felt in his life engulfed his chest.

Oh, God! Oh, God! You can't! Again he called to a foreign god.

The plea didn't help. The black void he'd been fighting claimed him at last.

Le Coq d'Or was quiet and subdued. The waiter did not hover over their corner booth, but kept a discreet distance. It was the right place for uninterrupted conversation.

"What are you doing in Chamonix, of all places?" Alicia asked.

The Raven smiled. "Just passing through."

"To where?"

The Raven shrugged.

"How did you know I was here?"

"Pops told me."

Alicia's face registered a look of surprise. "Then you know he's here?"

The Raven's chest tightened, but he kept a calm exterior. "Pops? Here in Chamonix?"

It had slipped out, and now her heart was fluttering. "Yes. Didn't you know?"

The Raven shook his head. "No, I didn't. I bumped into him in Paris and he told me you were here."

"How long have you been in Chamonix?"

"Not long," the Raven said. His heart was pounding, adrenaline gushing into the pulsing streams of his arteries.

"How long will you be here?" she asked.

"I don't know. I kind of like it here."

"What've you been doing with yourself? We have no skiing this time of year, unless you go high up."

"I go up to the glacier. It's nice. I walk there alone to think. Away from people. It's peaceful."

He peered across the table at her, a strange glint in his eyes. "Maybe you'd like to go with me. Maybe this afternoon."

The invitation slipped by Alicia. She had been looking at him carefully. "You don't look well, Nicky." Much as she considered him a creep and a ne'er-do-well, she had some feelings for him.

"What do you mean, I don't look good?" He expanded his chest. "Decided to take off some weight, that's all. I feel great! Just great!"

"You on a diet?"

"Yeah, you might say that."

"Well, just don't turn into a skeleton," Alicia said. "There're people who love you."

"Who?" He laughed bitterly.

"Daddy, for one."

An expression of contempt crept across his face.

"You don't understand Daddy," she said.

"I don't understand *him*! Bullshit! I understand him like he was the back of my own hand!" The Raven's face was reddening.

"Well then, how do you see him?" Alicia asked.

"I see him as a prick! A cold, aloof, perfectionist prick! If people don't measure up to his standards, he has no use for them," he said, pounding a fist on the table. The ashtray jumped and fell to the floor. "That shit! He ruined my life!"

The Raven's outburst came as a shock to Alicia. The rift was wider than she had thought, but maybe she could heal it. She kept her eyes steady as she reached for the ashtray and set it on the table before her.

"You've got it all twisted," she said.

"Oh, yeah? You tell me, sis, how do you size him up?"

She pondered, flicked an ash off her cigarette. "Introspective, as a writer should be. Cynical perhaps, but I think that cynical approach to life is a defense mechanism to conceal his emotions."

"Emotions?" the Raven said with deadly calm. "I never noticed."

"Oh, he has them all right," Alicia said, her eyes wet with her own emotion. "He loves deeply, but he's ashamed to admit it. And he's got a guilt complex a mile wide."

"About what?"

"About you, me—everything."

The Raven couldn't digest this complex thought. To him, things were either black or white. He stared glumly into his snifter of Grand Marnier. He had not eaten a particle of his lunch.

Alicia studied him, her eyes flicking from his food to the drink—his second—and to his gaunt face.

"That's quite a diet you're on."

"Yeah," the Raven said without raising his eyes. "Where's he staying?"

"At the Richemond."

The Raven changed the subject. His eyes took on a brooding look. His lower lip extended in a half pout. "You were always his favorite."

"I don't know that he has a favorite. He loves you, too, Nicky."

The Raven grunted.

A silence ensued, and for want of anything else to say, Alicia added, "Daddy's got a woman with him."

"Young, I'll bet," the Raven said sourly.

Alicia laughed. "Not much older than me. But she's lovely. Very smart."

His interest awakened, the Raven asked, "What's her name?"

"Allegro. Don't you think that's a beautiful name?" she asked. "Allegro Stern. She's a writer-photographer. Does articles for magazines and newspapers."

Everything seemed to come together in the Raven's mind, like a slowly developing picture. He raised his eyes to Alicia as it took form in his twisted brain. A glazed expression suffused his gaunt but still handsome face. He finally found his voice.

"Look," he said, "when you see Pops, don't tell him you met me or that I'm in town. I don't want to see him."

This is more than a rift, Alicia thought. Exactly what was it Allegro had said to her? *If you see or hear from Nicky, don't tell your father.*

"What's the matter, Nicky? You two have a fight?" she managed to ask, her throat dry, her voice almost a quaver.

"Yeah. Sort of."

"Anything I can do to patch things up?"

"No." His tone was firm, closing the subject.

Alicia looked at her watch. "I've got to be going." She rose from her seat.

He looked up at her. "Is he in love with her?"

"Yes. Very much, I think," Alicia said. "Nicky, I've got to get back to work. Thanks for the lunch."

Alicia left the bistro, confused and puzzled. The enmity between Nicky and her father was much more than she had bargained for. More of a chasm than a gap. And she had been powerless to do anything about it. She wondered about it, what had started it, what it was all about. She would talk to Allegro as soon as she reached the hotel.

At Le Coq d'Or, the Raven ordered another drink and sat staring into it for a few moments. It acted like a film developer in his mind, and the picture became full-blown and finely grained.

O'Rourke's message from the *American Brandy* that Allegro Stern was on board. That she was accompanied by

two older men. Well, he knew who one of the men was
now!

His father was following him!

He sipped his Grand Marnier and it brought rage and
vengeance to his clouded mind.

Is he in love with her?

Yes. Very much, I think.

Well, he'd fix that! Never mind Alicia. No one was
closer than the woman one loved. He would take her away
from him and it would destroy him, more than a bullet or a
knife or a nuclear bomb ever could. It would leave him
devastated. The old man's life would be a waking nightmare.

He would kill Allegro Stern.

He lifted his glass and drank again, laughing inwardly.
He knew where she was. Somehow he would have to get
her alone. He began to think of a plan and in the process
felt strong again. The old Raven had returned.

He need not have planned. It happened by chance on the
streets of Chamonix. Just as Allegro had turned a corner a
few blocks from the local police station, he saw her.

She had advised the police that she suspected the Raven
might be in the village. The sergeant had yawned, but
when she had identified herself, had shown her credentials, had informed him the Raven's sister worked at the
Richemond Hotel, the man showed more interest. He had
taken her to his superior, who had listened with detached
coolness, and, when Allegro suggested he inform the
Deuxième Bureau, had nodded and picked up the phone
immediately. Apparently, he knew of the Raven by reputation, and if Allegro's deductions were correct, he would
need all the help he could get.

Now, a few blocks from the station, she was face to face
with the Raven himself.

The son of the man she loved smiled at her, a lascivious, mocking smile. "Hello, Miss Stern."

Allegro's pulses quickened, but she answered him in a
cool, controlled voice. Don't let him see you're afraid!

"Hello, Nicky," she said.

For a moment the Raven was taken aback. He frowned.
"How do you know I'm Nicky Alden?"

"Your father told me."

"What? I saw him in Paris last week, and I *know* he didn't recognize me as the Raven!"

"It was two days later. Walter Trask showed him your picture."

"Trask?" That *shit*!

Allegro was appalled at his appearance. She had to keep him away from his father at all costs. He would kill Philip.

"They're looking for you, Nicky."

"Who?"

"The CIA, MI6, the Deuxième Bureau. Maybe the KGB. And they all have your picture now," she lied.

"So what! So let them look! They'll never find me! I'll elude them, hear? I'll elude them." A giggle came from his throat.

"You're asinine, Nicky," Allegro said.

He looked shocked. "What was that word?"

"Asinine. Silly. You're silly if you think you can evade the world's police."

"Bullshit!"

Allegro was trying to gain time. Any amount of time. Maybe a gendarme would come upon them, recognize the Raven from the photograph she had given them, the one she had taken from Philip's pocket earlier that day.

"How about another interview, Nicky?" She patted her camera case. "No pictures this time. Just the story of your life. What led you into it. Why you formed ARM. Why you blew up the Israeli Travel Center and the Southwest Limited," she said, desperately stalling for time. "We could talk about your connections with international gangsters—the terrorists you associate with," she went on. "People want to know how you feel about it, what makes you do it." She smiled. "It would make interesting reading, Nicky. Interesting history. After your demise."

"My demise? Bullshit, my demise! I'll live! I'll live longer than God!" But he was shaken. His lips trembled and spittle formed on them.

"Just one more for the road, Nicky. I promise to treat you fairly, even objectively."

The Raven was silent for a moment. Then he said, "All

right. I'll give you an interview. My way. Let's take a walk."

"Where to?"

"Don't ask asinine questions," he said, and giggled again.

He moved his hand beneath his jacket. Allegro looked down in horror at the muzzle of an automatic pistol. He waved it at her, then covered it again.

"Let's take a walk," he said. Then more firmly. "Move!"

Good God, he's going to kill me! Allegro thought. Kill me to get even with his father! He's been second-guessing me all the time. He knows I love Philip, that Philip loves me. This is his revenge.

She turned in the direction he indicated and began to walk. The thought of the 7.65-mm automatic in her lens case brought little comfort. How would she get it out?

He led her to the cog railroad near the Central Station. He paid the fare with one hand, depositing some loose bills and change into the agent's hand, never taking his hand from the gun.

"Ever see the glacier?" the Raven asked.

Allegro said nothing.

"It's beautiful," he said. "Reminds me of the moon. A dead planet. A place for burial."

They were alone in the rickety old car. Every so often, on the ride up, Allegro felt the hard muzzle of the pistol poke into her side. She winced.

When she looked at him, he was grinning.

"Beautiful scenery," he said. "Look at it. Enjoy it. Drink in everything you can, reporter lady. It's your last chance." He laughed, a harsh laugh filled with bitterness.

CHAPTER 36

At the Richemond, Alden was pacing the floor in a whirlpool of anxiety. When he and Allegro had returned from their usual morning drive and target practice, she had left him in the lobby saying she was going out to take some pictures of the quaint village and do some shopping. That had been a few minutes past twelve-thirty. It was now approaching three-thirty.

He forced himself to relax, placed his hands behind his head, and breathing deeply, tried to ward off his fear about Allegro. The chances of Nicky being in Chamonix were just too slim. It was just another wild goose chase. Allegro was probably having a long lunch with Alicia. He'd called Alicia's office time and time again only to learn she was out.

Suddenly, he heard a knock on the door. She was probably loaded with packages, unable to reach her keys. He jumped up, walked quickly to the door. Smiling, he turned the knob, swung the door wide.

"Allegro! I've been—"

But it was not Allegro. It was Alicia. She looked at her father and saw the holster under his arm and the butt of the 7.65-mm automatic. She raised her eyebrows. "Is Allegro here?" she asked. "I need to talk to her."

"No," Alden answered. "I thought she was with you."

"I had lunch with Nicky." It slipped out. *Don't tell your father*, Allegro had said.

360

"Nicky?" Alden's voice was strained. "Is he in Chamonix?"

"Yes. But I wasn't supposed to tell you. Allegro made me promise." Her eyes went to the holster again. "Daddy, what's wrong? Why are you carrying that gun?" she asked, her voice faltering, revealing her concern.

"Where is he staying?" Alden's voice had hardened.

"Nicky? He didn't say. Just said he was passing through."

"Where could he be?" He had crossed to the phone.

"There's the Mont-Blanc," Alicia said, "and Étrangers, but I doubt if he'd stay there. Then there's the—"

Alden was barking into the mouthpiece. "The Mont-Blanc Hotel. Yes, that's right, Mont-Blanc." He looked up at Alicia. "Where else?"

"Some *pension*—"

"Hello? Hello, do you have a Nicky Alden registered?" A pause. "I see. Thank you."

He looked up at his daughter. "What was that other one you mentioned?"

"Étrangers? But I doubt if he's staying there. It's too cheap for Nicky's taste."

Alden dialed the operator again and asked for Étrangers. He waited, received the same answer. No Alden registered. He cradled the phone slowly, looking at the floor. He realized the calls would be fruitless. The Raven would never register under his own name.

Alicia had sunk to her knees before her father, her wide eyes glistening with tears. "Tell me, Daddy," she pleaded. "Tell me what's wrong. *Please.*"

He passed his hand through her reddish tresses, and as he spoke, she began to sob. He started from the beginning, with the Southwest Limited, the *American Brandy*, the crossing to Liverpool, the car chase, London, Paris, and now Chamonix. He told her Nicky was the Raven.

When he had finished, his lap was damp with her tears. She looked up at him, swallowing deeply.

"Do you think he has Allegro?"

"It's a possibility." As he said it, fear shot through him like a shard of ice.

She opened her mouth to speak, hesitated, then went on. "Nicky told me he spends a lot of time on the glacier."

He rose slowly from the chair, reached in the closet for his coat, and made for the door.

"Daddy!" Alicia screamed, but it emerged as a choking gasp.

He was gone.

The cog railroad left for the glacier every fifteen minutes. The twenty-minute trip to the Mer de Glace seemed like twenty years to Alden.

Doubt assailed him. Suppose they were not there? Suppose he had done away with her someplace in Chamonix? Some lonely, stark alley?

He shuddered, pushed the thought aside. The glacier fit the Raven's psyche. It was more dramatic.

From time to time, his right hand went to the bulge in his coat, to feel the outline of the 7.65-mm weapon.

If the Raven hurt Allegro, he would kill him. All doubt was gone now.

On the glacier, the Raven and Allegro had reached his favorite spot, the lonely spot where he had brooded earlier, hidden away from the crowds.

Gun drawn, safety off, he pushed her to the ground.

"Take off your pants," he said, and grinned down at her.

"No, it's cold," Allegro said with a hint of sarcasm.

The Raven giggled. "I'll bet you've done it in the sand on a hot beach. Many times. Haven't you ever done it on a glacier?" He giggled again.

"No," she answered. An old saying raced through her mind. In case of rape, lie back and enjoy it. But how could she? How could she accept rape from this animal, this deranged human . . . or anyone for that matter. Besides, he intended to kill her afterward. She knew that. She glanced quickly at the lens case at her side. Her gun was in it. But now was not the time.

"Take those off or I'll take them off for you!" the Raven shouted.

Receiving only a contemptuous glare, he knelt down,

the gun still in his hand, and with the other unbuckled her belt and ripped her zipper downward.

Standing again, a look of triumph on his face, he unzipped himself.

He was hard as a rock.

Allegro looked away in disgust.

"This is for the old man," she heard the Raven say. "And believe me, you never had it so good. You'll never have it so good again."

On the glacier, Alden slipped and stumbled. Once he fell on the icy terrain. He had stayed close to the scree slopes at first, to obtain a footing on the rocks. But he thought the center of the Mer would give him a commanding view of the entire glacier. So he started up, tripping on chunks of ice, stopping to rest at times to catch his breath. The thinness of the air made his breathing shallow.

He kept moving toward the glacier's source, from time to time leaning back against a spire of ice, a tall, frozen monument cast in hues of blue, purple, and russet.

He gathered his strength, then shouted out into the frozen sea, "Allegro! Nicky!" And again, "Nicky! Allegro!"

But his answer came back only as an echo. He went on, slipping, sliding, falling time after time, but always going on, calling Allegro's name.

A light snow had begun to fall. Above Alden, in his secret lonely place just at the edge of the moraine, where it met the ice of the glacier, the Raven lowered himself on Allegro, gun still in hand, penis seeking.

Allegro lay limp and supine, giving in to his advances. She had a plan, a desperate one perhaps, but in any event she would try.

She would allow him to penetrate her, and when he was in the throes, at a high pitch, she would go for the gun that lay in the lens case a few inches to her left.

"You're going to love this," the Raven said, grinning. His grin was the grin of death, a skull beneath the drawn skin.

"This'll be your last lay." He giggled. "Might as well enjoy."

Then he was inside her.

Allegro lay still for the first few plunges, then began to buck, writhe, thrust up to him. She wanted to bring him to a pitch quickly. It would be *his* last lay, not hers.

In a moment, the Raven's eyes began to roll, his breath came faster, his grunting full and hoarse.

Now!

Slowly her left hand crept to the lens case . . . fumbled inside . . . felt the cold steel of the automatic, gripped it . . . brought it out.

But the Raven's eyes had caught the movement and in a savage downward slice of his own gun he smashed her hand.

The gun went spinning and sliding across the ice out of reach. He had broken one of her fingers, and when she drew her hand to her mouth in pain, he pistol-whipped her across the face.

"Bitch!"

A full-throated scream escaped her, rising from her lungs and reverberating above the glacier in a fearful shriek.

"Goddamn bitch!" He smashed her in the face again.

Alden heard it. It stopped his heartbeat for a moment, and stopped his forward movement. He stood still.

"Allegro!" He shouted into the void. "Allegro!"

"Philip!" came the answer. "Philip!"

He looked in all directions but could see nothing.

A rasping voice turned his head around. "Stay away from me, you prick! Stay away!"

"Yes, Philip! Stay back! Stay back!" she screamed.

Through the falling snow, Alden's eyes caught two indistinct figures, one standing, the other supine on the ice, approximately seventy-five yards to the left.

Nicky was fumbling with his zipper. Allegro was pulling on her pants. Alden looked at them in silent wonder, then slowly, foot by foot, he started toward them.

"Stay away, you cocksucker! I've got a gun!"

"So have I," Alden shouted. "I'm going to kill you, Nicky."

Insane laughter echoed down the glacier. "You wouldn't do that, Pops. You wouldn't kill your own son!"

"You're a gambler," Alden said. "Want to bet on it?"
He kept moving forward. The snow had stopped as suddenly as it had started. Now everything stood out in sharp, cold relief, like a frozen frame from a motion picture: the Raven standing, gun pointed; Allegro on the ice, eyes frozen in horror.

Alden had closed the gap as he walked and now stood but thirty feet from his son, ready to kill.

The Raven dragged Allegro to her feet, never taking his eyes off his father. He held Allegro close to his body, in front of him.

He smiled wickedly. "All right, Pops, shoot. But you'll kill her!"

Alden noticed the blood on Allegro's face and a blinding rage boiled up within him. "You're a coward, Nicky," he said without inflection. "Always were. You're *dirt*."

"Whatever I am, you made me that way. Prick!"

The voice carried off the ice, echoed through the canyons on either side, could be heard for miles.

"How?" Alden asked, stalling for time.

"Ever since I was a kid, all you've done is pull me down. Criticize me, try to make me measure up to you and your fucking ideas. Alicia was always your favorite. Alicia *was your favorite!*"

Alden shook his head.

"You even called me a stinking crow! That's why I took the name Raven! You forced me to!"

"I never called you a stinking crow," Alden said calmly. "That's in your mind. You're crazy, Nicky."

"You did. *You did!* When you were chasing me in the field with the rifle! And I had to turn into a bird to escape you! But you turned into a bird, too! And called me a stinking crow, and said you were going to kill me, just as you say now! I'm not a stinking crow!"

"Of course not," Alden said. "You're not a stinking crow." A sob escaped his throat and his eyes filled with tears. His son was insane. "Let the woman go," he said. "She's not part of this. We'll have it out—man to man."

For a moment, the Raven hesitated. Then he pushed Allegro forward savagely. "Here! Take your cunt! She's no good anyway! I'll kill you both!"

Allegro had fallen with the shove, and was slipping on the ice. But she slid, scrambled, holding onto jagged clumps of ice, making for Alden. When she reached his feet, she clawed her way up his legs and stood in front of him.

"Don't kill him," she panted. "He's your son!"

"He hurt you," Alden whispered. "Get out of my way."

"No." And she pressed harder against him, shielding his body with her own. "I don't want to die," she said. "But if this is the time, I want to go with you. I want to die with you. I want to die close to you, like this. Please. *Please!*"

"Get away, Allegro," Alden said. "Don't sacrifice yourself for me. I'm going to kill him." He raised the gun and sighted.

"No!" Allegro said. "He's your son, your seed—and he's mad. We don't kill madmen anymore."

The Raven's high-pitched laughter came again. "What's the matter, Pops? Ain't got the guts? Is that it? Ain't got the guts? Who's the coward now?"

Slowly Alden began to squeeze the trigger, taking careful aim. But his hand was trembling, and the figure of his son wavered against the frozen landscape. He began to shudder. Then he tossed the gun onto the ice, where it hit with a metallic sound and slid away. He turned his back on his son and, holding Allegro by the shoulders, started to lead her down the glacier.

"Don't turn your backs on me!" the Raven shouted. "You're dead! You're both dead! Nobody turns his back on the Raven! Nobody! You hear? *Nobody!*" The Raven raised his gun with two hands, taking careful aim at them, legs spread and bent at the knees.

Alden and Allegro continued to walk away slowly.

"*Shits! Cowards!*"

Two shots cracked, echoing off the glacier walls and reverberating across the frigid landscape. One nicked Alden on the left biceps. The other missed Allegro by inches, and struck the ice twenty feet beyond them.

Allegro let go of Alden's arm, turned, and charged at

the Raven, her scream of fury sounding across the uneven levels of ice.

The Raven grinned and raised the gun again. A tall figure stepped from behind a column of ice. Trask leveled a gun at the Raven and shouted at him to turn around.

The Raven turned. "You bastard!" he yelled at the CIA man. "You told them. It was *you!*"

The two shots sounded as one. Ice particles broke loose above. Allegro threw her hands to her head and went down. Trask fell to the ice. The Raven's bullet had shattered his skull, splattering his brains on the glacier's slick surface.

Alden had been immobilized by the action, but when he saw Allegro fall, he flung himself toward her, screaming her name.

The Raven turned from the crumpled body of Trask and aimed the gun at his father. Alden had Allegro in his arms, rocking with her, tears pouring down his face.

"Kill me! Go ahead. Kill me and it will be over!" he screamed.

"Good-bye, Pops. It's your time."

The demented son leveled the gun at his father. Alden closed his eyes. It didn't matter anymore.

"It's your time, Raven." Another voice, weak and quavering, came across the ice. "*Your* time."

The Raven turned. An old man faced him twenty feet away.

"Grushenko!" the Raven shouted. "I wondered when the KGB would show." His mad laughter rolled across the frozen landscape. Again, two shots rang out across the ice.

The Raven fell, blood gushing from a bullet hole in his throat. Grushenko also went down, slid along the ice and disappeared.

The sight of his son falling, blood spurting forth, brought a choking sob to his throat. Loss and despair filled his soul. His son was a misshapen, sprawled mass on the glacier.

"Oh, God!" Allegro said.

Alden whipped his head around. "You're alive!" he gasped in disbelief.

"Grazed my head. I'll be all right."

"Thank God!"

They were distracted by a new movement. About twenty-five feet away from the Raven's body, a lone figure, small, wretched, stood leaning against a pillar of purple ice. The figure limped slowly toward them. It was Grushenko, his eyes reflecting sorrow, pity, and remorse.

He sat down on the ice beside them, blood seeping from a flesh wound in his left shoulder. He stretched out his legs, the cast shredded, almost useless. A long silence followed.

"Why? Why you and not me?" It was all Alden could think of.

"Because it is against nature," Grushenko said. "A son shall not kill his father, nor shall the father kill his son."

He offered the Smith & Wesson to Philip, butt first. "You can kill me if you want. I'm old. I have no time left."

Alden stared at the gun that had killed his son, then shook his head dumbly, and turned his gaze back to where Nicky's body lay sprawled upon the ice. A light snow had begun to fall again, and as it fell, it reddened with his son's blood. He stood up.

He looked at Allegro with concern. "How are you?"

She pulled a bloodied hand from the crown of her head. "Look to your son. I'm all right."

"He was never my son," he said bitterly.

"He wasn't sane, Philip. He wasn't sane through it all." Allegro watched him walk slowly to his son's body, saw him stop and look down. She watched him shudder, then saw him bend over Nicky Alden, once known as the Raven.

As Alden stared at his boy's face, at the gaunt drawn features, eyes open, staring at nothing, at the blood on his chest and throat, he started to cry. He sobbed deeply as he lifted his son's body, surprised at how light it was. Then he turned and started walking slowly downward to where Allegro and the man he knew as Ernst Eisenstadt waited.

"You weren't dirt, son," he murmured into a deaf ear. Tears streamed down his cheeks as he said it again. "You were never dirt."

L ater that day, after a local physician patched his wound, Grushenko went to police headquarters to inform the prefect he had killed the Raven. The prefect listened as he had listened to Allegro, in a detached, cool manner, nodding now and then. "Are you sure it's the Raven you killed?"

"Positive," Grushenko said. "The other dead man is a CIA agent, who also came here to kill the Raven. They had fired at each other before I arrived on the scene. The bodies are still up there."

The prefect called over one of his men, directed him to take a team up the mountain.

"I want to see Henri Girard of the Deuxième Bureau," Grushenko said. For once, he wasn't covering his tracks. It didn't really matter now. Pain shook him, tearing at his chest. For a moment, he felt faint. But he forced himself to go on. Maybe one more day, or a few hours.

"Girard is on his way. We had information from the Stern woman earlier today that the Raven might be here," the prefect said. "Girard is our head man where the Raven is concerned."

"When will he arrive?" Grushenko asked.

The prefect looked at his watch. "Soon."

"I'll wait," Grushenko said.

An hour later, a lifetime of pain for Grushenko, a portly man with a handlebar mustache pushed his way through the door of the prefect's office.

"*Comment ça va, Charles?*" he said to the prefect.

369

"Pas trop mal. Not too bad."

Girard turned to Grushenko. "This is a surprise, Vladislav—to find you here."

Grushenko did not answer.

"Well," Girard said, "why don't we all have lunch?"

"This is business between you two," the prefect said. "Anyway, I'm up to my ears in paperwork. But I'd appreciate a report."

Outside, Girard voiced his concern. "You look like hell, old friend. Are you sick?"

"Just tired. I'll be fine. Let's get this over with."

At Girard's suggestion, they made their way to the Mont-Blanc Hotel. Girard was a gourmet. Grushenko thought it was a waste of money. He would have preferred Étrangers, where he was staying.

They had known each other for many years, were friends on opposing sides. They formed a mutual admiration society, each respecting the other's talents and intelligence.

"So," Girard said after they were seated and had ordered. "How are you, Vladislav—really?"

"Old," Grushenko said.

"Aren't we all?" Girard poked his fork into a Coquille St. Jacques. It steamed in front of him, a mixture of fish chunks and scallops and other shellfish in a white wine sauce. He turned a piece of lobster on his fork, examined it, and placed it in his mouth. Chewing, he said, "So you killed the Raven. How am I to believe that?"

Grushenko removed two pictures from his pocket and placed them on the table before Girard.

Girard continued to eat as he scanned the pictures. "Where was this one taken?" He used his fork to indicate the photograph of the Raven having his cigarette lighted.

"In Paris."

"And this one? From your files, I suppose."

Grushenko nodded.

"Where did you get the one from Paris?"

"From his father," Grushenko said.

"His father took it?"

"No. It was given to him by a man named Trask."

Girard's bushy eyebrows rose. "The CIA's Trask? We've had our eye on him for some time. He's been shipping arms to terrorists and people like Qaddafi. We have proof. Well, we'll take care of that." He brought the last morsel of Coquille to his mouth and nodded to Grushenko. "Okay. From the beginning"

Grushenko told him the whole story, including the fact that Trask, like the Raven, was probably on the way down in a body bag.

Girard sighed, burped, and ordered dessert. "Are you sure you won't have something? *C'est merveilleux.*"

"I'm sure," he said, knowing he couldn't keep any food down for more than a minute.

Girard looked at the pictures again. "You trained him, Vladislav? You and the KGB?"

"And we destroyed him."

"I'm convinced," Girard said, and burped again. "You know you'll have to come with me this time?"

"I know," Grushenko said, swaying in his chair. "It doesn't matter." As he said it, he swayed too far and toppled to the floor like a felled tree.

While at dinner with Allegro and Alicia, Alden was called to the manager's office.

"A call for you from the police, monsieur," the tall, almost emaciated manager said.

Alden picked up the phone. "Who is this?"

"Henri Girard of the Deuxième Bureau. The man you know as Ernst Eisenstadt is in the hospital. It looks serious. He is asking for you."

Aldén didn't know what to say, sat mute for a few seconds, the receiver in one hand. Too much had happened. He couldn't react.

"I'll send a car," Girard said, then hung up.

Alden returned to the table, told Allegro, insisted Alicia wait for them at their suite.

The police car arrived, took them to the hospital. It was a one-story building with, Alden thought, no more than ten beds and a couple of examination rooms. Like all such structures, it smelled of rubbing alcohol, of the stale remains of human excretions.

Eisenstadt was in a private room. A large man sporting a handlebar mustache stood up as they entered. "I'm

Girard,'' he said in a whisper, holding out a hand. ''I don't need to be here with you. I'll go for a walk.''

Ernst Eisenstadt lay in the midst of white sheets and pillows, his parchmentlike skin almost as white. His eyes were closed.

''Ernst,'' Alden said, taking his hand.

Grushenko opened his eyes, tried to smile. ''I am not Ernst,'' he said, his voice a low croak.

''It doesn't matter,'' Alden said, knowing it did. He dreaded the whole truth, but had to know.

''I am not looking for absolution or your forgiveness. Too late for that,'' the voice said, almost too faint to be heard.

Alden and Allegro pulled up chairs, leaned as close as they could.

''I am from the KGB,'' he said, looking at the saddened faces, knowing the telling wasn't going to help at all. ''We trained your boy. Took a mind slightly twisted and gave it purpose. Helped him to become what he was in the end.''

''If not you, Ernst, then somebody else,'' Alden said with resignation. ''He was destined to this end.''

''Not Ernst. Vladislav Grushenko of the State Security Committee.'' The old man was rambling, his thoughts half in the past, half in the present. ''They took my son,'' he said. ''While I was with you in Arizona, they took my son. They put him in prison . . . sent him to the gulags.''

The old man coughed up blood. It dribbled down his chin, staining the sheets. Allegro pulled a tissue from her bag and tenderly wiped his face.

''I'm sorry, Ernst . . . Vladislav. I'm sorry,'' Alden said.

''We have been wrong in many things, Philip. I want you to know that,'' Grushenko whispered, his voice getting weaker. ''You are a man I admire in many ways.'' He stopped, his face screwed up in pain. When he continued, they could hardly hear him. ''Wrong . . . all the years . . . wrong . . . took my son . . .''

As he uttered the last few unintelligible words, the old head seemed to melt into the pillow. Only a still, withered silhouette could be seen. Vladislav Grushenko was dead.

* * *

Nicky was buried in Chamonix under his own name—Nicholas Alden. Philip, Allegro, and Alicia stood on one side of the yawning hole, a saddened Girard on the other. He had put Grushenko's body on a Soviet helicopter earlier in the day.

As the cleric droned on in French, chaos and confusion reigned in Philip's mind and soul. Random clips flashed before the screen of his mind. Memories: of Nicky catching his first fish in the Sierras; Nicky building a snowman; Nicky in Barbara's arms.

Barbara. He had notified her of Nicky's death. She had not flown over. He had not said anything about the Raven.

Tears rose to his eyes as he remembered himself, Nicky, and Barbara in the early days, days full of promise and hope. He was surprised he still had feelings for Barbara. He realized what had begun in hope had ended in chaos.

Chaos. A Greek word meaning formlessness, the void, confusion, randomness as the scientists put it for want of any religious affirmation.

Chaos.

Alden was hopeful. He knew that from chaos came form, structure, life, according to Greek mythology. And that from his personal chaos, there would arise a new beginning, like the phoenix rising from the ashes.

He looked over at Allegro. She was crying.

Daddy, is that the moon up there?

THE BEST IN SUSPENSE